Margaret Graham has been writing for thirty years. Her first novel was published in 1986 and since then she has written a further fourteen novels, and is now working on her fifteenth. As a bestselling author her novels have been published in the UK, Europe and the USA. *At the Break of Day* was previously published as *The Future is Ours*.

Margaret has written two plays, co-researched a television documentary – which grew out of *Canopy of Silence* – and has written numerous short stories and features. She is a writing tutor and speaker and has written regularly for Writers' Forum. She founded and administered the Yeovil Literary Prize to raise funds for the creative arts of the Yeovil area and it continues to thrive under the stewardship of one of her ex-students. Margaret now lives near High Wycombe and has launched Words for the Wounded which raises funds for the rehabilitation of wounded troops by donations and writing prizes.

She has 'him indoors', four children and three grand-children who think OAP stands for Old Ancient Person. They have yet to understand the politics of pocket money. Margaret is a member of the Rock Choir, the WI and a Chair of her local U3A. She does Pilates and Tai Chi and travels as often as she can.

For more information about Margaret Graham visit her website at www.margaret-graham.com

Also by Margaret Graham

After the Storm (previously published as
Only the Wind is Free)

Annie's Promise

Somewhere Over England (previously published as
A Fragment of Time)

A Time for Courage (previously published as
A Measure of Peace)

Easterleigh Hall

Margaret GRAHAM
At the Break of Day

arrow books

Published by Arrow Books 2015

2 4 6 8 10 9 7 5 3 1

Copyright © Margaret Graham 1991

First published in Great Britain in 1991 by
William Heinemann Ltd as *The Future is Ours*

Arrow Books
Random House, 20 Vauxhall Bridge Road,
London SW1V 2SA

www.randomhouse.co.uk

Addresses for companies within The Random House Group Limited can
be found at: www.randomhouse.co.uk/offices.htm

The Random House Group Limited Reg. No. 954009

A CIP catalogue record for this book
is available from the British Library

ISBN 9780099585848

Printed and bound by CPI Group (UK) Ltd, Croydon, CR0 4YY

Penguin Random House is committed to a sustainable future
for our business, our readers and our planet. This book is made
from Forest Stewardship Council® certified paper.

For Mum and Dad

I would like to thank
Sheila Doering of the United States,
Helen and Danny Buckley of Dorset,
Jackie Gaines, Marian Farrow,
Miss E. M. Glass of Somerset and
of course Sue Bramble and her library team
for their invaluable help with
the research for this book.

CHAPTER 1

Rosie gripped the ship's rail, feeling the throb of the engines, feeling the surge of the ship through the sea, seeing Frank and Nancy standing so far away on the quay, so far away and so small. The wind was harsh and hot but it didn't matter. It was 1946 and she was leaving America. That's what mattered. She was leaving to return to a family and a country she had almost forgotten after six years as an evacuee and it was unbearable.

The wind carried spray into her face but still she stood there; there was nothing else she could do. Just stand and watch the two people she had grown to love become smaller. Just stand and wonder whether she would ever see them again, whether she would ever see the bedroom where she had read Grandpa's letter three weeks ago and heard the jazz sweeping out from the gramophone, as always, across the sloping Pennsylvanian lawn.

No breeze had ruffled the maples, the sycamores or the chestnuts that day as she stood at the window. There were skis in the corner of the room, Cougar pennants on the wall. She had wanted to be a cheerleader but that wouldn't happen now. The letter had said it was time she came home – there was a job waiting for her at Woolworths – it was only fair on Norah – the war was over and the two sisters should be together again.

From the ship, Rosie had to strain to see the two small figures. How could they be so small? Frank was big, with arms that had held her when she had finished reading the letter out to them in the kitchen. Nancy was large too, and had put her arms around them both and said, 'We'll write to your grandfather in London, Rosie. We'll ask him to let you stay and complete your education, and become the journalist you want to be. We'll tell him how much we have grown to love you.'

'Woolworths, goddamn it,' Nancy had said while 'Rinso

White, Rinso Blue' filtered out from the wireless. 'Woolworths for Christ's sake.' They had all had tears in their eyes which Frank blamed on the onions sliced up on the side for the evening's barbecue. 'Goddamn onions,' he said and then stamped into his study, his pipe clenched between his teeth, and Nancy had laughed gently.

'This'll be the third he's broken this year if he's not careful,' she said, 'and the Sub-Editor will just love that. They've got a bet on that this year it'll be three within six months.'

But Rosie hadn't laughed. She had stood with Nancy's arms around her, wanting to cling to this plump, grey-haired, blue-eyed woman who had become her mother, who had watched her grow from a ten-year-old English girl into a sixteen-year-old American. But she didn't, because Nancy wasn't her mother, was she? She had no mother. She had a grandfather whom she knew she had once loved, and a sister whom she had never known whether she loved or even liked, a sister who had never written.

The wind on the ship was steady, no longer snatching at her cotton jacket, just streaming past her, through her, and now she looked out to the yawning emptiness of the sea and the sky, beyond which lay England. But she wouldn't think of that, or of Manhattan which was fading behind her. She would think instead of the lake, where they had gone the day after Frank had written the letter.

They went upstate each summer but this time it was different. This time they were waiting.

They had driven down through small towns which smelt of diesel as they passed the petrol stations. Her tanned legs had stuck to the seat in the heat. She could still feel the stubbled kiss from Uncle Bob who had wrapped his arms around her before she climbed into the car. His new jazz band had played at the barbecue the evening before.

He had hugged her and said, 'If you go back, Rosie, don't forget that it's the half valving that sets jazz apart, gives it the variation in pitch, oh hell, which sets it above other music. You remember us, you remember jazz, you remember that we love you. You hear me now. And you scout out for bands to send me. I want one with a middle tone, hear me? I love you, hear

2

me? I'm glad you came. You made me glad we fought with Europe.'

She heard him. She had heard him on a dark evening five years ago too when he had been an isolationist shouting at Frank in the living-room that there was no way the States should be drawn into a war. There was no way they should supply the Britishers. For Christ's sake they wouldn't even pay their debts. She had stood then, gripping the banister, shouting at him, 'You silly old bugger. Over there the 'ouses are being bloody bombed. Me grandma's been killed and there ain't no kids in London any more. Even me best friend Jack's 'ad to go to bloody Somerset and you carry on about bleedin' money.'

The banister had been hard, but warm, unlike the ship's rail she was still clutching.

Bob had called up, 'Why did you run away then?'

And now she heard her voice as it had been then; so young, so different.

'I didn't. I was bloody sent. No one asked me. I was just sent.'

Rosie said those words again now, into the wind which stretched them out then scattered them. 'No one asked me.' And her voice was now an American drawl and there was the same anger in it that there had been then. 'No one asked me, did they, Grandpa?'

They had stopped to eat at a roadside diner surrounded by walnut and ash trees and the earth had oozed out the last of its heat as they drove the last leg towards their wooden lake house. Rosie had stood in the hall. It had smelt the same, dry and warm, filled with the scent of pine. Frank's rods were there, the old clock. But this time there was the dark sense of waiting.

She barely slept and rose with the dawn, not allowing herself to look out at the lake. She never did. She liked to feel the cool of the polished floors as she walked silently, barefoot, through the house, and then across the grass, and then the mulch of the woods before she saw the water. It was a ritual. It would keep her safe. But it hadn't this time, had it?

Still beneath the trees she had heard the lake, rippling in across the stones and on up to the sand which might still be cool. Then she was out into the light and at last the lake was there, glinting, easing in across the shore. And yes, the sand was still cool and loose and fine-grained. There had been no storms recently then. No storms to force the water into three-foot waves, to smash down beyond the pebbles, soaking the sand.

Rosie looked out on to the grey sea now. The prow of the ship was slicing through the waves, her hair was thick with salt and still she could see the skyline of Manhattan and she knew that Frank and Nancy would remain there, waiting until she disappeared.

And so too they had waited at the lake, day after day, swimming, sitting, beating time to jazz; Erroll Garner, Billie Holiday, Bix Beiderbecke, always Bix, and Grandpa's reply to Frank's letter had not come.

On Nancy's birthday, towards the end of June, they had driven to the Club, taking their costumes, swimming in the pool. She hailed her friend Sandra who was up here from town too. They sat on white wrought-iron chairs which dug into the grass at the edge of the terrace overlooking the pool. They slid ice-crowded glasses to the table's edge to break the vacuum the condensation had produced. They sipped their Cokes, slowly. Behind them was the lawn which stretched back to the Clubhouse.

Frank passed them bourbon-soaked cherries from his and Nancy's cocktails and the talk was of the latest jazz band Uncle Bob was promoting, or the parched grass back home behind the rhododendrons where the hose did not reach; anything but England. Anything but Grandpa. Anything but the waiting.

And then Joe came towards them from the Clubhouse – Joe who had been here last year, who had been a Senior at their school, who was now at College. Joe who she had thought was beautiful since she had arrived in Pennsylvania, who was even more beautiful now that she might be leaving. But no, she wouldn't think of that. If she didn't think of it, it might not happen.

He was nodding at the girls, holding his hand out to Frank.

4

'Hi, Mr Wallen.' His voice was deeper than last year. He was taller, more blond. The hairs on his arms were bleached by the sun. Sandra nudged her and grinned. Joe didn't look, not then. But then he hadn't looked last year either. He did after dinner, though, when he smiled, his teeth white against his tan, his watch gold against his skin, and he asked her to the Subscription Dance which was being organised to raise funds for a new tennis court.

That night she had dreamed that she was on a ship, like this ship, being pulled in half by Grandpa and Norah at the prow and Frank, Nancy and Joe aft.

But she'd gone to the dance, goddamn it, she thought as she pulled her jacket round her throat and let the wind tear more strongly at her clothes. Yes, I went to the dance.

She shut her eyes because the wind was dragging tears across her cheeks. That was all. Only the wind.

She had gone to the dance because the letter had not yet come, and therefore there was still time. And now she laughed, but it was not a proper laugh as she thought of Joe's arms around her, the taste of vermouth and lemonade, the talk of College, of majoring in Politics, of his wish to enter journalism, his hopes that he might work on Frank Wallen's newspaper.

She had listened to his ambitions, which were also hers, and pushed away the thought of England. Later she watched the lake as they drove back to the house in his Buick, and then smelt his skin as he leaned down, his lips touching hers, but then his tongue pushed into her mouth and she drew back, uncertain. She had never kissed like this before.

Her feet crunched on the gravel as she walked towards the porch. 'I'll see you, Rosie,' he called as he drove away, his wheels spinning.

'Sure,' she said and had hoped that she would, in spite of drawing back, because he made her heart beat faster and her lips feel full, her skin feel as though it needed to be touched, and if she felt like this, she thought, it couldn't all end. Could it? Grandpa? Could it?

She did see him again, within two days, because Sandra had rung and asked her to a barbecue on the beach, where Joe would also be. She had answered the phone then grinned at Nancy as, later, they both strolled down to the lake and Nancy

5

sat while Rosie swam in the cool clear water out to the raft. She lay on the wet wood, then dived into the water again, swimming back to shore, to the beach house.

She had rolled down her costume, running her hands down her body, brushing at the wet sand which had caught between her breasts and along the top of her cold buttocks, and between her thighs. Should she let his tongue search her mouth? What did she do with her own? What did other girls do?

She returned to Nancy, and sat against her chair, taking handfuls of sand and letting it run through her fingers on to the ground.

'So why don't you ask that Joe over for a swim?' Nancy had said, handing her a salad roll.

The tomato was warm and the lettuce limp. It was the taste of summer by the lake for her.

'I don't know really, Nancy. I guess I just don't want to somehow.' She had bent her head down, resting it on her knees.

'You know, when you've just come out of the water and your hair's wet it's just the same as when I used to wash it back in 1940 when you first came,' Nancy said, her voice lazy. 'I remember my first date. I didn't want him to see my body, even in a costume. Too kind of personal if you know what I mean?'

Yes, she'd known what Nancy meant and now she remembered the feel of Nancy's hand stroking her head, her voice as she said, 'You've really grown, Rosie, and I guess Joe has too. I remember it was difficult to know what to do with a new date at your age. Sometimes things that you've read in books become real and you don't know what you think about it.'

Rosie remembered now how the lake had lapped at the shore while Nancy continued.

'I guess my mom was right, Rosie, when she said that you do what seems right at the time but don't let yourself get hustled, if you know what I mean, my dear. Letting a boy go too far is wrong at your age. Kissing is enough, I think.'

And Rosie remembered saying, 'But Grandpa is hustling us. Can't we just say I'm going to stay here?' She had gripped Nancy's hand, looking up at the woman who had come to her in the night when she had been ill, the woman who had smiled from the front row when she collected her literature prize. The woman who now said that Grandpa had the right to make the decision for them all. Rosie was sixteen, not twenty-one. It was only right, but Nancy had turned away as she said this.

At the barbecue they had all jitterbugged in the humid heat which was heavy with the smell of hamburgers and onions. Joe was good, very good, but so was she and they picked up the rhythm and didn't talk, didn't laugh, just danced as a breeze at last began to ease in from the lake. Dave, Sandra's date, tapped Joe on the shoulder and they swapped partners and danced again, but though the rhythm was the same it wasn't Joe's hand which caught her and turned her and threw her up and then to one side, and so it was good to be called to eat, over by the glowing barbecue.

She didn't eat the onions but sat with Sandra on blankets out where the woods met the sand and they laughed while the boys fetched root beer which Sandra's mother had brought from the ice-box. The parents smoked cigarettes which glowed in the dark and Rosie watched the lanterns blowing near the barbecue. Frank and Nancy hung up lanterns in their garden when they had a barbecue and people danced and ate. Did Grandpa? Of course not. But it hurt too much to think of that, so she watched as the moths beat against the lights.

'Don't they know it's hopeless?' she murmured.

'D'you remember that darn great Polyphemus the old coach stopped the game for in ninth grade?' Joe called across to Dave. 'He stopped play and we watched it crawl out all wet. We had to wait until it dried and the wings got as tough as Flying Fortress wings. Jeez, those moths are more like birds. Six inches from wing-tip to wing-tip. We swatted it.'

The breeze had become a wind as the music played again and Joe pushed his fingers between hers, pulling her up, dancing so close. Her head had lain against his shoulder. The humidity remained and they were drenched with sweat and Rosie had thought of the wings beating about her face. She hated moths. She always had done and she remembered Grandpa swatting at a hard-bodied one which had banged into the kitchen light but it was Jack who had come in, cupped it in his hands, taken it into the yard, set it free. Grandpa, let me stay.

She shivered and Joe held her, looking into her face, but it wasn't the moth, it was the thought of England. Joe kissed her

7

and she felt his lips on her forehead, in her hair, his breath on her skin, and it was what she had wanted all evening.

The music was slow and she felt his chest against hers, his hips, his legs. She wasn't going to think about moths any more, about anything any more. Not about school, not about ninth grade – only kids were in ninth grade. She was sixteen, Joe was eighteen. They were no longer kids.

Her breath made a wet patch on his shirt and she concentrated on this, not on the mailbox which would one day soon hold the letter.

Then they were dancing in the darkness beyond the lanterns, and all she could smell was him, all she could feel was him, as he moved his hand all over her back and kissed her, again and again, and her mouth opened under his, but this time his tongue didn't flick into hers.

The hand which led her off to the shelter of the wood was soft and sure and kind. The ground was dry, his kisses were on her face, her neck, and hers were on his, but then he unbuttoned her dress, slipping his hand across her shoulders, her neck. Her breathing felt strange.

She put her hands either side of his head, holding his face so that she could kiss his mouth, see his eyes which looked at her, then through her, heavy-lidded. At his lips which were as full as hers felt. Now she let his hands stroke her breasts and she knew the adults would not approve and she thought they could go to hell.

She closed her eyes as he pushed her dress back off her shoulders and it was now that he kissed her breast with his open mouth, with his tongue. She felt it, soft and warm, and allowed him to do all this because the adults were making decisions, had always made decisions, and this was hers. And they wouldn't like it.

But then she opened her eyes. The wind was howling now and she saw his head down against her skin, her body felt his hands along her thighs and his mouth was no longer soft and neither were the sounds which came from him. She was frightened, wanted Nancy. Everything was so quick. After six years everything was rushing, too fast, too goddamn fast, even this, and she didn't know how to stop Joe, how to stop anything, anything at all.

8

But then the rain came and Joe lifted his head, pulled back her dress, took her hand, helping her from the ground, laughing, running, and that night the waves on the lake were three feet high as they drove along the surface of the water. Tomorrow the sand would be solid and wet as she walked on it and she knew now it would be all right because the rain had fallen tonight when she needed it. So that meant everything would be fine, wouldn't it? And she and Joe would have the time they needed to take everything so much more slowly.

But she did not walk on the sand the next day and everything was not all right, because there was a letter from England in the mailbox. Norah insisted that she came home and Grandpa agreed. The waiting was over. There was only grief and anger to take its place.

Rosie lifted her hands now, leaning against the rail, standing on her toes, looking back, and, yes, Manhattan was still visible, she hadn't quite left, not yet.

She hadn't said goodbye to Joe, or to Sandra. Frank had driven them back to the house on the last day of June and there had been an ache inside her which seemed to reach into the air, taking the colour from the maples, the sky, the whole world. The ache hadn't left her still. She wondered if it ever would.

She had packed her trunk, listening to Louis Armstrong, ignoring the visitor from the Children's Aid Society who called to speak to Frank and Nancy. She folded her clothes neatly but left her baseball bat, skis, her pennants on the shelves and on the walls, because there would be no place for them in London.

She looked out at the baseball target set up by Frank on the back of the garage, then took the ball from the shelf, feeling its stitches, its leather-covered hardness, the slap as she whacked it into her other hand. The mitt was there on the shelf. She put the ball with it. It was all over and the tears would not stop running down her face.

They took a cab from the house the next day and she waved at Mary, the domestic help, who cried, but Rosie did not, she seemed too empty, too grey, too tired. But she had cried all night. Had Frank and Nancy?

They talked on the train to New York but the words were dry and flickered from her mind and it was as though everything

9

were happening two feet above the ground and there were no shadows.

At Grand Central Frank showed her the bulbous clock above the information desk.

'This is a good meeting place,' he said, taking his pipe from his mouth. 'You just remember that when you come back.'

For a moment she had seen the colours and shapes of Grand Central Station and then it slipped back to the flatness and to the noise which whirled around her, sweeping in and out of her head but never staying, and she turned away but Frank pulled her back, put his arm around her. His brown eyes close to her brown eyes.

'You've got to fight a good corner. Make something positive out of the next three days before you get on that boat. We want you to soak it in, remember it. Remember America. That's why we're filling in the time here, not back home. The future is yours, Rosie. You must make something positive out of the rest of your life. Have we got a deal?'

Rosie looked at Nancy and then back to Frank and wanted to shout, But there's this pain, deep inside and it's because I'm leaving you, the lake, Sandra, America; and Joe. And I'm angry with Grandpa and Norah and you, for letting this happen. And I'm frightened because I'm going to a place which used to be home but which isn't any more.

Nancy touched her face as the people parted around them. 'None of this is the end of the world, you know. We can write. You'll come and stay, or we'll come over.' Her voice was heavy with sadness, her eyes shadowed as Frank's were, and Rosie knew that these two people were hurting too. That they loved her, that they didn't want her to go, any more than she wanted to leave.

They walked on through the pillared hall and the noise was greater. People clustered at the ticket booths. Were they going home? Were they laughing and smiling because they were going to people they knew and loved?

Frank had gripped her then, as Rosie now gripped the rail again, her hands down from her face, Manhattan all but gone, though not quite.

He had gripped her, pulling her back to him. His hands had

10

been the same as they had always been, short-nailed, strong. Would they be old when she saw him again?

He had said, 'Nearly sixty cleaners come in the early hours, just so you can put your toots down on the great big shine. Now isn't that something?'

She had nodded, but it was nothing in amongst the pain. She had leaned her head back at Nancy's command and looked at the picture of the zodiac on the towering ceiling.

'There's something wrong with it, so people say. Maybe Orion is back to front or something. But it looks pretty good to me.' But it was nothing.

They called in to the Oyster Bar, then passed the movie house and stood and looked at the bronze doors behind which the trains waited at their platforms. There would be one taking Nancy and Frank back to Pennsylvania on the fourth, but not her. No, she would take a ship and a train and then a cab, each one taking her further from them, from Joe, from them all.

'These trains leave at one minute past the scheduled time. Always one minute past. Remember that when you come back,' Nancy said.

They took a cab to the Plaza Hotel but Rosie turned before they left the station and saw 89 East 42nd Street in gold lettering above the main doorway. Did Euston have its address written up? She couldn't remember. She didn't care.

She still didn't care, standing here, surging away from America, remembering the avenues they had driven along and across, the streets they had turned down which were plunged into darkness by the shadows of the skyscrapers. They had driven beneath bridges, slicing in and out of the shadows of the girders.

'In winter the tops of these skyscrapers are sometimes in the clouds,' Frank had said, his hand clasped over the bowl of his pipe because Nancy would not tolerate that goddamn smell in the car.

The buildings reared up, jagged against the blue of the sky. They were complete, untouched. But the place she was going to wasn't. The bombs had made sure of that.

In the Plaza lobby there were plants with rich green waxy leaves. They looked so cool in the heat, like the lake. She touched one. It was plastic and warm.

11

Her bedroom was silent, empty. She had no energy to draw the drapes across the full-length window, she just let her clothes drop to the floor in the bathroom and stood beneath the cold water, wanting the sharpness, the intake of breath, the soothing of the pain which could not be soothed.

They walked in Central Park. There were tennis courts.

'Will the Lake Club raise the money for another one?' she asked and Frank nodded.

'They usually do.'

Would Joe take someone else to the next Subscription Dance? Would he kiss her breasts too? If she had stayed, would they have been able to take it all more slowly? Would she have been able to ask him to kiss her gently, to hold her in his arms, not press his lips against her nipples, not yet. Not until she was less of a child. Not until they really knew one another.

Would Frank and Nancy still sit around the pool, would the glasses still stick to the table? Would the world go on?

Frank had stopped and was pointing his pipe towards the grey rocks, the drying grass.

'This was covered with squatters' shacks in the Depression but wars are good for us. We make money, we save money. Now we need something to spend it on, so we'll have a boom. Poor old Europe won't. It's been drained white. It'll be tight back home, Rosie.'

But London wasn't home, and neither was Pennsylvania any more. She was in no man's land. Didn't anybody see that but her?

That night when midnight had been and gone she stood at the window of her room, a strange room in a strange city. She listened to the garbage trucks wheezing and clanking, the air-conditioning humming, the police sirens wailing, and knew that she had felt this lonely before. She recognised the panic which surged and tore into her, gripping her hands into fists, squeezing the breath from her throat. She recognised the pain which tumbled along with it.

It was the pain Grandpa had tried to hug and kiss away so long ago on the wharf at Liverpool but he had not been able to touch the rawness inside her because he was the one saying she couldn't stay.

He was the one saying those words again.

Rosie held the drape tightly, screwing it up, holding it to her mouth, leaning her head against the glass. All around her was the humming, the wailing, the clanking, and now there were tears too. Tears which turned to sobs and the drape was creased and damp when she turned to her bed, but even then there was no peace because the waves of the lake lapped and rippled and its glare hurt her eyes as she dipped in and out of sleep. In and out. In and out, until she woke, sweat-drenched, the sheets twisted about her limbs.

But it was still night, and the water was cold from the shower as she let it run over her face, her body. She was almost a woman now and had been a child when Grandpa had held her with the cold September wind whirling around them on that Liverpool dock.

'My little Rosie,' he had said. 'My darling little Rosie. It won't be long, my love. I promise you that. It really won't be long but I want you safe.' And he had cried. Tears had smeared – not trickled – just smeared all over his face which had been old even then.

Rosie turned the shower on harder. 'It's been too long, Grandpa. It's been such a very long time and I don't remember you any more. I don't belong any more. You are tearing me away from my home again and I think I hate you.'

In the morning they watched the riders exercising their horses in Central Park, then took a steamer which smelt of diesel. They looked at Staten Island, Ellis Island, the ancient ferries which plied to and fro, one with funnels, and it had meant nothing because she was leaving.

They took a cab up to Fifth Avenue, driving past the steam that drifted from manhole covers and came from the cracks in the hot water system carried in underground piping.

They shopped in stores for a crêpe de Chine nightdress for Norah which Nancy chose and Rosie knew should have been flannelette, but then, Norah might have changed. But what did it matter?

She looked up. Behind her, captured by the mirror tilted on the counter, was a red-haired girl, and for a moment she thought it was Sandra. But of course it wasn't.

They moved on to the candy department and bought maple candies, butterscotch and toffee because, Nancy said, the neighbours would like sweets especially now that the rationing was so intense.

She bought gum and fruit-flavoured envelopes. And stockings for herself, for Norah, for Jack's mum – and Camel cigarettes, too, because Maisie was a twenty a day girl. She bought a toy car for Lee, Jack's new brother, but she didn't mind whether it was a Buick or a Cadillac. None of it mattered. She bought a sweater for Grandpa and another for Jack, another for Jack's dad, Ollie.

For lunch they put nickels in a slot in a diner and she saw a boy who she thought was Joe. But of course it wasn't and by this time tomorrow she would be drawing away from Manhattan, hearing the gulls, losing Frank and Nancy, losing them all.

Now Rosie, standing by the rail, looked up at the sky. She hadn't noticed the gulls before.

They hadn't been able to eat their meal and had taken a bus to the Rockefeller Center and Rosie had watched the coins clink through the driver's change machine, like the hours and minutes of these last few days. They had stood on the sidewalks as Nancy told them of the cleaner employed full-time to keep the Center floor clear of gum and she had thought of her Grandma who had worked as a cleaner at the bank. It was there that she had died when the bomb had fallen just before Rosie left for America.

That evening they went to Chinatown and she bought a jar of spice from a shop which had varnished ducks hanging in the open shop-front. An old woman passed with shoes that slopped as she walked.

They sat and drank cold tea at an outdoor café and Rosie bought a book of Chinese art from an old street vendor. Maybe Jack would like that. And still the minutes clicked away.

The cloud layer had not dispersed with the coming of night and reflected the Manhattan lights. The London skies had been aglow on the nights before she left. Not with light but with flames.

It was nine o'clock now. It would soon be the fourth. They flagged down a cab and drank Manhattans in a restaurant which spilled seats out on to the pavement.

They sat and watched the women in hats, the men in smart

14

grey suits, the boys in shirtsleeves, the girls in cotton dresses. Each girl looked like Sandra, each boy like Joe. She picked out the ice-cube from her drink. It numbed her tongue, but not her pain.

'I'm saving the best for tomorrow,' Frank said, taking her hand in his. 'It's somewhere you'll never forget, somewhere that'll warm you on the long trip home, on the nights when maybe you can't sleep.'

Nancy touched her shoulder and smiled.

Frank continued. 'It's a place I always think of when times are tough. It's the street where Bob and I used to visit to soak in jazz. Real original jazz.'

Rosie looked at him and saw that his eyes had lost the shadow of pain which he had carried over these last days.

She stood at the window again that night listening to the lorries, the garbage truck, the sirens. She showered, she cried and drifted in and out of sleep and there was Joe, his wristwatch glinting, his hand on her skin, his mouth too. There was Grandma, lying beneath the rubble. Jack reaching out to her. Then Frank and Nancy holding her, sure and strong, then Grandpa calling her from their arms but she couldn't see his face.

They didn't talk over breakfast. The pecan waffle looked good, the celebrations in the street outside were loud for the fourth of July but it didn't matter. Nothing mattered.

It was hot again, so hot. They took a cab to Frank's favourite place. She stretched out her arm along the window, loosening her fingers, breathing slowly, keeping the panic in, mixing it up with the pain. They passed in and out of shadows and the noise of the streets was loud. Life was all around them but not in her. Not with her.

Frank was clenching his unlit pipe between his teeth, his fingers tapping on the armrest of the door.

'Charlie Parker and Dizzy Gillespie played in clubs next door to one another down fifty-second Street, this goddamn great street. I heard them. Billie Holiday sang too. Dixieland and New Orleans just roared out across the street all day and into the night.' He was stabbing the air with his pipe now. 'There was nothing to pay, just the price of a beer and the love of the music. It's stayed with me. It'll stay with you, keep you warm.

15

It's special for me, and for Nancy, and Bob. Now it'll be special for you.'

The cab slowed, turned into the street and Rosie watched as Frank leaned forward, his face eager, and then she saw the bleakness begin in his eyes and his mouth set into a tense line. She had looked then, out of the window, at the clubs which would warm her, remind her, and she saw what Frank had seen.

She saw the smoky brownstone buildings which were still there, but without the clubs. There was just paper which scudded about the street and paint which was peeling off doors and window glass which was cracked or gone. Dented cars lined the street, a trash can rolled on the sidewalk.

They drove down slowly and where there had once been jazz sweeping out of the windows were groups of men lounging, staring. There were more standing in dingy doorways, buying drugs, selling drugs, taking drugs, and Rosie held Frank's hand and told him that it was jazz sweeping across the sloping lawn that she would remember. It was Uncle Bob's groups, the barbecues, the baseball target, the maple syrup on pancakes at breakfast – those were the things that would warm her.

'This is nothing. This doesn't matter.' But then she could speak no more and her pain was gone as she saw his in the tears which were smeared across his face, as Grandpa's had been. Frank looked old too.

And now, standing on her toes again at the rail, she could no longer see Manhattan. They were gone and she finally turned from the wind and wept. It was over. All over.

Frank and Nancy stood hand in hand now that the ship had quite gone and Frank didn't look at Nancy as he said, 'When I saw those clubs had gone and everything had changed I felt my heart break. It looked like us with her gone.'

Nancy put her arms around him, holding him.

'It's over,' he said. 'Those six years are gone and I love that girl more than I ever thought I could love anyone, other than you.'

Nancy said into his jacket, 'We knew she had to go back. We chose to forget. That wasn't fair on her. We let her down, but maybe we could go visit in a few months, make sure she's OK?'

They were both crying and the sun was too hot.

Frank said as he looked back to the ocean again, 'No, she must settle back with her family and only come when it's right for her. She's had a safe war and it's over now. We all just have to get on with the rest of our lives.'

Neither could speak any more and they caught a cab, and then a train and then drove back to the lake, but Frank did no more fishing that summer. He and Nancy just sat and listened to the waves on the shore.

CHAPTER 2

For the first three days of the voyage to England, Rosie lay on her bunk, not eating, not sleeping, just pushing the sheet into her mouth to smother her tears. The other three girls thought she was seasick.

On the fourth day she dressed, showered and walked the deck, feeling the rise and fall of the ship. There were loungers lined up near the rail, quoits to play, music in the evening, and space. She leaned against the rail, the sun was hot, the wind fierce. It tore at her hair. She was going back to England because she had been told to and that was that.

But there was all this anger and pain which seemed trapped inside her body, inside her mind, and she wished it would break free and be swept into nothing by the wind. Hadn't Grandpa realised that she'd grow to love her new life? Didn't he know how she would feel being dragged away again? But then he didn't know her any more. She didn't know him.

She walked on, holding the hair back from her face, watching as a child threw a bean bag to his mother, and then to the father. Some others were playing French cricket. There was room for that on the upper deck.

On the trip six years ago there had been no room, no parents. Just children with labels pinned to their lapels, wearing plimsolls, gumboots, their faces grown wary and tired. There were destroyers and other ships ploughing through the grey waters, not the space about the ship that there was now.

One morning Rosie had come with the others to the rails to wave but the destroyers were gone and each ship had to make its own way. It was that dull grey expanse of sea that Rosie remembered because that was when she realised that she and all the other children really had left their homes. They had to make their own way too. There had been a bleakness in her then, deeper than tears, and anger too.

But that night some of the boys had rolled marbles across the dance floor and the children's escorts had fallen, in mid foxtrot, on to great fat bums. Rosie and the boy who reminded her of Jack had laughed, along with so many others. The escorts hadn't laughed, they had gripped the children's collars and with red angry faces had told them of the dangers of a cracked coccyx. One lad had said that he didn't know you could break your flaming arse on a marble and they had laughed again.

Rosie stopped now, near the stern, watching the flag streaming out and the wake frothing and boiling. Yes, they had laughed a lot, and cried with despair and anger, but in the end it had been all right, hadn't it? She looked down at her shoes – open-toed, leather – and the tanned foot, and remembered the plimsolls, the child that she had been.

Yes, that had turned out all right, and so would this. Wouldn't it? But the child was almost a woman, and the pain seemed deeper, more sharply etched, and she wondered who would be there to meet her when the ship docked.

There was no one to meet her at Liverpool. She took a cab to Lime Street. The streets were so small, the sky so grey, the rain so heavy and no one had come to meet her.

There were no gold letters above this station, no drawling men in short-sleeved shirts, no women in slacks and dark glasses. No one who called her honey and showed her a bulbous clock under which they would meet when she came back. No one to meet her here at all. She wouldn't cry, not here, in this strange land. Later she would though – in Grandpa's house in Middle Street, but only when it was dark and everyone else asleep.

She bought tea from a trolley and handed over a sixpence.

'That's swell,' she said, picking up her case, shrugging so that her bag wouldn't slip from her shoulder, moving to one side to let the man with the cap buy his.

'Yank, eh?' said the woman, passing the man his cup without looking. Her headscarf was knotted at the front and her hair hung down her forehead. She looked tired and thin.

Rosie sipped the thick stewed tea and looked at the woman,

the man, all these people who spoke in a thick scouse that she could barely understand.

'I don't know,' she replied, putting the cup back down on the trolley and moving towards her platform, tears stinging the back of her throat. I don't know goddamn anything. I only know I'm hurting. I only know I shouldn't be here. And nobody has come to meet me.

The train shuddered out along the tracks, through suburbs which were torn and jagged, splashed with purple from the rosebay willowherb. There were great gaps in the streets and bomb-damaged houses with rooms hanging open to the air, their damp and peeling wallpaper still clinging to the plaster. She had seen photographs in the newspapers but nothing had prepared her for this.

The train was taking her further from the sloping lawns, making her see what she had escaped. But that wasn't her fault, was it? Grandpa had made her come back and he hadn't even come to meet her, and neither had Jack.

She wiped the train window clear of condensation, felt the wet on her skin as she made herself count the telegraph poles, made herself smell the train, taste the tea thick on her tongue and teeth, watch the rain, because all this was England. The raindrops jerked down the pane as the train rattled slowly over the points.

Poor little country. Poor goddamn little country – and she saw tired brownstone buildings where no jazz played.

Guilt came then and it was shocking in its forgotten strength. It was the same guilt which had come on heavy heat-laden nights when she was safe and thousands of miles away from the bombs, the rationing, the grind. But the feeling had faded with the years and she had forgotten it until today. And now there was so much pain, so much anger, so much guilt that she thought her head would burst, but then this too faded. All of it faded. Nothing stayed. She was too tired. Right now she was too tired but it would all come again, along with the panic. She knew. It had been the same six years ago.

She wiped at the window again then sat with her hands clenched. She watched as the man opposite took out a packet of Woodbines, and struck a match. The smell of sulphur filled the carriage before being swept away in a rush of noise and wind as he hauled on the window strap, flicked out the match, then snapped it up again.

She watched as he drew deeply and read his paper again. She watched as the woman opposite took out sandwiches wrapped in greaseproof paper. The tomato was warm and had stained the bread. The child in the corner was kicking his leg against the opposite seat. He had soft brown eyes like Jack's. She looked away quickly.

Why hadn't Jack met her? She pressed her hands together tightly in her lap. Why? He had written all through the years and had said he would come. Frank had cabled Grandpa telling him the time and date. Why hadn't one of them come?

She looked at the boy in the corner again and then out at the fields, so green, so lush, even in the greyness, even in the rain. She had forgotten how green it was, how small the fields were. They passed old houses made of deep red Cheshire stone, and copses. She'd forgotten there were copses.

Yes, why hadn't either of them come? She had known Norah would not. 'Norah's walking around like a flaming great purple bloodhound,' Jack had written in his first letter to her. 'She'll not forgive you for going, leaving her here with iodine and impetigo. It'll be your fault that the programme was scrapped before she could come too. Just shrug her off.'

Rosie had, she'd forgotten about the older girl who had increasingly pushed, shoved and scowled her way through life the older she became, but now they would be meeting again. Would it be any better?

The man opposite stubbed out his cigarette on the floor, grinding his heel down, squashing it, mixing it with the dirt from the floor.

Rosie remembered salvaging dog-ends with Jack before the war then rolling them into new fags and selling them for two-pence a pack. She and Jack had done that together and his mum had laughed but Grandma had never known. She would not have laughed and now so much of the past was coming back. Grandma would have told Grandpa he was a fool not to tan 'that girl's backside'. He had always loved Rosie so much, but he hadn't come to meet her, had he? He had just issued the order.

Rosie hadn't cried when Grandma died beneath the rubble

of the bank. Norah had cried while the funeral guests were there and then she had gone up and sorted through Grandma's mothballed clothes trying on the coat with the fox fur and the paws and the head with eyes which followed you around. It hadn't suited her purple face, Rosie thought.

Norah had kept that and the cardigans and given the jumpers to Rosie to cut the arms off and sew into blankets. They had smelt of sweat until Rosie had washed them. Norah had sold the rest to the rag and bone man and kept the money.

Rosie shifted in her seat. Surely she had changed? They were grown up now, things were different. The seat prickled and the view of Arundel Castle on the wall above the man's head was faded.

Jack had unscrewed the one of Weymouth on the evacuee train carrying their school down to Somerset when war first began. He had sold it to the owner of the village pub to get them enough money to travel back at Christmas when the bombers still hadn't come.

His mum had sent him again though, after Rosie had gone and the bombs were falling night after night and after old Meiner's house down the road was crushed. Rosie had liked Mr Meiner. Jack had fiddled them both a job lighting fires at his house on the Sabbath by saying they were older than they were. 'Meiner left Germany but the buggers killed him anyway,' Jack had written and his mum and dad had sent him back to Somerset then. But it was to a different area. Norah had gone too.

Rosie watched the woman next to her peeling off the crust of her last sandwich, eating it piece by piece, licking her finger and stabbing up the crumbs. Then she folded up the paper and put it away again in her bag.

Rationing was still on in England. They had debts to repay, the country to rebuild, and Rosie couldn't take out her great slab of cheese, or the fruit, and the biscuits prepared on the ship. Instead she put her hand into her bag and pulled out a bread roll she had saved from breakfast.

They were passing through towns now and these were damaged too. They pulled into stations; doors slammed, whistles blew, and there was never the long mournful hoot of the American trains.

22

The man smoked another cigarette and this time the sulphur filled the carriage, and Rosie remembered the oast-houses and the hops, and smiled. Then there were the candles which the fumigation man lit when she and Norah had scarlet fever. How ill they had been, how the bed bugs had bitten, how they had tossed, turned, sweated, ached.

Rosie threw the little boy a sweet and his mother smiled.

'How old is he?'

'Seven.'

Their father and mother had died in the year of Rosie's seventh birthday. She knew she was that age because her grandpa had said Martha, his daughter, her mother, 'had seven years of sunshine with you, my little Rosie'.

Grandpa had bought the house then, because the landlord wouldn't improve it. How he had managed she didn't know. He wouldn't tell, he had only muttered that his daughter hadn't worked herself to death in that laundry and he hadn't worked two shifts twice a week to see it all slip through his hands. So he had bought it off the landlord and together he and Ollie, Jack's dad, had chipped at the plaster, stripping it down, disinfecting the bricks, replastering, reflooring both houses, because Ollie had bought his too.

Since then there had been no cockroaches to scuttle from beneath the wallpaper and no bed bugs. No tins of paraffin at the foot of each bed leg. Rosie scratched herself as the train gushed into the blackness of a tunnel.

There had been no more bed stripping, mattress scrubbing, but there had been . . . what was it? Oh yes, roses. Roses whose fragrance filled the yard. She had forgotten those until this moment.

The train slapped out into the light and Rosie put up her hand to shield her eyes. The rain had stopped. It was four p.m. and they would be in London in an hour.

She leaned her head back, letting it roll with the train, watching the man opposite tap his knee with his newspaper. The child was asleep, his head against his mother's arm, and she missed Nancy and felt the pain again, raw, savage, and the sky seemed darker.

There was no one to meet her at Euston either and she gripped her case more tightly as she queued for a cab. 'Putney, please,' she told the driver, leaning forward, easing her case into the taxi. The trunk was tipped on end by the porters and juggled upright in the front. She tipped them half a crown.

'Bloody Yanks,' she heard a man say behind her, and his voice burst through her pain.

She turned as she got into the cab. 'Bloody Britishers,' she said. But she wished she hadn't as they drove through a ruined London. The skyline was different and there was uncleared wasteland where there had once been streets.

She pulled herself forward, looking out. It was drizzling now. It would be hot at home in Pennsylvania. But no, that wasn't home. This was home. She pushed the strap of her bag from her aching shoulder, remembering the same ache from her journey to Liverpool so long ago. But then it had been her gas mask which was heavy, filled with sandwiches and fruitcake.

A man with a long nose and dark suit had taken the gas mask away from her. He had given it to Grandpa to take home because she wouldn't be needing it where she was going. Had Grandpa given it back to the Town Hall?

They were getting closer now. The streets were clustering. The lampposts had cracked bulbs. There was rope on one of them. So children still swung on them as she and Jack had done. Why hadn't he or Grandpa come?

She sat back, pressing herself deep into the leather seat. She didn't want to go on. She didn't want to reach Middle Street, leave the cab, see Norah, see Grandpa. She wanted to go home.

But they were there now, turning into Middle Street, and the taxi slowed.

'Which one, miss?'

She didn't know. It was all so small, so narrow, and the far end had gone; flattened into piles of bricks, tiles, rosebay willowherb. Grass spurted out of the hard-packed earth and there was a surge of sadness within her for the people who had once lived and laughed here where children were now scrambling, shooting guns made out of wood, cowboys shooting Indians.

'Your grandpa's been watching too many bloody Hopalong Cassidy films at the flicks,' Jack had said when she had told him she was leaving for America.

'Will you write?' she had asked, sitting on the kerb rolling marbles, trying to get his tenner, and he had, though he hadn't come to meet her. But she mustn't keep saying this, she must try and remember which house had been her home. She must try and stop the panic.

'Which one, miss?' the cabbie asked again, almost coming to a halt, and then she saw it. Number 15, with a front door which had once been bright red and was now dark, dirty, almost colourless. It was only now, with the taxi halted and the meter still clicking over, that she remembered the colour it should have been. It was all so small.

The panic was gone. There was nothing in its place, just an emptiness.

She couldn't leave the cab. She couldn't move. She fumbled in her bag, looking for money. But it wasn't money she was looking for, it was just time, and then Norah came out, standing by the open dirty door, leaning back against the wall, staring at her, her face just the same but her hair frizzed up into a perm, tight like her face. She looked more than her eighteen years and Rosie felt a rush of pity for the sister who had been left behind.

She pulled on the handle, pushed open the door and walked towards her.

'Hi, Norah,' she said, leaning forward, but Norah stiffened and so Rosie pulled back without kissing her cheek and the emptiness was filled again.

'You're back then,' Norah said, and her voice was the same too. Sharp and hard. 'Grandpa's asleep, don't disturb him.'

Rosie could hear the children playing on the rubble at the end, where Mr Sims and Mr Elton had lived, Mr Meiner too. She looked down there, not at Norah. She had come back as she had been told to, and Grandpa was asleep, Jack was nowhere and Norah had not changed. So this was it, was it? This was goddamn it. But she wouldn't cry. Not yet. She had no right to in this ruined street.

'Mr Sims died then, did he?' she asked. 'It seems kind of sad. He used to give us toffee, do you remember?' It was better to talk, to drawl out the words slowly and make sure her voice did not shake. It was better to do that than stand here making no attempt to reach out and touch this girl she had not seen for over six years.

25

Norah moved back into the house. 'That trunk will have to go into the yard. There's no room in the house,' was all she said.

Rosie knew there was no room. The small hall ran into the only downstairs room and upstairs there was just a bedroom and a large boxroom which she and Norah had shared, head to toe. Would that be the case again?

'Hey, miss, how're we going to get this lot in?'

The cabbie was out now, heaving at the trunk, and Rosie called after Norah, but there was no answer and so she dumped her bags on the sidewalk and tried to help him edge it out and lower it to the road, but it was too heavy for the two of them.

'I'll see if those kids will help,' she said, running on down the road, calling to them, wishing that she was running back to Liverpool, back to Frank and Nancy. But then she heard her name, and then again, and footsteps sounded behind her, closer, catching her. Then a hand caught her arm, slowing her, stopping her, and it was Jack. At last it was Jack, turning her to him, gripping her shoulders, shouting, 'Where the hell have you come from?'

'I'm back from the cowboys, didn't you know?' she whispered. 'Didn't you know? Why didn't you meet me?' His eyes were brown as they had always been, his smile the same.

He picked her up now, swung her round.

'Where are your plaits? I've always thought of you with your plaits. Where are you going to bung your rubber bands now?'

It was so good to feel his arms, hear his voice, see the hair which still fell across his forehead, because he was her friend. He had always been her friend. She laughed and cried and held him close and he put his arms round her.

'God, I've missed you,' he said and it was almost more than she could bear.

He pulled her back towards the cab. 'I didn't know you were coming back.' He squeezed her hand then dropped it as they reached the cab.

'But Frank cabled Norah to tell you.'

'Then it's your own bloody fault I never got the message. You should have known better.' He was heaving at one end of the trunk and they had it up, and he and the driver went down the alley between the houses, through the alley at the back

26

where the gutter was damp from the drizzle which had now stopped.

Jack was so tall, his shoulders were wide and his body was thick. He looked more than sixteen. He sounded more. His voice was deep like Joe's but there wasn't the tan, there wasn't the soft quality of the clothes, of her clothes. He was like England, worn and tired. Norah was right. It hadn't been fair that she had missed all this. She turned and looked at the crumpled skyline of the houses backing on to the alley.

They were at the back gate and she didn't want to go in, she held it for them because the yard was home and she couldn't go in, not yet, because Grandpa was in there, and he hadn't come to meet her, he hadn't even stayed awake. He had just dragged her home and she thought she hated him even though he had once loved her so much and she had loved him.

They walked back to the taxi. She paid the fare, tipped half a crown and didn't care what Jack thought, even if it was 'bloody Yank'. He said nothing, though, and she watched the taxi drive away, leaving her here. Her journey was over. She turned to Jack, to his warmth and his smile, and looked at the hands which had written her letters when others hadn't.

'So where *are* you going to put your rubber bands then?' He was leaning back against the wall, putting his hands in his pockets, sloping one leg over the other.

'Round my little finger, I guess,' Rosie said, leaning back on the lamppost which threw light into Grandpa's bedroom.

'Will Woolworths like that, I ask myself?'

'Woolworths will have to get stuffed if they don't,' Rosie answered, looking up into the sky where a weak sun was filtering through.

The sun would throw sloping shadows across the lawn tomorrow. It would glitter on the lake. Nancy would wear goggles to sunbathe. Frank would fish.

'Are you glad you're back?' Jack asked.

'Now you're here,' Rosie said, and flushed because the boy she had known was gone and this half-stranger was in his place. 'Can I come and see your mum?'

She said this because he had blushed too and she felt awkward and wanted to include his family in her feelings, in her words. She loved his mum anyway. She was full-breasted like Nancy, and kind too.

Jack took out his cigarettes, ducking his head down to catch the flame of the match. Something was different between them. Had there been too many years? Too many miles? Had they grown too far apart to be friends? But that could never happen, not for her anyway. This was the boy who had swung her at the rec, who had beaten her at flicksies, helped her tie string to all the knockers in the street, then pulled them with her, heard the knocks. This was the boy who had run whooping through the streets with her when their neighbours had come to their doors, shouting and swearing at them. Who had written.

'Make it tomorrow,' Jack said, pushing himself up from the wall. 'Come and see me on the stall first, down Malvern Lane. We'll talk, catch up. Things aren't the same in there.' He nodded to his house, his face angry, and then he smiled. 'Get in there and see your grandpa. He's been waiting. He's missed you.'

He sauntered off, nodding at her, not going into his house but on down the street. Then he stopped and called back, 'Got any gum, chum?'

'Sure, a goddamn trunkful,' she called back.

He walked on. Then turned again. 'Glad you're back, Rosie. I would've met you. We've only grown, we ain't changed, you know. Not really. Tomorrow then.'

The hallway was dark and so small and there was no sound in the house. No Bix Beiderbecke, no Erroll Garner, no New Orleans with the banjo cutting through the jumble of sounds, keeping the rhythm going. Rosie stood still, her hands on the wallpaper. It was the same; she could feel the pattern running on down beneath her fingers. She had done this when she left. She remembered now.

She thought of the houses she had passed on the train, with their rooms hanging open to the world, wallpaper torn and flapping. That could have been this house. Her grandpa could have been one of those who died, and she pushed open the door into the room where they cooked and washed and lived because she couldn't bear the thought of that and knew now that she still loved him.

28

There he was, sitting at the table with the brown chipped teapot in front of him. It was the one Grandma had bought. So that hadn't changed. But, dear God, he had. He turned as she entered.

'Rosie, you're here. I didn't know when you were coming, if you were coming. I couldn't rest. I've waited all week for you.'

Somehow she smiled, put down her bags, her jacket and walked towards him, her hands held out. He stood and pulled her to him, holding her close. Her arms were round this man who had once been strong and firm, who had held her with nailmaker's arms and told her he loved her. He was thin, and so small, so old with an old man's smell and he had always been so clean.

She looked past him to Norah. You bitch, she thought, you've just lied to me, you lied to him, kept my cable from him. You black-hearted bitch.

'I'm sorry, my Rosie.' His voice was cracked, stumbling, and his words were loose, clumsy, as he whispered, 'I'm sorry for bringing you back. Norah wanted you here and I promised your grandma you'd come home. I thought you'd want to. Norah said you'd think we didn't want you back, if we let you stay. Sometimes I can't think straight, like I used to.'

She held him, remembering how much she had loved him, knowing how much she still did.

Norah was washing dishes in soda, her head up, listening for the words Rosie knew Grandpa did not want her to hear.

'I love you, Rosie. I couldn't have you thinking we didn't want you back,' he repeated.

'I know, I know,' she soothed because the man was now the child and that hurt more than all the pain so far. 'I love you too.'

Rosie moved back, holding his hand, guiding him on to the chair again, pulling another round to sit at the table with him. He wouldn't release her hand. His joints were loose, his face long, his jaw slack and he had no bottom teeth.

'I've sure missed you, Grandpa. Every day. I guess I couldn't wait to get home, to you.' A lie, but what did it matter.

Norah banged down a cup she was washing on the draining board. 'Took your time, then. Planning to stay for more school. That wasn't fair. I told him so.'

29

You talk too goddamn much, Rosie wanted to say, but she didn't because Grandpa didn't move, didn't say anything, just dropped his head and Rosie rubbed the back of his big veined hands, touching the swollen knuckles with her fingers.

'Woolworths not good enough for you, then? It suits me.' Norah was wiping the cup with a teatowel.

Rosie sat back. 'Woolworths will be fine. Just fine. I can't think of anything I would rather do, Norah.' But she wanted to say, You still got that dandy fox fur? You must think you're the tops waltzing in wearing that, but she didn't because Norah had been left behind and no matter what she'd said or done since, it wasn't fair. And that was that.

Norah turned back, tucking the edge of the towel into the cutlery drawer beneath the drainer.

'You'd better get down to the Food Office tomorrow to get your ration book. You're eating our points.' She gestured to the pan on the old gas oven. 'Put that on the table.'

Rosie wanted to tip the pan upside-down on that prissy perm but instead she smiled at Grandpa, who brought out a handkerchief with a trembling hand and raised it to his mouth, wiping the corners, putting it away again carefully. So careful, so slow; like his writing had looked, but she hadn't noticed.

Too many years had passed and Rosie saw the old brown-stones as she fetched the pan full of mashed potatoes. She looked for a bowl.

'Put it on the table in the pan. Or have you forgotten how we live?'

Rosie flushed. There was nothing she could say because she had.

'I've got tins of ham in the trunk. Shall I go get them?' She moved towards the door.

'No, the Spam's cut. We'll save the ham for something special.'

So there we are, Rosie thought as she sat down. I'm home. I sure am home. But she wouldn't cry, not here, and she reached again for Grandpa's hand. Now she was here she remembered the room and it hadn't changed. Along one wall were all Grandpa's books. He'd read each one and had wanted her and Jack to do the same, but she'd run out of time, and so had Jack. Norah had refused to read them.

She looked round as she cut the pink Spam, eating it with mashed potatoes but no salad. The dresser was the same, the bread board, the bread knife with the burned handle, the worn lino, and there were no cockroaches, maybe no bed bugs. There was a bed in the room though, the folding one that her mother had slept on whilst her father used the chair.

She turned to Norah. 'Is that my bed?'

Norah pointed her knife at Grandpa. 'No, it's his. He has accidents. It's not worth soiling a proper bed and he can reach the privy quicker.'

Grandpa continued to chew but flicked a glance at Rosie, then reached for his handkerchief and wiped his lips, again.

Rosie talked then about the trip over, the train, the damage, the bombs. She talked of anything and everything because she couldn't bear to see the shame in Grandpa's eyes, to hear that voice slashing and wounding as it had always done. The war had changed nothing in Norah.

Norah ate on, chewing, drinking her water, not listening. Rosie knew she wasn't listening but at least she wasn't speaking.

Grandpa rose and walked to the back door, out to the privy. 'Won't be a moment,' he said.

Norah continued to eat. Rosie talked then of New York's rundown East Side, the 'lung blocks', those tenements which gave their people TB.

'Like Mum and Dad,' she said. 'If we hadn't had Grandma and Grandpa, what would we have done? He was just great to us.'

'They wouldn't have been working in the laundry anyway if he'd stayed in Bromsgrove.' Norah pointed her knife at the yard. 'What was wrong with being a nailer? He goes on about it enough. Grandma didn't want to come down. She told me.'

Rosie said, 'Grandma was always complaining. You couldn't take anything she said seriously and you've got awful like her. You've got a tongue like a . . .' but Grandpa came back and so she hurried on and spoke of the hop-picking they'd done in the years before the war. The sun, the smell, the fun.

'Couldn't go to Kent like the rest though, could we? Had to be up in Malvern because that's where the Midlanders used to go.' Norah didn't look up as she spoke, just hooked a piece of mash at the corner of her mouth with her tongue. 'Why couldn't we be the same as everyone else? That's what I want to know.'

Rosie cut in. 'So, how was Somerset then, Norah? Did you settle in?' She wanted to draw that sour tongue away from the old man who had sent her away and then brought her back, but only because he thought it best for her. She knew that now. She had always known it really, but the anger was still there, inside her, mingled with the pain.

'Not as good as America. Country life is hard. I skivvied, worked my fingers to the bone.'

Rosie looked at her. 'Got enough flesh on you now then, Norah, you could slip on a marble any day and not break that goddamn backside.'

No one was eating now. Norah sat back, her eyes dark with rage, her mouth closed into a thin line. Then she finished her potatoes, stabbing them with the fork. Rosie took the plates, washed them in the kettle water. It was nearly dark now and the cracked clock above Grandpa's bed said nine o'clock.

'I've got presents in the trunk,' Rosie said, turning, leaning back on the sink. 'A great nightdress and stockings for you, Norah, a sweater for you, Grandpa.' Her voice was conciliatory. She must try again if they were to live together. She must keep telling herself that, because Norah had suffered, while she hadn't.

Norah was reading a magazine at the table but she looked up now.

'You're sleeping in the boxroom. I've got the front bedroom.'

Of course you've got the goddamn front room, Rosie thought, and I bet that goddamn fox fur is hanging on the back of the door, his goddamn eyes glinting, but she said nothing.

She pushed open the door into the yard and took Grandpa's arm, feeling him lean on her as she helped him to the bench under the kitchen window. The air was full of the fragrance of his roses.

She put the newspaper on the bench which was still damp and then they sat, neither speaking, for what was there to say? So much, too little.

'Of course he wouldn't dig up his precious yard to put in a

shelter. It would have disturbed the roses,' Norah called through the door.

Rosie put her hand on Grandpa's. 'Quite right too,' she said quietly.

'Wouldn't go down to the shelter in Albany Street either. He wouldn't sleep with strange people. Got to be different.'

'I like my privacy,' Grandpa said loudly now.

'I guess we all do,' Rosie nodded, patting his hand, glad that he was answering Norah, jerking his head up, sticking his chin out. Glad too that she need not sleep in the same bed with that girl ever again.

She leaned forward, smelling the dark red cottage rose which was growing well in the raised bed which Grandpa had built years ago. There was a trailing pink clambering up the privy.

Rosie walked round the plants now, looking closely. There was no greenfly. She drew near the shed which still smelt of creosote but only faintly.

'I guess we need to do this again,' she called to her grandfather.

'If you can find any, go on and do it. Don't forget we're rationed even if you haven't been,' Norah shouted. Rosie didn't bother to tell her that America had in fact been rationed. She knew it couldn't compare with British measures.

In the shed the trunk was laid down flat and behind it was an old upended pram turned into a cart. Rosie edged past the trunk. She had forgotten all about the cart. Ollie and Grandpa had made it and she and Jack had raced it against First Street. Norah wouldn't race with them. She might get hurt, she might get dirty. Rosie leaned down and smelt the old leather, spun the wheels.

'I told him to get rid of it but he wouldn't.' Norah was there behind her now. She was waiting for her present. Well, she'd have to wait a little longer.

Later, when it was quite dark and the curtain had been drawn round Grandpa's bed, Rosie called good night.

'I couldn't let the pram go,' he replied softly. 'It reminded me of you, see.'

Rosie did see and she called, 'I love you, Grandpa. I've missed you so much.' And to begin with she had.

That night Rosie didn't shut the door of her bedroom. She

33

hadn't shut the door on her first night at Nancy and Frank's either. She had felt too lonely, too homesick and had cried silently. She cried now, silently too, thinking of Frank and Nancy, of Sandra, of Joe, of the lake. Crying more as she thought of this house where she'd been born and which wasn't home any more, of this country which was strange to her, of the anger, the pain, the confusion which swept over her in waves. And the despair.

She clenched the woollen knitted blanket she had made before she left and sleep would not come as she tried to cling to Frank's words. 'The future is yours. Make something positive out of the rest of your life.'

Downstairs, Albert lay back on his bed. He could see the table, the cooker, the sink in the dull moonlight. She was back, his Rosie was back. She had looked like her mother when she came in, her hair short, her plaits gone, but the same love in her face that Martha had always had for him.

He coughed, his chest was bad. He was old. The rubber square beneath his sheet made him sweat and it smelt, but then, he smelt too. He turned from the room, lying with his face to the wall. Perhaps he shouldn't have brought her back.

He turned again, back into the room. It was hot now and he was tired but he didn't want to sleep. He sometimes had accidents when he slept.

Perhaps it had been too long, he thought, for he had seen that behind the love there was despair. But he had to believe he had done the right thing as he had had to when he waved her off from Liverpool. It had broken his heart to see the ship becoming smaller and then the loneliness of the war had broken him somehow.

He struggled now, pushing himself up, looking at his books. Maybe Norah had been wrong to think that Rosie would feel deserted if they left her there. And there again she was right, it wouldn't have been fair if one sister had advantages denied to the other. It was all so confusing. He just didn't know. Norah was wrong too, about Nellie not wanting to come to London.

Nailing was dying in Bromsgrove, there was nothing to be made from it any more. His wife had wanted to come south and he remembered with bitterness her face that day when she had insisted they move. But then he pushed the memory from him

34

and thought instead of the land of his roots and Herefordshire too; the sweeping hills, the lush green of the fields, the hops strung so high – and he smiled at the comfort the memory brought.

Yes, there had been despair behind Rosie's love, and he knew it was because she'd left a land and people she'd grown to care for and there was an ache in his chest at her pain. He eased himself back down, pulling the sheet up round his shoulders. He understood that and he would try and take her back to those hills where the scent of the past would ease the present, perhaps for them all, even Maisie and Ollie.

CHAPTER 3

The night had been long, and as Rosie washed in the sink she longed for her own shower and scented soap back in Lower Falls, but there was only the tin bath which hung on the yard wall. Tonight, she thought, she would drag it in when Grandpa was asleep and Norah in bed. Tonight and every night, not just once a week like before she went away.

Grandpa was sitting at the table. Rosie had washed through his drenched sheets and his pyjamas and they were hung on the line, along with his rubber square. She had hoisted them high with the pole but not too high, because he had said that he did not like the neighbours to know.

'Even Jack's mum and dad?' she had asked gently as he dipped his bread in some warm milk after he had sponged himself down standing on newspaper behind the curtain.

'Even Ollie and Maisie,' he had said.

She carried her tea out into the yard, standing by the shed in the spot the sun reached at this hour of the morning. She listened to the sounds of the street, the dogs, the children, the whistling bike-riders, the rag and bone cry. She looked up at Jack's house. The windows were blank and there was no sound. Before she left there had always been laughter and music and shouting.

Her grandfather walked out now and sat on the bench, his back against the wall. He had a walking stick which he propped between his knees. When she was young he would bring peas home on a Saturday wrapped in newspaper and on Sunday they would shell them, sitting on the back step, eating some, putting the rest into Grandma's pan.

Jack would come in and pinch five, always five, throwing them up and catching them in his mouth. Then Maisie would shout across the wall that there was bread and hot dripping from around the piece of scrag-end. She, Jack, and sometimes Norah would go while Ollie and Grandpa went to the pub on the corner for a pint.

The pub had gone too, she realised now. She had forgotten that it had existed, down next to Mr Meiner. She fingered the peach rose, The Reverend Ashe, which grew up against the shed. It had taken a fancy to the creosote, Grandpa had laughed in the year before the war. She had made perfume with its petals. The water had gone brown but there had been a weak scent.

She had given a bottle to Grandma, Norah and Maisie. Maisie had laughed and dabbed some on behind her ears, heavy with earrings, throwing back her head, patting her hair, telling them it made her feel like a ruddy duchess. Ollie roared and slapped her on the backside. Grandma and Norah had thrown theirs down the sink.

As Norah grew older she had always copied Grandma, though Rosie could remember that when they were small sometimes they had laughed together. But as Grandma grew more bitter, more angry, Norah copied her. They froze Rosie out. They formed a team. A team 'who knew better', who were older, wiser. Just more crabby, Jack had always said.

Rosie drank her tea, which was too cold now, then threw the dregs around the roots.

'You remembered then, Rosie,' Grandpa called.

Rosie smiled. 'Yes, I've never forgotten.' But she had until this moment. She had forgotten that the tea leaves nourished the roots.

She moved into the shadow, sitting with him, tucking her hand in his arm. It was thin and his armbands sagged above the elbows. His cuffs were drooping on his wrists. 'I'll sew a tuck in those sleeves for you, shall I?'

She smiled as he nodded and patted her hand. His joints were swollen, his skin was dry and thin, stretched too tight. They sat in silence now and still there was no movement from Jack's house. At home there would be the smell of waffles cooking and the sound of jazz playing, and she had to talk to muffle the memory.

'Do you remember the peas, Grandpa?' Rosie asked as she watched a bee weave in and out of the rose bushes.

37

He chuckled. 'They were good times.'

Rosie nodded, looking up into the sky, which was pale blue with small white clouds that seemed to fit the size of England. Yes, perhaps they were but she had seen another world and she couldn't leave it behind yet. Would she ever be able to? She looked at Jack's house again.

'What's wrong next door? Jack seemed strange. He told me not to go in. There was something in his eyes.'

Grandpa leaned forward, poking the ground with his stick, rubbing it backwards and forwards across the cracks in the concrete. 'You'll have to ask Jack. People have a right to their privacy. He'll tell you what he wants you to know, if there is anything. It's maybe just the war.'

He brought out his handkerchief and wiped the corners of his mouth. 'It's maybe just the war, Rosie. It changes so much.'

'Yes, Grandpa. But you haven't changed and neither have I.' Did he know she was lying?

Rosie left him in the yard then because she was thinking too clearly of Frank and Nancy, of Sandra and Joe, and there was no place for them here where there was no shower, just a tin bath. Where her grandpa's skin was tight and old, where there was no laughter from Maisie.

She was glad she had to sort out ration cards, jobs, shopping. That would do for now. Later, when the sun was past its height she would talk to Jack. Later still she would write to Frank to refuse his offer of money to finance further education. All that was over. They were no longer responsible for her. She was back in her old world. She looked at the list Norah had written, this was her reality now.

Rosie spent an hour at the Food Office waiting for a ration card, then joined a queue forming outside a small shop and waited for half an hour shuffling forward slowly while the sun beat down. Norah had said, join any queue you see, there'll be something at the end of it, but today it was dog food and they didn't have a dog. She bought a pound anyway and gave it to the woman at the end of the queue with two crying children. She knew Jack would have sold it to a man without a dog for twice as much and she smiled at the thought.

She registered with Norah's grocer round the corner whom

she had known as a child, collecting tea and cheese at the same time. The shop seemed so dark, so small. The goods on the shelves were dull, meagre. He nodded to her. 'Back then. Norah told us you'd had it easy.'

'I guess I did,' she replied and watched his tight withdrawn face, wanting to apologise, wanting to take the years back, stay here, be one of them again. But at the same time, wanting to shout her anger at him.

'Next please,' he called, hurrying her, looking past her.

'I'd like some Players, please,' she said, resisting the push from behind.

'Only available to our regulars.' He was reaching forward for the next customer's ration card.

'They're for Grandpa,' Rosie insisted, not moving over. She had just enough for a packet and then her money from Frank was gone.

The man sighed. His brows met across the bridge of his nose and his eyes were tired. He bent below the counter and passed her one pack.

'Thanks.' She paid and walked past the queue which was jostling behind her.

'These Americans think they can come here and throw their money about. Isn't right, it isn't,' one old lady said to the woman next to her. Rosie didn't look at them, she didn't look anywhere but in front, thinking of the lake, of the sloping lawns and the soaring music. I didn't choose to go, she wanted to scream at their shadowed faces and resentful backs.

She walked back down the street towards the Woolworths in Albany Street. She wouldn't cry, she mustn't. Whatever she did, she mustn't let these Britishers see her pain, or even her anger because she had no right to that. They had stayed and endured. She had fled.

Outside Woolworths she stopped, looking in through the glass doors, seeing the lights, the long alleys of counters. She and Jack had pinched a 6d car from here when they were eight. She'd longed to work in amongst it all. But that was then.

At eleven she stood in an office before a white-haired supervisor, her hair permed like Norah's.

'So, you're Norah's sister. Good worker, that girl.'

The woman had run her lipstick outside her top lip to

thicken it. Her breath smelt of tea as she moved behind Rosie to take out a file from the cabinet and then returned to her seat.

'Sit down then.' There was a cup half full on the desk with a cigarette stub floating in it.

'Thanks,' Rosie said, smoothing her skirt, not looking into the cup.

The woman brushed at the corners of her mouth with her little finger. There was a brass ring with a bright red glass stone on her wedding finger. 'Well, you'll have to do something about your voice, if you know what I mean.'

Rosie looked at her. 'No, I guess I don't.'

'Well, listen to that. You sound like a Yank. I don't know what our customers would think, I really don't. This is Albany Street, not Hollywood.' The woman frowned. 'But Norah did put in a good word for you. You've got that old man at home to support, haven't you? Need all the help you can get, I should think.'

'My grandfather, you mean. He has his own money. He doesn't need ours. Norah and I have to work to keep ourselves, not him. It's his house, you know. He gives us a home.' She was tired now, so goddamn tired of it all, so sick of Norah. 'He's a real nice man. Kind of quiet but nice.'

She looked out across the store with its counters glistening with goods. Norah was on jewellery, leaning back talking to the girl at the other end. She was smiling, her mouth a slash of red.

'Oh well, we need someone on records anyway though the stock is very limited these days. Maybe the voice will fit in there. All American anyway, aren't they, these singers?' The woman's voice was slower, kinder. When she smiled the lines cut deep. 'My dad was a nice man too.'

Rosie looked at her closely now and felt her face begin to relax.

'We had a lot of Americans here in the war. They'd come and talk. My friend married one. She's in California now.' The woman was pulling her overalls across her breast. 'Yes, proper little meeting-place in here. It's very dull now. England is very dull. I expect you've found that.'

Rosie looked out again, across the aisles. 'I only got in yesterday and I guess it's real good to be here.' If she said it often enough it might help it to be the truth.

40

'Oh well, that's nice.' The woman was moving towards the door. 'Perhaps we can move you into the snack bar when we get one. You seem like a good girl. Start tomorrow, why don't you.'

Rosie walked out of the office into the hub of the store. The Andrews Sisters were singing 'The Three Caballeros' and she wondered how Albany Street would take to Bix Beiderbecke. She walked past Norah and smiled – after all they were not children feuding any longer. Norah had been unfairly treated and Rosie must damp down the anger.

'I'm on records,' she said.

'Well, don't be late. Grandpa needs his lunch. There's a nice bit of Spam in the meat-safe.' Norah turned away, then back again.

'I suppose you're meeting that Jack. Well, not until you've done the chores, you're not.'

'One day, you'll find yourself being pleasant and it will be as much of a goddamn shock to yourself as it will be to the rest of the world.' Rosie walked away, leaving Norah to close her open mouth, and all the way home she was glad she had let the anger out. It helped her to lift her head, but from now on she must rein back in.

She opened a tin of American ham for Grandpa instead.

'This is our celebration,' she told him. There was no ice-box so Rosie drank lukewarm milk, then sank the bottle into the pail of water again. She stood a bowl in water and left half the ham in it for Norah's meal that evening. It was only fair.

She and Grandpa ate tinned peaches which slipped on the spoon and were easy to eat. Juice trickled down both their chins and they laughed as they had done before she left.

It was only when he was asleep and the floor was washed, the dishes too, when the cooker was cleaned and her arms were black from the grime, when the beds were made, that she left, wondering how Norah could sleep with those fox's eyes glinting on the back of the door. But what did it matter? She was going to see Jack, but then she heard her grandfather calling. She turned. He was in the doorway, waving to her, leaning on his stick with the other hand.

'You forgot your matchbox.'

For a moment Rosie paused and then she remembered the ladybirds which she used to catch in a matchbox she always carried when she went out. She called, 'No I didn't, I've got one in my pocket. Don't worry, we'll keep the roses clear of greenfly.'

He smiled and waved again and turned back into the house. Rosie stopped at a tobacconist, bought a matchbox and tipped the matches out into the bin. He mustn't know that she had forgotten.

Malvern Lane was too narrow to receive much sun and Rosie watched as Jack moved backwards and forwards in front of his stall, holding a flowered teapot high above his head, laughing with one woman, nodding to another who picked up a saucer and turned it over in her hands. She dropped money into his left hand and pushed the saucer deep into her shopping bag.

'Come on then, ladies. Don't let the rationing get to you. Look, it's a lovely day up there above the clouds, let's have a smile, shall we?' He was laughing now and the crowd laughed with him, Rosie too, but he hadn't seen her yet and she was glad. She wanted to stand here, listening, watching, trying to ease into London just for a moment. Trying to push away the thought of the intersections, the streetcars, the ice-cream parlors.

'Just look at this.' Jack pointed to the teapot which he still held high. 'When did you last see a splash of colour like this then, eh? Can't buy it now, can you? Certainly not. Only white can be made the chiefs have said.' He looked round at them all. 'Well, that's as may be, but today is your lucky day. Here – ' Jack turned and gestured to the back of the stall – 'I have just a few little treasures so who's going to give me five bob for this then?'

It went on like that for half an hour and by that time all the coloured china had gone, as Rosie knew it would, and as the crowds thinned he saw her and called across.

'Did you remember your matchbox, then?'

The woman in front of Rosie turned. Her cheeks were red and her smile broad. 'He's a one, that lad. Could charm the bleeding birds out of the trees.'

Rosie laughed and held up the box. She didn't want to speak, to drawl. She didn't know if the woman would stop smiling.

'Be with you in half an hour. The gang's coming,' Jack called

42

again, then he laughed as a woman came and slapped his arm, giving him money for two plates and telling him she'd take another if he threw in a kiss with it. He looked at Rosie again and pointed to his watch. It wasn't gold, his skin wasn't tanned. Was Joe playing tennis now? Was Sandra?

She wandered off, down the lane, moving out round a heap of yellowed cabbage leaves whose smell followed her on down past the potatoes, the lettuce, and drowned the scent of the pinks tied in small bunches and left to stand in a tin jug.

There was a tea stall and she bought a cup, sipping it, hearing the past all around her, the noises, the voices, breathing in the smells which had faded and vanished with the years. But they were here again, all here.

So, the gang was coming too. She didn't remember them, not their names or their faces. It was only Jack she had pictured over the years and the miles. Would Joe and Sandra forget her too?

When she returned Jack was waiting, his old leather money apron now tied around the waist of his father, Ollie, who had run the stall for as long as Rosie could remember. She started to walk towards Ollie but Jack caught at her arm.

'Leave it for now.'

They walked to the rec where they had scuffed the ground with worn plimsolls on hot days as they pumped themselves higher and higher on swings already raised by being thrown over the bar. They didn't talk as they walked through the streets, and Jack had to lead the way because she had forgotten. He sauntered, hands in pockets, his two-tone shoes worn, his hair hanging down over his forehead.

She remembered her shoes, and the sweater she had worn back to front as all Lower Falls girls did, but they were in her room, on the shelf below the Cougar pennant and she mustn't think of that.

They crossed wasteground which had once been three houses. The rec was across the road from Oundle Street where there were houses with black-tarred casement sheets instead of glass. They were all deserted and two were ripped apart; just as she felt.

She remembered the park with railings but they were gone and now Jack told her how his mum had written to say that they had been taken away by men with oxyacetylene cutters to build Spitfires.

'How's your mum?' she asked. 'It was so quiet today.'

His eyes were dark as he turned, then looked past her. 'Race you to the swings.'

He ran, catching her arm, running with her across worn asphalt where weeds were breaking through, running faster than her, goddamn it, and so now she spurted but he was still ahead and the breath was leaping in her throat as the swings drew nearer. But he was first, throwing himself on to one, pushing back with his feet, lifting them high and then surging forward, up into the air.

She sat on hers and looked at the sign that said, '12 YEARS AND UNDER ONLY.'

'Hey, we'll be done.'

She heard his laugh. 'Come on, Yank. We've just been through a war. No one's going to stop me swinging if I want to.'

She pushed off now, feeling the air slicing through her, half pain, half pleasure. The links were rusty and stained her hands and then there was only the squealing of the chain and their laughter. She leaned back, the sky was blue. It was the same sky over America. Maybe it wasn't so far after all, but she knew that it was.

Afterwards they talked, still sitting on the swings, Jack's legs gently moving his, his shoulders leaning hard into the chain, his hands between his knees.

He told her then that Ollie was drinking, snarling. Sleeping a little. Working a little. That Maisie seldom laughed now.

'But they were so different. Was it the war? What about Lee? Hasn't he helped?'

There were two small children standing by the swings now and Jack winked at them, standing, nodding to them.

'It's all yours,' he called and they ran past him and Rosie, who stood too and watched as they scrambled on to the swings.

'Give us push, mister,' the boy with red hair said.

Jack did and Rosie watched as his broad hands pushed and caught, pushed and caught the swing.

'I'm OK now,' the boy said and they walked over to the bench. The dark green paint was flaking. Rosie brushed the seat with her hand, rubbing the paint off as she sat.

'Didn't Lee help?' Rosie insisted, watching the two children, hearing their yells clearly across the intervening space. She didn't want to hear of Ollie snarling, of Maisie silent. She wanted to hear of laughter, of bread and dripping, of earrings jangling.

Jack shrugged. He reached down, pulling at a dandelion which had lifted the asphalt. 'He seems to have made it worse and he's a lovely kid. It can't have been the war either. Dad didn't get called up. It's his chest you see, collapsed lung. He built the new airfields, that sort of thing. Did a bit of dealing.' He smiled slightly but his eyes were so angry.

Rosie smiled, looking away. 'I just bet he did.'

'I wasn't there, you see. The kids that came back after the first evacuation went away again with the Blitz, like you did.' He flicked the shredded dandelion at her. 'She was good to me though, Mum was. She came down visiting, you know. All the time. It was good fun.'

'Was your dad jealous of that?'

'No, I don't think so. He didn't change until later. When he came to see me first he was fine. Took back a few hams, sold them well. Even did a bit of dealing with the GIs who were camped in the village.' He paused and looked up at the sky, and his voice became angry. 'But then, all of a sudden like, he stopped coming. Didn't see Mum much come to that after D-Day. Busy, I expect, and then there was Lee. He's got red hair too.' Jack flicked a piece of grass off his trousers, nodding towards the boy he had pushed on the swing. 'I don't know what's wrong. It's just wrong. I wanted to tell you before you came. I didn't want you upset.'

His face was red now and he didn't look at her. She wanted to reach across and hold him as he had once held her when she cut her knee and needed stitches. But they were children then. They were grown now and there was a difference somehow.

He looked at her now and the anger had gone, there was just tiredness, like hers. 'Come anyway. They want to see you but it's funny, me dad doesn't like Yanks.'

Rosie looked at her hands. 'He's not the only one.'

'Oh, I reckon it's this rationing, you know. Makes people crabby.'

There were voices behind them now, calling, shouting, and a

football bounced behind them and over them and Jack looked at Rosie. 'Remember the gang? I thought it would help you settle back in.'

She did remember when they were all around, touching her clothes, laughing at her tan, at her voice, asking about Lower Falls and New York and the skiing. Telling her about Somerset, where they had all been evacuated. She looked away, wishing she had been with them, wishing that she belonged as she had once done.

It was Sam, the old second-in-command, his hair in a crew cut, who showed her that for him at least she no longer did.

'So you came back. Slumming, eh?' he said, not looking away when Jack told him to shut his mouth. His pale eyes held hers as he bounced the ball, then threw it to Ted, then Jack. Then bounced it again.

Her eyes were blurred but it was tiredness, she mustn't think it was tears. She remembered Sam all too clearly now. He had tied her to a lamppost when they were nine and fired arrows at a potato he stuck on her head. She hadn't cried then and she wouldn't now.

There were laughs and jokes, and always the ball was on the move. She watched, listened, smiled, waited and then Sam threw the ball to her, hard. She had known that he would and batted it straight back at him with a clenched fist as Frank had taught her. He caught it and threw it again, talking to Ted as he did so, but looking at her all the time.

She threw the ball to Jack. He looked at Sam, then back at her. There was a question in his eyes and she knew he had brought them together deliberately, to face up and get it over with. She shook her head. She was angry now and she would deal with this herself. This was her rec too, her gang, and nobody was going to take it away from her. They'd taken enough already.

She hurled the ball hard at Sam, and nothing more was said as they caught and threw, caught and threw, just the two of them. Her arm was tired and she was hot, but it didn't matter. Frank had trained her well.

It was Ted who broke the silence. 'So, how's po-face taken to you coming back?' he asked.

Rosie kept her eye on the ball, waiting for it to come again, feeling the stinging in her hands, seeing the two small boys running over from the swings, leaving a space beside her for them to join in. Waiting, too, for Sam. The ball came. She hurled it back. He caught it; she heard the slap of skin against leather. She needed her leather mitt.

'You can't blame Norah, she had a lousy time, like the rest of you,' she panted.

She caught the ball again, then batted it back but Jack intercepted and passed it on to the small red-haired boy. Rosie felt the throbbing in her hands, but she wouldn't look at them. She looked instead at Sam. What would he do now?

'No way that old bag had a bad time. Come on, let's sit down,' Dave called.

Sparrows were sitting in the clubbed trees around the rec, singing and flying. Jack walked to the bench and the others followed. Sam took Woodbines from his pocket, shaking his head, looking at Rosie, his eyes still cold. His hands were red, like hers. Did they throb like hers too?

'Your Norah should have gone too. Bloody unfair, I call it.'

Jack looked up at Sam, then at Rosie and she shook her head again.

Ted said, 'That's a load of rubbish. She was billeted with the doctor over in the next village. Had a life of old Reilly, never even had to flick a bleeding duster.'

They were sitting and leaning on the bench now, cigarette smoke drifting up into the air, watching the two small boys kicking the ball from one to another, hearing the thuds. Rosie said nothing, not yet.

Sam flicked his ash on to the ground, rubbing it in with his shoe. 'I bet Rosie never had to flick a duster either. Bet she never had to queue for food. Bet she stuffed herself with ice-cream, steak, got taken out by flash American boys, the brothers of those GIs who swanked over here.' Sam laughed but it was a hard sound. 'Well, go on. Did you?'

Rosie flushed, looking across at the two boys, then back at Sam again. 'What's wrong, bud, did a GI steal your girl?'

Ted laughed, clapped Sam on the shoulder. 'She got you there.' They were all laughing now, Jack too, but his eyes were still watchful. Sam did not laugh.

He stubbed out his cigarette carefully on the sole of his shoe and put it back in his cigarette packet. Rosie watched. She had forgotten people did that. She had forgotten that they needed to and she wanted to say she was sorry, but no, she had to fight Sam. That's all there was to it, or there was no place for her here, with them.

'No,' Sam said, 'nobody stole my girl. I just don't like freeloaders who come back home and lord it about in their new clothes, expecting everyone to bow and scrape because they're back. This is the real world here.'

They were all standing now and Rosie looked at all their faces. They were uncertain, all except Jack, who was looking at her, waiting to see if she could make it on her own. It was only if she couldn't that he would come in. He had always been like that. He had always been there behind her.

Sam turned to her. 'You've had it on a plate. No rationing, no bombs, just bloody everything you want. So just don't come back here, Rosie Norton, and drawl all over the rest of us.'

There was silence. Jack was still watching her. 'There *was* rationing,' she said but that was all because they were never really short of anything, and there was no danger for her.

'Oh yeah, when did you last have a banana?' Sam said, his eyes narrow. Jack's were, too, but they were looking at Sam.

Rosie couldn't answer because Frank had exchanged a piece of pork for a hand of bananas last year and the year before. She looked at them all, at their pale skins, their tired faces, and said, 'You're right. I had it cushy, I have a drawl. I had bananas last year and I'm sorry. It's not fair. Do you think I don't know that? But I'm back. I haven't changed.'

There was silence as they stood around her. Sam's lips were still thin. Jack's eyes were steady. The others were nodding, smiling, all uncertainty gone.

Sam still didn't smile though. He said, 'OK, you say you haven't changed.' He looked at Jack. 'You tell her about tonight, then bring her along. We'll see if she's changed. We'll see if she's got too good for us all.'

Jack's face set, he took Sam by the arm, moving him along towards the pavement. Ted followed. Dave and Paul too. Rosie didn't. She watched them, then the delivery boy cycling past. He rode 'no hands' and sat with his arms folded, whistling. She looked back at the gang. What was happening tonight? Whatever it was, she'd do it.

Ted turned towards her, then nodded to Jack, so did the others. Sam just stared and then called to her, 'Be there.'

The delivery boy had reached the corner. Rosie called back, 'Bank on it, Sam.' But what was it?

As they walked back without Sam and the others, Jack told her about the bomb which had killed Sam's mother, the GI jeep that had killed his sister. But he wouldn't tell her about tonight. 'Not yet,' he said. 'I didn't want you involved. I have to explain some things first.'

They passed the black-tarred replacement windows in a damaged house and he told her how in this time of shortages he, Ollie, Sam and the gang had bought demob suits off the men coming home and resold them at a profit, and that didn't hurt anybody because the soldiers didn't want them anyway.

He told her about the drivers who would deliver twenty-one pigs to the wholesalers and be given a receipt for twenty. How the odd one would be sold, piece by piece. For a lot of money. It was big business. Nasty business.

'But what about tonight?'

He told her about the police swoop on marketeers in March designed to end the racketeering. About the major roadblocks around London and other cities. About the lorries and vans the police searched for eggs, meat, poultry. He told her about the market stalls being raided. He told her that the police were still stopping and searching anyone who seemed suspicious. That it was a dangerous time to be out and about if it looked as though you were up to anything shady.

'But what about tonight?'

He asked her if she remembered Jones who had owned their houses. Jones was getting very flash, he said, because he took people's money for black-market produce like that extra piece of pork – and only sometimes delivered the goods. He also pinched produce from the local allotments, but they could find no proof. Last of all, he had taken two cheeses from a farm where the neighbourhood owned two cows and had a cheese club.

'Sure I remember him, now what about tonight?' She

49

grabbed him now, turning him to her, laughing, and it was the first time she had done that for so long.

'Tonight we are not banging door knockers, we are not cutting up sleepers for fuel and selling it, we are not making cigarettes out of dog-ends. Tonight we are breaking into a warehouse owned by Jones and taking two of his cheeses. You, me, Sam and Ted. All the gang. We're taking back what's ours. Are you coming?'

He was still facing her, his eyes serious, though his mouth was smiling. She thought of the lake, but all that was slipping away from her. Just for now, it was more distant.

She thought of Grandpa, the police action Jack had just explained. 'We could get caught?' He voice was serious.

'Yes.' He didn't hesitate. 'Yes, we could. It might be big trouble.'

'Does this cheese really belong to the street or is it all for money?'

'No. The cheese is ours. We're sick of getting taken for a ride, and being pushed around.'

She smiled, walking on now, hearing him catch her up.

'When do we start?' she said because she knew all about being pushed around.

It was dark when she left the house. She had bathed in the tin bath as she said she would and felt better. She wore a loose dress, it was so hot.

They met outside Jack's and walked quietly, neither speaking until they reached the end of Middle Street, then cut across to Vernon Terrace, up the alley, down to Futcher's Walk, picking up the others, picking up Sam. Nothing was said as they approached the wall which ran round the warehouse.

There were dogs but Jack knew them and called to them quietly. Then he was bunked up and over by Sam who shot Ted up too. Sam went next, the others after. She was to be look-out. Sam would wait the other side of the wall to relay any warning.

A cyclist approached and Rosie walked slowly on, then back again when he had overtaken. She listened and looked and wished they would goddamn hurry. She thought of Grandpa asleep, of Norah too. She thought of Joe and Sandra, Frank and

Nancy, but still she looked and listened for over half an hour and again wished they'd hurry because she was out here on her own.

There were sounds now, the soft bark of a dog, voices, and Jack called, 'All clear?'

It was, and so he threw one cheese, then the other, then scrabbled over himself. It had all been so easy. She had proved herself to Sam, to them all.

But then they saw the police, walking towards them, dipping in and out of the lamplight, and Jack grabbed her, told her to run, told the others to stay – for Christ's sake stay behind the wall.

She felt her fear and his. She thought of Grandpa, and then of Sam, and now the fear was gone. She turned to Jack.

'No, put your arm round me, kiss me.'

He looked at her, then at the police. He ducked his head and kissed her with soft lips and she hugged him, turning her back, pushing the cheeses up inside her dress, and then they walked towards the police. Everything was quiet, all they could hear were the footsteps walking in time towards them. She didn't know if they had seen. She didn't know if a hand would grip her shoulder and her Grandpa would know what she had been doing.

She held her stomach, walking with legs slightly apart, feeling Jack's arm around her. It too was tense, trembling, and then she started to cry, asking him why they couldn't marry, especially with the baby due so soon. She clutched the cheeses to her.

They were level with the police now and Rosie turned her face into his shoulder. It was warm, as Joe's had been.

'Just don't leave me, that's all. If you won't marry, don't leave me.'

The police looked away, embarrassed, and Jack held her closer, his breath warm in her hair, and his arm was relaxed, warm now because they hadn't been stopped yet, and maybe they wouldn't be. He held her close and said that he would stay for ever, but she must eat more calcium, more cheese. Then they were well past the police and near the corner.

'Oh Jack,' she said, 'I know the baby will look just like you.'
And now they were round the corner and running, laughing.

51

That night she lay in bed, hearing Jack's voice, feeling his lips on hers. Sam had bought her a ginger beer. Ted had said it would be bad for the baby. She had laughed with them. The anger in them had eased because they had taken what was theirs and she knew she could do that too. She could take back the future which had seemed to be hers until last month. She would have her journalism, somehow, and she would start tomorrow.

Welcome back, Jack had said when she told him.

CHAPTER 4

The next day Rosie enrolled at evening secretarial classes which would begin in late September. Frank had joined his paper as a cub reporter after teaching himself shorthand and typing. If college hadn't been necessary for him, it wouldn't be for her.

September was too long to wait, though, so she brought home a shorthand book from the library because she was working towards her future now, this very day. It was the only way she would survive the loss, the separation from that other world, those other people she still loved, still grieved for even though she had Grandpa, the gang, and Jack.

July turned to August which was heavy with heat and with rain too, but by then Rosie had learned the rudiments of shorthand on her own late at night in her room, though she still had no speed. But it would come. Goddamn it, it would come. She would make sure it did.

The weather didn't matter during the day either because she had coaxed Mrs Eaves into letting her play Bix Beiderbecke through the speakers so that his mellifluous cornet-playing filled the store. But only once a day, Mrs Eaves, the supervisor, had said, jangling the keys on the belt of her overalls, leaning across the mahogany counter, because the public prefer the Andrews Sisters, Glenn Miller – the romantic, the slick.

So too did Norah, but Rosie didn't care so much about that now that she knew. Norah had not had such a bad war. She had pranced around, showing off, drinking tea with a cocked little finger, putting the milk in last.

'So why lie?' Rosie had asked Jack.

He had shrugged and so she had asked Norah that same day, leaning on the rectangular counter, talking quietly so that the other assistants could not hear.

53

Norah had flared with anger. 'I'm not lying,' she said, 'not really. You had a much better time. It should have been me. I'm older.'

Perhaps, Rosie thought now as she ticked records off against the stocklist, Norah was still trying to adjust, to come to terms with leaving Somerset. Perhaps she yearned for the people who had been her family for that time. If so, she understood and so she played the Andrews Sisters and smiled at Norah, who didn't smile back.

Rosie turned as a customer, a woman in a felt hat, asked for 'Chattanooga Choo Choo'.

'It's sure nice. I really like Glenn Miller,' Rosie said as she wrapped it. Grandpa did too. He had heard it on the wireless and tapped his foot as he read *Silas Marner*. Rosie had laughed and told him that she would try to buy a gramophone and he could bop to Duke Ellington. He had stopped having accidents now. There had been no soiled sheets, no embarrassed lowering of the eyes, and he even wanted to hear of her evenings at the Palais with the gang.

She told him how she and Jack jitterbugged around the floor, feet moving fast, swirling in and then out, up and over his hip, his shoulder, while the MC shook his head, tapped them on the shoulders and pointed to the sign on the wall: ABSOLUTELY NO JITTERBUGGING ALLOWED.

They didn't stop. No one stopped. They all danced. The war was over. They had all fought it, Rosie too, Jack said. They all bore the scars. He could see hers, he had told her, in her eyes, and they were still fresh, but they would go. One day they would go. And we're alive so we'll jitterbug like the others and no one will tell us we can't. So they jitterbugged and it kept the shadows and the pain away.

But there were nights when Ollie lurched home drunk and there was shouting and banging to be heard through the walls. On these nights Jack didn't come dancing, he stayed behind to stand between Maisie, Lee and Ollie. It wasn't the same without him. Dancing with Sam and Ted, Dave and Paul didn't stop her wanting Frank and Nancy. It didn't stop her wanting Maisie and Ollie as they had been before the war. It didn't stop her wanting a much earlier time when there had been no pain or anger in Jack's eyes. And it made her think of Joe.

Rosie tipped the Beiderbecke record back into its sleeve. Her legs ached. There was no air in the shop and the heat was thick about her. She longed for a draught or the cool of the evening. She pulled her burgundy overall away from her back and then stood still. Nancy had said it was the best way of cooling down. It did no good to fret. Maisie had said that too last night when at last she had come round and Rosie stood still now, thinking of Maisie's plump arms, so like Nancy's.

For a moment it had been like Pennsylvania again but then Nancy had never smelt of lavender. Maisie did, always had done, Rosie realised as she was pulled against that warm, plump woman who had pushed open the yard gate as she and Grandpa were hugging mugs of tea between their hands and breathing in the roses.

What were they talking about? Rosie served another customer, smiling, giving change, settling back against the counter. She couldn't remember, but she smiled again at the thought of the pushchair coming through the gate, the child wide-eyed and unsure. Then Maisie, her red hair brown at the roots, her earrings jangling and her face bright with a smile.

Rosie had stood her mug in the earth of a rose bush and run to Maisie, flinging her arms round her, smelling the older woman's lavender scent. She had looked at Maisie, taking in the circles beneath her eyes and the lines from her nose to her mouth. But the smile was the same and the voice too.

'You took your time coming home. We've missed you,' Maisie said, pulling her close again. 'We've really missed you.' Rosie hadn't spoken. She knew she would have cried, for these arms were Nancy's too and she could hardly bear the pain.

She squeezed Maisie, then turned, her head lowered, to Lee. He was squirming round, his eyes watching her; his smile was Jack's but his skin was pale, freckled. Not like any of the others.

He reached up his hand and gripped her finger and she said how cute he was, and lifted him from the pushchair, taking him to Grandpa, sitting with him on her knee. Maisie poured tea from the pot for herself, fetched Rosie's from the rosebed, dusted the earth off the bottom with her hand, and called Rosie the same mucky devil she'd always been. They laughed together, as they used to do, and then just looked at one another.

'You look tired,' Rosie said, rubbing her cheek against Lee's head. He pulled away and looked at her, his smile there, his eyes watching hers.

'Don't fret at what you hear,' Maisie said, her face drawn. 'It sounds worse than it is.'

Would she come again tonight? Rosie wondered. She'd said she would.

Maisie did come, with Lee again, while Rosie washed clothes in the sink. 'Sit with Grandpa,' she called through to the yard. 'I'll bring the tea out in a minute.'

Norah slammed through from the hall. 'I'm going out, especially now that kid's here. There's no bloody peace.'

'Why don't you stay?' Rosie said as she wrung out the blouse and dress. 'We should try to get on.'

She had decided to be pleasant again, to try and build some sort of a bridge between them this summer because they needed one another. Couldn't Norah see that? Families were important, but then it seemed that Norah preferred her friends.

Norah pulled her cardigan over her shoulders and checked her make-up in the mirror, tucking the lipstick she had melted down last night into her bag.

'I've got better things to do,' she said. 'We're going dancing. Not at the crummy Palais but up West.'

Rosie smiled, wanting to wring her neck instead of the blouse. She shook her hands over the sink, dried them, then picked up the tea tray. Norah's dress didn't fit. It was too tight over the hips.

'Have a good time,' was all Rosie said.

Lee put out his arms to Rosie as she sat down between Maisie and Grandpa.

'Go on, pick him up then,' Maisie said. 'He gets nothing but spoiling from Jack too.'

She was smiling as she pulled out the Camel cigarettes from her bag. 'Thanks for these, Rosie. I should have been in sooner to say thanks – and to say hello. Here you are, Albert.' She leaned past Rosie, handing him one. 'Got your own matches, have you?'

He nodded.

Rosie let Lee walk up her legs and body, holding on to his hands while he arched away, and then she put him down, watching his unsteady walk. He reached into the raised beds, picking up soil, looking at it, dropping it.

Grandpa laughed. 'It's good to have you here, Maisie. A bit like old times. Can't believe this little nipper is one and a half. Seems only yesterday it was Jack and Rosie digging up me roses.'

They flicked their ash into their hands and Rosie leaned back, her face to the sun, watching the smoke spiralling, disappearing. She didn't like the smell and moved to the upturned pail, hugging her knees, laughing as Lee tottered towards her.

'Yes,' Maisie said. 'Just like old times.'

There was silence except for the grunts from Lee.

'Can you put back the clock then, Albert?' Maisie said.

'Yes, can you, Grandpa?' Rosie echoed.

That night Rosie replied to the letters she had received from the previous week. She was glad the lake was so warm, and the swimming good, that the Club tennis court was already being built. But, she wanted to say, how can it all continue as though I've never existed? How can all these things go on when I hurt so much inside?

How many Subscription Dances had gone into the court? she wondered. How many girls had danced with Joe? Had Frank leaned back in his chair and said, 'You make sure you don't drink when you drive that girl.' Of course he hadn't. He only said that about her. But not any more.

She told them of the evening classes to begin at the end of September with Miss Paul over the piano shop – shorthand, typing, book-keeping. She told them of the rationing, of the cheeses; of the roses which were still free of greenfly. She did not tell them about Woolworths, nor about Norah or Maisie. She cried all night and she thought her sobs were silent but they weren't. Grandpa heard them and it was more than he could bear.

The next day, which was a Sunday, he held her hand and said that they would go to Herefordshire again this year. They would go hop-picking as they used to, before the war, before things changed. All of them, Maisie, Ollie, Jack and Lee, just like they used to, and perhaps there she would learn to laugh again deep down inside, and the others would too, and they would cast the war from their lives.

They did go, even Ollie. Even Norah. They took a train on 1 September and then a bus along the roads which wound round and along the rolling green hills because here no one had sliced through nature, but had fitted in with it. Or so Grandpa had always told them when he brought them here each year before the war. Rosie remembered the American street grids, slicing up the towns, and the long straight roads of Pennsylvania, thinking of Frank and Nancy returning to Lower Falls without her now that it was September.

She pushed that from her. She looked out at the fields. There were cider apple orchards. There was space, sky, air. It was green in the distance, not grey and cramped, and slowly she began to remember what had once been, so long ago.

Close by, the barley had been harvested and the ground re-ploughed and that was still the same. Though not each field, not yet, and now those that were left unploughed must wait until the hops were in because for those few short weeks of the harvest all else was put to one side. Would her pain be put to one side too, and everyone else's?

Jones's farm with its large spacious pigsties was the same too. Swept, scrubbed, white-washed, for this was where they always slept. Jack laughed as they stuffed straw into the palliasses, chasing Lee with a handful, pushing some down Maisie's back, then Rosie's. Maisie crept up behind him and they pushed him on to the heaped pile, sitting on him, stuffing straw up his trousers and down his shirt until he begged for mercy, and even then they stopped only when he had gone down on his knees.

Grandpa, Ollie and Jack slept in the end partition. Rosie, Norah, Maisie and Lee were in the next. The rest of the sties were taken by Black Country people and a few from Bromsgrove, and this was why Grandpa came here, and not to Kent. It was here that he heard his Bromsgrove dialect, his roots. Where were hers? Rosie thought.

'Just you wait, he'll be calling us "me dooks" before the day is out,' Maisie said as she gave Lee a biscuit to chew. As they ate supper heated over the primus in the end building he did and they all laughed, even Norah, even Ollie, even Rosie, and it was from deep inside.

Jack and Rosie walked down the lane to the road, watching for the caravans that they knew would come bringing gypsies on from the plum-picking at Evesham, the cherries at Shropshire and the peas at Worcester. The gate was warm from the sun, deep cracked, chipped with the initials they had carved in 1938. Jack covered it over.

'Your Grandpa would catch us with his stick,' he laughed.

Rosie nodded, looking down the lane, hearing the caravans, the barking of the long dogs and lurchers, the ponies which plodded, the brasses which jingled. She felt the wind in her hair and was happy because for the four weeks they were here, this place belonged to her, just as much or as little as it belonged to the others.

The gypsies came now, the women walking at the pony's head, one smoking a clay pipe. The men sat, the reins in their hands. The children sat too, looking ahead, not at Rosie or Jack.

'Never changes, does it?' Jack murmured, watching as they rolled past.

They walked then, up to the hop-fields, neither speaking, taking the path which ran along the top of the kale field. She remembered where to go, she realised. Somehow she knew where to go.

She walked ahead now, confident, hearing Jack close behind. On round the kale which looked like small trees, then further to the ragwort-spotted meadows. At the bottom of these, past clumps of purple-crested thistles, lay the stream. They used to picnic there at the end of the day. She turned.

'Do you remember . . . ?' she began, but stopped for Jack was nodding.

'Yes, I remember. Tinned salmon sandwiches.' He was smiling and there were no shadows in his eyes today. Rosie hoped that there would be none as the four weeks went by. Would Ollie and Maisie be able to go back in time, enough for a fresh start? Would she?

In the distance rooks clawed up into the sky from the copse planted on Trafalgar Day. She turned further up the hill and they were on to the worn top path and into the hop-fields where the bines swung fifteen feet above them in the wind and Rosie stood still, looking about her, remembering.

Her mother had come every year before she died. They had picked all September and her mother had said it made her feel safe, standing here, as Rosie was doing now. Safe from the world. She had died though, her father too. They hadn't been safe. Was there such a thing as safety? Everything changed. It always changed.

'It's like being under the sea,' Jack said, standing close to her, looking up.

It seemed so quiet, no dogs barking, no cyclists whistling, no children playing. She loved this first evening before the picking began and the hops were stripped.

'I love this first evening,' Jack said.

When they returned to the sties the Welsh had arrived and were in the barn, singing, shouting, laughing. One child was crying but Lee was sound asleep and Maisie too. Norah lay on the straw mattress. It always itched the first night, Rosie thought as she settled on hers, but she could see the sky through the window, the clouds scudding over the moon, and then she slept and dreamed of nothing.

In the morning she was up early, walking along the lane again. The mist lay still over the land and there were blackberries on the bushes as she passed. She picked two and they stained her fingers. They were sweet and cool.

The oasts were shrouded by the mist, the farm buildings too. A cockerel crowed. She was at the kale now and there was dew on the leaves. She reached down, rolling the drops off into her hand. There were ferns at the edge of the field and everywhere the earth was red and smelt of a long warm summer.

There were partridges flying up before her, and a lurcher dog over from the caravans was leaping and bounding in the kale, making more birds rise. There was smoke from the gypsy caravans and washing strung across the bushes. The hedges nearby were stripped of branches for their fires. Rosie turned now, back to the farm, to the white-washed, partitioned sties, because the sun was breaking through, the mist was rising and soon the picking would begin.

As they left for the hop-fields, the sun was casting sharp shadows from the two oasts and the distant Welsh hills were black. Rosie tightened the hessian sacking around her waist and took Maisie's bag from her, passing it on to Jack when he nodded. It left both Maisie's hands free for the pushchair.

'That's better,' said Maisie, pushing the chair and laughing.

The hop strands had been strung in the spring by men on stilts and now the pickers pulled at the bines, flip-flipping the hops into the wattle bins. The Welsh were ahead of them, the Black Country people with them, and Grandpa was laughing and talking, his voice soft, almost young again. The gypsies were further back, the children silent as they worked. One had a ferret and carried dock leaves in his pocket as a cure for its bites. Rosie looked at Jack and they laughed.

The hop-leaves hung down from the strings, deep etched by the sun filtering through. The sprays of hops were a delicate green, the pollen-like powder was yellow on her fingers. It made the beer bitter.

Her fingers grew sore but soon she was picking without looking, flipping the hops into the bins, smelling them on her hands as she pinned back her hair. Norah wore grips in hers.

'Sensible,' Maisie whispered, 'but not going to set anyone's heart on fire.'

They worked until lunch, then sat in the shade eating sandwiches, drinking water that was warm from the heat of the day. Grandpa went back to the sty to lie down but he returned at four looking rested and happy. Rosie lost count of the hours, measuring time by the level of hops in the bin, watching the pale green piles rise. The hoverflies were all around, humming, buzzing. Butterflies too. There were moths at night, she remembered now.

The busheller came round again and again, dipping his bushel basket into the bin, counting aloud each time as he filled it. He tipped the hops out into one of the big sacks, giving them a card with the number written on, and Ollie initialled it each time. They heard him counting as he went down the next aisle and the next.

So it went on from day to day and the sun never faltered and in the evening they sat around the fire and never raised their voices, even Ollie, even Norah.

Rosie told them of the moth as big as a wren and shrank back as smaller ones came, attracted by the kerosene lamps. She watched as Jack gently brushed them away. Joe would have crushed them.

On Sunday this hop-farm did no picking and there was a stillness in the hop-yard, but the kiln was still in use, drying off the hops picked late yesterday afternoon. She and Jack walked into the oast-house and below the hop-floor was row upon row of long white sacks waiting for collection by the brewers who would come when all the hops were in.

'Tidy little sum,' Rosie said, breathing in the scent of the sulphur, the sweetness of the baking hops.

'Yes, I'd like to live here amongst these hills,' Jack said, fingering a sack. 'I like the country.'

'What about Somerset?'

'Yes, I like that too, but this is more like home, somehow, if you know what I mean.'

She did know what he meant. The lake was fading from her dreams, the baseball target too.

They packed a picnic and went to the stream where the cattle came down to drink. They laid blankets on the dry warm grass and lay back, listening while Maisie and Ollie laughed together and Grandpa took Lee down to the water and Jack told Rosie about Somerset.

He told her about the cart he had driven through a stream like this to soak and tighten the wheels. About Elsie, the farmer's wife, who wore cord trousers, and Tim the farmer, who gave him books to read because they only had a morning of lessons in the school below the big hill where the locals had quarried for hamstone before the war.

The quarry was fenced off in the war, Jack said, used for 'something 'ush 'ush' the old men had said. He told her about the cows he had to milk, the udders he had to wash, the apples he had to pick. How he had stayed down there to work on the farm when he was fourteen, rather than come back to the V1 and V2 raids, but really because he didn't want to leave the country.

He told her about the hams that had hung from the ceiling, the blackberries he and the other lads picked down by the fields which were joined to the next village by a long path.

He told her how Maisie had come down and how they had laughed with the farmer and his wife over thick fat bacon and pints of cider. How Ollie had come too, released from his job building airforce huts for a weekend. How they had herded in the cows for milking. How he had shown his dad the pigs he was rearing, how Ollie had kissed him when he left, and Maisie too. They had been happy then.

He told her about the Blitz and how he had worried, though he had never written about this in his letters to her. How he had thought of his mum and dad beneath rubble, burned, suffocated, but they had never been hurt, not so you could see anyway, he said.

He rolled over then, pulled at a shoot of grass, chewed the end, spat it out. He told her of the GIs who had come and pitched their tents opposite one of the village pubs and further up too, opposite the blackberry bushes. How they had danced each week at the social club, how they had made friends. And he told her of big Ed who reminded him of his mother because of his laugh and his hair.

'He gave me candy,' he said to Rosie, lying on his back now, his arm over his eyes. 'He sort of adopted me. He was good, and kind, and clumsy. He'd meet me on the green. I'd lend him me bike to go to the village across the main road for the bigger dances. That was where Norah lived.'

'Do you miss him?'

'Yes I do. We laughed a lot. Those GIs were good to us kids. Really good, they took us under their wings a bit, one to one. They were warm and friendly, not like us. D'you know what I mean?'

Yes, she thought. She did know, because that is what her American family were like. Then Rosie told him about Frank and Nancy because they, too, had taken *her* under their wing. She had not seen her real family for six years and so they had become unreal, too distant, too different. She told him about her pain, but he already knew, he said. She told him about the lake, and about Sandra. But she did not tell him about Joe.

She told him how she would not pledge allegiance to the flag as she was supposed to each morning before the start of school. She told him about the barbecues, and about Uncle Bob – of the jazz and the long shadows across the sloping lawn.

Then Grandpa called from the stream and she took Lee,

dipping him in and out of the water because Ollie and Maisie were talking to one another at last.

Jack felt the sun on his face and he thought of his own pain. He remembered how Maisie had come again and again to Somerset, how she had laughed when she met Ed, how she had popped out when Jack was asleep and he was glad that she did because the war was long and dirty for her in London.

He looked across at Rosie, at her legs, which were tanned as his were not. Tanned and strong, she lifted her skirts higher as the water rippled around her. She was pretty, not really changed. She reminded him of Ed, the way she spoke, and it warmed him. He had trusted Ed, liked him.

He looked across at his father. He loved him, too, he knew he did, but he didn't know this dark, fierce man that Ollie had become. He didn't know this father who wouldn't throw Lee up in the air, or blow on his stomach to make him laugh as he had made Jack laugh. No, he didn't know him at all and he didn't like him. Jack sank back on the blanket. His father had taken the laugh from his mother's face and didn't love their baby. Is that what the war did to you?

Rosie was calling him now and he pushed himself to his feet.

'Go on, son,' called his dad. 'I bet she splashes you.'

Jack laughed then because his dad looked like he used to and sounded like he used to and he hoped it would last so that the anger, confusion and pain which swept through him and frightened him would go.

The sun kept shining and the hops were brought in and neither Jack nor Rosie wanted the weeks to end. They walked to the shop pushing Lee and bought him liquorice shoelaces. They all sat outside the pub with the Welsh and the Black Country people and watched the gypsies running their ponies up and down. They drank ginger beer and cider while one old gypsy bought a pony 'With All Faults'.

They paid the sixpence deposit on the glasses just to sit outside in the last of the sun, and talked again of Somerset and America and watched as Ollie and Maisie sang 'Roll Out the Barrel' after three glasses of beer and Grandpa asked, 'Will you have another drink, me dooks?'

They sat round the fire on the third Sunday night and

listened as Grandpa told them, as he always used to, how the nailers would put their babies on the bellows to rock them to sleep. How he had been bellow-rocked by his parents, and had then pumped the bellows when he was a bit older than Lee, standing on a box. How he had learned to have the irons in the fire ready for his father as he finished one batch of nails, so that a few seconds could be saved on each nail and a few more pennies earned from the middleman.

He told them how some children had stood in the roof with their backs against a beam and pumped the bellows with their feet. He looked at his hands as Jack put more wood on the fire and told how he had grown tall enough to work at the nail bench. How he had made his first good nail. How he was given a penny dated for that year.

He told them how one boy had not wanted to work. How he had been nailed by the ear to the doorpost and left until he promised he would work.

Rosie held his hands but Norah just looked bored.

That night Rosie wrote to Frank and Nancy, telling them that she was living in a pigsty, and about the smell of hops on her hands, and the feel of the water about her legs in the stream, telling them that she was happy. And she was. She still missed them, but she was happy. She had been taken back to her childhood, reminded of so much, and, yes, now she had found her English family again.

As the last week drew to a close, all the pickers dragged down the longest bines from the end of the rows and Rosie picked up the hop-dog caterpillars which fell out and carefully laid them to one side.

'They'll turn into moths, you know,' Jack teased.

'I know but I guess I can handle it.'

They carted the bines to the oast-houses, the largest of which had been scrubbed and swept that afternoon. Jack and the rest of the boys stood on ladders and draped the bines, because tonight there would be a dance. There was always a dance.

Everyone came, and the band played jazz for half an hour and Jack told Rosie how much he liked it too, but his favourite was Duke Ellington, not Bix Beiderbecke, and then the band played swing and jive and they danced in the heat, their bodies touching and then away again. And always there was the smell of the hops. Norah danced with a Welsh boy. Their bodies did not touch but she smiled, and that was good.

Rosie went outside, sat with Grandpa and drank cider while he had a beer. Maisie and Ollie drank too, and laughed and then Maisie pulled out her cigarettes and Grandpa took one, and Ollie too. Then he stopped, his hand too tight on her arm. His face was hard and Rosie looked at Maisie, at the tension on her face. Now Jack was there, leaning over, trying to take his father's hand from his mother's arm.

'Where did you get those bloody Yank fags?' Ollie shouted and those about them looked. Lee was in his chair and he was crying now.

Maisie winced at the tightening grip. People closed in and now the band were playing 'I'm Dreaming of a White Christmas'. In goddamn September, Rosie thought, even as she moved closer to Maisie, pulling at Ollie's arm, wanting them all to be safe again, as they had been just a moment ago.

'I gave them to her,' Rosie said. 'I brought them back from America, don't you remember?'

It was over then, over as though it had never been, and Jack took her back into the dance and the heat. The music was slow as Jack took her in his arms.

It was too hot but it didn't matter, he was with her, touching her, and she almost felt safe again but she could still see Ollie's anger and Maisie's fear. She didn't tell Jack that she had given Maisie Camels, not Lucky Strikes.

Jack was leading her out now, into the dark cool air, away from the music and the people, and they stood down at the gate again, feeling their carved initials with their fingers, seeing the wild hops winding round the hedge and the telegraph pole, seeing the lights from the farm, hearing the owl in the distance, the music from the oast-house. It was now that he kissed her, with soft, gentle lips, and it was as though she had known this feeling of warmth and safety all her life because his tongue did not intrude into her mouth, nor his hands move to her breast, and his skin had the smell of the boy she had grown up with.

She kissed him back, holding his head in her hands, wondering at the children they had once been, and the people they had become, and it seemed that their friendship had become something stronger. Something good. Yes, she was home at last, safe at last, and the cigarettes meant nothing.

CHAPTER 5

On their return Mrs Eaves had assigned them to different counters. Rosie didn't mind. She stacked the notebooks, laid out the pencils, the few sharpeners clutched inside the tiny globes. She looked at America. So large. And at Britain. So small. And as Glenn Miller played 'The Boogie Woogie Bugle Boy of Company B' she thought of Nancy and Frank, of Sandra and Joe, and it didn't hurt so much, because she had spent September in the soft warm hills with Jack and was at her evening classes twice a week.

Norah minded though. She had been put on haberdashery and measured out quarter-inch baby ribbon, cord, and tape and added up on a pad, her face set, her voice sharp.

At home she sat nearest to the fire, her stockings rolled down round her ankles, her slippers trodden down beneath her heels, and would not talk of hop-picking, or the sun which had turned their skin brown, or the stream which had lapped at their legs, because if they hadn't been there she would still be on jewellery.

Rosie and Grandpa talked though, long into the night, and his skin was tanned too, his eyes bright again. They talked of the bines which floated like seaweed in the evening breeze, of the gypsies who danced on that last night as though they were part of the earth and sky. They talked of Maisie and Ollie whom they often heard laughing in the yard now, of Lee who was tossed into the air, Ollie's hands strong around his waist. They talked and they laughed but Grandpa did not discuss Jack, he just took her hand one night, and said, 'I'm glad you've found your friend again. Sixteen is difficult, it's half child, half adult. You need someone you can trust.'

Rosie told Jack as they walked to the Palais, Sam and Ted behind them, and Jack nodded. 'Yes, that's it. It's the trust.'

Jack came dancing with them every night now, because Ollie wasn't drinking and shouting and sleeping. He was working on the stall, selling nylons out of a suitcase, his finger to his nose if he was asked what else.

On Mondays, Wednesdays and Fridays the gang went dancing, slipping 1/6d on to the pay desk, making for a table at the edge of the floor. Sam and Ted looked at the girls who clustered down one side, deciding, choosing. Then they danced beneath a great glass revolving chandelier while the band played swing and jive, but never jazz. They coasted around the MC who stood in the middle of the dance floor, checking that no one kissed, that they all danced in the same direction, that they did not jitterbug.

Few kissed. All went in the right direction. All of them jitterbugged and her hand didn't sweat in Jack's and she could smell his skin as he swung her close, and then away.

They drank warm ginger beer mixed with cider and it brought back the buzz of the hoverflies in amongst the bines, the smell of the hops on her hands, the sun which washed her past back into her bones.

They walked home, dropping Sam and Ted, standing in the alley at the bottom of their yards. They stood looking at the light thrown out across the roses, looking at the shed rotting in the left-hand corner, looking at one another.

He would kiss her, gently, lightly, squeeze her hand and then leave her, walking in through his gate, she through hers. She would hear his steps in time with hers, and it was only with the closing of the door that the sound of him left her, but the knowledge of his presence in the bedroom next to her wall kept him close.

Tuesdays and Thursdays she went to Miss Paul's above the piano shop and typed to Chopin, chasing the notes, rubbing out the errors, blowing the rubber dust from the keys, cursing inside her head because Jack was watching Jane Russell at the Odeon whilst she was here.

But each week she was faster and her shorthand was better, and she wrote to Frank and Nancy that next spring she would find a job in Fleet Street. Just you wait and see, she wrote, and she knew that her letter was strong and positive, and that they would be glad.

By the middle of October she was moved back to records and played Duke Ellington for Jack and he touched her face when he walked in and heard. He stood still, listening to the piano as it beat its rhythm.

Norah was on spectacles and would stand waiting while customers read the printed card with the letters that diminished in size. Her nails clicked on the metal frames that she held in her hand while she waited, her face long as she fitted them around strange ears.

Rosie played 'I'll Be Seeing You', and smiled across as Norah scowled, but then regretted that she had done it, because the bridge between them had not yet been rebuilt.

October became November, and though there was still grief in the quiet hours of the night, she no longer kept her bedroom door open. There was hope, there was fun, there was Jack.

They danced and they kissed but still lightly, gently, and his hands didn't slide beneath her blouse nor his tongue probe her mouth and she was glad. She didn't tell him about Joe though, even when he told her of the girlfriend he had had in Somerset, the one he had kissed in the apple orchard. She said instead that it was only another five months until her exams and that she must work until midnight again.

She said this too when she wrote to Frank and Nancy but she also told them of the rationing, and the wind which grew ever more cold. She told them how Maisie called over the fence every Sunday and passed bread and hot dripping and how she and Grandpa ate it on the bench, wrapped in scarves and coats.

She told them how she, Jack and Ollie had helped Mrs Eaves's sister move into an old Army barracks north of London along with two hundred other squatters. They had pushed an old barrow with some furniture down the road from the flat she shared with her son and his wife and three children – a flat which had only one bedroom.

She told them how the people were taking over these empty buildings because there was nowhere else for them to live. How the Local Authorities were accepting them and connecting water and electricity, for what else could they do? There were no houses available. She told them that these were the things that she would write about when she started her proper job in the summer.

Frank wrote back asking why Mrs Eaves's sister hadn't moved into one of the prefabs they had been hearing about. If she didn't know, she should find out, get the complete picture, start thinking like a journalist.

Rosie asked Grandpa as they sat in front of the coal fire while the rain teemed down as it had done for the last seven days. Jack had collected some wood from a flooded bomb site and this was stacked on its end to one side. There was a smell of wet dust from it which crept through the whole house, but it would make the coal last longer.

'There aren't enough. They're having lotteries in some Local Authorities, though why anyone would queue to live in one of those I don't know,' said Grandpa, flicking the ash of a Woodbine into the fire. He coughed. The damp November air was making his chest thick again and his tan was fading, but he had had no accidents for months.

'Well, I can,' ground out Norah. 'A nice clean bungalow with a neat garden, a nice sort of neighbour. A nice new town away from London's mess. I'd want it.'

Rosie looked round the room, at the books either side of the fireplace, the American oilcloth on the table, bought from Woolworths. She thought of the house by the lake, the house in Lower Falls, and knew now that all three were home. At last all three were home.

As Christmas drew near she sewed cotton sheeting into two small pillowcases and filled them with hops, sending one to Frank and Nancy, hiding one for Grandpa. She bought a Duke Ellington record for Jack and Evening in Paris perfume for Maisie, Californian Poppy for Norah (because Norah needed all the sweetness she could get, she told Jack).

She bought Ollie paint brushes because he was always talking of doing up the house, but there were so few materials available. She bought Nancy a Union Jack brooch which was left over from the war. It was luminous 'so Frank will be able to track you down wherever you are', she wrote as she put their card in with the parcel.

She told them that her typing was still improving, the Palais was still fun. She did not tell them how Jack kissed her good night or that, as she crossed off the days to Christmas, her grief

70

was deep and dark again because she remembered Lower Falls and the times they had spent together.

Instead she sat by the fire with Grandpa on 20 December until ten p.m. colouring, cutting and sticking paper chains together as they had always done.

'I've missed this,' he said, his hands folding the strips slowly, holding the ends between thumb and finger while they stuck together. 'I've missed our Christmases.'

'So have I, Grandpa,' she said. But she was not thinking of paper chains. She was thinking of the thick snow where here there was rain. Thick snow which had turned the world into a Christmas card as they had travelled by tram on her first American Christmas to the main shopping centres which were decorated with lights, and with streamers and garlands, snowmen and Father Christmas. The air had rung out with carols and there had been a Father Christmas on each floor, wilting in the central heating.

That night she didn't sleep at all. The next day when she walked home from work, there were no lighted trees in the windows, no people on skis and horse-drawn sleighs, no sparkling snow. There was nothing of the excitement she had known in Lower Falls for Lee, who was looking out into the street, his face pressed against the window. It wouldn't goddamn do.

At home there was a small piece of fatty bacon to boil along with carrots and potatoes. She did this but didn't talk. She poured Grandpa's tea, smiled at Norah and then went in to Maisie, wrapping Lee up warmly, taking the pushchair, going to the market, talking to Jack who nodded and asked Ollie to mind the stall.

They went by bus up West, and walked down the streets where there were some decorations, but not many and no Christmas lights. They saw the tree in Trafalgar Square, a gift from the Norwegians, then went into an Oxford Street store, up in the lift, Lee looking, laughing, touching, until they reached the grotto.

They queued, Jack's arm about her waist, holding the folded pushchair with his free hand. She held Lee, kissing his face. His skin was soft and warmer now than it had been in the street. He pulled her hair and she laughed.

71

'You should have kept your plaits,' Jack said. 'He could have swung on those.'

He leaned the pushchair against his leg, and took Lee from her, holding him up, turning him round in the air, laughing as he laughed, dropping him down against his chest, blowing on his neck.

'I love him,' he said, looking at Rosie.

She nodded. 'Silent Night' was playing on the gramophone. The record was scratched but it didn't matter. She wanted Lee to see and feel the magic as she had done because it would help her own grief this Christmas; her first away from Frank and Nancy.

She told Jack of the sleighs, the Christmas tree they had put up in the front garden, the garlands that hung on every wall and from every ceiling. She told him of the trams which had flattened the nickels she and Sandra had laid on the tracks when they were eleven. Jack blew again on Lee's neck, then bent and kissed her cheek.

Lee cried when Father Christmas took him on his knee in the dimly lit grotto, but Jack dropped down beside him and the crying stopped. The present was wrapped in red paper and Lee tore at it as they left. It was a wooden car. Blue and red, with wheels which spun.

Rosie remembered the bald tyres which Frank had heaped into the boot of the car during the war in case the worn ones he was using punctured. There were no new ones available.

There were plenty now, though, and new cars too, but here, in England, new cars were to be sold abroad to help the national debt and people patched up their old ones and made do. In America they were pitching into a boom, Frank said. Over here they were trying to pay for the war which had bled them dry.

'I don't mind queuing. I don't mind being rationed, or being cold,' Rosie said as they walked back down Oxford Street. 'It's time I had my share of that. But I wanted Lee to see another world, just for tonight.'

That night she slept, at least for a while.

On 23 December Jack called as she was settling Grandpa by the fire, his newspaper on his lap, his Woolworths glasses catching

72

the light from the flames. The coal was wet, hissing and smoking. As Jack came in she put a sheet of newspaper to the fireplace.

'Leave the door open for a moment, Jack. Let's get a bit of a draught.' She held the paper with her fingertips as the fire roared suddenly, blazing red, browning the paper, which she snatched away, the heat hurting her face.

'That's great.'

She dug into the coals with the poker.

'There you are, Grandpa, that's a bit better.' She turned to Jack. 'Are we going up the Palais?'

She was reaching for her gloves, catching the coat which Jack tossed to her from the back of the chair.

Jack looked at Grandpa and winked. 'What d'you think, Grandpa? Shall we go up the Palais? D'you reckon this girl could take a change?'

Grandpa looked at Rosie. He rubbed his hands together, then picked up the paper. 'I expect she can. It sounded a good idea when Maisie told me.' He looked over the top at Rosie. 'Just put the guard up, there's a good girl, and don't hurry back.'

Rosie looked from one to the other. The guard was warm, she pushed it up against the fireplace, pulling the hearth rug well back.

'What are you two goons talking about? What's wrong with the Palais? It's the special Christmas night.'

She was pulling her coat on now. The buckle was cold as she threaded the belt through. Jack pulled up her collar.

'Keep that up, it's cold enough to freeze the balls off that monkey in Elm Street.' He pushed her towards the front door. 'Bye, Grandpa,' he called. 'Be good. And if you can't be good be careful.'

Rosie heard Grandpa laugh and said, 'If I'd said that he'd have lathered me.'

Jack marched through the yard, past the hard-pruned roses, out down the alley to the Tube station where people were rushing, their faces pinched. Rosie was tired, cold. Presents had arrived from Frank and Nancy for them all this morning. She had asked Norah what she had sent to the doctor and his wife in Somerset. What had they sent her?

Nothing, Norah had replied. They have their own children. There was nothing in it for me. Everything will go to the kids. All they offered was college, like yours did. I don't want that, too much hard work. Why keep in touch?

Rosie told Jack now what her sister had said.

'I don't know why she can't love or why she's so bitter,' she added.

Jack shrugged. 'She always has been. When will you realise that? Nothing will change her. It's in her bones. She's just getting more like your grandma every day. Nothing is ever enough. Nothing is ever right, but I think she misses your grandma too. It was always the two of them against you and your grandpa.' He shrugged. 'It's made her more spiteful. Maybe she'll change when she gets a boyfriend, someone of her own.'

The Tube train lurched and swayed through the tunnels and Jack held her hand. He never wore gloves.

'I'm hot,' she said, removing her own, because she wanted to feel his skin against hers.

'Nearly there,' Jack said, standing up as the train stopped in Bond Street station.

'Nearly where?' she asked as she was pulled along behind him, still holding his hand but jostled now by the crowds surging up from the train into the evening air.

'Nearly reached your Christmas treat,' Jack said, turning and grinning at her as they reached the pavement, slowing until she was up with him. 'You've been looking as though you've been hurting, deep inside. Can't have that, can we?'

He wasn't looking at her as he said this. His cheeks had flushed. 'Thought this might help. You gave Lee a treat. This is yours.'

They were south of Oxford Street now, in Soho. They were strolling along with many others and Jack told her that Soho had been the hunting cry of the Duke of Monmouth and that he had built a rather 'super' house on one side of Soho Square.

Rosie laughed. 'This is my treat, is it? A guided tour of Soho?' She dug him in the ribs.

'That's right, but there's more, my dear girl. Just you wait and see.'

They were walking past an accordionist who held his cap

74

between his teeth. There were two sixpences in it. Jack gave him another and then they turned into a pub, past two tarts who stood either side of the door.

'Not tonight, ladies,' Jack said.

'Too young anyway, ducks,' the blonde with black roots called back. Rosie flushed but Jack laughed.

Inside it was dimly lit but warm . . . There were sailors at the far end, sitting with civilians, all men.

Jack ordered a beer and a ginger beer for Rosie. Rosie stood back in case they were thrown out because they were too young. Jack was grinning, chatting, and he was served with a beer after all. Charm the bloody birds out of the trees, Rosie echoed the woman in the market.

She moved towards the end where the sailors sat, and Jack pulled her back as he sipped the froth and edged her towards a table nearer the other end.

'That's a pick-up,' he said, nodding towards the sailors.

Rosie looked again. 'But they're all men.'

Jack smiled and leaned his head back against the dark wood panelling.

Rosie looked at her own drink. 'I haven't seen this in the States,' was all she said.

'Or this.' Jack nudged her, pointing to the onion seller who wore his strings of onions over his shoulder. One woman sneaked up behind and cut a single one off, disappearing into the crowd. No one said anything.

Rosie remembered the cherries she had put over her ears in Frank's back garden. Rich red shiny earrings and they would be having Christmas over there without her.

They finished their drinks and moved out past the tarts again.

'A little older but not enough,' the blonde said again, rubbing her shoe up the back of her leg. 'It's a bit bloody cold.'

'You're right there,' Jack said, steering Rosie past them, strolling with her along the street. The restaurants were busy, holly hung from the ceilings and the white-bibbed waiters looked like the dippers which flew in bursts around the hopyards. Rosie felt the tears gather in her throat because it was dark and cold and she was a long way from Lower Falls, a long way from Herefordshire.

It was further on that she heard the cornet, wailing up from the basement of a house just ahead of them, and then another and another and it was like the brownstones, though here, this time, the buildings weren't empty and dead. Here, close to her home, there was jazz.

She said nothing, just clutched at Jack's arm as they stood on the pavement, hearing Dixieland, New Orleans, hearing the drums. It was 'Take Your Tomorrow'. Pure Bix, pure gold breathing life into the streets, and into her mind. She looked at Jack, his head bent towards her, watching her face carefully.

'Does it make it better, little Rosie?' he asked, his voice quiet.

She reached up and kissed his cheek because she couldn't speak. He drew her towards him and this time their kiss was not soft and gentle, but filled with an excitement which left them both breathless, both awkward, until Jack turned towards the steps leading down to the door.

'You coming then?'

Inside it was dim and smoky. Rosie sat at a table near an opening which led to a counter where Jack bought coffee and rolls. Rosie watched as he put sugar in using the spoon which was chained to the counter. She wanted to hold the kiss in her mind but the music was surging and as Jack joined her she sat back and listened, feeling the heat of summer, hearing the jazz across the lawn. Seeing the faded, empty New York brownstones. But here, in England, they were not empty, and she was sitting with Jack, breathing in the rhythm once again.

All evening they sat as the trumpet played that deliberately impure tone which distinguishes jazz from straight playing.

'He's using his lips,' Jack said quietly.

'No he's not, he's half-valving.' But then she saw that he wasn't. 'OK,' she said. 'You win.'

'I like the banjo, it's cleaner than the guitar.'

'No, it's not. Charlie Christian showed us that.' Rosie pointed towards the guitar player. 'See, that guy's using his fingertips to strike the strings as well as stop them. How about that for a clean note.'

'How about that for a know-it-all.' Jack was leaning towards her and they laughed together quietly while the music played and all pain ebbed away. They kissed, lightly, but they were older tonight, closer tonight.

76

They listened to the trumpet's break, tapping the table with their hands as the player improvised and the others in the band fell silent. He was good, a young man with long hair, and then the rest came in. Jack picked at the wax which had clumped around the candle which stood in a jam jar. 'Duke Ellington is right not to like improvisation. He plans everything, you know.'

Rosie looked at the candle. They had used candles to burn the bed bugs from creases in the mattresses when they were young. They had used candles for the Christmas table in Lower Falls but it didn't hurt to think of that here. She picked at some wax herself. It was slightly warm. She rolled it into a ball. Looked at the band again. Did they play to a written arrangement or to one made familiar by use?

'Their improvisation works though,' she said as the band broke for a coffee.

'Yes, you're right, but it can turn into a right mess. Like your shorthand when I read to you too fast.'

Rosie sipped her coffee. It was cold but it didn't matter. 'What about you?' she said. 'What about your plans. Will it always be the stall? Once you were going to be an artist.'

Jack sat back, tipping the chair, resting it against the wall. 'Don't know. Me art's not good enough. Not much point sorting anything out. Not yet anyway.' He turned round to look at the band. The trumpet player was standing near them, talking to a girl with long black hair.

Rosie drank the last of her coffee. It was bitter at the bottom. 'Why not? What's stopping you?'

Jack turned and smiled. 'Look, you had a good schooling. We had very little. Just mornings and then it was bloody chaos. All the evacuees in the one large school hall.' He leaned forward taking her hand. 'It's not that though. Got to do me National Service, haven't I? Not worth starting anything until then.'

She had forgotten about that. Forgotten that he would be going away for eighteen months. It was too long. She couldn't bear to be without him. She squeezed the wax, looking at that, not at him. 'When?'

'Not until I'm eighteen. There's loads of time. Bit more than a year when you work it out.'

The band were playing again and she looked at him as he sat four-square on his chair again, his hands slapping on his thighs in time to the beat, and then he turned to her.

'I'll fix something up afterwards, like everyone does.'

They didn't leave the club until eleven p.m. and then travelled home, talking and laughing because tonight had been filled with music, with talk, with gently held hands. The kiss he gave her at the back yard gate was soft again but as he held her there was excitement too.

She slept that night with scarcely any dreams, only one about a silent brownstone house that turned into a noisy jazz-filled Soho basement. She woke in the morning and scratched the frost from the window. The cold didn't matter because they were young and the war was over. Their lives were just beginning and they had a year before he had to go and that was a long time. Besides it was Christmas Eve.

Maisie cooked the turkey in her kitchen on Christmas morning and Rosie helped Jack to carry the table from Grandpa's house and they all ate together, pulling home-made crackers, drinking beer that Ollie had 'found'. They ate tinned peaches and tinned ham for tea and Grandpa raised his cup of tea.

'To Frank and Nancy, God bless them.'

Yes, God bless them, Rosie thought, thinking of the stockings which had hung at the mantelpiece last year, the turkey, the Christmas lights, the smell of spruce throughout the house. The wine, the liqueurs, the guests, the warmth, the skiing in the afternoon, and the ache wasn't as sharp, and she knew it was because of the jazz, and Jack.

She fingered the light woollen scarf which Nancy had sent. It was warm draped around her shoulders and she barely felt the draught coming from the ill-fitting windows and the gaps in the doors. All the houses were the same after the blast of the bombs which had rocked and cracked the buildings.

She looked across the table which she had helped Maisie to set for tea and smiled at Jack. His bed was down here now, moved from the boxroom to make room for Lee. Rosie wished he hadn't moved, she wished she could still hear him shut the door, sink into bed, cough. Lee climbed on to her knee now and she hugged him, rubbing her face into his neck, making him laugh, making herself laugh.

'That's a nice scent,' she said as Maisie leaned over her shoulder to put a toast soldier into Lee's mouth. 'What is it?'

'You should know, you gave it to me,' Maisie said, turning from the table quickly, moving towards the sink. Ollie stopped eating his Christmas cake, looked at Rosie and then his wife. He dropped his knife and the noise was sharp in the sudden silence. Maisie's back was still and Ollie's face was dark again as it had been before the hops were picked.

Rosie looked at Jack. His face was tense, his eyes wary, pained.

She turned to Maisie and laughed. 'I'd forgotten. It's Evening in Paris. It's nice, isn't it? I've got some myself at home.' She poured another cup of tea for Ollie. 'Drink up, Ollie, that cake of Nancy's is pretty dry.'

He looked from her to Maisie, his eyes guarded, his thoughts elsewhere.

'Don't make those bloody crumbs,' he said to Lee.

Rosie looked at Norah. 'Did you like your Californian Poppy? Maybe I should have bought you the French one too.' Norah wasn't listening, she was reading the book of women's love stories which Maisie had given her.

Ollie was relaxing again now with his cake and tea and Maisie brought Lee another toast finger, smiling at him, at Jack, at Ollie, at Rosie. But Rosie looked into the fire instead because she knew the perfume was not Evening in Paris. But she saw that her words had taken the anxiety from Jack's face.

CHAPTER 6

January 1947 brought bitter cold and a letter from Nancy.

Lower Falls
January 1st

My dearest Rosie,

We were so very pleased with your presents and the good wishes from your Grandpop. Please give ours to your family for a happy and safe New Year.

I say safe because Frank is getting real uptight. He's been seeing bogeymen in the woodpile ever since Churchill's Iron Curtain speech at Fulton, Missouri. He sees East Europe falling under the Communists and Truman's Government getting real upset about it. Thinks they'll have bad dreams about the Reds sweeping over here too.

Already that goddamn busybody, Gallagher, in Local Administration, is getting busy sharpening his knife, asking questions about Art, our friend in planning. Do you remember him? Had some kind of a soft spot for those revolutionaries in Russia in the thirties. He's got a wife and kids now. Doesn't think of politics any more but this LA is really sniffing. Does he think that there are Reds under every bed or something crazy like that? Even came round to the newspaper offices asking how long Frank had known him.

But, let's not go on about that now. I guess Christmas without you has made me mope. I can't tell you how we miss you. We took a ride into town. It wasn't the same.

We're off skiing for a week at the end of January but that won't be the same either, without you. Sandra is busy, having a good time as always. Talking without drawing breath. We see Joe from time to time. He'd like a job on the paper. Maybe he will, but we'd rather it was you.

How are things with you, Rosie?

All our love,
Nancy

Rosie read the letter standing in a queue during her lunch-hour hoping that at the end of it there would be some sort of meat. But there wasn't and she walked back to Woolworths, her feet cold in her Wellingtons even through the thick socks she had knitted from a pulled out jumper.

It hadn't mattered until she read the letter, saw the round handwriting, remembered the feeling of Nancy's arms, the smell of Frank's pipe. Perhaps it would be better if they didn't write, didn't stir up memories, but then she shook her head. No, her feet would still freeze and she wanted to feel Nancy reaching out to her.

She shook her head at Norah and Mrs Eaves as she went in. 'The soldiers couldn't get through with it. They're slower than the lorry drivers. Maybe tomorrow.' She shrugged and pushed her numb feet into her shoes before taking her place behind the counter, feeling the letter in her pocket.

She wrote back to Nancy that night telling her that the road haulage workers were on strike, the meat was rotting in the warehouses, the soldiers were slowly getting it through. She told her how they thought they'd bought some from a guy called Jones at the pub who had meat which would otherwise rot, but he took their money and ran. We never seem to learn, she wrote.

She told Nancy how the greengrocer was rationing potatoes to two pounds a head a week. But there *was* corned beef – 'So we party every night, Nancy. You'd love it.'

She switched out the light and lay back in her bed. Did her letter sound angry or just plain tired? She felt both as she lay here listening to Grandpa moving about beneath her. She sat up, read the leader column of *The Times*, and analysed a report which Frank had enclosed for her as practice. Wrote it up. Transcribed her shorthand because there was no time to waste. It was 1947. She was moving forward. She had to keep telling herself that.

She had said it as she heaped the fire with ash before she came upstairs, banking it up, hoping it would stay in until the morning. They were wrapping coal in soaked newspaper to make it last longer and Jack's wood from the bomb site helped.

She lay down and pulled the blankets up round her ears not thinking of the food in the American shops, not thinking of the

81

skiing slopes. Beating back the anger at the ease of the world which she had left behind.

Maisie hadn't been any luckier with her meat queue either. Lee had been so cold after two hours she had come home and Rosie had rubbed his hands between hers to warm them up. She listened to his crying and coughing through the wall.

He was ill, his temperature was high. She put on the light again and added to her letter, telling Nancy that on New Year's Day flags had been raised at all Britain's collieries as they were nationalised. It hadn't meant more coal though, not yet. A fuel crisis was threatening.

Here Rosie put down her pen. Lee was still crying and now she could hear Jack's voice, soft and gentle, and Maisie's too. She listened, wanting to speak through the wall to Lee, to reach out to him, but she didn't, she just waited until there was no more sound and then she wrote again, wondering how long it would be before the new National Health Service took effect. She did not mention the Local Administrator or Eastern Europe and the Iron Curtain. It was too far away, too trivial against Lee's cough and the bitter cold.

The next day Jack came round. It was Sunday and Lee was a bit better, he told her, his muffler up round his mouth, his dad's old coat worn at the cuffs, the belt missing. Rosie nodded, heaping Grandpa's sheet from the sink into a bowl, drying her hands, pulling down her sleeves, throwing her coat around her. The accidents had begun again, but Jack was here and nothing else mattered.

Jack carried the sheet into the yard and they each took an end, twisting it, hearing the water pouring on to the yard, seeing it begin to freeze even as it hit the concrete. Again they twisted. The water splashed on his coat.

'Why are you wearing that thing?' Rosie asked. 'It's so darn big.'

Jack just shrugged and grinned. 'Makes me look older. Maybe those tarts up West would take me on now.'

Rosie looked at his face, then flicked a corner of the sheet, splashing him. 'There'd have to be a pretty thick fog, and a Derby win to make it worth their while.'

She carried the sheet in and Jack hung it over the airer which hung from the ceiling above the fire while Rosie lifted out the other sheet from the sink. They did the same a second time and Jack asked how Nancy was, and Frank. As the cold sliced into her wet hands she would not let herself think of the skis which would be propped up in her old bedroom. She would not let herself think of the central heating, the washing machine, the hamburgers oozing out of toasted buns. Nor would she think of the Local Administrator, or Art, or Frank, because as dawn had come she had realised it wasn't trivial, or Frank would have written himself. Nor would she think of the big coat that Jack was wearing because she thought she knew what it meant.

She made mugs of tea with twice-used leaves and they cupped them in their hands, Grandpa too, his eyes not meeting theirs because he was ashamed. Jack pulled a newspaper out of his pocket.

'Ollie sent it round. He's stuck on the crossword. Wants you to finish it, if you've got the time.'

Rosie smiled as Grandpa took it, concentrating on this, not that land across the sea.

'Number five down. Can't get that at all. None of us can.'

Grandpa took the stub of pencil from Jack, read the clues, knew the word and they all smiled as his eyes met theirs.

'Hypothermia, that's what it is,' he said.

Rosie looked at Jack. He had known all along, she could tell from his eyes.

'Where are we going?' she asked, blowing on the pale tea, feeling the steam damp on her face. The room was damp from the sheets too.

Jack drank his tea, wiping his mouth with the back of his hand. 'Nowhere today, Rosie. I'm a bit busy.' He reached forward, giving her his mug. 'Thanks for the tea.'

She had known he would say that. Ever since Jones had taken the money and not brought back the meat, she'd been waiting for this because she had seen the anger in his eyes, and knew it was reflected in hers. And today he was wearing that coat which would cover any amount of meat.

'I'll come.' Rosie was up again but Jack was at the door now.

'No, you won't come. Stay here. I've just got a bit of work to do.'

He didn't turn back as he moved quickly through the yard, stepping over the ice from the sheets, slamming the gate behind him. But then he heard the latch lift and she was there, shaking in the cold, her coat slung over her shoulders. There was a freezing fog coming down now, its droplets were on her hair.

'Rosie, get the hell back in the house. Do as I ask, just for bloody once.' His voice was angry but she looked so small, so cold, and so he came to her, taking her in his arms. 'Go on now, get back in. It's nothing. Nothing, just a job.'

'Like the cheeses?' Her voice was indistinct, muffled by his coat.

He laughed. 'Yes, a bit like the cheeses.'

She stood back from him now. 'Well, I'm coming. He owes my grandpa too. And we should do this together.'

Jack looked at her. 'You're crazy. You won't give up. I'm getting it for all of us. Let me and Dad do it. You don't have to be involved. Just go back in and wait.'

But Rosie was walking into his yard now. Didn't he know that waiting was too hard?

Ollie drove out of London, grinding the gears of his friend's car but using kosher petrol. 'Don't want to be stopped before we start, do we?' he said as he wiped the windscreen again, scraping his frozen breath from the screen, passing Jack the rag. 'Here, you keep at it. Make sure I can see my way. And you keep quiet in the back, Rosie. You shouldn't be here anyway.'

Jack looked out through the small patch he had cleared for himself, scrubbing the windscreen in front of Ollie. The fog was freezing on the screen, the wipers were scraping some of it away. His dad was peering down at the map then out again at the road signs. Fog was seeping thickly around them now.

'Don't matter. It could help,' his father murmured, pointing to a turning on the pencil-drawn map. His nails were thick with dirt from the tyre they'd had to change ten miles back. They turned at the next crossroads. There were factories either side, flat-roofed. Two in ruins, burnt out by incendiaries. There was another old three-storey building with blackened bricks. The edges were indistinct, the fog was thicker now.

'Bert said it's along at the end. Might be guards though. Do you want to go through with it?' Ollie was looking at Jack now.

No, I don't want to go through with it. I'm frightened. I

want to go home. I want me mum, I want to turn round and take Rosie back with me. I don't want the bloody meat. But all he said was, 'Course. Why not? That old bugger should have let us have it. He took our money.'

He wiped at the windscreen again. Lee needed it. He needed some good red meat inside him. He was pale, his cough was bad. It was crazy to let the meat stay in there – and besides Rosie was here. She had made him bring her. She wouldn't give up. It warmed him, made him smile, gave him courage.

They were close now and it was quiet as Ollie turned off the engine and drifted into the side of the road. Had old Jones posted guards? Jack wondered. He must have known that if he cheated them they'd come after him. He knew Ollie too well, didn't he?

'He did the same with the Wind and Flute regulars. Took their money, said they could come and transport their own meat, then said the meat had gone off. They'd paid their money, it was their loss, the old devil said.'

Ollie was tapping the dashboard, peering through the fog. Jack wound down his window. He could hear nothing but church bells. He looked at his watch.

'What time are the others supposed to be here?'

'By now,' Ollie said. His voice was short. His eyes darting to the mirror and then to the front again.

'What if the meat has gone off?' Jack asked.

'Then we've done all this for nothing but at least we've tried. You see, he stamps on us, that bugger, always has. Runs the Pawn, runs the betting shop, thinks he runs us. Someone pinched two of his cheeses, you know. Upset him for weeks that did.'

Jack nodded, remembering Rosie walking beside him with a swollen stomach and now, as he leaned his head out of the car, he grinned, banging lightly with his hand on the side of the van, hearing her knock back.

She was his past and his present. She was everything and she was tired and hungry because Grandpa had all that she could spare. Rosie had never told him that, but she didn't need to, he had seen it for himself.

Ollie pressed his mouth to the grille between the cabin and the back.

'We can't wait any longer. You come through to the cabin,' he called softly to Rosie. 'Keep a look-out for the cops, for anyone. If you see them, come and get us, don't hoot the horn.'

Jack followed Ollie from the van, walking on the grass to deaden the sound of his footsteps. They could see the fence ahead. There was barbed wire on the top. Ollie gestured and Jack crept round to one side, Ollie to the other. There was a gap, but it was too small for Ollie so it was Jack who went through alone, carrying cutters for the padlock, carrying his fear.

The fog was thicker now, he could taste the sulphur in his mouth. It stung his eyes and was thick in his throat. His feet were frozen in his plimsolls but they were quieter, like the GIs' rubber-soled shoes had been, like Ed's had been in the Somerset village. Had they worn them in the Ardennes? Had Ed been frightened? Had he shown it? He'd always said there was nothing wrong with fear. It kept you alive. Why had he never written? Why do I think of him so much? Why do I lie awake at night and think of him?

He stopped, gripped the cutters. Keep your mind on the job, you bloody fool. He listened again. Had there been a noise? He waited. No, nothing. Fear kept you alive, Ed said. He repeated it to himself. There was nothing wrong with it. The door was ahead, the padlock dripping in the fog.

He eased the cutters round the chain, bending his elbows, putting his weight behind it but it was no good. He tried again and they slipped and fell. He froze, his breath loud. He couldn't hear. He breathed through his mouth. That was better. There was nothing. No one.

He stooped and picked up the cutters, tried again, and this time fear had put strength into his arms and he ground the cutters through, catching the chain before it fell, laying it gently on the ground. Ed was right, it helped. He took the sack from beneath his coat, opened the door, and crept on, into the cold store. Looking. Listening. Breathing. Christ, why was he so loud? He could see his breath. He had seen Rosie's in the yard. Shut up, concentrate. Listen. Look. Breathe.

There were carcasses hanging on hooks, others cut into joints. He took only what they had paid for. There was no rancid smell. This meat was good. He turned, easing his way back out, shutting the door, running now, back to the fence, but

86

where was the gap? He edged along. The fog was thicker now. He couldn't see. The meat was heavy in the large pockets inside the coat. His hands were numb, his feet too.

'Dad,' he whispered. 'Dad.' But there was no answer, there was just a noise behind him, an arm round his throat, a fist hard into the side of his head and pain which for a moment crushed him but he didn't drop the cutters because he knew they could be traced back to Ollie.

There was another punch and he felt his lip burst. He spun round, out of the grip because he didn't want to be locked up, he didn't want to be kept from Rosie, from Lee, from his mum, from Dad.

No, he didn't want to be kept from his dad and he swung his fist at the large dark man whose face he couldn't see in the fog. He felt the shock of contact up into his shoulder, saw him fall, begin to rise. He swung at him again. Rosie needed her meat. Lee needed his.

'Dad,' he shouted. 'Dad.'

But his father was already there, the fence planks that he had torn away thrown across the yard.

'Get out now, son.' Ollie was struggling with the guard, his breath coming in grunts, warding off the blows, parrying, grabbing an arm, twisting it up behind the guard's back now, bringing him to a standstill.

'Quick. I'll cover you. Get to the van. If I don't come, drive off. There might be more than one.' He was tying the guard's arms together.

Jack ran off through the gap, the meat heavy in the coat, but then he stopped and waited by the fence. His dad had come for him. His father was putting the guard into a hut.

'Out of the cold,' he told him as he ran back. Together they went to the van, pushing the meat beneath sacks, keeping Rosie in the cabin. Together they drove until they found a phone box. Then Ollie rang the police, telling them that there was a guard tied up in a shed in Jones's warehouse, nothing more. They drove back, neither speaking, scared the police might see them, might stop them, but they didn't.

They threw the sack into the back yard, then drove the van back to Bert. They were stopped and searched but Rosie had wiped the blood from Jack's face with her handkerchief moistened from the yard rainbutt and there was nothing to be seen but the sweat on the palms of their hands, the fear in their eyes.

That night those who had paid Jones received their meat and Jack held Rosie and told her that he hated the cold, he hated to feel such fear, but Ollie had been like he was before the war – strong and reliable – and it had been worth it for that. She kissed his bruised cheek, his swollen lips and remembered that she had never been able to see him hurt, even when they were children.

That night she wrote again to Nancy, asking about the Americans' fear about Russia. Asking about Frank and the Local Administrator because she couldn't bear to think of Frank being hurt either.

As January turned to February the cold was like nothing anyone could remember. The snow heaped itself in drifts over the roses and up against the windows. They dug paths through to the road and walked in the gutter. They slipped and fell but went on and heard in the grocer's queue that Mr Philips's son, a conscript, had been killed in Palestine.

Nancy wrote that it was suspected that the Polish elections had been rigged to allow in the Communists and that the United States Government feared that the Soviets had atomic secrets. Would they too build a bomb? Would the Government feel forced to stand out against the Communists?

Rosie didn't want to read this. She wanted to read words of love that she could hug to herself at night, keeping out the darkness of the winter, the worry that the world was going crazy again. That there might be war. Is that what they were saying? Hadn't they all gone through enough in the last one? Weren't they still going through it?

Wasn't it enough that there was snow *and* that there was a fuel shortage? That there was no power during the morning and afternoon at home, so Grandpa had to go to Maisie's to huddle round one fire, and one set of candles? For Christ's sake, wasn't that enough?

She was standing in her room, tearing up the letter, talking aloud, going mad. Is that it? Am I going mad? She took down her books and her pencil and transcribed long into the night because none of this mattered. She must keep saying that. All she had to do was get through to the summer, because then her career would begin.

In March the snow turned to floods and drowned sheep that would have been part of the meat ration. Violence continued in India, terrorist attacks continued in Palestine, and President Truman told Congress that America must be prepared to intervene throughout the world to oppose Communism.

There was another letter from Nancy.

Lower Falls

My dear Rosie,

The snow sounded like fun. Are you getting in any skiing? How is the rationing? That doesn't sound fun.

Here it's pretty mopey. The Local Administrator has interviewed Frank again. His friend Art lost his job. He was once a Communist. He'll never work again unless Frank can take him on. He's looking at it. The LA asked Frank if he is, or ever has been, a Communist. Of course he threw the goddamn man out.

It'll all settle. A few people are getting a bit uptight but it'll pass. Your exams are soon. Keep working but have fun too.

Sandra says she'll write but you know her. Too much partying, too much talking. She means well though. Mary sends her love. Wonders if you're missing her hamburgers.

Will write again soon.
Nancy

That night Rosie danced with Jack at the Palais, she swung, danced, smiled and clung to him. That night she couldn't sleep. Hamburgers – what the hell were they? All she knew about were the sheets from Grandpa's bed to be washed in the morning, the coal to wrap in newspaper, records all morning, queuing all lunchtime, like the rest of this country.

March turned to April and the blossom came, filling the parks with colour, the daffodils too and hyacinths which scented the paths. While Rosie queued she read her shorthand book, testing, thinking, transcribing in her head. She had no time to dance in the evenings because she was practising on an old typewriter of Maisie's.

'It's the exam in two months. It's so important,' she told Jack, and he understood and read to her from a book. She took it down in shorthand, typed it up while he timed her, sitting at the kitchen table, his feet up on another chair, chatting with Grandpa. Norah wouldn't help.

In June she took her exams and they danced that night and kissed in the yard because she dared to believe she had done well. Ollie brought round bottles of beer and Grandpa had some too, and Norah. Jack winked at Rosie.

In July, the results came through and that night they celebrated again and then danced at the Palais until midnight because there was no more shorthand, no more typing to be learned.

'We've done it,' she told Jack, kissing him on the mouth, tasting the beer on his lips, knowing that he could taste it on hers. 'We've goddamn done it.'

Tomorrow she would walk up and down Fleet Street and find a cub reporter's job and she ignored Norah's scowl as they danced in through the yard, because now she was really on her way and Jack had said that he was proud of her, and so too had Grandpa.

CHAPTER 7

The newspapers would not take a girl of seventeen. They wouldn't take her if she was older either. She was not sufficiently well educated. She was a girl. There were too many men back from the war. They wouldn't even take her as a messenger. It wasn't suitable work for a girl.

She thought of the baseball she had thrown, the bike she had ridden, chasing down other kids on the block, down the street, in and out of cars, trams, hunting for Indians when she was the cowboy. The nickels she had pushed on to the tram lines for the trams to flatten. That wasn't suitable play for a girl either. This was the end. Somehow it brought everything to an end.

She didn't go back to Woolworths for two days because she couldn't stop the tears. She lay on her bed, the curtain drawn across the small window, but there was no light anywhere, anyway, any more. Everything had gone, nothing was worth getting up for, going on for. It was not only that her plans had failed but her protection had been stripped away and now she faced again the pain of her separation from the two adults she had loved with all her heart and it was all too much.

Jack came. He sat on her bed, held her hand but she couldn't feel him, she couldn't hear him as he told her she must not give up. She must get angry again, he said. She must fight. Remember the cheese, and the meat. Remember the rec, the hop-yards where it had been warm, where things had changed for them all.

'Don't let yourself lose, Rosie, not now, not ever. Don't let yourself despair. You'll see Frank and Nancy again.'

She turned from him. She was too tired, couldn't he see that? And she hurt too much. She wanted Nancy's arms to make it better. To take the ache away and to wipe out the hours of work which had all been for nothing. It had all been taken from her, as she had been taken from America. She felt dead and to tell him would be to hurt him. How could she do that?

Maisie came too, and Grandpa sat with her, but how could she tell any of them about the emptiness, the pain? How could she hurt them like that?

On the third day she returned to work because there was nothing else to do. She must live every day, Frank and Nancy had said. What would they say now, when she had failed to use all that they had given her? How could she hurt them like that?

Mrs Eaves gave her Erroll Garner, Louis Armstrong, Duke Ellington, Charlie Parker to play because Jack had been in to explain her absence. She took her by the arm, and led her to the office.

They sat and drank Camp coffee while Mrs Eaves talked of the Americans she had known, the GI, Stan, she had loved, although she was married.

'My husband came home in the winter of forty-five. Desert Rat he was. I was white haired by then and he thought it was the Blitz that had done it. It wasn't though. Stan had been killed in the Ardennes. It broke my heart and turned me white nearly overnight.' Mrs Eaves was holding Rosie's hand tightly.

'It's all right,' Rosie said. 'Don't talk. Don't say any more. Don't hurt yourself like this.'

Mrs Eaves swallowed but then continued. 'War breaks hearts. It breaks lives too. There's so much love that can never be spoken about; so much pain. There's so much death. So much injury which takes away futures. Really takes them away, Rosie.'

Mrs Eaves leaned back and lit a cigarette with trembling hands, letting the match drop into the ashtray. They both watched the flame die.

'Life's not a bowl of bloody cherries you know, Rosie.' Mrs Eaves's voice was tired, quiet. 'You're growing up. Frank and Nancy aren't here. Your Grandpa's old. You're on your own, my dear. Everyone is.' She flicked her ash into the ashtray, picking a shred of tobacco from her lip.

'But . . .'

'No buts. You can either sit down and give up or get out there, find a job as a secretary on a magazine, a paper. Get into it that way. Then maybe go back to America if you want to.

You're lucky, you have people who love you. You have a life and a future. So many haven't any more.' Mrs Eaves was crying now and Rosie held her and wept too and then she went back to her counter and played Bix, smelling the hamburgers cooking on the barbecue, feeling sand beneath her feet, seeing the hops on the bines. She thought of the cheeses she had clutched to her, Jack's bruised face in the van, Frank's struggle with the LA and she knew she'd have to go on. She wouldn't let herself lose, not now, not ever and this is what she told Jack, when he came in, but although his smile touched her pain, it didn't make it go away.

When she returned that evening, Grandpa was ill; he had the same cold as Lee had struggled with. She sat by his bed all night and every night for ten days and though he was better he was not the same, and she knew that she couldn't go on with her plans. Not yet.

He needed her at lunchtime and when she finished work and during her tea breaks, and she was there because she loved him, not because Norah shouted at her, 'You've got to. It's only fair.'

She was young, only seventeen, she told herself as she brushed her hair, tucking it behind her ears. There was plenty of time. She would wait, but waiting was so hard.

The next day she made Norah queue at lunchtime while she came home and sat with Grandpa because Norah had shouted at him this morning.

When Norah complained she said, 'You're not fit to be near him. You're cruel, you always were and you still are. But you'll do the goddamn shopping. It's only fair.' She no longer felt guilty where Norah was concerned. The feeling had faded when Rosie had begun to look after Grandpa day and night, out of love but out of duty too. She and Norah were equal now and there was no room in her life for guilt any more – or almost no room. Besides, there was too much pain in the darkness of the night and she wondered how many tears a person could cry.

It was on Friday that they went to the jazz club again, and Jack told her he had won twenty pounds when Pearl Diver won the Derby and that the bookmaker had been Mr Jones. She laughed but stopped when he said she must have the money to go towards a ticket to America, to see Frank and Nancy. To go back for ever, if that is what would take the shadows from her eyes. Maisie had said she would look after Albert, and Jack would too.

The smoke was all around them in the club. A man in the corner was rolling a reefer, his girlfriend was smoking hers. The smell was sweet.

'Go on, you use it,' Jack said, pushing it across to her. 'It's your birthday present. A bit late, I know.' He was drinking his beer, not looking at her, and Rosie thought of the sweater she had knitted him for his birthday, out of two of Grandpa's old ones, and here he was, offering a way of life back to her.

He looked tired too, and she felt like a spoilt child who had kicked and screamed because she had been hurt, ignoring him. Thinking he couldn't see what she was feeling.

She pushed the money back. It was held together by a rubber band. 'I couldn't leave you,' she said. 'I couldn't leave any of you. And anyway,' she said, leaning back and drawing circles in the beer which had spilled on the table, 'now my plaits have gone, where would I put the rubber band?'

He laughed, very loud, and the boy rolling his reefer looked across at them, nodding his head at his girlfriend, licking the cigarette paper, lighting it, breathing it deep into his lungs.

Rosie drank some of Jack's beer and knew now that she loved him, more than anyone else, and the pain receded and she slept each night and woke to sunlit days.

Since Rosie would not use the money, Jack took them to Butlins in August instead, after a summer of austerity with rations reduced yet again. Mr Attlee said, 'I cannot say when we shall emerge into easier times,' and Rosie nodded as she read these words. She was already emerging.

Grandpa was pleased because Marshall Aid appeared to be a possibility.

'I knew humanity would prevail,' he said.

But Frank had written to tell her that in the spring President Truman had embarked on an American crusade against Communism. He wanted the West strong enough to buffer the US and Rosie wondered if this was the only reason they were receiving aid. She didn't tell Grandpa that. She didn't tell him either that Frank had been visited again by the Local Administrator because Nancy seemed to think it was just a nuisance not a problem. And maybe she was right.

Only Norah, Rosie, Ollie and Jack went to Butlins. Not Grandpa, he was still weak but feeling much better, and not Maisie, who stayed behind with Lee to look after the old man. She wanted to, she had insisted when Rosie went round. Lee's too young. You all go and enjoy yourselves. And I don't mind about the sheets either.

They travelled by charabanc past verges sown with barley which were now being harvested. They saw a man scything an entry for a reaper-binder into a field of wheat. They stopped and watched him rake up the wheat he had cut. It was too precious to waste.

As the charabanc engine started again they began to sing on the back seat, Jack and Ollie drinking beer, and soon the whole coach was joining in, even Norah. The camp had rows of flat-roofed chalets, a swimming-pool, a gym, a dining-room, and over on the edge where the hedge leaned over from too many years in the path of the wind, there was a fun-fair.

She and Norah shared a chalet and Norah walked around touching the wardrobe, the dressing-table, the basin.

'This is what a prefab must be like,' she said. 'Nice and clean, fresh and new. That's what I want. My own new prefab. You can win competitions for the best gardens, you know.'

Rosie sat on the bed and nodded. Norah had never gardened in her life. She looked around. She preferred Grandpa's house with his books, the fireplace, bricks which had been there for years. Bricks which had housed him, and her.

Jack and Ollie had a chalet in the next row.

In the morning the tannoy woke them, shouting 'WAKEY WAKEY', but she didn't mind because she had no sheets to wash and wring. They straggled with the other campers past rose beds clear of greenfly into the dining-room, to eat beans and bacon, and Ollie wondered whether the roses had been there when the services took over the camps in the war. Rosie felt in her pocket for her matchbox. It was there. Why had she brought it? Would Maisie remember to catch the ladybirds for Grandpa?

She drank her tea and smiled at Jack. They were here together for a week and it was as though the years had fallen from her and she needed nothing else. Just him. They ran to the pool when breakfast was finished. She stood in her swimsuit on the edge of the pool, the tiles cold beneath her feet. She felt Jack's eyes on her. She flushed and dived into the cold water. Jack's body was strong and as pale as hers was now. Her lakeside tan was gone.

She hauled herself up on the edge, then stood and dived again, hearing the water gushing past, kicking out, reaching the other side. It was as good as the lake and it was fun. She hauled herself out, dived a third time, heard the water again. Yes, it was just as good. She surfaced, wiped back her hair and smiled at Jack.

Now the Redcoats were blowing whistles, and they were formed into teams for racing. Jack's team won. Again and again they plunged into the water, throwing balls, racing when the whistles blew, then filing into the dining-room again for lunch.

At three Rosie went with Norah to keep fit in the gym, throwing her arms up and down, feeling the sweat on her face. Again and again until she was too tired to think of Frank and the LA, Grandpa, even the journalism, but not too tired to think of Jack.

That evening they danced in the ballroom. She and Jack did not jitterbug but held one another close while the lights caught the chandelier and the MC called out numbers, giving prizes to those who won.

Jack smelt of chlorine, and his hands were cold and dry against her skin. She wore nylons he had bought for her, for Norah too. He pulled her closer and she felt him down the length of her body and they danced as though they could never be apart.

'I love you, Rosie,' he murmured, his breath warm in her hair.

'I love you too,' she said and she did. She always had, she always would.

The band struck up now, loud and fast into the Hokey Cokey, and they both laughed as they formed a circle, Rosie holding Ollie's hand, Jack holding Norah's, and it was like the ship's dance as they sailed away from Liverpool. But tonight she was home, her pain had been faced and this was better than the Lake Club had ever been, better than the barbecue with Joe.

That night she dreamed of Gallagher in Lower Falls. The next day she wrote to Frank and Nancy, asking them if there was any danger that Frank would have to give up the paper because of this LA. It was his life.

She wanted to know what they were facing because she could think of them without pain now. She licked the envelope as the tannoy called 'WAKEY WAKEY'. Breakfast was an egg, a soft-boiled egg, and she dipped her soldier into it, remembering the egg cosies her mother had knitted, asking Norah if she did too. She nodded and smiled.

They swam again, watched by other campers in deckchairs, some with knotted handkerchiefs on their heads, and Jack put Ollie's name down for the Knobbly Knees Competition in the afternoon.

At twelve-thirty they rushed to queue for lunch because the food was put on the tables exactly on time and yesterday it had been cold but that hadn't mattered to Rosie, because she hadn't had to buy it, or cook it, or wash up afterwards. Rosie wrote a postcard to Grandpa and Jack sent him one of a fat lady and a thin man doing something with a banana and Rosie was glad Grandpa needed new glasses.

Ollie didn't win the Knobbly Knees Competition, a sandy-haired young man with a moustache did. He was on holiday with his mother. Jack gave him a wolf whistle and Rosie gave Jack a slap.

They swam again though it was cloudy and cool but she liked to feel the water around her.

'Do you remember the stream at the bottom of the hop-yards?' Jack called over from the other side.

Oh yes, she remembered it. The pebbles beneath her feet, the water lapping around her calves, Jack lying on the grass, his hair hanging over his forehead, his sleeves rolled. Oh yes, she remembered it.

She put make-up on that evening, wearing lipstick for the first time. It felt sticky and tasted of peppermint. She wiped it off again. They went to the Tyrolean beer garden before dinner, singing along to an accordion player. Jack bought Ollie

97

a beer while Ollie went to phone the local pub back in London, where Maisie had said she would be.

He was angry when he came back, throwing his jacket on the back of the chair, furious that she hadn't been in the bar.

'You said you'd ring Monday and Friday, didn't you? Maybe she got muddled. Or maybe Grandpa's cough's not so good?'

'Maisie said she'd ring us here if he wasn't, didn't she?' Norah said, looking over Jack's shoulder at the sandy-haired young man, primping her hair, pulling out her mirror and checking her lipstick, which had smeared on to her teeth.

Rosie looked at Jack, then at Ollie who was sipping his beer, his eyes dark again, his foot tapping beneath the table, on to the tiles, clicking, clicking.

'No, only if he was very bad. She'll be there on Friday night.' She wanted to slap Norah because Jack's eyes were darkening now and she remembered the months following her return, the shouting, the pain and anger in the boy she loved.

The accordion player was near them now, playing 'Roll Out the Barrel', and Jack bought another drink and they talked of how they used to collect tat for the rag and bone man and keep it in the old barrel at the bottom of Ollie's yard, but the laughter in Jack's voice was forced.

'You remember, don't you, Dad?'

Rosie watched as Ollie looked up from his beer, wiping the froth from his upper lip.

'You remember the tat, don't you?' Jack repeated and Rosie watched the accordion squeezing in and out, the fingers pressing the buttons and keys. Where the hell was Maisie?

'Yes, I remember.' And now at last Ollie was smiling. 'What about you two finding those dog-ends and selling them? Bloody cheek, that's what it was.' He was laughing now.

Rosie remembered the saliva-limp ends which Jack had made her tear off and which made her feel sick. She remembered the man on the train on her way back from Liverpool, stamping out his cigarette end. She remembered the Lucky Strikes Maisie had been smoking in the hop-yards. She looked at her hands.

Ollie had stopped laughing and was just staring into his beer. Rosie spoke again because she wasn't going to let Ollie and Maisie ruin Jack's holiday. They'd already hurt him enough.

'We sold them for twopence. Pinched your cigarette paper too.' She paused as he looked up. 'I bet Jack never told you that.'

Now Ollie laughed again and Rosie looked at Jack, who smiled, but his face was still tighter than it had been. She took his hand and as they hurried to dinner with the rest of the campers she said, 'It'll be all right. She got the time wrong. We're together. We're safe together. Forget about everything. Now come on, catch me.'

She dodged ahead of Norah, weaving in and out of the people streaming to the dining-room, doubling back round the rose bed and then up to Norah again. He hadn't caught her, though it had been close and he was really laughing now.

After dinner they sat in the ballroom and shook hands to left and then right as the compère directed. The young man with knobbly knees was on their right, sitting with his mother. Norah shook his hand, and Rosie watched as she smiled, her head tilted, her mouth pursed.

'Good evening,' Norah said.

His reply was lost in the chorus of 'Hi-di-hi' from the campers to the compère. What would the Lakeside Club think of all this? Rosie thought, laughing, happy, free. Frank and Nancy would love it.

The band played Glenn Miller numbers most of the night and Rosie tapped her foot to 'Little Brown Jug'. At the Ladies' Excuse Me she watched Norah, who stayed in her seat, her neck rigid, her eyes lowered. The young man had not yet asked her to dance.

Rosie nudged her sister, who ignored her but turned to Ollie and said, 'I think I'd like to try one of your cigarettes please, Ollie.' Her mouth was rounded, her vowels careful.

Ollie turned, his hands red from clapping to the music, his forehead sweating in the heat.

'Eh, what's that?' he said.

Rosie stood, walked round the table and tapped Knobbly Knees on the shoulder, drawing him to his feet. Norah's neck became even more rigid.

99

'Well, hi there.' Rosie's voice was more of a drawl than it had ever been. 'Sure is a great little dance hall.'

She was leading him on to the floor now. His hands were sweaty, his nose was too and the pores of his skin were big. His glasses were steel-rimmed and glinted beneath the chandelier. She stood with him, her hand on his shoulder, waiting for the beat, feeling Norah's eyes drilling through her, to him.

'Say,' she said, 'I guess this dance is way beyond me. You come on over and we'll get Norah to show me how it's done.'

She pulled him behind her. He still hadn't spoken.

'Say, what's your name?'

'Harold Evans.' His voice was high-pitched.

They were almost at the table now and Norah turned from them. Jack was looking down at his drink.

'So, Norah,' Rosie said. 'This is Harold Evans. We can't seem to get the hang of this dance. How about helping us out?' Rosie pulled at her arm, hauling her up.

'Harold Evans, this is Norah Norton. Naughty Norah for short. That's Jack and Ollie Parker. Now off you go, before you miss the music.'

Rosie stepped round them, walking off to the bar to buy a cool drink, not watching to see if they danced. She had done her bit. It was up to them.

Jack was still laughing when she got back, his head down, his shoulders shaking.

'I didn't recognise him with his trousers on,' he said. 'And where do you get the brass nerve?'

Rosie sipped her drink, winking at Ollie. 'I just pretended I was Nancy. I didn't want Norah's long face all week anyway and it would be nice for her to have someone. I have.' She touched his hand.

The dancers wouldn't leave the floor that night, even when midnight had been and gone, so the Redcoats formed a crocodile and danced them out in a conga and had to do that each evening from then on.

The next day Norah met Harold and sat on the deckchairs around the pool, watching as others swam. His mother sat with them, knitting, but Norah looked happy.

'He's a clerk in a bank,' she had told Rosie the previous

100

night. 'An office worker, not just someone selling things off a stall.'

'I expect he likes prefabs too,' Rosie had said, not showing her anger.

Rosie went to the gymnasium on her own, Norah was too busy sitting round the pool. She met Jack and Ollie and they walked to the fairground and shot at pitted yellow ducks which flapped up and down on a revolving belt. Jack and she pulled ropes in swinging boats and the wind rushed through her hair and Jack whistled as her skirt blew up. Ollie laughed and went to watch the Beauty Competition.

Jack and she sat on the ghost train. She screamed when the cobwebs dangled in her face and she remembered the Polyphemus moth and screamed again, glad that it was Jack's arm around her, not Joe's. Glad that it was his lips which touched hers, clung to hers, and his hand that now stroked her breast, but gently on top of her blouse.

They looked ahead as the train burst through the rubber doors, out into the daylight, past laughing campers, past a Redcoat who called 'Hi-di-hi'.

'Hi-di-ho,' Rosie yelled back and Jack too and they looked at one another as they walked away, their hands touching. His closed round hers and squeezed and now they smiled. 'I love you,' they said together.

They stopped again at the yellow ducks. Jack shot three down out of four. He tried again and shot down all four.

The Redcoat behind the counter handed him a pink teddy bear.

'When your turn comes, you should do well on the ranges. I was bloody hopeless.' He was fair-haired and hazel-eyed. Jack handed the teddy to Rosie.

'What was it like?'

'Not so bad if you like being kicked around a square, having no sleep, and peeling spuds until your arms drop off.' The Redcoat picked up his cigarettes from the counter, flicked one out to Jack who shook his head. 'Just put one out.'

The man laughed. 'You'll be smoking sixty a day before you're through your first week.'

Rosie knew what he meant and she gripped Jack's arm. She

had forgotten about National Service. She had forgotten that Jack would go.

'It's not dangerous though, is it?' she asked.

Jack jogged her arm. 'Come on, don't be daft. We've got loads of time anyway.'

Rosie didn't move. 'But it isn't, is it?' Because they were talking about Jack and this was important.

'No, you have to volunteer to go to the hot spots. Most of the time.' He nodded and winked at Jack. 'Go on, have a free go.'

Jack picked up the air gun. 'You sure?'

'Well, can't nick any money with these jackets coming down over me trouser pockets so you have the perk instead. Even have to keep me fags on the counter so I don't need to reach in me pockets.' He shrugged. 'Go on. Won't hurt anyone.'

Rosie paid anyway and gave Norah the second teddy.

The weather held up all week and Rosie wouldn't think of him leaving her. It was so far away. Conscription might be stopped by then. By Friday her tan was deeper and his lips were on hers and nothing else mattered.

That night Harold sat with them and told them about his brass-rubbing weekends. He told them how he travelled round churches and was always losing his cycle clips. Norah laughed, her finger dabbing at the corner of her mouth.

'Yes, fascinating hobby. I used to do some in Somerset.'

Jack spilt his beer and Norah frowned at him.

'We have some very old churches near us in Middle Street, you know,' Norah continued. 'I should think you might find some rather nice things to rub.'

Ollie coughed, then stood up. 'Must go,' he said hurriedly, 'need to phone.'

Rosie said, 'Why don't you come over, Harold? You live near Putney, don't you? Could be a change of scene for you.' She was shaking Jack's leg. 'That would be nice, Jack, wouldn't it?' It would be lovely, she replied to herself. It would be 'real swell' to have Norah happy and away.

They rushed to dinner as usual and Jack said that Norah had never been near a brass in her life, let alone rubbed it.

Ollie didn't come for his meal. They found him in the Tyrolean Bar when they had kicked their legs out in the last conga, singing, whistling out of the dance hall with streamers draped round their necks, and hats lopsided on their heads.

He was drunk. Maisie had not been in the local as they had arranged and his anger was frightening.

CHAPTER 8

When the charabanc dropped them Maisie came to the front
door and pushed aside Ollie's hands which were shaking from
the beer of the night before. She pushed aside his muttered
oaths and questions and took hold of Rosie who had been
bracing herself for the row that would come, wanting to shield
Jack from the tensions of these two.

Rosie watched Maisie's lips, heard her words, then dropped
her bag, turned and began to run, up the road, past the grocer's
down First Street, then Wellington Avenue, past the glue
factory and through the smell which always hung so thickly in
the air.

'Grandpa's very ill,' Maisie had said. 'He wouldn't get the
doctor. It was too expensive. He made me get medicine from
the chemist but it wasn't enough. The doctor came in the end. I
fetched him. It's his chest and his heart. He's in St Matthew's.
He's never going to come home, Rosie, but he wouldn't let me
bring you back. He wanted you and Jack to have that time
together.'

He's never going to come home, come home, come home.
Her feet were beating it out now and the breath was harsh in
her throat. He must come home. He's Grandpa. He mustn't
leave me. She was dodging round people, leaving them staring.
One man pulled at her arm. She shook him off.

'It's me grandpa. He must come home,' she shouted at him.
'He mustn't leave me.'

Then Jack was with her, running alongside.

'It's all right. It'll be all right,' he said, his voice coming in
bursts as he ran, but how could anything be all right now? she
wanted to scream at him. I left him alone and now he's dying.
But there was no breath left and at last she had to slow down
and walk, bent over, the stitch digging into her side, her mouth

104

dry, her shoes scuffed and dirty from the street dust. Then she was off again as it eased, Jack alongside. Norah hadn't come and she was glad.

There were long tiled corridors in the hospital with green ceilings and notice boards on chains, like the swings in the park.

'But they're not rusty,' she said, walking quickly, her shoes clipping along the floor, hearing the squeak of the swings, remembering the smell of rust, the scent of summer.

Jack pulled her back. 'Slow down, calm down.' But she pulled away. Grandpa was in here, alone. Didn't he understand? She had left him and now he was in here, alone.

They found his ward but the Sister stopped Rosie at the doors, her cap starched and upright, her face thin.

'Visiting hours are between three and four or six and seven,' she said. She held a clipboard in one hand and her watch was upside down. Why was that? So that she could see it of course. There was another sign hanging outside the ward. WARD 10. Would that squeak?

'It's my grandpa. He's been brought in and I've just arrived. I have to see him.' Rosie was calm now, her voice strong. She could see him down at the end, pale against the white pillow, the white sheets. He was her grandpa but somehow he wasn't. His eyes were sunken, his chin had dropped and his mouth hung open. She looked again at the Sister. 'I must see him and then I must talk to you.'

The Sister looked at her, then down at the clipboard, tracing a pencil along a list of names and words and numbers. Rosie didn't move, just waited. She would wait all afternoon, all evening, all night. She was used to waiting. Didn't they know? All her life she had waited.

A staff nurse eased past carrying a covered bedpan. An old man sitting next to his bed in a checked wool dressing-gown was picking at the air with clumsy fingers, again and again.

She looked back at the Sister whose navy uniform drew the colour from her tired face. The woman looked up at her, smiling slightly.

'Well, Doctor has finished his rounds. Perhaps it would do Mr Norton good. But just this once, mind. And I shall be in my office just behind you, to the left.' She pointed over Rosie's shoulder and Rosie felt Jack turn, then saw him nod.

105

'Thank you, Sister,' she said and walked down the ward, alone.

She talked gently, quietly to Grandpa who smiled at her but did not speak. She told him that he was looking well, that he would soon be home. But he wasn't and she knew he wouldn't. She held his hand which was so much thinner. How could people become so thin so quickly?

She talked of swimming in the pool on holiday, telling him how it had been boarded up when the Navy had taken it over.

'It would have been more good to them as it was,' she said. 'They could have practised their battles.'

She told him about Norah's clerk, of the Knobbly Knees, of the fun-fair and all the time she held his hand and wanted to say, 'I love you, Grandpa, and I can't imagine life without you. I've just found you again and I can't bear it if you die.'

But part of her remembered the words Norah had shouted down the pavement after her. 'You'll be pleased. Now you can get on with your bloody job.' Was that true? She looked down at his hand in hers. No. She would rather there was never a job for her if he could come home again.

She kissed his hand, held it to her cheek and couldn't say how much she loved him because she would cry and then he would know how very ill he was. So she listened as he tried to talk of the roses but, halfway through, the words died behind lips which were too clumsy to be his.

'I'll look after them, don't worry. There are no greenfly,' she murmured, watching his face.

'There are no roses here,' he murmured, nodding at the dark and grimy yard outside his window.

She touched his hand. 'Just rest,' she said.

Though his eyes were sunken, they were the same. They were dark and kind and the eyes of the young man he had once been. The lids, though, were heavy and closing and she reached forward and stroked his cheek. He hadn't been shaved properly. There was stubble beneath his chin and it was this that made her weep as she walked home with Jack because Grandpa had always shaved each day.

Norah was sitting in the kitchen eating Spam and boiled potatoes. There were some left in the pan. They were overcooked and in pieces. Rosie drained off the cold, thickened water, tipped the potatoes on to a plate, cut a slice of Spam, then a tomato.

'It's his heart and his chest,' she said as she sat down. 'The Sister says that he might die tomorrow or in three months' time, or in six months' time.'

Norah took a drink of water. 'As long as we're not expected to have him home.'

Rosie looked down at her plate. 'No, he's too ill. But he misses his roses.' She was tired and the tears were too close to tell Norah that she had a voice like a goddamn saw and the soul of a witch.

As she lay in bed that night she thought of the bleak yard, the soot-stained walls, the emptiness of it all.

At lunchtime Mrs Eaves said she could leave half an hour early because Rosie told her she must sort some things out for Grandpa. She walked home and put two of the smaller roses which grew in pots into the wheelbarrow. They were not strongly scented but their colour was rich. She pushed them through the streets in her Woolworths uniform. The same streets that she had run along yesterday.

Her arms were taut, her shoulders ached and people stared at her again, but it didn't matter. None of this mattered. Didn't they know what had happened to her grandpa?

She passed the back of the terrace which fronted on to the rec and turned left down the alley, coming out opposite the slide. She pushed the barrow across the road along to the swings and the footworn grassless earth. She pushed a swing. It squeaked. She looked back at the houses, ripped apart, unrepaired. There was more wallpaper than ever flapping on the end wall.

The park in Lower Falls had been grassed. Picnic tables and ice-cream vans had spotted the ground. She preferred this one. She looked down. The rust from the chains had stained her hand again. She moved behind the swing and pushed the seat, sending it soaring, hearing their laughter from the long lost years.

She pushed the barrow in through the hospital gates and past an ambulance which was parked with its back doors open. She edged round to the left-hand side, walking beside the main building, checking where she was in relation to the annexe which housed Grandpa's ward.

107

She walked alongside the soot-blackened walls until she saw the peaked roof of Ward 10. She pushed open two gates which were set into the wall. There were dustbins in one yard and old trolleys in another. She moved on. There was no one else walking, or standing, or watching. There was just the distant smell of cooking; the distant clink of plates, pans, cups.

Rosie stopped. Her hands were blistered. There was a lower wall now and she looked back at the building, shading her eyes against the sun. Then back at the wall. This had to be where the yard was but there was no gate.

She clutched the handles, pushing the wheelbarrow on again, welcoming the pain in her hands because it deflected her grief. She wheeled the roses round to the other side. Here was a small brown gate with a rusted latch which she lifted and then brushed back her hair. She could smell the swings on her hands.

She eased open the gate, looking towards the ward. There was no face looking out but she could see Grandpa eating in bed with a bib on. She lifted first one, then the other rose, putting them where he could see, checking for greenfly though she knew there was none.

She pushed the wheelbarrow home and bathed her hands. The blisters were bleeding. She bound them and then she climbed the stairs, taking a chair from Norah's room and heaving herself up into the loft, searching through old boxes. At last she found his nailer's penny. Grandpa had looked diminished in other people's pyjamas, in a ward which was not his home and she wanted him to remember who he was. She wanted to remember who he was.

That evening she took it in to him and he held it, holding her hand tightly too.

'They call me Bert here, but my name's Albert.'

'I'll tell them, Grandpa.'

'I tell them all the time, but it doesn't make any difference.'

'I'll tell them now,' Rosie said, leaving him, feeling his hand about hers as she found the Sister and told her, and then found the Matron and told her also.

Grandpa was asleep when she returned but he still held the penny. She kissed him and started to leave but as she reached the end of the bed he opened his eyes.

'There are roses in the yard. They'll have a gentle scent.' He was smiling at her, his eyes full of love.

She came the next day and he gave her the penny to put away safely.

'They called me Albert today,' he said.

'Of course they did. They know that's what you like.'

It was hot in the ward and the water in the jug was warm but he didn't mind and sipped as Rosie held the glass and then he told her how hot it had been around the nail furnaces, how thirsty they had all become. Rosie stroked his arm and listened as he told her how he had made Flemish tacks, so small that a thousand weighed only five ounces, but he had made hobs, and brush nails, and clinkers too.

He sat up, and she straightened his pillows and he told her how the fire and the chimney were in the middle of the shop, how he used to watch the different colours in the flames when he was a child, how he had woven stories in his mind then, but once he was a nailer he didn't have the time.

He told her how he would take one of the three iron rods from the fire, turn it with one hand and hammer out the tang, or point, to make the iron harder. He told her of the special coke that was bought from the gas works. It had already been used but was good enough for them once it had been broken up.

Rosie asked him about the boy who had been nailed to the doorpost by his ear, the one he had taken down. Grandpa stopped smiling then and asked for more water. It was still warm and Rosie held the glass to his lips and now he was crying.

She stood up, putting her arm around him, feeling like the parent he had been, listening as he said, 'He repaid me, you see.'

He wouldn't talk any more about nailing and she left that night wondering if his heart had broken each time she had cried throughout the years, as hers had just done. And wondering why it was that the tears had come.

As August turned to September and September to October, Rosie and he talked of other things, other people, but never of the nailers. He told her of the books he would like to have written and how he had read them instead.

She told him of Norah's clerk who had ridden over on his

109

bicycle. How Norah had taken him brass-rubbing at St Cuthbert's, how she had come back with sore knees and a mouth like a sparrow's bum which had flashed into a smile the moment he looked at her. They were going again next week, and the next and the next.

'With a bit of luck and a following wind,' Rosie said, and Grandpa laughed.

She told him of the letters she had received from Frank and Nancy. They had asked her to write a feature for their paper because, Nancy said, it would cheer Frank up to think of her working at something like that.

'Why does he need cheering up?' Grandpa asked as the leaves swirled into the yard, over the wall, snatching at the roses, scudding into corners.

'Things are a bit difficult on the paper right now. You know how work gets, Grandpa. There are ups and downs.'

But it was more than that, she knew, as she slipped into the yard and pruned the roses before she left that night, putting the old blooms into the canvas bag she had brought. Frank had spoken up for the Anti-Nazi League during the war and the Local Administrator had discovered this. Frank had been questioned by two other guys now, Nancy had told her, adding that Commie-hunting was getting to be quite a sport.

Rosie put away her secateurs and waved to the nurses who were watching from the window. They hadn't minded about the roses. They had been pleased.

That night and for the rest of the week she worked on an article about Austerity Britain, telling America of the fuel cuts the Midlands would have to suffer, losing power for one day a week; of the imports which still had to be kept at a minimum; how Britain had to export or die; how in 1946 even the new cricket balls for the Test Match had had to be rationed.

She sent this off with a letter to Frank and Nancy telling them that Grandpa was a little stronger but really no better and that she needed to be able to delay her lunch-hour and visit at three, which Mrs Eaves allowed. Maybe another employer wouldn't and so her career would have to wait for just a while longer.

In October she read that the film star Ronald Reagan had appeared before a Congressional committee investigating

Communism in the USA. She read how he had opposed a Hollywood witch-hunt against Communists or anything which might compromise the democratic principles of America. She read that already there was evidence against seventy-nine Hollywood subversives but Nancy wrote and told her that none of these had been named and hysteria was the order of the day.

'Where the goddamn hell is it all going to end?' Rosie asked Jack as they walked to the hospital in the afternoon on 1 November. He shook his head.

Frank wasn't too well, it was the strain of being questioned about activities which were deemed patriotic during the war years. But now the enemy was different and she felt the anger rising again as the wind whipped through her coat.

She kicked the leaves, angry and confused that the world had broken into enemy camps again, before anyone had yet recovered from the last war, and even in America, the land which had always seemed so free, so happy, there were victims.

Nancy had also written to say that the feature was not what they had wanted. They could read that in any paper. 'What we want from you, my girl, is something from the point of view of the people and don't leave the new career in the air for too long.'

Rosie and Jack leaned against a lamppost, watching as children swung from a rope tied on the next one, playing chicken with the bikes which raced past in the gloom, listening to the curses of the riders who shook their fists and told the kids that they should be at home in bed.

'I'll try again,' she said to Jack.

That evening Grandpa talked of Bromsgrove again. He sat high up against his pillows, his eyes looking into hers as he told her of the foggers. His breathing was too loud tonight and the Sister had said he was not so well again. He was speaking quickly, as though there was no time, and Rosie felt the fear tighten within her.

He told her how foggers were middlemen who employed nailers and sold their products to the nailmasters. How the nailmaster liked them because the fogger could provide him with whatever he wanted at short notice. This meant that the nailmaster did not have to carry large stocks. It also meant that he did not have to supervise the nailers.

111

'The fogger did that, you see,' Grandpa panted.

Rosie gave him more water. 'Not now, Grandpa. There's no hurry.'

'But I want you to understand, little Rosie. Can't you see that?' He paused, coughed and she held a handkerchief to his mouth. 'Can't you see that?' he repeated when he could talk.

Rosie nodded. 'Yes, Grandpa.' But she couldn't.

'Those foggies could play tricks, you see. They could say them nails weren't a proper job. Give you less for them but charge nailmaster the same. They could bore a hole in the weight. Weigh up your nails light, so you gave him too many. They were smart. They made money. They were hard.'

Rosie patted his hand. 'Sshh now.'

There were screens round the bed next to Grandpa's and a doctor had gone in.

'But I want you to see how he made his money.'

Rosie looked at him. 'Who made his money, Grandpa?'

'Barney, the boy with the nail through his ear. Your grandma loved him, you see. That's why we came to London. He moved down here.' He was panting, leaning forward. His shoulders were so thin beneath his jacket. 'He moved with the money he'd made. That was when she wanted to come down here. It wasn't me at all. But he was married when we got here.'

Now Rosie couldn't see the screens, she could only see Grandpa's face as he picked hops in his beloved hills, his body easy, his eyes at peace. And then she thought of Grandma, whose eyes had seemed devoid of warmth. Could a woman like that ever have felt passion, love?

Grandpa was coughing again and it was longer before he could catch his breath this time and while he did she smiled and said, 'Oh no, Grandma loved you. You know she did.'

Grandpa lay back, his eyes closed. 'Maybe you're right.'

'Anyway, Grandpa, she was married when she met this Barney, wasn't she?'

'She met him the week after we'd wed. After she'd come over from Dudley, and somehow the light went out of her face, if you know what I mean.'

Rosie could say nothing because suddenly she saw Maisie and knew exactly what Grandpa meant.

His hand was clasping hers now. 'You must marry someone

you love, someone who loves you, Rosie. You wait for that person and don't you settle for anything less. Do you hear me, Rosie?'

The screens were being moved back now and the visiting bell was ringing.

'Do you hear me, Rosie?' His grip was firmer than it had been since he had come in here.

'I hear you, Grandpa, and I promise. But she loved you, you know.'

She kissed him, smoothing the sheeting around him, brushing his hair to the side with her fingers, smiling into his eyes.

He watched her walk up the middle of the ward, waited for her to turn and wave. She always waved, she always smiled and thought he couldn't see her tears. But he saw them, all right. He had seen them when he had taken her to Liverpool. He had seen them as she had walked up the gangplank and he had felt her gas mask in his hand and had wanted to run after her, push everyone else away and take her back with him.

But she had needed to be safe. That was what had been most important, that the children were safe. He lay back on the pillows, looking out into the yard, at the pruned rose trees. He remembered the children waving from the portholes, singing 'Roll Out the Barrel' as the tugs eased the ship out into the fairway.

He had still heard them singing as the ship moved away. He hadn't heard for four weeks whether she was safe and then each day, each week, each year had been empty without her. He loved her, like the air he breathed, like he'd loved Martha, like he'd loved Nellie, and Norah. He'd been down to Somerset to see Norah every three months but she'd been ashamed of him and had no more love for him than she'd ever had. She was her grandmother's child and had learned all her bitterness at that woman's knee and now there was no love left in him for Rosie's sister, none at all.

On 20 November Ollie said he would visit Grandpa while Rosie slept out overnight along the Mall with thousands of others to cheer as the King and Princess Elizabeth drove to Westminster Abbey.

Jack arrived at midnight and they lay side by side on old

113

blankets and newspapers and it was good to hear him breathing so close and to drink steaming tea together from thermos flasks as dawn came.

She wrote it all down, the bitter cold, the woman who sang 'Knees Up Mother Brown' at dawn and toasted the Royal couple with stout. She toasted Jack and Rosie too.

'Because, God bless us,' she said, 'I like to see some love in this bloody awful world.'

Jack's kiss had tasted of tea, his lips had been soft, and now, as she peered over the heads of the crowd and snatched a view of the Irish State Coach escorted by the Household Cavalry in their scarlet uniforms and riding black horses, she could still feel his body alongside hers.

She wrote of the tulle veil which hung from a circlet of diamonds and the coupons which had been needed. She wrote of Lieutenant Philip Mountbatten who had been born in Corfu, the son of a Greek Prince, and would now be known as Prince Philip, Duke of Edinburgh.

Rosie wrote of the cheers from the crowd after the service as Princess Elizabeth and the Duke of Edinburgh travelled to their wedding breakfast at Buckingham Palace, cutting the five-hundred-pound wedding cake with Prince Louis of Battenberg's sword.

She knew this because she and Jack had moved along to the Palace and she had listened to the reporter in front of her. Jack had laughed and said she'd go far with ears that could flap that well. Rosie turned to laugh with him and as she turned she thought she saw Maisie at the back of the crowd. The light was back in her face and she was looking up at a big man with red hair who stooped and kissed her mouth.

Rosie typed up the story that night and sent it to Frank, then visited Grandpa and wouldn't let herself think of Maisie, or Grandma and the fogger. She wondered whether to tell Jack but she couldn't bear to see the pain in his eyes return and besides, she might have been mistaken. Yes, that was it. It was a mistake. It wasn't Maisie, the crowds had parted and then closed, it could have been anyone.

At the end of November Frank wrote and said he loved the

piece and it would be used. He also said that the Russians had tested an A bomb which was putting some members of the town into a total sweat. But do they seriously think anyone would use those bombs? he wrote. Rosie didn't know because the world seemed crazy enough to do anything and she held Jack tighter that night as they walked back from visiting Grandpa because he would have to register for National Service in April.

A letter from Nancy arrived at the beginning of December, when there had been a flurry of sleet which had frizzed Norah's perm.

Lower Falls
November 26th, 1947

Dearest Rosie,
  We think of your grandpop every day and wonder how things are. You know we send our love to you all and only wish we could be there to help.
  Great things are happening in Lower Falls. Our Local Administrator is becoming positively peacockish with importance and self-righteousness. A deadly combination. The big boys of the film industry have blacked ten Hollywood writers and producers who were cited for contempt of Congress after allegations that they were Commie sympathizers.
  They have said that none of these will be re-employed until 'he is acquitted or has purged himself of contempt and declares under oath he is not a Communist.' Many liberals feel that in America we should not have to declare anything at all. This should be a free country.
  I guess I lie awake at nights now because all that work Frank did in the war to encourage people to support the Britishers against the Nazis is beginning to look as though it is going to cause him pain. It somehow makes him an automatic Red. He is very tired, very strained. But I can't believe that any of this can go on for long. Sanity will prevail, as my old mom used to say. I have to go. The old boy has bitten through another pipe. We will write soon.
  Nancy

115

The next evening Jack and Rosie went to Soho, to walk down the street and hear the music pitching and soaring because she had dreamed all night that the jazz had become silent and the buildings were derelict brownstones.

They stopped to listen to banjos, pumping tubas, four-square rhythms. They leaned against railings and drank in the Chicago-style jazz which was drifting up from a basement window, closing their eyes at the solos with their riff backing, squeezed between snatches of the theme.

Later, back in Middle Street, they kissed in the yard and Jack stroked her breasts and kissed her neck, her shoulder, the soft rising flesh, and Rosie didn't feel the cold which had earlier chilled her. Then they held one another close, so close, because they were both new to such passion, such longing and wanted more, much more.

On 20 December Rosie took paper and glue to the hospital and together she and Grandpa cut and stuck paper chains. They gave some to the ward and some she took home, and could not forget those swollen hands which could barely hold the paper together as it stuck.

The next night they just sat and there was snow in the yard, settling on the rose bushes, and Rosie said that in no time at all the spring would be here.

'Not for me, my little Rosie,' Grandpa said as a nurse walked past with the old man who still picked at the air. 'Not for me.'

But Rosie wouldn't listen because she couldn't imagine a time when he wasn't there and so she talked of the jazz which had played in Soho and Lee who wanted a cart for Christmas. She talked of the pram in the shed which she and Jack had raced on and Grandpa just sat and smiled and listened until she fell silent, watching the clock, wanting to go, but not wanting to ever leave.

'It's because of Barney and your grandma that we got the house. I want you to know because you'll need to understand this when I'm gone.'

He shook his head as she interrupted. 'No, Grandpa. It's Christmas . . .'

'Rosie, listen to me.' It was the voice he had used when he was younger and firmer, and she knew she must listen, and so she did, holding a handkerchief to his mouth as he coughed, again and again before he could begin.

'You know that man Jones. The one who owns the warehouse. He owned our houses too. He was going to sell. To kick us out. Ollie and me and all the families.' Grandpa coughed again and Rosie poured a drink, holding the glass for him, then wiping his chin. There was still stubble and his hair was too long.

'We needed to buy the house and your grandma told me to go to Barney. To borrow enough and for Ollie too. I had to go with me cap in me hand. I can remember twisting the brim so much that I couldn't wear it again. The words sort of stuck in me throat but he lent us the money and that was what was important. Nothing else. Nothing else at all.' He was coughing again and Rosie didn't want to listen. She didn't want to see the tears smearing over his cheeks. This was her grandpa, and she didn't want to see him like this but she had to.

'Your grandma always said it was her house. Barney did it for her. She was right. I tried to think it was because I took him off the doorpost but it wasn't. He told me so. He said he'd had her on the foggers' floor. That she'd loved him, followed him to London. But he didn't love her. So he owed her something. He laughed, you know.'

Rosie wiped his face. 'Don't, Grandpa, please don't. It was probably just words, to hurt you. He was jealous that you'd got Grandma. That's all.'

'But you've got to understand that it was your grandma's house really. And you mustn't blame me. I've made sure you're all right.' He was gripping her hand now. 'Promise you understand. Go on, promise.'

'Sshh. It's all right. I promise.' But she didn't know what she was promising and before she left she said, 'But why did you go to him? Why not just find somewhere else to live?'

He was lying back now, his jaw slack, breathing through his mouth, his eyes following the movements of the nurse behind Rosie. He said nothing for a moment and then lifted his head, wiping his mouth with a clumsy hand.

'Your mum and dad were dead. How long would we live? I had to work hard and pay it off so you always had somewhere to live. It was for you children. It didn't work out quite like I wanted, but you'll be all right. I promise.'

117

Grandpa didn't die that night, or the next, but on Boxing Day, after Rosie had kissed him, and held him, then left. There had been the peace of Herefordshire on his face all evening and so she was not surprised, but that did not make it any easier.

CHAPTER 9

Rosie stood in the churchyard, hearing the vicar but not watching him, hearing Maisie's sobs, but not watching her, or Norah, Ollie, Jack. Instead she looked above the heads of all of them to the trees which lined the cemetery. There were no leaves, there was no sun. There was no Grandpa any more but she still could not believe that.

She picked up the handful of earth and dropped it on the coffin but it meant nothing. The vicar's words meant nothing. He was gone. That was all. He was gone.

At the solicitor's office she sat with Norah on raffia-seated chairs. A strand was broken and dug into her leg. It meant nothing.

In his will Grandpa left the house to Norah, in pursuance of his wife's wishes, the solicitor intoned. With Rosemary to have residence for so long as she required. The nailer's penny and his books were to come to Rosie, along with the letter which was now handed to her. It all meant nothing. Because he had gone.

Rosie walked with Norah towards Maisie's for sandwiches and tea and to accept the condolences of the neighbours. She listened to her sister, saw her smile, felt the letter in her pocket which she would read alone, because Grandpa had said that people needed their privacy.

They walked past the torn houses but she didn't feel torn, she felt nothing. When they reached Maisie's she smiled at Ollie and the people who kissed her with sweet tea on their breath and kindness in their faces. She drank sweet tea herself. She didn't take sugar. Had Maisie forgotten? But what did it matter? She didn't eat though. Even with the tea her mouth was so dry, her eyes were dry, her heart was dry.

She put down her cup, carefully, still smiling, still nodding, still thanking Grandpa's friends for their kindness as she walked out through the yard, past Jack, who didn't stop her because he knew she had to be alone. But there was love in his face and grief too.

Grandpa's yard was empty. The rose trees were stunted from her autumn pruning. She touched The Reverend Ashe, running her fingers along its thorns, remembering its summer scent mingling with the creosote of the shed, seeing the roses which she had left in the hospital yard to bloom for someone else.

She went up to her room, taking her jacket and her dresses back into the kitchen, fetching Grandma's green wicker sewing box from beneath the bottom of his bookshelves. She measured and cut the black tape she had bought from Norah's counter and then sewed, stitch by stitch, a black armband on the left sleeve of the jacket. And then there were the dresses.

The needle went in and out, in and out. The scissors cut the thread cleanly. One done. The needle went in and out again and again. The fire was burning low. She had wrapped the coal in damp newspaper last night. She had heaped the fire with ash before she climbed the stairs. She had riddled it this morning, holding up newspaper to draw the heat, but Grandpa would never sit here again.

Middle Street

Dear little Rosie,
Please try and understand. Your grandmother felt that Norah should have gone to America too. She felt it was unfair that it was just you. She felt the house was hers and when the bomb fell and she was dying she made me promise that Norah would have it in my will. She knew then that the impetigo would keep her from America.

I couldn't cry for her. Not after that. But I promised, you see. You must stay in the house for as long as you need to. That was the best I could do. I find it hard to forgive myself. I leave you my penny and my books. I loved them but not as much as I love you.

Grandpa

Rosie put the letter back in her pocket. She felt nothing. She picked up the needle again, in and out, in and out.

There were footsteps in the yard. They were not Jack's or Norah's but Maisie's and her arms were plump and warm as they hugged her, but Maisie's face was without light, and as Rosie let the last of the dresses fall from her hands she thought of the big red-haired man but it was all too distant. And what did any of it matter?

'I wasn't there with him, you see, when he died. And I left him for too many years. He was so alone and I even left him to die alone,' Rosie said.

Maisie's arms were no help. They didn't reach inside her. But there was a lavender smell in the crook of her neck and Rosie rested on her shoulder for a moment and wondered how you could take away the years and return to where the sun smiled and you shelled peas on the back step.

'Come to me next door whenever you need help or you want to talk.' Maisie stood up and Rosie didn't watch her but looked instead at the flames of the fire as Grandpa had watched the flames up in Bromsgrove.

'I know things are bad again but come. Don't be put off by the rows. We love you. All of us. Jack especially. And we all loved Albert. It won't be the same.' Now Maisie was crying and Rosie turned from the flames which were easing round the lumps of coal. Maisie's eyes were red and her skin was blotched and Rosie stretched out her hand.

'No, it won't be the same. But nothing's been the same for so long.' And she wanted to say, why are you quarrelling again? Who is that man? Did he exist or did I imagine it? But she wasn't imagining the pain in Jack's eyes.

She said nothing though, just watched Maisie walk away through the smog that was creeping into the yard, edging her hair and clothes with droplets.

She looked around the room, at Grandpa's books, at his ashtray bought in Malvern. At the slippers which still held the shape of his feet. At the table covered in oilcloth. At the back step where they had shelled peas. No, nothing was the same.

All this was Norah's and she couldn't believe this had happened. That she no longer belonged in the house she had been brought back to. She couldn't believe that Grandma could do this to her. That Grandpa hadn't fought her. But she shouldn't feel angry because Grandpa had told her why and she should understand. She should goddamn understand.

But there was a noise now from the yard and then another, sharp and loud. She saw through the window that the shed door was open and that Norah was pulling and heaving at something, her coat rising at the back and her petticoat hanging down beneath her frock.

It was the pram she was pulling out, dragging it to the alley, chucking it at the children waiting outside playing flicksies in spite of the fog.

'Have that, and good riddance,' she said and Rosie watched as she went back into the shed. It was Norah's house now. Rosie couldn't stop her, and she would stamp down on the rage which was making her head burst.

But then Norah came out with the saw which was rusted and hadn't been used for years. She took hold of the thick trunk of the peach trailing rose, The Reverend Ashe, which had held the warmth of the summer. She took hold, leaning down, her breath thicker than the smog, and now Rosie moved.

She wrenched open the door, calling, 'Leave that alone, you greedy bitch.' She didn't recognise her own voice as she tore through the yard, pushing Norah backwards, snatching at the saw, feeling the raw cut it made on the palm of her hand.

'Get away from his roses.'

She held it to one side as Norah grabbed at it, hitting and slapping Rosie, pulling at her arm, shoving her, shaking her, but she couldn't reach the saw. Rosie was on her knees now, forced back by Norah, who shrieked and gripped her hair, pulling it hard, forcing Rosie backwards, her eyes pulled into slits, pain searing through her.

Norah's face was close to hers now. She was bending over and Rosie felt the spittle which sprayed from her mouth.

'This is my house now, Miss bloody Hoity Toity. If I want those roses down, I'll take them down.'

Now Rosie twisted free, slapping Norah hard across the face and then again, hearing the saw crash to the ground. 'You leave them! You leave them or I'll tell that apology for a man you've got that you've never rubbed a brass in your life. That you sulked all through your time in Somerset because you didn't get a GI button.'

Norah came at her again, her hands like claws, fury, rage, hatred in her face, and Rosie held her wrists, keeping her away, forced back now on to the rose, the thorns digging into her scalp, her back and hands as Norah pushed back, harder.

Then Norah stopped, pulled away, stood there panting. 'This is my house. His roses can stay. You can't.'

Rosie eased forward, the thorns dragged at her hair, at her cardigan, snagging, pulling.

'His roses will stay and so will I. Go and look at the will again.'

Norah wiped her nose with the back of her hand.

'Then you'll be in the way. Harold will marry me now I have the house. Why don't you just get back to where you belong? Nobody wants you over here now that he's dead. Grandma never wanted you, only me. Now they're both dead. You haven't got him to stand by you.'

Norah turned, pulling her coat straight, walking into the kitchen, slamming the door. The light came on and Rosie cried in the yard that was empty and cold.

The fog was catching in her throat and her tears were warm. She'd never noticed that tears were so warm. She leaned against the shed and then Jack came and held her, saying nothing, just holding her until she walked to the bench where she used to sit with Grandpa.

'Will you go back to Frank and Nancy?' Jack asked, still holding the saw that he had taken from her. 'There's nothing to keep you here. Not now. It's the sensible thing to do.'

He propped the saw against the shed, squatting, taking a packet of Woodbines from his pocket. Rosie saw the match flare, smelt the sulphur. Saw the oast-houses, saw Frank striking a match against the kitchen tiles. Heard Nancy say, 'Get that goddamn thing out of here.'

'You must do what makes you happy, Rosie,' Jack said, smoke pouring from his mouth. His face was pinched, pale, alone. He didn't go to the Palais any more because the rows were so much worse, and Rosie held out her hands to him, watching as he pushed himself upright.

'You're here. That's what makes me happy,' was all she said because he was alone and she loved him and she couldn't leave him, not as she'd left Grandpa.

123

The next day she applied and was accepted for a job as a typist at a magazine and handed in her notice at Woolworths. The day after that she took the train to Herefordshire and watched the winter claw deep into the earth and into her body where there should have been pain, but there was nothing again.

She took a bus from the station to the village, driving along mist-draped roads which curled around the base of the hills, then up between them, weaving and turning. There were oast-houses drained of colour, their cowled vanes motionless. Sulphur would not sting anyone's eyes today.

The bus passed a broken wagon with its shafts upended at the entrance to a field. Cobwebs were moisture-laden in the hedgerows. No birds sang as she stepped from the bus and walked up the lane to the farm along the frost-hard track. The blackberry leaves were dark, torn, furled. Her fingers had been purple last year from the juice. Norah's face had been purple all those years ago.

She walked past the yard where manure steamed through the mist. A dog barked. She didn't stop until she reached the pigsties, the sties where Grandpa and she had slept. Where they had all slept and laughed and talked.

The cold was deep in her now, her hair was heavy and damp. She dug her hands deep into her pockets and turned towards the path to the hop-yards. The dog still barked but there were no other sounds.

The grass had overgrown the path and its wetness soaked her shoes, but it did not matter. The sloping yards were empty of bines, as she knew they would be. There was no sea of green, no Roman Candles of green sprays. She took her hands from her pockets, lifted them to her face and remembered the hop smell of sticky hands, the yellow powder under nails, Grandpa's last season.

She cried, standing in the long wet grass with snow spattered on the distant Welsh hills and his 'me dooks' echoing again and again. It was here, standing in the hop-yards, that she said goodbye and at last believed that he had gone.

She waited for the bus at the end of the track, next to the telegraph pole where no bines wound today. But in the spring they would grow again, twining up clockwise, always clockwise, two feet in a week, and the pickers would come. She could hear the bus now, lurching up the lane, and turned again to the hop-yards.

One day she would come again because this is where the sun had always shone. One day she would come back, with Jack. And in the meantime she would stay at 15 Middle Street, to be near him, to make something positive out of her life.

The office was pleasant to work in. She watered the flowers, typed all day, listened, watched, learned and asked how she could move into Features. The Editor laughed.

'Give it time,' she said. 'At least now we know you're keen.'

She wondered if Frank had liked her feature on the jazz clubs. She had heard nothing from him or Nancy.

She and Jack no longer went to the Palais for Jack had seen Ollie hit Maisie after the funeral and now he didn't like to leave them alone. So they spent their evenings walking up and down the alley behind the houses and listening for the sounds of angry voices.

In February Frank sent her twenty dollars for the feature, which had drawn letters from his readers. More, please, he said, when you have time. He didn't talk of the Local Administrator, just of Grandpa and how sad they were for her and would she be coming back to Lower Falls?

That night she sat in her boxroom and wrote, telling them that she would come back but only when Jack had gone for his National Service because she couldn't leave him. She didn't tell them she loved him and that he was her reason to breathe, to live. But he was.

Each night they would just be together. Sometimes they talked, sometimes they kissed, but it was enough that their hands were joined and that their voices mingled, that their lips touched and then drew away because they were both frightened of too much passion.

In March Frank wrote of his distress at the news that the Communists had staged a coup in Czechoslovakia, and journalists who had attempted to get through to the President's Palace had been turned back by police and militia wearing armbands and carrying guns. Coming only nine years after the Nazi takeover it chilled the blood.

Nancy also wrote and said that the Local Administrator had written a letter to the newspaper calling on all good Americans to be extra vigilant as the Communist Menace crept forward yet again. Frank had not published it, of course. 'And come when you can,' she wrote. 'We love you. We grieve for you. This Jack must be important to you. I'm glad. Keep going with the writing.'

On 23 March Harold and Norah were married in St Cuthbert's. Rosie wore a new hat and so did Maisie. There was to be a small reception at a local hotel which Rosie had paid for because Norah had cried and said that Harold's mother would expect one.

Rosie had nodded and given her the money as her wedding present as Grandpa would have done, and besides, it would stop her goddamn crying. Maisie made the cake, though she had wanted to use hemlock as the flavouring, she told Rosie as Norah came down the aisle while an elderly man played the wedding march. He had a drip on the end of his nose.

Norah looked almost beautiful but Jack said that was because the veil was thick and hiding her face. Rosie nudged him and then held his mother's hand because Maisie had begun to cry. Her tears were silent but Ollie saw and looked away. Rosie watched his hands tense, but then Lee wanted Jack to lift him so that he could see Harold put the ring on Norah's finger. They kissed.

It was the first time Rosie could remember Norah kissing anyone, even Harold. Usually they cycled to their latest rubbing or sat either side of the fire, neither speaking, while she sat at the table, working up a Feature, practising, always practising.

At the reception Ollie toasted them, his voice thick from the beer he had already drunk, while Maisie held Lee and kissed his neck and Rosie saw that there was no light in her face, and that her eyes were bleak and red.

Norah didn't thank Rosie for the reception, she just simpered to Harold's mother, who was cold and distant because her son was leaving her alone in her small flat for something bigger and better.

Rosie squeezed Jack's hand and moved through the people who were crowding around Maisie's cake. They were mainly

Harold's friends. Sam and Ted had already joined up. Dave and Paul too, and Norah didn't seem to have many. But Mrs Eaves was there and Rosie touched her arm.

'I'm so glad you could come,' Rosie said, leaning forward and kissing her powdered cheek.

Mrs Eaves smiled. 'I've missed you, young Rosie. Is it going well? The job, I mean.'

Rosie nodded. 'But I miss you and the girls.' It was true. She did.

'And will you stay over here, now your grandpa's gone?'

Rosie looked at Harold who was pushing cake into his mouth. There were crumbs on his chin and his glasses were crooked.

'Yes, I'll stay but when Jack goes I'd like to visit back there.' She wanted to go, but more than that, much more than that, she didn't want Jack to leave. She couldn't imagine life without him, not for eighteen months. But at least he would be safe. There wasn't a hot war now, only a cold one, and you had to volunteer for the dangerous postings.

She had another drink. She mustn't think of April, of losing him too. She moved from Mrs Eaves, back to Jack and the warmth of his arm as he held her closely to him.

In April Jack heard that he had to report to the Ministry of Labour and National Service. He woke up Rosie, throwing stones at her window because Norah and Harold would play hell if he woke them by banging on the door. It was still cold and Rosie, wrapped in her cardigan, stood at the back door and laughed while he held her, kissed her, because she thought he was just impatient to see her but then he told her the news.

She felt cold inside at the thought of the months without him. Haven't we all been through enough, all we children of the war? Haven't we spent enough time away from the people we love? What did their Lordships want – our souls too?

'Don't go,' she said. 'You can't go.'

She was holding his sleeve, tightening her grip, pulling at him.

His face was still pinched and pale as he kissed her, held her, and the lines from his nose to his mouth were deep but his smile was the same.

'Don't worry, my little Rosie. Trust me. I've got to go and

see someone I know to try and sort something out before I report. I'll come back later. Don't worry.'

But she did worry. She forgot to water the plants at work. She made mistakes. She couldn't eat and wasn't interested in the letter which had come this morning from Frank. Frank was worried about the turn events were taking in Europe with the Berlin Blockade and the possible murder of the Czech Foreign Minister, and, worst of all from an American point of view, Truman's guarantee that US troops would step in in case of Soviet aggression in Europe. What did she care what was happening out there in this crazy world when Jack might be leaving her?

But then all afternoon she did care because was Frank saying there might be another war? She was tired. The world was mad and Jack was leaving as Grandpa had done.

He was waiting for her in the garden on her return. He had been taken on as an apprentice by old Jones. A phoney apprenticeship but at least his National Service would be deferred and he could stay home and look after Maisie and Lee.

'And you, Rosie,' he said, his breath warm in her hair.

Rosie held him, breathing in the smell of his skin.

'But Jones, you hate him. He'll squeeze you dry, rub your nose in it.'

'I know, but it's worth it to make sure Mum and Lee are all right. Dad hit Mum again last night. I don't understand him any more.'

That night Rosie dreamed of Grandpa twisting his cap in front of Barney.

In June Ollie put money on My Love to win the Derby. It won and he gave money to Maisie for a new dress but still there was no light in her face and the quarrels continued.

Harold and Norah seldom took their cycles out now, because Norah didn't want to. They didn't quarrel though, they sat either side of the fireplace while she knitted and he watched Rosie and sucked his teeth just because she was there. But Rosie just looked back, because there was nowhere else she was goddamn going, not yet.

On the day that the Berlin airlift began and the Dakotas shuttled in the food that would break the Russian blockade, Jack had to attend for his medical, which he passed but he wasn't required to report. He was an apprentice, wasn't he, he told Rosie when he met her from work.

They picked Lee up and went straight to the rec to push him on the swing. The wallpaper was still hanging off the damaged houses but there was more and more grass pushing through the caked earth over by the slide.

'The bines will be growing,' Jack said, his voice lurching as he pushed. 'One day we'll go back.'

Rosie watched his hands on the back of Lee's seat, the muscles in his arms, his shoulders. His skin was tanned now and she wanted to reach forward and kiss him.

She remembered their most recent trip to Soho. They had listened to jazz and he had said that Duke Ellington was always changing, that was why he liked him. She had said that she was tired of change. That was why she liked New Orleans, Dixieland. Bix Beiderbecke. He was dead. He couldn't change.

She did move now, putting her arms around Jack as he swung Lee, wanting him close. Because soon he might go. How long could he get away with all this?

In August, the Olympic Games were held in London but without Germany, the Soviet Union and Japan. Frank and Nancy had written to her asking for a feature on it from her point of view. They sent money for her travel expenses to Henley for the rowing, to Bisley for the shooting and to Cowes for the yachting. She arranged for some time off work and they said that she should show them her work and they would consider it for publication.

Norah was jealous and angry and told her as she slopped potato out of the pan on to her own plate that she should go back to America with her superior ideas and leave them in peace.

At Cowes she loved the feel of the wind in her hair and as she leaned on the rail of the ferry leaving Portsmouth she thought how Grandpa would have enjoyed this. She had Lee with her to give Maisie and Ollie a bit of peace.

They stayed the night at a small cottage where they ate scones and homemade jam. The landlady's son was in the Army, a National Serviceman who was fighting the Malayan Communists. His friend had been killed next to him, three

129

weeks ago, in the jungle, Mrs Mallory said, but so far her son was fine.

The tablecloth was crisp and white and Lee picked up the crumbs he had made. His hands were like Jack's and Rosie held them and kissed them, wanting to catch the ferry back to Jack. Not for the first time she was grateful to the man whose cheeses they had stolen.

Lee pulled away, and reached for another scone, so she stroked his hair instead and looked at the horse brasses on the wall, the black beams across the ceiling and thought that one day she and Jack would have a home like this, but within scent of the hops.

The next day they watched the yachts and the crowds and Rosie described the gulls which wheeled and dived on to a bald man's head. She wrote of the blazers, and the women in sleek dresses who burst into cheers as Britain won a gold medal, of the ice-cream which tasted almost as good as maple walnut, of the trees around Osborne which were almost as tall as the white oaks. She wrote of all this but thought of Frank disappearing out round the point to fish. One day she would see them again because Frank was still stressed, but there was no time now. Each moment must be for Jack.

She took Lee to Wembley too and wrote of the thirty-year-old Dutch housewife who was cheered on by the British women because, though she was world record holder in both the high and long jump, she competed in neither and won four track events instead.

She wrote of how the cinder track seemed to beat back the heat and the disappointment when Britain failed to win an athletics gold. She lifted Lee on her shoulders to watch the Czechoslovakian Emil Zatopek win the 10,000 metres and thought of Frank and his love for that small country as the crowd rose to cheer the runner. Tears were pouring down her own face and Lee laughed, bent over, digging his heels into her arms, and wiped them for her with his sleeve.

She bought him a drink and a sandwich from a stall, and they sat on some steps, Lee tucked in next to her in her shade, laughing as he pushed some bread into her mouth. The egg was warm. The sun was hot on her neck. She put her arm round him and held him to her.

'I love you,' she said, rubbing her face on his hair.

'Love you, and Jack,' Lee said. 'Still will when I go to school next year.'

'And we'll still love you, even though you'll be really big.' Rosie unwrapped some biscuits she had made and poured him some milk from the flask. The ration had gone up to three and a half pints.

Lee turned his face away.

'Go on, it's good for you.' Rosie held the mug for him, hearing the crowds cheering in the background. He wouldn't drink it.

'Why should you?' Rosie murmured as she poured it back into the flask. 'There's too much you have to do because someone tells you to.' She thought of Jack and the landlady's son in the Malayan jungles. He must have volunteered. How crazy.

She watched Lee eat his biscuit and then took him by the hand because she wanted to watch the Americans running in the relay. It reminded her of Lower Falls School somehow, the heat, the ice-creams, the fun. They pushed their way up, squeezing on to seats, looking down at the track. Maybe there should be majorettes. She saw her old room, the Cougar pennant, the programmes.

It was hot and she pulled Lee's hat from her pocket, and made him wear it although he wriggled. She sat him on her knee, holding his legs, knowing her dress would crease but not caring because he was Lee and she and Jack loved him.

The crowd were noisy, the relay hadn't begun. People were still going up and down the stairs, seeking seats. Rosie wiped her forehead. It was so goddamn hot. She shielded her eyes. The race must begin soon. The athletes were limbering up, shaking their arms and legs. She could almost hear the cinders crunch.

But then she saw Maisie walking down the steps between the seats twenty feet away. She watched her turn, and stretch out her hand towards a big red-haired man and her face was full of life and full of love and Rosie could not breathe, but held Lee tightly. It was a mistake. She looked away, then back again, and knew it was no mistake. The man was the same one who had been at the Royal wedding, and there was still the same love on both their faces.

131

Rosie didn't watch the race, only those two people who walked on and disappeared, and then she took Lee down the steps too, pulling his hat even further on to his head because his hair was the same red as that man who had looked with love at Maisie.

That evening she heard Maisie carrying washing into the yard and left the roses she had been dead-heading, throwing the faded blooms into the compost in the corner, opening the yard gate, shooing away the children that played in the alley, entering Jack's yard.

'I saw you today,' she said, not looking at Maisie but helping to peg up the sheets, smelling their freshness, hearing the dogs and children further down the alley, knowing that Lee would be out there soon kicking a football with his friends.

'I saw you, Maisie, and you've got to decide. You can't go on like this. It's not fair on Jack. Or on Ollie. You're tearing them apart and yourself.'

She still didn't look but heard Maisie throw her pegs back into the old cocoa tin and lean against the back wall, her face to the sun.

'I can't decide, you see, Rosie. That's just it. I'm torn between two worlds. But don't tell them. Please.' Maisie moved now and took her arm. 'Please. I'll sort it out. I'll make it all right. Just don't tell anyone. Albert always said you had a right to privacy.'

Rosie shook out the last sheet. Lee's laughter was loud as he ran past her and out into the alley, dribbling the ball, kicking it to his friend. She and Jack had done that.

She turned now. 'Of course I won't say anything but just don't hurt them. Especially Jack. Please don't hurt them.'

Maisie touched Rosie's hair. 'I won't. I promise I won't. I'm glad you know. It will help me to be firm.'

Rosie's magazine didn't take her pieces because they were geared to the American markets, but they thought she had talent and when there was an opening they would give her a chance. They celebrated because Jack came round to say that Maisie was being nice to Ollie again. She seemed more settled, he told Rosie.

'It's strange. I don't know what's happened but something has,' he said.

They went up West and ate in Lyons Corner House while a small band played and then they danced and she felt his body next to hers, dancing in step, always in step, and the evening was warm and long and that night they kissed in the yard, and his mouth was as urgent as hers, and his hands were strong on her body.

'I love you, Rosie. I love you and I want you. But we must wait.'

He drew back and his face was beautiful in the light from the moon and there was the fragrance of Grandpa's roses all around. It was not the place for words, and so Rosie said nothing about Maisie and the man. She could not break her promise.

There was a letter on the hall floor for her next morning, which Norah and Harold had not picked up. They never did, if it was for her.

It was from Nancy enclosing sixty dollars.

Lower Falls

My dearest Rosie,

I do hope that perhaps soon we shall see you. It would cheer Frank up so much. He loved your features. They were published last week. Again to great enthusiasm.

Our local band of defenders against the Commies is in full cry yet again because two Congressional committees have been set up to investigate allegations that 30 US officials belong to a spy ring. Thank God most people don't believe it but there are two men, Karl Mundt in the House and Senator Joe McCarthy, a Wisconsin Republican, who most certainly do.

It would be laughable if it wasn't so serious. A manhole blew up in the street yesterday and Frank yelled, 'It's those Commie bastards.' Some people believed him.

But he is kind of down. He's got himself all worried about Korea now. I keep telling him it's all getting too stupid. He's seeing a new war where there is none. I'm kind of worried about him. The paper's readership is suffering. We have had a brick through the office window, but he won't stop writing common sense. The LA doesn't like that of course.

133

The Lake was great. Sandra sends her love and that young guy Joe too. Do you remember him? He's doing quite well on the paper now. Wish it could have been you.

All our love,
Nancy

Yes, Rosie thought as she folded the letter and brushed her hair. Yes, she did remember him but like a distant shadow because Jack filled her life now. She put down her hair brush and read the letter again. How serious was all this?

That evening Jack came home, straight to her, his eyes angry, his lip swollen. Jones had wanted him to deliver stolen meat. He wouldn't. He was sacked. He was no longer an apprentice. Jones would inform the Ministry of Labour and the Army would send for him. But when?

CHAPTER 10

January 1949 was cold but there was still no call-up for Jack and so they didn't feel the wind which cut into their chapped skin as they walked to the Palais. Sometimes they walked because it was better to be alone than with either family.

Spring came. The clothing ration ended and there was still no call-up but now, with each day, their kisses were getting stronger, their bodies pushing closer because it could not be long and there was so much love between them, and so much that was beautiful when they were together, so much that was dark when they were apart.

They walked to the rec on the last Saturday in April, when all the plates had been sold, and Ollie had gone to the pub, yet again. Rosie wouldn't think of that as Jack swung lightly, his face tense. Instead she watched the shadows of the clouds scud across the park. There were buds on the clubbed trees. She heard the scrape of his shoes on the earth, the shriek as the chain jolted to a halt, felt him reach out and pull her to him.

'Look after Maisie and Lee for me. Promise me. Promise me,' Jack said as he sat on the swing and she moved to stand between his legs. He always asked her this. He pressed his head against her belly and held her tightly.

'I will, don't worry. It will be fine,' Rosie said, looking at the fence which was being erected around the bomb-damaged houses. Work would begin soon. Then all this would be changed. She hugged him. Everything would be changed.

They'd had a letter from Sam this morning. He had only another six months to go before he came out.

'See, it went quickly,' she said now, listening to the foreman shouting as one section of the fence fell down.

'He'll be home soon. Nothing can happen in eighteen months. You wait and see. It'll all be fine. Maisie and Ollie will sort it out. It's already better.' And sometimes it was, but not always.

She could feel his back lifting and falling with his breathing, feel his body heat, smell him. She didn't need to say that each day for her would be endless without him. He already knew. She didn't need to remind him that there were twenty-four hours in each day, seven days in each week, fifty-two weeks in a year.

She wouldn't tell him that Norah was longing for him to go, so that she would also leave. That Frank and Nancy had written to her telling her to come when Jack had left. But she must stay here for now, alone, without him, without Grandpa, because she had promised him that she would. She would just hold him because he ached at the thought of the future too.

In May his call-up still had not come but the Berlin Blockade ended. Again there was a letter from Nancy talking of Sandra's new hairstyle, Mary's new Hoover. The target on the garage door which Frank had repainted for when Rosie came back out. She mentioned Frank's stress again, but that was all.

The summer was hot and blistered the pavements. The stall did good business and Jack's voice was hoarse at the end of each day but his lips were as soft and warm as always, his hands as gentle, his words of love as tender as they had always been.

And she wrote and told Nancy again that she would not be coming, not yet.

In July the sugar ration was put down to eight ounces a week, the sweet ration was back at four ounces and there was a further cut in tobacco supplies. Another letter from Nancy told her that Truman had tried but failed to dampen the hysteria which was spreading across America after the latest Soviet spy conviction. And had Rosie heard about the attempt to screen all school books by the House Committee for Un-American Activities? Didn't they know that Goebbels had burnt books in the streets? Did this always happen after a war? Boy, is that goddamn Local Administrator having the time of his life!

It's great that Jack hasn't been called up. We're sorry you can't come. So sorry. But maybe later?

But Rosie wouldn't think of this, she pushed it all from her because each dawn so far had brought the knowledge that Jack was next door, so close, so dear and nothing could spoil this love they had. Nothing. Not even absence, nothing.

They went to Southend with Maisie, Ollie and Lee. They ate winkles and she felt the wind in her hair and heard the laughter of the children who pushed go-carts, racing them, screaming as they won, screaming as they lost and she remembered the feel and smell of the old pram which Grandpa had kept and she missed him. But then she missed him every day.

She sat with Maisie, their skirts held around their knees, the wind tugging at their hems and sleeves, and they laughed as Jack rolled up his trousers to his knees, then ducked Lee down into the sea, then across to Ollie, who took him and held him.

Rosie looked at Maisie. 'So, it's all right?'

Maisie took a Marmite sandwich from the OXO tin, squashing the bread together, eating it with small bites. There were teethmarks in the bread. 'Of course it's all right, Rosie. Just you wait and see. You mustn't worry your head about us.'

But behind the dullness of her eyes there was pain. And Rosie did worry. And all any of them seemed to do was wait. She didn't ask about the man. She didn't want to know; all she wanted was for it to be all right.

She watched Jack again, his strong back beneath his shirt, his pale legs in the rolled-up trousers. She wished they could both be by the lake, lying in the sun, tanned. She wished she could see his body. She wished they could lie together and she could feel his hands on her, his kisses on her breasts.

That night she clung to him in the yard, tasting the salt on his skin as she kissed him, seeing the pallor of it clear in the late evening light. She gripped his jacket, searching his face. She never wanted anything to come between them. Their love must never die and pain take its place as it had done with his mother.

'I want to sleep with you,' she said, holding his head close to hers, talking against his mouth, and she felt his arms tighten.

'I want to sleep with you.' His mouth was on hers. 'But not yet. There's time, my love. There's time.'

But there wasn't time. His call-up papers were in the hall when he came down the next morning and in her hall was a letter from Nancy telling her that the last American occupation forces had left South Korea. What would happen now?

She screwed it up and threw it across the yard because Jack

was there, beside The Reverend Ashe, reading out his enlistment notice, and what the hell did she care about Korea, or Truman, or bloody witch hunts which were so far away and which had nothing to do with her or the boy who was now holding her, the lashes of his brown eyes throwing shadows on his cheeks?

They both cried, there, within the scent of the rose, and Jack felt he couldn't bear to go and leave her here where he couldn't touch her, hold her, love her. He couldn't bear to go and leave his mum whose pain he could still see deep down but couldn't understand, or Lee who would start school in September without him. What if the shouting began again?

He left two weeks later, on Thursday, from King's Cross. Rosie came, but only Rosie. There were couples kissing, crying. There was the rail warrant in his jacket pocket. There were doors slamming, porters pushing through them. 'Mind yer backs.'

The station smelt of dirt and heat and loss and he held her to him. Breathing in her smell, which drowned out all else, holding her face between his hands, kissing her lips, her eyes.

'Be careful. Come back soon. Come back,' she said, tasting his lips, but the whistles were blowing now and he heaved his case into the corridor, scrambling in after, leaning out of the window, sharing it with another boy, holding her hand, bending to kiss it, but the train was moving and he was leaving and he let her fingers slide from his grasp.

'Stay with Mum. Look after Lee. Promise me.'

She was running along the platform now and her lips were smiling and she was nodding but there were tears all over her face, dripping down on to her blouse.

'I love you, Rosie. I love you, little Rosie. I'm sorry I have to leave you.' He gripped the window. Had she heard?

The station was still busy, there was another train leaving from the next platform, there were whistles, doors, calls, the tannoy, but all she could hear were his words. I love you, little Rosie. And they were Grandpa's words too and now she was alone.

The train picked up speed as it left the station. Jack still waved, though he could no longer see her. The wind was too strong in his face, it made his eyes water. It had made his eyes water when he left for Somerset, leaving his mum behind in the bombs. He was leaving her again, with Ollie. He was leaving Rosie but there was nothing else he could do. He had to go. He had been told to go.

He drew his head back in, pulled up the window. It was quiet except for the voices along the corridor. He rested his head on the window. There was nothing else he could do.

He shoved his case back against the sliding door which was open then eased himself into the compartment, between two other boys. The air was thick with Woodbine smoke. He drew out a cigarette and struck a match, cupping his hands, sucking, smelling the sulphur, trying not to think of the oast-houses, the stream where she had paddled, her legs so slim, so brown. Trying not to hear Lee's laugh, or see Maisie's smile, Ollie confused, angry.

He leaned back, feeling the heat of the conscripts either side, hearing their jokes, their coughs, their laughs, and at last he was talking too, pushing them all down deep inside because there was nothing else he could do. Just nothing and it hurt too much.

And so he listened, but did not really hear, and laughed, but did not really mean it, and talked, but only with his mouth, not his mind. The train lurched and rattled over the points and a boy who spoke with a plum in his mouth sat by the window and told them how he had been a sergeant in the OTC and was going to apply for a commission.

'Frightfully good management experience you know,' he said. The compartment door slid shut, then open again. A boy looked in.

'Seen Joe?'

'Who's Joe?' asked the lad next to Jack, stubbing out the cigarette with his foot.

The boy walked on. There was laughter in the corridor and a packet of cigarettes was thrown past the door, caught and thrown back and still the train travelled on, roaring through tunnels, shafting out into sunlight, further from Rosie, from Maisie. And he didn't want to leave them. Didn't want to be sent to God knows where to do God knows what. He wanted to get on with his own life. But he had no choice, had he? Had any

139

of them? He closed his eyes. There had to be more to life than all of this.

He thought of the sign, ABSOLUTELY NO JITTER-BUGGING ALLOWED. thought of the sign, 12 YEARS AND UNDER ONLY. thought of Ollie slapping Maisie, of himself pulling at his father, heaving him out into the yard, wanting to shout at them all to stop.

But it was all right, he told himself, as he drew on his cigarette, feeling the heat in his lungs, coughing, stubbing it out, leaning back. It's all right, Rosie's there. She's strong, she'll take my place. She'll always love me. I'll always love her.

He shut his eyes, shaking the thoughts from his head, making himself listen to the talk which was flowing past him. Really listen, hanging on to the words, the jokes, the questions, taking a newspaper when it was offered, reading it, passing it on.

He talked to Sid, next to him. He was just eighteen, never left his mum before. Never been evacuated. His hands were shaking. Jack, at nineteen, felt old. But they were all the same. None of them wanted to be here. They all had other lives.

The towns had gone, there was wild free country, not the sloping hills of Herefordshire, or Somerset. He remembered the picture he had unscrewed and sold, the milk chocolate they had been given, the corned beef. He had been sick.

'I mean to say, basic training is absolutely nothing. When you're experienced, as I am, it's a doddle.' The boy with the plum was speaking again.

Sid leaned forward. 'What'll we do then?'

'A bit of marching, a bit of polishing. Getting fit, improving ourselves, you know.'

But they didn't, not yet. All Jack knew was the ache inside, the loneliness of it all, the missing. What was Rosie doing now? What was Maisie cooking for tea? Had his bed been folded and taken from the kitchen? Was Ollie drunk?

The train pulled into the station at a platform which held kiosks selling books and sandwiches and tea, but Jack moved past with the others, his case heavy in his hand, banging against his leg, but this time there was no gas mask.

They hurried along, Sid beside him, skirting through the others, keeping ahead of Nigel, the OTC Sergeant, trying to

140

lose him in the crush. They headed towards the branch line and the train full of conscripts. They tried one door. A boy with a crew cut and no front teeth leaned out.

'Sorry, cock, full up.'

They moved on to the next and the next and by now Nigel was with them again and Sid cursed. Jack winked, opening a door, throwing his case in, Sid's too, Nigel's too. Whistles were blowing, boys were leaning out of windows whistling and shouting, and then they were in but there were no seats. There was singing though, and rampaging up and down the corridor, and Jack remembered how they had pretended to cry on the evacuee train as they passed through stations so that the onlookers got their money's worth.

The moors stretched either side and there was beauty in the sky, in the bleakness of the dales, the scattering of sheep, the heather, the short-cropped grass. But Rosie wasn't here, Maisie wasn't here, and it was fear as well as loneliness that stirred him now because Sam and Ted had told him too much about the Army.

In the station yard there were lorries backed up with their tailboards down. They heaved their cases into these now and Sid lit a cigarette, his hand shaking.

A Corporal pacing backwards and forwards glanced at his millboard, then shouted at Nigel to 'get his bleeding legs working and hurry over'. Then he turned.

'Put that ruddy fag out, you ruddy nig.'

Jack turned, and his eyes met those of the Corporal.

'Got anything to say, nig?' the Corporal shouted at Jack. 'Got any comments to make, any suggestions you would like me to send back to Mother?'

Jack shook his head as Sid stubbed out the half-smoked cigarette, put it back in his packet.

'You see,' the Corporal shouted, stabbing a finger at Jack and Sid, 'we don't like dirty 'abits in the Army. We don't like people bringing their nasty little ways in with them. Put that bleeding fag over there, in that bin.'

He pointed towards a bin fastened to a lamppost over by rusty railings near to the station entrance.

Sid stumbled towards the tailboard, jumped down, ran across, and picked out the cigarette from the packet, but his hands were shaking so much that they all fell into the bin. He reached down, then saw the Corporal, looked again at the cigarettes, and ran back, pushing himself up and into the truck.

'You'd better get yourself back down and go and fetch those cigarettes, hadn't you? You forgotten there's shortages? Or maybe Mummy lets you have hers.'

Sid moved to the tailboard again, hunched down beneath the lorry roof. He ran back, picked the cigarettes out, brought them back. They were stained, dirty, smelling of old fruit.

The Corporal nodded and turned, calling, 'Come along please, Mr Sanders, Mr Nigel Sanders, or Nanny will be cross. Come along. Don't be afraid. You're only leaving civilisation behind. You're not humans any more, you're nigs.'

Sid was shaking and Jack felt anger drown his fear as when the Billeting Officer in Somerset had separated two sisters, sending one to the town, the other to a village. There was nothing any of the children could do. There was nothing he could do now. Nigel hoisted himself up and the lorry rumbled away from the station yard.

They drove into the camp and a wooden barrier fell behind them. Jack felt trapped, lost, but so did the others, he could tell from their faces, even Nigel. They passed bleak married quarters, barracks, squares, huts, black stencilled notices, and then they stopped, jumped out, listened to the shouts of the Corporal, watched the spittle on his chin, the red cheeks which reddened, the eyes which narrowed.

They were lined up, their suitcases still in their hands. They were marched, out of step, to their barracks. They left their cases, turned, marched to the quartermaster's stores.

There were counters, Corporals shouting, battledress, beret, boots – some that fitted, some that did not.

'What a shame, poor little boy wants Mummy to change them? Tough shit. Wear 'em.'

More kit was slapped down and they stuffed it into drab-green kitbags, collected their mattresses, which they draped over their heads, then hauled the bag and blankets to the barracks. Heard a siren. Reported to the cookhouse for tea as their Lance-Corporal ordered. Were sent back for wearing civilian clothes. They changed. The Lance-Jack laughed, standing in the corridor to his room. They were too late for tea.

Jack felt anger come again but it mingled with strangeness, fear, loneliness, all of which he had felt before in Somerset. Rosie had felt it too. Little Rosie.

They marched back again to the barracks, to the thirty wire-framed beds, to the windows which were nailed down and unopenable. To the stove which would have been too small to heat Grandpa's shed, to the tall metal lockers beside each bed, to the stone floor which struck chill into them, although it was August and hot.

They were given pen and paper to write to their families.

'To say that you're having a lovely time,' the Lance-Jack said, walking up the centre of the room, looking them up and down. They were hungry, lying on their beds in prickly khaki, feeling in their pockets for change to go to the Naafi.

Jack wrote home, saying he was having a lovely time, saying his clothes would be sent back, saying it was just like being evacuated and that had turned out all right, hadn't it? No problems, he wrote.

He wrote to Rosie, saying that he loved her, that he would be home for two days at the end of basic training, in two months, that she must look after Maisie, please, and Lee, and herself. Please.

As he, Sid and Nigel walked to the Naafi and bought a sandwich and a beer, he thought of Elsie, the fat farmer's wife in cords who had lit an oil lamp each evening so that he would not be afraid of the shadows in the old farmhouse. The smell of it had eased into his room from the landing. The others were silent too, sipping their beer which dripped on to the formica table. Their thoughts were elsewhere too.

They bought boot polish before they returned to their billet and all night long they bulled their green-corroded brasses, rubbing with emery paper for hours. Their hands grew cramped and stiff, their necks too, from bending. There were Woodbine stubs in the tin ashtrays on the two tables, there was a sourness in their mouths, a loneliness in their eyes which were heavy-lidded, tired, unsure. And always there was the radio playing, but there was no jazz.

Sam, from Liverpool, brought out a candle and a spoon, and heated the handle, rubbing it over the dimples of the boots, squeezing out the oil, rubbing away the waterproofing with it, but who cared? It would make them shine.

He showed them how to spit, then rub the polish which they had all bought in the Naafi round and round. It produced a shine. A bloody shine, and so they all did the same or ironed their boots. They laughed and swore and said they weren't afraid of the Lance-Jack, or the Corporal, or the Sergeant, but they were. Finally at 0400 hours, they slept, though the radio still played through speakers controlled by the Lance-Jack. In their sleep they rocked to the rhythm of the train, to the lurching of the truck, to the voice of the Corporal.

They were woken at 0530 hours. The Sergeant screamed 'Wakey Wakey', and thumped his swagger stick along the end of each bed, swearing, tipping every other metal locker over, standing over the spilled contents, calling them whores who had turned the place into a bordello, telling them their kit would be stacked properly or they wouldn't live long.

Jack shaved in cold water, and dabbed at the cuts which ran red. He thought of Butlins but he didn't smile. Hi-di-bloody-hi, he thought. His eyes were red and sore, his hands and shoulders ached and he hadn't even dreamed of Rosie in that brief hour of privacy, he had been too tired.

Nigel's face was without cuts. He had no need to shave. The cat calls followed him out but he flicked his towel over his shoulder and smiled, walking away, giving a royal wave. They had to fold their sheets and their blankets just right. Put back the lockers, just bloody right.

Then they were out, into air which smelt sweet, into a summer day where birds sang, and Jack had forgotten for hours that anything pleasant existed. They marched with knife, fork and spoon held in one hand behind their backs as the Corporal ordered them to, but were screamed at because they were not swinging the other arm. No one had told them.

'You should have known,' he screamed again.

They marched, out of step, into the cookhouse, drinking sweet thick tea, eating greasy tinned tomatoes, and bacon, then tipping the remains into slop bins whose putrid smell reached out into the steamy hall. They moved along, sluicing their cutlery in the lukewarm tank. Bits clung to the forks and the knives.

144

Then back to the barracks and the lavatories. The floors were swept, the windows polished. Jack took the ablutions instead of Sid because Sid was shaking and pale. He had called out for his mother just before dawn.

Jack handed him his window cloth, and with Sam from Liverpool hurled buckets down the clogged stinking pans so that the inspecting officer wouldn't complain, wondering all the time how this mad-house could be allowed to exist.

They had their hair cut, the shears pulling and scraping far up their necks. They had a medical inspection in the afternoon, sitting on benches in a building which stank of urine and disinfectant and gleamed with green and white paint. They all passed and all groaned.

That night they blancoed their webbing, pressed their clothing, ironing over a sheet of brown paper which had been wetted with a shaving brush. They breathed in the pungent smell of steam and scorched paper, feeling the heat on their faces, their heads already bursting with the ache of tiredness. There were only two irons between the thirty of them. The night was endless. The music blared. Sid slept and Jack pressed his then wrote to Maisie asking her to send spare pyjamas and underpants so that he could keep the Army issue ready at all times for inspection.

He wrote to Rosie, sitting on the floor because the bed was laid out for inspection. He told her that all he could smell was scorched, damp, brown paper, all he could hear was cursing, all he could feel was the ache of tiredness. The ache of missing her.

'God, I'm bushed,' groaned Nigel.

They spent the last hour of the night on the floor, to avoid messing up their beds, Sid and Nigel too. They were scared, Jack was scared, of the Sergeant with the swagger stick and eyes like bullets and for the second night he was too tired to dream of Rosie.

They were right to be scared. The Sergeant tipped their pressed clothes, their lockers out on to the cold stone floor but they didn't turn and look. They stood to attention at the foot of their beds, their faces set, their minds raw with anger, with despair, with the confusion of tiredness.

'You're a bloody shower,' the Sergeant shrieked.

They had their injections that day then they polished the studs on the soles of their boots, the brasses again, the windows, the tables, the buckets, the floors. They polished the words off the lid of the boot polish tin, set it to one side for inspection and bought another for use.

They pressed the military frieze into sharp creases again. They covered everything in newspaper so that nothing would get dirty between the evening and the morning. They moved by numbers, they didn't think, they didn't feel, they didn't dream.

'God, I'm bushed, exquisitely bushed,' Nigel groaned.

'Go to sleep then,' Jack murmured. 'Give us all a break.'

The next day they drilled. The rifles were heavy, their shoulders were sore from them. They marched, they halted, they turned, they about-turned. Sid stumbled on the turn, every time. The Corporal swore. They stopped for a smoke break, Jack, Nigel and the others, but Sid was marched up and down, up and down, and still he stumbled and his face looked like the faces of the sisters who had been separated in Somerset, like Lee's when his father turned from him.

Then they all marched, again and again, and their boots rubbed but they were not allowed to stop for lunch because Sid still couldn't turn and that night Sam cursed Sid, and the others did too, and tipped him out of his bed and threw his locker over because the minutes had ticked away for tea break too, and still he had made mistakes.

'Get out of it,' Jack shouted and Nigel helped him push them away.

They picked up Sid's things, turned their backs to his tears, giving him privacy, shielding him so that the others couldn't see either. They were tired, dog tired, but they laid out their beds for inspection, then Sid's, and walked him to the Naafi though their feet were raw and burned with each step.

'Just a quick one,' Jack said.

'Builds up the sugar level,' Nigel murmured, his lids drooping.

They bought Sid beer and listened as he told them that he got so worried he couldn't think and it was then that he made mistakes and he didn't think he could bear it.

They bought him more beer so that he would feel too ill to think and the next day he didn't stumble or the next, or the next, and he bought them the beers those nights. But the next week the Corporal shouted at him, rode him, cursed him again until he stumbled on the turn again the next day and the beers in the evening didn't help.

Jack watched as the boy's hands began to shake, and the taunts began again as the whole squad was punished, missing lunch, missing tea. He watched as the light faded from Sid's eyes and felt anger above his tiredness.

So when the Corporal lined them up and the Sergeant marched with clipped strides down the ranks, pointing his stick at Jack, he moved it to one side, his eyes hard like the Sergeant's, his hands sweating with the fear he wouldn't show. He didn't want Sid to suffer any more.

He could cope. He was stronger, he was nineteen, a man. Much older than the sister who had been killed by a car when she ran away from the town to the village to see her Sarah. Much older than Lee who had been pushed aside by Ollie.

He was marched away, sworn at, cursed, pushed, his head yanked back by his short hair.

'Got a nice little job for you,' the Corporal said, his voice low, his lips thin. 'You're not going to know what day of the bleeding week it is when you've finished, sonny.'

He was handed scissors and spent the afternoon on hands and knees cutting the grass around the parade ground. The ants scrambled amongst the grass, the dandelions were acrid, their milk spilling white on to the ground. His thumb and finger were blistered. He changed hands. That thumb and finger became blistered too.

He changed again, the sun sharp on his neck. He could hear the Corporal, and the boots.

'Forward march.

'Halt.

'Turn.

'About turn.

'Smoke Break.

'Forward march.

'Halt.

'Turn.

147

'About turn.'

His thumb and fingers were bleeding, he padded them with grass he had cut. It was cool but with each cut the pain dug deep.

He didn't break for tea. He worked on until the ants and the sun had gone. And then in full kit, he doubled around the tarmacked square on blistered feet which bled warm blood into his boots. But Sid was left alone and that helped the pain of his hands and feet as he lay on the floor all night because there was an inspection in the morning.

The next day he was told to shin up, then jump from gym ropes he could hardly clasp by a sweating instructor who moved the mat as he jumped and laughed as the rope burned his hand and then the mat burned his shins. He laughed as his elbow, then his shoulder crashed on to the hard polished floor.

'Think you know more than the Army, do you?' the instructor ground out. 'Think you can cheek a Sergeant, do you? We'll see about that.'

He was put on fatigues because he was last out of the changing rooms when the instructor hid his boots, slapping his rubber slipper in his hand as he laughed, whipping it across Jack's back. But he wouldn't show the pain, or the anger.

The next day he drilled with raw feet, threw his rifle against his bruised shoulder and held the butt in a hand that throbbed and bled but he showed nothing. There was no smoke break for him and he winked at Sid and Nigel as he marched, looking at the sky, the clouds, thinking of Lee, of Rosie.

He scrubbed the walls in the cookhouse all evening and watched the cockroaches scuttling out from behind the pipes. But none of this mattered. He was tough, he could take it. He was alive. He was nineteen. Rosie loved him. Lee was all right. Maisie and Ollie were all right. Rosie had written and said so.

The next week the Corporal found a speck of dirt on the back of Jack's buckle and grinned as he extended his punishment. He spent the evening syphoning petrol then rubbing graffiti off the lavatory walls with it, tasting it, smelling it. He vomited all night in the latrines.

But he could take it, he told Sid and Nigel who came and stood by him. It was Sam's bloody handwriting.

'How exquisite,' Nigel said.

They laughed, all of them, even Sam, who polished Jack's boots for him that night, and bought him a beer, while Sid stayed behind and laid out his kit. Nigel bought him another and because he was such a tight arse Jack wondered why.

'You're keeping that bastard off our backs. We're extraordinarily grateful, you know.'

He didn't understand why Jack laughed, why he laughed even when he lay on the floor beside his bed, and neither did Jack himself, especially in the dead of night when the laughter choked into silent tears and he churned between images of the sisters and Lee and Rosie.

He peeled potatoes when the Corporal decided his locker was a disgrace, though there was nothing wrong with it. He watched the squad run to PE in baggy shorts and singlets, carrying their plimsolls, wearing their boots, their pale hairy legs thickening already from the drill. He thought of Butlins, of Harold, and cut into the potato once more. Rosie had written, she still loved him. Lee was happy. Maisie and Ollie were fine. And he was fine. He was nineteen. He could take it.

Sid shared his food parcels with Nigel and Jack. They were all fitter by the fourth week. The Corporal still shouted, still punished, but Jack hadn't broken. The men were his friends, they cheered as he cut the grass, yet again. They helped him off with his pack after he had been doubled round the square, yet again.

They woke him when he slept too soundly during the education talks in a room thick with smoke as they were told, yet again, of the Empire, and the pox, and they grinned when he winked at them. But he was nearly finished. He was nearly broken. He had no dignity left, no power to save himself. No nothing. Just Rosie's letters and the thought of the hand that had written the words.

In the fifth week the Corporal left his bike outside the hut when the Sergeant had ordered it to be put away and the Corporal left their squad with the Sergeant's language still thick on the air. The men blew up johnnies bought from the barber and let them fly from the door as he passed.

The Lance-Jack took his place, a new stripe on his arm and a voice which was not so loud, not so cruel, and now the fatigues ended and Jack slept at night. At last he slept and had the time and the privacy to dream of Rosie.

In September his squad cursed and swore on the assault course, feeling the skin scrape off their stomachs as they scrambled up and over the nets carrying packs filled with bricks, feeling the straps cutting into their shoulders, humping Sid up before them because last one home got fatigues.

They plunged from logs into murky water-filled ditches, spitting out filth, pushing against the weight of the pack, forcing their heads up and the panic down. They raced and beat the squad from Waterloo barracks in the cross country and the Lance-Jack bought them all beers.

They sat up that night and cheered as Nigel sang and danced and Sam called, 'You'd make a lovely tart.'

Jack wrote to Rosie and told her. They watched new squads arrive and stumble and scramble, and tossed them cigarettes and told them it would be a bleeding picnic.

They shot on the rifle range, feeling the Yorkshire breeze in their hair, the first hint of winter in its coldness, lying full stretch on their stomachs. He wrote to Rosie and told her of the smell of the ground which still had the summer tight in its grasp, of the men, who were now moulding into a team, almost in spite of themselves.

They were paid.

'One pace forward.

'Two, three, salute.

'Two, three, take pay.

'Take paybook.' Open top left pocket.

'Pay and paybook correct, sir.' Place pay and paybook in pocket.

'Two, three, salute.

'Two, three, about turn.

'Left right, left right.' Three bags full. Sir. There were drinks in the Naafi. Only a few days more then a transit camp. Postings came in. Sid was a clerk, Nigel a Sergeant in Education. He didn't want a commission now. He was one of the men. Jack was a squaddie.

The next day, the last before the passing-out parade, they squatted on the grass with the weak late summer sun on their faces around a Sten gun which was taken to pieces by a dirty-fingered NCO.

Jack said, 'Be gentle with the grass, Corp. It's been very carefully cut.' The squad laughed, the Corporal too.

The Corporal put the gun together, then took it apart again. Jack could smell the oil, see it beneath the Corporal's fingernails, and he remembered Ed in that Somerset village. The oil beneath his fingers as he threw the ball to Jack, the drawl as he shouted at him to pitch it higher next time, the sun shining on his red hair. Where was he now? Why had he never written?

The gun was in pieces again. They tried to put it together and failed. They tried again and succeeded and the smell of the oil was heavy and it was the same as the smell on Ed's hand as he had ruffled his hair and asked when his mom was coming down again.

'The aim of war,' said the Corporal, 'is to kill the enemy.'

Sam murmured, 'Don't tempt me, sunshine.'

The others laughed and the Corporal called the comedian out to the front, standing Sam there, pointing to his head.

'Don't aim at his head. You'll miss, and if you hit it, you'll find there's no brain, just air if it's like this specimen.'

Jack pulled at the grass, floating it down in the faint breeze.

'Don't aim at his legs. You won't kill him.'

Had Ed killed anyone? Had he sat in the sun and listened and learned. Ed had needed to. They didn't. The war was over. Frank got over-worried. There was the bomb now. There wouldn't be another war.

'Aim at the body. That'll get them.'

Jack had applied to become a clerk. It was a cushy number but he had been refused. The officer said his schooling was incomplete though his IQ was high and that he would be directed towards the Infantry because his rifle range report had been good. Jack looked at the Corporal and then at the Sten. At least he'd never have to kill anyone. And nothing mattered now, because basic training was over. He was going home after passing out tomorrow. For two whole days he would be home, with Rosie.

CHAPTER 11

The carriage was as full of smoke as it had been on the journey up to Yorkshire, and the floor as littered with cigarette stubs, but now it was different. They had passed out. They would not have to go through anything like that again. Nothing as bad ever again.

They were to be clerks, teachers, wireless operators, or squaddies and then their lives could begin again. And for the next thirty-six hours they were going home. They all laughed again, as Sid won a hand of cards and Nigel dealt another on the table they had made by heaping a coat over a kitbag.

Jack looked out of the window, the cards worn and slippery in his hand. Rain raced down and across the glass, jagged from the slipstream, and he could see little, but as they drew near London the houses grew thicker. There were chimneys belching smoke, there were the same damaged buildings. Nothing had changed in two months. But what about the people? What about his family? Were they all right?

The train was drawing in, shunting, slowing, stopping. They hauled kitbags out on to the platform, then up on to their shoulders, walking in a group. The smell of London was the same but Jack felt as he had done when he returned from Somerset. Strange, different. And his home had been different too. Was it now?

They took the Underground or other trains, waved, slapped shoulders and couldn't say to one another how they felt. This had been a family, and now they might never see one another again. So they waved, laughed, looked away, looked back, and Nigel, Sid and Jack stood still, looked, nodded then drifted into the crowd. What else could they do?

Rosie was waiting at home, at the entrance to his back yard. The rain had stopped, the fog had settled, raw, close. He saw her as he walked down the alley, leaning against the wall, her scarf round her mouth, her coat belted, the collar up. He watched her straighten and run and heard the thud as his kitbag rolled from his shoulders into the drain and then she was there, in his arms. He pulled down the scarf, kissed her warm lips, searched her mouth with his, felt her against him, her arms around him, and the strangeness was gone. She was here. He was home.

'They're all right,' she said into his neck. 'There's been no rows. No trouble.'

Then there was the sound of running feet, panting breath, and Lee was there, clasping his leg, crying, laughing, punching, and Jack picked him up, threw him into the air, caught him, hugged him. He hadn't changed. It had only been weeks. It seemed like years.

Ollie and Maisie bought in beer from the pub, and Rosie ate with them because Maisie said every minute was precious when you were in love. Rosie looked away from the bleakness of her eyes, back to Jack who sat balancing on two legs of the chair. He was broader, fitter. A man. And when he had held her she had felt shy against his strength, against the roughness of his stubbled chin, against the voice which was deeper, stronger.

'Do you still love me?' she had asked.

'More than ever. You are what I dreamed of at night. You are my world. You keep me going and you keep my family safe for me. I shall never love anyone else.'

She had felt the pulse in his throat as she touched his neck and then his hands where the scissors had scarred. She picked up his hands and kissed them.

The two days passed too quickly. Rosie waved from the back yard. He wouldn't let her go with him to the station where they would be pushed and pulled by the crowd, where he would see her face as the train left.

She watched as he walked up the alley, listened as his footsteps grew fainter.

She wrote to him at the transit camp, and then to the Barracks when he moved on there. He wrote to her of guard duty, the inspections, the charging of his friend because of a dirty buckle.

He wrote of the Corporal who read out the Guard Duty orders, issued them with bicycle lamps, whistles and pick-axe handles, allocated the stags, or shifts. He drew second stag – 2030 to 2230 then 0230 to 0430. He wrote of the route they walked, the huts they guarded. He wrote of the hours they spent guarding nothing against nobody.

As November became December he wrote of rifle practice. How he would lie on a groundsheet, feeling the iciness of the earth seeping up into him, seeing his breath white before his face, feeling his fingers hurt with the cold as they held the rifle, then the numbness.

He told of pushing home the ammunition clip with the palm of his hand, seeing a red and white flag for a miss, but more often it was a bull.

He told her he loved her, missed her, and knew that she must love him because she stayed for his sake to help Maisie and Lee, when she could be in America.

On 20 December Rosie made paper chains with Lee, but in Lee's house, not Norah's because Norah would not allow the mess, and she was glad that Jack was lying on groundsheets firing at targets because the British were launching the biggest drive yet against the rebels in the Malayan jungle and that could have been Jack, but it wasn't. Thank God, it wasn't.

She strung the paper chains around Norah's kitchen, though she had not wanted any, but Grandpa had always liked them. She helped Maisie do the same. Balancing the step ladder while Maisie reached up, pushing the drawing pin in, laughing because Lee was laughing, and soon they all were, even Ollie who came through the door with a bottle of wine for Christmas and a message from the pub that Jack was coming home for two days' leave.

They ate the turkey at Maisie's because Norah and Harold were going to his mother's for two days. She looked at Jack, and he at her, and she barely tasted the turkey, because he was back. This year there was no perfume for Maisie, no need for Rosie's lies, and she drank her wine, her shoulders easing, because soon perhaps she could go to Nancy and Frank. 1950 promised to be a good year.

Jack walked her back, into the empty house, up the silent

stairs into the boxroom where ice crept up the inside of the windows and the chill dug even through their coats. He wouldn't let her stay up here where it was so bleak and carried her mattress, her bedding, and laid it where Grandpa had slept, where he slept next door.

She watched the muscles in his back beneath his shirt as he stirred up the fire, straightened the blanket made of cardigans. She watched his arms as he tucked the blankets under the mattress. She watched his face as he turned and held out his arms to her and the bed was soft and warm now as they lay together, and his hand undid her blouse, traced the shape of her breast, and his lips too touched her flesh and his tongue licked her skin and it was the right time where Joe had been the wrong time and the wrong person.

She undid his shirt, pushing it back from his muscled shoulders, remembering the boy who had played flicksies, the boy who had raced in the carts, the boy who had pinched the cheeses, the boy who had been beaten by Jones's man. They were not children any longer. They were nearly twenty.

'I want you, Jack. I love you.' She was breathing in the smell of his body, kissing his shoulders, his chest, his arms.

His voice was soft as he drew her close. 'I want you too, but there might be a baby. We must wait.'

But she was kissing his words away because she was alone and soon he would go and she couldn't bear it.

His kisses were stronger, his leg was between hers, his hands on her skirt, but then he moved, pushing her back, sweat on his face and chest.

'No, not now. Not yet. We must wait.' He stood up and drew on his shirt, turning from her, doing up the buttons, looking into the fire, stooping, scooping out the ash, banking it up. Then just standing, watching the greyness that was all that was left of the smouldering fire.

'We must wait, little Rosie. Wait until we're married.' He turned now and sat with her, pulling up the blanket, wrapping it round her.

'I've never seen your body. I've never felt your skin against mine. I don't need marriage. If you do, we'll marry now.' She leaned against him. Didn't he know what it was like, living with a sister who wanted you to go? The snow would be crisp

155

now in Lower Falls. Frank was under pressure because things had become much worse for liberals in his town. She could go back, lean into Nancy's arms. But more than this, she longed for him and his love.

Didn't he know that, though she had promised to stay for his sake, she was lonely? That the days were long and the nights longer still? But then she looked at his hands, the scars, and knew that it was a time they both had to live through.

January pushed into February and she heard little from Nancy and Frank. She wrote to say that she missed them, loved them, and would have come but Maisie and Lee needed her help and support, but maybe she could come in the summer. Did they understand? Were they angry?

Nancy wrote saying that of course they understood, but they had been a little busy. Mao's victory in China and the friendship pact between China and the Soviets had caused a bit of an upsurge in the Reds under the Bed campaign. McCarthy had launched a true blue Red Crusade, saying that he had the names of over two hundred Communists working in the State Department. Three more of their friends had been fired – one had had his house burned down. Another had killed himself. Frank was still fighting through his paper, through letters to other papers, and he was becoming a target.

But she also said that this was only a wrinkle and Rosie mustn't worry. It was just that it was taking a lot of their time. Maybe it would be better if she didn't come for a while anyway.

Rosie chose to believe her, because there was nothing else she could do. She went next door to Maisie. It was Saturday and they took Lee up West, had lunch in a Lyons Corner House and Maisie held her hand and said, 'It's easy when I have you.' Her smile reached her eyes and Rosie squeezed her hand. What else could she do? And things were getting better for Maisie and Ollie, she was sure they were.

Jack wrote telling her about the trench digging they were doing. And then the trench refilling they were doing, day after day.

In March Norah heard that there was to be a new town built in Corby, Northants.

'If you weren't here then we could go. Why don't you get out and find a place of your own?'

'Because this was Grandpa's house and I can stay as long as I goddamn need to. I don't enjoy it. I just have to stay here.' Rosie sat at the table, watching them both sitting in the armchairs, looking at the space where her mattress had been when they were away, and Grandpa's had been before that. Yes, for now she had to stay here, she had promised Jack.

In April she laughed because customs men raided a liner and seized thousands of pounds' worth of smuggled nylons and Jack wrote to say it was a crime, all those stockings being kept from the streets.

At the end of May the sun was hot and on the first Whitsun since petrol rationing ended Maisie and Rosie took Lee to Southend by train, and walked from the station past streams of cars. Rosie held her face up to the sun. Jack was more than half way through. The sun was out, the world was good today. They would marry when he left and had sorted out a job. He had written and asked her. Soon, all the grey years would be over.

But on 25 June North Korea invaded the South and Rosie wrote to Frank because she wanted to know what it meant. He had always said Truman was afraid of appeasement. Would the United States become involved? Was this the conflict he had dreaded? Come on, Frank, she wrote, tell me what's going to happen. Jack's a soldier now.

She didn't have to wait for his reply because on 26 June President Truman offered military aid to South Korea and Attlee endorsed his actions in the House of Commons. On 27 June the UN backed the opposition to the Communists, making it a police action, not a declaration of war. But did that make any difference? Boys would die anyway, wouldn't they, she wrote to Jack. It was not a question.

The Soviet Union was boycotting the United Nations and was unavailable to veto the motion. On 28 June British ships were placed under the command of US General Douglas MacArthur, the same day that the South Korean capital, Seoul, fell to the North Koreans, and that night she didn't sleep. But so far British troops were not being sent. And anyway the boy at the Butlins fairground had said the only conscripts who went into action were volunteers.

She wrote to Jack in the first week of July, sitting out in the

157

yard as dawn came up, breathing in the fragrance of the roses, sure that England would not send troops into yet another conflict. They had done enough. Yes, here, with the yellow roses unfolding and dew thick on the petals, she told herself that England had done enough.

For God's sake, the houses still hadn't been rebuilt, food was still rationed, unexploded bombs were still being found. Yes, they had done enough. And so she wrote not of the conflict in Korea but of Sinatra's visit which she had written up as a feature and would send to Frank.

She wrote of the new Zephyr that Jones was driving and how she had let his tyres down because of the beating he had given Jack, and the apprenticeship he had terminated. But before she could finish the letter the post came, and a letter was brought out by Norah because it was from America, and not in Frank or Nancy's handwriting.

Norah waited as Rosie peeled it open, looking at the address. It meant nothing to her, neither did the writing. She turned it over. It was from Joe. She looked up at Norah standing beside her. Rosie stared at her, then walked from the yard, remembering his blond hair, his tanned skin, his lips on her breasts, but he meant nothing to her. She leaned against the wall which was not yet warm from the sun and read the letter.

Lower Falls
27 June

Dearest Rosie,

I'm writing to you because I feel you should know that Frank has been ill for some considerable time. It's his heart. They didn't want you to know, which is why they were glad you couldn't get over. The pressure of the last few years, the rise in the anti-Red feeling – though for God's sake Frank isn't a Commie, just a liberal – were giving him problems. They didn't want to tell you. Felt it was better not to.

But Korea was the last thing really. Frank kind of takes all this to heart. He is so scared it will make things much tougher over here for those guys already in trouble with this un-American thing as well as involving our boys in war again. I guess he feels that with MacArthur in Japan it could get real nasty. That guy's such a hot head.

158

Anyway Rosie, Frank has had a heart attack. He isn't well. He could die. He thinks of you as his daughter. I know that it would do him more good to see you than anything else. I work for him now. I know him. Please come if you can. I'm sending you a ticket. Pay me back later if you can. I still remember that summer before you left. It was really great to be with you. Do you remember?

Yours,
Joe

Rosie folded the letter, putting it back into the envelope, taking out the ticket. Hearing Frank's voice, his laugh, seeing his broken pipes, seeing the love in his eyes for Nancy, for her. She mustn't cry. There was no time for tears. She must go now. She had waited too long already. She had neglected them.

'I've got to go, Maisie,' she said, wiping Lee's chin with her finger and licking it. Her finger was sticky. It had been sticky with hops that first summer back here, when her heart was so raw at leaving the lake and the Wallens.

'I've got to, Frank's ill.' She looked at Maisie who was cutting bread, holding the loaf to her body, against her apron, sawing a slice from the top. There were crumbs on the table.

Maisie stopped, her face paling. 'Don't go. Don't leave me. I'm not strong enough.' She threw the knife down. 'Don't leave, Rosie. Don't leave us. Not with Jack gone too.'

She hurried round the table, took Rosie by the arms, shook her, looking at Lee who had gone quiet, and stopped eating.

Rosie smiled at him, at Maisie. 'It's not for long. I have to go. I have no choice. I'll be back. Soon. Hang on. Please, let me go. Promise me you'll stay. Jack loves you so. You and Lee and Ollie. Promise me. If it gets very difficult, I'll come back. Just write.'

Maisie promised to stay, promised to write if it became too hard, and kissed her, held her tight, and there was the smell of lavender on her neck.

Rosie wrote to Jack too. She said that she knew she had promised but she had to go. It was only for a while. You'll understand. He's ill, they've written. I'm needed. I love them but I love you more. Write to me. I love you, I love you.

She forgot about Korea. She forgot about everything but informing the office, packing her clothes, posting Jack's letter, taking the train which rattled from the station, and now she cried because she feared that she would be too late.

CHAPTER 12

On the ship, Rosie thought of Jack receiving her letter, reading it on his bed, the only private space he had. She stood by the rail, watching the gulls wheel above the wake as they left Southampton, and wished that he was with her to take her in his arms and tell her that he understood. Surely he would when he knew that Frank was so ill?

She thought, too, of Grandpa standing on the dock so long ago as the children sang 'Roll Out the Barrel' and her voice broke so that no words came from her. Had he heard them as the ship moved out? She would never know now.

As the days went by and England faded, she remembered the leaves on the north shore of the St Lawrence as the ship carrying the evacuees at last drew into Canada, of their colours which she could not believe even now. She thought of the three cheers on deck when they docked, the high arched dining hall where they were taken, the lights in the streets, the food. But most of all the lights because England had been so dark.

On board now, she wrote to Maisie, talking as she would have done had she been there, pulling her back to them all, talking of days gone by; the good times. She would be back soon, she said, and Jack would finish with the Army next year. She wondered to herself how long it would be before Maisie had no more need of their support. They had their own lives to lead, their own love to enjoy. Their futures to explore and work towards.

She wrote to Jack, explaining again, telling of her love, again. She wrote to Norah.

She sat in deckchairs, feeling the breeze on her face, breathing in the air which was free of London smog, free of smoke, thinking of the balls which Frank used to throw to her to catch, the mitt that was warm on her hand, thinking of the balls which he threw for her to hit, the bat which she could swing as well as any boy. Thinking of Jack because she was sailing far away from him and already it was hurting her.

She ate food which was plentiful and fresh and sweet, and felt again the guilt which she had felt as a child a million years ago. But this time she had chosen to come. It was her decision – and she could have made no other. Jack would surely understand that.

She rested in the day because she didn't sleep at night, and each morning asked the purser how much longer, until at last he smiled and said they would dock within thirty-six hours. But she knew that because the gulls were back over the wake again and as they moved along the Hudson River the next morning she saw the cars on the Brooklyn Shore Road, the Staten Island ferries passing the ship. She saw the towers of the city glittering in the morning sun from the starboard side.

She moved to the other side. Here there was the Statue of Liberty, Ellis Island and the low outline of the New Jersey shore. She was back, she was almost home and she was crying.

Merchant ships lay at the piers, steam was surging up from the streets beyond, streets filled with new shining cars. Britain could not afford to keep its goddamn cars, they were exported, and she realised she was gripping the rail, taut with anger.

She took a cab to Grand Central Station and there were no damaged streets, no queues outside the shops, and the tears came again now because she was going home, but she had left home too. She belonged in both, but really she belonged with Jack.

The cab plunged in and out of the shadows of apartment blocks and sped along the double highway of midtown Park Avenue which Frank had said covered the New York Central and the New Haven railroad tracks.

'You a Britisher?' the cab driver asked, his jaws never ceasing to chew gum. He flicked her a piece.

'Yes, but I spent six years here. I'm glad I'm back.'

The gold lettering was still on Grand Central. She walked through the pillared hall, bought a ticket from a booth, thought of all the cleaners, looked up at the zodiac on the ceiling. No, she couldn't see what was wrong with it. She remembered Frank's face and hurried. She didn't stop to look at the Oyster

Bar, or the movie houses, and there was no one meeting her beneath the clock. She felt alone and longed for the feel of Jack's hand in hers.

She moved straight towards the bronze doors, checking her watch. The train would go at one minute past the scheduled time. There were redcaps wheeling trolleys to the silver grey trains, conductors standing by the doors. There was air conditioning on the train. It hummed like the ice-box would hum in the kitchen in Lower Falls. She sat down, she looked at her watch. Come on, for Chrissake. Frank was ill.

But he wasn't at the house. No one was. The blinds were drawn and it looked smaller than she remembered. She walked round to the back. The target was painted as Nancy had said. The rhododendrons were glossy, the lawn was green except where the hose wouldn't reach. There was no jazz sweeping out across the lawn. She stood with her hand to her mouth and longed for Jack because she couldn't bear to think that Frank was dead.

But he wasn't. A neighbour rang the newspaper for her because Frank and Nancy had gone to the lake, and it was Joe who came, driving across in a silver grey Buick which flashed the sun into her face. He drove her to the lake, the hairs on his arm still bleached, his watch still golden against his tan. His voice was deeper, his shoulders broader, but she couldn't look at the hands which held the steering wheel, or the lips which had kissed her breasts.

Instead she listened to the swing music on the radio, and longed for jazz. She looked out at the small towns they were passing through and the petrol stations with their pumps right beside the road and longed for Jack, only for Jack.

'Frank's getting better,' Joe said, reaching forward, pulling out the lighter, drawing on his cigarette. 'He doesn't know you're coming. But I sort of guessed you might use the ticket. I left word with the neighbours.' He was looking at her and she nodded.

'I know. I should have wired to tell them. It was stupid. I was busy getting ready, saying goodbye.'

'Uh huh. So how's little England?'

It was hot, and her legs stuck to the seat. She wound down

163

the window. There was a smell of petrol, diesel and dust. Heat hazed the distant mountains. She thought of the soft hills of Hereford, the stark dales that Jack spoke of. She looked at Joe's hands now. There were no scars on his fingers and thumbs.

'England's just fine,' she said. 'It was good of you, Joe, to send me the ticket. I'll let you have the money when we get to the lake.'

'Say, no hurry. We know things are tight with you Britishers right now.'

She wound up the window, feeling in her purse. She had the money. It was her savings.

'Things aren't tight with us little Britishers,' she said, putting the money on the dashboard, swallowing her anger. She closed her eyes, pretending to sleep as the next four hours crept by. Pretending to sleep until they drove in amongst the walnut and the ash trees and then the rhododendrons which were purple in June.

Just wish there was still the wild plum and the white oak like my dad knew, she mouthed, as Frank had always done at this stage of the journey, and wondered if Frank had been well enough to do it this time.

She was sitting up now, leaning forward, as the sun went down below the hills and the earth was oozing out the last of the heat. She heard the crunch of the gravel beneath the tyres, saw the wood-lapped house, smelt the lake. Yes, she was sure she could smell it.

She opened the door before the car stopped, ran across and up the steps, opening the door, and then stopped. She hadn't told them she was coming. How different would they be?

But then Nancy was running across the cool pine floor.

'Where the goddamn hell have you sprung from, my darling little Rosie?'

And her voice was the same and the arms that held her, but the face which looked closely into hers was older, so much older, and thinner and the lines were deep from the nose to the mouth and there were shadows beneath the eyes.

'Joe sent me a ticket. I've paid for it. I came. I love you both so much, so I came.' Rosie reached for the hand which was smoothing her hair and kissed it. 'How is he?'

164

They were walking across the floor and then she stopped and turned, looked back as Joe brought in her bags.

'I owe you, Joe. Thank you.'

He was still so tall, so strong, so tanned, but she longed for Jack, his slighter body, his smile, his pale skin, his drawn face. Her Britisher.

'Thank you,' she said, then turned and climbed the stairs because she had already forgotten the boy who had kissed her breasts after the barbecue.

She sat with Frank all evening, holding his hand, laughing when he chewed his empty pipe, listening as Nancy read him *Gone With the Wind*.

'It makes him fall asleep,' she said.

Rosie sat with him until he fell asleep, then she walked without shoes down the stairs, feeling the coolness of the floors, breathing in the smell of pine from the furniture, from the shellacked logs, from the very air which was cool as she stepped out on to the verandah. She walked with Nancy across the lawn, into the shadows of the trees, and neither spoke as they approached the lake.

She could hear its ripples slapping against the shore, smell it on the breeze, feel the mulch of the woods beneath her feet. She lifted her head. She could not see the star-strewn sky through the branches.

Then they were out on to the shore and the moon lit the air and the water and she dug her shoes into the sand, reaching down, scooping some into her hand, letting it fall through her fingers. Jack would be happy here. She would bring him one day and they would make love here, while the sand was still warm.

She put her arm through Nancy's. They walked down to the water, letting it lap their feet.

'So how is he really?' Rosie asked because they hadn't spoken of this until now.

'Thank God, he's going to be fine. They think anyway, as long as he doesn't get a lot of pressure again.' Nancy looked up at the sky. 'It kind of makes you feel the world's gone mad, Rosie. Here you have a good man, then things change and suddenly there's a suspicion he's a bad man because of the company he keeps or kept. Because of the words of reason he writes.'

She turned and they walked towards the boathouse.

'And what's even more crazy is when that company isn't bad either, but just had or have Commie connections. It kind of makes me want to puke. But it makes me goddamn frightened too because it's happening here, in our "free" country.'

The wind was gentle, there were no waves now, just a swell. It would be a good fishing night for Frank.

'Will he get completely well?' Rosie looked towards the point. Frank had looked older, like Nancy, thinner too. The lines were deep and his eyes sunken. He had no tan.

Nancy hugged her now. 'Sure, honey. Especially now that you're here. He is just so pleased and he knows it must have been hard to leave Jack and Maisie, especially now that they're sending British troops to Korea.'

Rosie drank hot chocolate in the sitting-room, talking about Uncle Bob, about Norah, about Grandpa, watching the moths beat against the glass, hearing their thuds, feeling the cold fear which Nancy's words had brought, but not being able to speak of it, because Frank was ill and needed her. Because Nancy did too.

It was only when Nancy had kissed her at the bedroom door that she could think. She moved to the window, opened it and breathed air which was so different to London. Then she wrote to Jack, thinking of the landlady at Cowes and her son's friend. You only have to go if you volunteer, the man at the fairground had said. She told Jack again now. She also told him again and again that he must not, but then, why would he?

The next day and the next and every day in July and August she sat with Frank beside his bed, with the windows and doors wide open, the drapes billowing in the breeze, playing records on his gramophone. They talked, but never about Korea, or McCarthy or his three friends who now had no jobs, about the 'hate' letters which Nancy said they had begun to receive in far greater quantities since North Korea invaded the South. Neither did they talk about the falling readership.

There were many hours when they just sat silently together listening to the piano of Erroll Garner, the voice and trumpet of

Armstrong, or the record by The Gang, Bob's new band, that had a tension and an urgency which Rosie liked and so did Frank.

She tapped her foot, poured him iced drinks and thought of the reports in the US papers of the American soldiers who were being mauled as the North Koreans pressed home their advance, and of the British 27th Infantry Brigade who were travelling to Pusan from Hong Kong. She thought of all the United Nations troops that were still being pressed back into the South Eastern coastal tip and thought that the world had gone mad.

Each of those days she walked down the gravel path to the mail box and once a week Jack wrote. His first letter was angry – worried about Frank, about Maisie – but she replied, telling him that Maisie was fine. She had seemed better, had promised that if there was trouble she would write and then Rosie would come back. Trust me, she wrote. I'm only here because I had an urgent letter. But she did not tell him that it was from Joe.

After that he sent her love and news of the assault courses they were clambering over, the football match his team had won, and she was glad that his letters were filled with news such as this. Not of battle which seemed to be in every paper that she read.

Nancy and she went to the Club and Sandra screamed and rushed over, her brace gone, her hair permed, her lipstick bright. She was in her first year at College, majoring in English. She was tanned, a gold watch hung loose on her wrist. They sipped vermouth from chilled glasses which stuck to the tables. They slid them to the edge to break the vacuum, and could only talk about the old times because their lives were so different now – Rosie was not at College, she did not have a gold watch – there was nothing between them and all she longed for was Jack.

Nancy held her hand as they walked to the car and Rosie told her then of her love for him, but Nancy knew already.

'Maybe it would have been Joe, if you'd stayed. He's a good man. Pretty ambitious, but a good man. He got you over. That was kind.'

Rosie nodded. Yes, it was kind, but he wasn't Jack. He didn't go back all those years, like Jack. Jack was her childhood, he was England. He was her life.

*

By September the leaves were falling from the trees and Frank was well enough to sit in the back seat while Nancy drove and Rosie looked back at the house as they left, wondering when she would come again. Because she would be back, but next time she would come with Jack.

In her room in Lower Falls her skis still stood, and the Cougar pennant hung as she had left it. The patchwork quilt was still on the bed and she sat and felt the ridges, then traced her hands along the pine headboard which Frank's grandfather had carved. It was the same, all the same, but she had grown.

The next day Mary returned from holiday and they kissed and hugged and Nancy built up the barbecue to catch the last of the mild autumn. As the light faded and the moths were dragged towards the lanterns, Rosie sat with Frank on the glider and listened because now he was home and there had been a stack of hate mail in the box, and he needed to talk.

His words were calm, slow, but his jaw was clenched as he spoke of the fear and suspicion that was rising in America. He wanted to be back where the trees and the lake hid him, but that wasn't possible. Someone had to print some sense.

He gripped his empty pipe with one hand and her fingers with the other, carving points out of the air as the smell of steak rose with the charcoal smoke.

'The fear and suspicion really got going when America heard that Russia was making headway with its own A bomb. Then there was China. How could the nationalists, supported by our wealth, go down to a peasant army? Now there's Korea. The North with Commie backing sweeping us aside as though we were flies.'

He was swinging the glider gently and his voice was calm. Tired but calm. 'They're frightened that another war will take all this wealth from them. Or maybe it's "we", hey, Nancy?' he called. But Nancy shook her head.

'You've never been afraid of poverty. You made all this, you could make it again. You might *have* to make it again if this goes on.' She flipped over a steak and laughed. Frank laughed too and Rosie felt the love flow between them and thought of Maisie and Ollie.

'That guy McCarthy, he's cunning. He wants re-election.

He picked out a hot chestnut to get in the papers. He's telling us he knows over two hundred Commies in the State Department. He hasn't named them. He can't name them, but some people want to believe what he says.'

'Steak'll be ready in five minutes,' called Nancy. Rosie nodded and Frank waved his pipe.

'But why?' Rosie asked.

'There was a backlash after the First World War. We had the Ku Klux Klan then. Now we have the Red Menace.' Frank rubbed his face with his hand. There were age spots on the back. 'And it's like I said before; it's hard for people to believe that this great big country of ours can get beaten by Mao, or Korean peasants. Look at our troops in Korea, pinned down by fire power. Cut off, whole battalions surrounded, thousands of our boys captured. It can't be the way we handle things, can it? It has to be betrayal from within. That's the only answer for some.' Nancy called them over now and Rosie helped him to his feet.

'Look at Hiss, a Harvard Law School graduate from a WASP family under suspicion of spying. McCarthy loves that. He tells the people that we are being betrayed by the high-ups within. He tells them that we red-blooded Americans could wipe our boots on the Commies, except for this betrayal.'

The barbecue was hot on their faces, the smell rich and sweet, and it seemed a world away from the harassment and fear of which Frank spoke, but that night there was a phone call, which Nancy took, and it was only when Frank went up to bed, his feet heavy, that she told Rosie that Uncle Bob had just been interviewed by the FBI. He had been reported last week for speaking out at an isolationist meeting back in 1940 and shouting that the Nazis must be beaten. It had been the day after Rosie had yelled at him from the stairs.

The doctor came the following week and now Frank was able to walk down the block, and drive into work for a few hours, and he came home with Joe, who stayed to dinner, his shirt white, his teeth white, his hair bleached. They talked of the jobs Frank had given to two of his blacklisted friends and Joe frowned as he drank from the crystal glass.

'I guess we should be seen to be even-handed,' he said. 'There should be a leader column alongside yours taking a more normal view. We'll be closed if we take too much of a liberal stand.'

Rosie put her own glass down. 'Frank's paper is even-handed.' Her voice was sharp.

Frank laughed. 'He's got a point. I haven't been publishing any of the crazy letters. I guess we'll let them roll. Maybe it'll shake some of these burghers up, make them see what's going on outside their picket fences. And maybe it's time Joe had a column. We'll give it a shot.'

They moved to the sofas and sat in front of a fire which flickered and swept heat into the room, and Rosie thought of the small banked fire, the queues, and Jack. She looked at Joe. He was so big. She wanted to be back in England, to feel Jack's arms around her, his lips on hers, to feel safe. There had been no letter from him last week, or this week, so that night in bed, she read all that she had received and slept with them beneath her pillow.

There was no letter from him the next day either but there was one from Maisie.

California
USA
7 Sept. 1950

Dear Rosie,
    You will see from the letter that I am in America too. I couldn't manage any longer. I love him you see. He came over for me again and this time I had to go back with him. Lee is Ed's boy. Forgive me. Jack left, you left. Ollie is a good man. I've hurt him so much. It was never his fault, always mine. Jack loved Ed too. I wrote to Jack but he didn't write back. Go to him.

Maisie

She left that day, throwing clothes into her cases, kissing Nancy and Frank, saying she'd come back. She had to be with Jack. She flew. The ship was too slow. Frank paid. She didn't mind. She had to get back to Jack and all the time she cursed the red-haired man and the woman who smelled of lavender because they would bring pain back into Jack's life and he might blame her.

170

She took a taxi down the narrow streets. They had still not rebuilt the houses round the rec. Why hadn't Maisie written? She would have come back. Rosie had known the man was Ed. Deep down she had known.

She jumped from the taxi, paid, tipped, and ran down between the houses to the alley, her cases banging into her legs. She dropped them in Jack's yard. He wouldn't be there, but Ollie would.

Ollie was sitting at the table, drunk. His face was unshaven. He smelt of stale beer. There were dishes in the sink. Lee's toys were heaped in the corner of the room, broken and hacked apart. Maisie's clothes were with them. There was no fire in the grate and it was cold.

Rosie walked over to him, putting her arms around him, holding him, rocking him, but he didn't cry, he just moaned.

'I'm so sorry,' Rosie whispered. 'I'm so sorry, Ollie.'

He was silent at last, then pushed himself away from her, turning back to the beer, pouring it into his glass, drinking again. She stooped to pick up the clothes, the toys.

'Leave it. I'm going to burn them.' His voice was cracked like an old record.

She moved to the fire then, cleaning out the grate, emptying the ashcan into the dustbin, feeling it in her eyes and throat. She laid wood, then coal, lit it. Held a paper to draw it, heard the crackle then felt the heat.

She boiled a kettle, washed the dishes, made tea. Came and sat at the table with him. She poured him a cup, and one for herself. It was hot and strong. He didn't drink his. He didn't even look. He just drank his beer. She should have stayed in England, but how could she? How the hell could she?

'I knew it was that GI,' he said as Rosie poured another cup. 'Bastard.'

He pushed his chair away, kicking at the toys, standing there, his hands limp by his sides.

'I just knew,' he repeated then he walked into the yard. Rosie followed.

'I loved her, you see. It drove me mad. If I'd been kinder maybe she'd have stayed. But it burned inside me. She wouldn't let me touch her, not after she met him.'

Rosie held his arm. It was dark now. There were lights in Norah's house.

'The boy was his. I knew. It was the hair. They both had the same hair. I used to buy ham off him. I liked him. Trusted him, but only in the beginning. Now they've gone.' He turned and looked at the house.

'Your granddad and me bought these two houses. Things were all right then. Now I've got nothing and he's dead.' He was looking at her now, in the light from the kitchen. 'It's you bloody Yanks. You knew, didn't you, and you never said. Maisie told me. You bloody Yanks, you stick together. Well get out of here. You don't belong. Just get out.' He was shouting, moving towards her, and Rosie backed away from him, out of the yard, because he was right. She had known and there was nothing she could say. But then he called, 'There's a letter here for you. From Jack.'

She stood at the gate, the latch was rusty, there was a slight fog, the dampness made her cough. Why was Jack writing to her here?

Ollie went into the house, came out. The letter was white in his hand. He thrust it at her, then pushed the gate shut. It was dark, too dark to read. She walked to the end of the alley, to the lamppost where Jack and she had swung. She ripped it open.

Rosie,
  Norah told me someone called Joe wrote to you. Who the hell is Joe? Is that why you went? Is that why you left Maisie? You promised. You said if I wasn't there, you would be, but one letter from a man I've never heard of and you're rushing back to the Wallens. Was Frank really so ill?
  I trusted you and all the time you knew about Ed. She's taken Lee. He was Ed's. You Yanks think you own the bloody world. Go to hell. Go back, you seem to like it so much. Don't let me see you again.

                                                        Jack

CHAPTER 13

Rosie spent the night at Norah's. Not speaking to her, or to Harold. She couldn't. She couldn't sleep, eat, think. All she could do was feel.

She travelled to Yorkshire the next morning, her mouth dry. She must see him, talk to him. She must make him understand. The leaves were down from the trees, the wind buffeted the train. There was a view of Harrogate screwed to the wall. What had happened to the one that Jack had taken and sold in Somerset? What had happened to her world?

She turned from the glass-framed picture, from the man who sat reading his paper, blowing his nose. She stood, left her paper in her place and walked up and down the corridor to dull the pain. Everything was dark. There was no colour. He couldn't leave her. He was her life. He was her childhood, her future.

She leaned her head against the window, letting it bang against the glass as the train rushed through long sweeps of countryside, watching the rain jerk down the pane. Yes, she'd known. But she couldn't tell. It would have made it worse. Or would it? She didn't know, for Chrissake. She didn't know. All she knew was that she had promised Jack, and Maisie too, and there was anger added to the pain. Why couldn't people live their own lives? Why reach out and destroy hers? Why, Maisie? For God's sake why?

She changed trains, buying a roll which she couldn't eat from a kiosk, buying stewed tea, feeling it coat her teeth; feeling despair. She had to wait two hours for a connection. This part of the journey was slower, and she wanted it to roar and rush. She had to talk to him.

The camp was large. Squat buildings lined the roads. Nissen huts stood behind barbed wire. White notice boards held stencilled letters. The taxi took her to the duty room. It was six p.m. He was out.

'Where?'

They wouldn't tell her.

She held the taxi, gripping the door as though it would drive off, asking each soldier who passed, ignoring the winks, the whistles. No one knew. But still she waited. Still she asked.

'In the pub, in the village,' a boy with a shaved neck told her. He looked a child.

'Which pub?' She still held the taxi door. The meter was ticking over.

He didn't know. But it was one in Little Somerton.

They drove there along unlit roads. Sheep were huddled on the moors and the trees were stunted and crouched before the wind. Faster for Chrissake, she thought, but she said nothing.

She paid the taxi, standing in the centre of a village which was more like a town and watching it leave. It was dark and cold. The grey stone of the buildings funnelled the winds in off the dales. There were soldiers in the streets and girls who smiled, their lipstick bright in the light from the street lamps and the windows of the houses. There were railings, sharp pointed, newly painted. She could smell it.

Rosie walked up the street, looking at the men, and they looked back, walking towards her, but they were not Jack. She moved on, shaking her head. There were catcalls.

'Give us a knee trembler then.'

She pushed open the door to The Red Lion. It was crowded, full of smoke. Soldiers were playing darts, the juke box was loud. There were girls at the tables, their laughter high, too loud. A man in front turned, he was drinking beer with a cigarette in the hand which held the glass. There was froth on his upper lip. He grinned at her, wiping his mouth with the back of his hand.

'I'm looking for Jack Parker.'

He shook his head. 'Never 'eard of him. What about me?'

She looked past him, at the man behind, the men to the left and right, all of them, but none was Jack.

She turned and left. The man followed, holding open the door, calling after her.

'Come on, sweetheart, I'll buy you a drink.'

174

She didn't turn, she just walked on. She had to find him, had to talk. She couldn't live without him. She couldn't live with this despair. It made her breath shallow, her skin clammy.

In the second pub there was the same smoke, the same juke box music. Lights pulsed from it, on the men, the women, the ceiling, but not on Jack. He wasn't there.

In the third pub there was no music. There was a pool table down one end and dominoes too. There were girls at the tables, soldiers right up to the door.

She pushed through them, looking, asking. Their khaki was rough and damp. It smelt. Was that the smell Jack had meant when he told her about pressing his clothes?

A man caught her arm. She pulled away. He spilt his beer.

'Bloody 'ell,' he said, shaking his head, 'I'm only trying to tell you, Jack's over there.' He jerked his head behind him and she gripped his arm.

'I'm sorry, so sorry.'

Then she was past him, sliding through another group, smelling their beer, their sweat, and he was there, sitting at a table flicking a beer mat over and over, his arm round a girl with blonde hair and black roots, and it was as though she was split apart, jagged and bleeding, as she heard a moan. It was her. It was like the noise that Ollie had made.

But no one else heard. No one saw her. No one was looking. Not the men round the table, not the girl who was leaning into his neck, not Jack whose lashes were still too long, whose face was still too pale, too drawn, so sad.

She didn't hear the others, see the others. Those that pushed her, jostled her, those that sat around his table. They were laughing. Their mouths were open, their shoulders were heaving but she couldn't hear them.

'Jack.' It was her voice. It sounded the same, not as though it came from the pain which was slicing through her body.

She watched as he looked up, his face changing. He moved, then stopped. His face became set, his arm gripped the girl. He turned from her. But for a moment he had loved. She had seen it.

She moved closer. 'Come and talk to me, Jack.'

He was turning to the others, his shoulder towards her, then his back. The girl looked over him, to Rosie, and laughed. There was lipstick on her teeth.

'Talk to me, Jack.' Rosie leaned forward, picked up a glass of beer that the Lance-Corporal who sat opposite him had just put back on the table. It was three quarters full.

'Talk to me,' she shouted and the laughter stopped around the table. But Rosie couldn't hear anything other than her own voice. Now he turned. 'Come outside and talk to me or I throw this goddamn beer over him.'

She nodded to the Lance-Corporal who sat still, doing nothing, saying nothing. There was quiet all around them. She could hear that now. The glass was heavy, and wet. The beer was sticky. The hops had made her hands sticky too.

She said, 'Remember the bines, Jack? Remember how sticky the hops are? How the dust gets beneath your nails? Come and talk . . .' She did not need to go on because he rose.

The girl caught at his hand. He shook her off.

Rosie kept the beer in her hand until he had passed and then she handed it to the Lance-Corporal, but wanted to throw it over the girl. Into her eyes, her hair, her mouth, because Jack had held her and she had leaned into his neck where the smell of him was strong.

She pushed through the crowds, those who were still talking, those who hadn't noticed. The rest opened a path for her, not looking, their eyes busy, and everywhere there was the smell of damp khaki.

She opened the door. It was cold, dark. Jack was down the street, leaning on the wall, his foot up against it, a cigarette in his hand then his mouth. He had done this when she had come home the first time. But then it had been different, he had wanted her.

He watched her come. Her walk, her hair, curling around her face, her neck. Her eyes which were heavy with pain, her lips which were trembling and he wanted to reach out and hold her, love her, but she had gone away. Joe had written and she had gone. Maisie had gone. Rosie had known about Ed, all that time. And now the love washed away and the anger came again, as it had done every day since Maisie had left, frightening him by its savageness.

He turned and walked on, hearing her footsteps behind him, just behind, never at his side because he walked too fast. She would never walk beside him again.

176

He would never let her. He had trusted her, loved her above all else. But she had rushed to Joe, to Frank, to America, and because of that Maisie had gone to Ed. His heart was full of pain, his eyes too, but she mustn't see that. No one must see his pain again. He pushed it away until only the anger was left.

Rosie followed him, out of the town, to a crossroads where the only sound was the wind, but when it dropped she heard the sheep too. He stopped now, sitting on the rocks off to the left, lighting another cigarette.

'I'm sorry, Jack. I'm sorry I left.' She wanted him to reach out and hold her but he didn't and so she put her hand out. He knocked it to one side and threw his match away. It fizzed in the damp grass.

'I had to go. Joe wrote. To say Frank was ill. He works for him, you see.'

Jack sat slumped on the rock, his head down, his cigarette glowing. 'Is that so? Norah gave me the letter. You left it in your room. You knew him well. You had a summer together. You never told me. Maisie knew Ed well. She never told me either. You knew though. But you didn't tell me.'

Rosie put her hands in her pockets, bunching them. This was all wrong. Joe meant nothing. How could he come into this? How could he touch her life with Jack? This was about Maisie and Ed, not her and Joe. The panic was rising, she wanted to hold him, kiss him, tell him she loved him, only him, but there was such anger in him. It changed his face, now, as she looked at him.

She spoke slowly, carefully. 'It wasn't like Maisie and Ed. Joe works for Frank. I knew him, that's all. Long ago. We dated. He wasn't important.'

Jack didn't look up and his voice was dead. 'I told you about the girl in Somerset. She wasn't important. I wanted you to know. So that you could trust me. So that I could trust you.'

Rosie wanted to reach out, make him look at her, make him see her love. She said, 'I don't know why I didn't tell you, Jack.' But she did know why. It was because Joe had touched her breasts and his tongue had found her mouth and she was ashamed, but how could she tell him that?

He flicked his hair with his hand. It was longer now. She wanted to reach out and stroke it, stroke his face, see him smile.

'Anyway, what about that girl? What about the trust I have in you?' she asked, her hands clenched tighter now, with anger as well as pain. The red lipstick, the mouth, the hair, all in her mind.

Jack shrugged. 'What about her? She's here. You aren't. You went to America. Maisie left. You knew about Ed. You didn't tell me. You deserve nothing better. I thought I could trust you.'

He was standing now, shouting at her, screaming at her. 'Don't you understand? It was Ed. I loved Ed. Ed was like my father. But he wasn't mine, he was Lee's. After all that he's Lee's father and Lee has gone.' He was gripping her shoulders, shaking her until her head jerked backwards and forwards. Then he stopped and turned.

'Tell me you didn't know, Rosie. Please. Tell me it was a mistake.' His voice was tired. The anger was gone in her. She knew his face would be drawn but he wouldn't turn for her to see.

She couldn't tell him. She stood there as the cold wind caught at the trees behind her and at her hair and wanted to be back in Middle Street, back with Grandpa and Jack, back with the roses, with the life they had had. Back where she could understand why this was happening.

'I did know. I saw them. I didn't know it was Ed then, or I didn't think I knew. But when Maisie told me in her letter it wasn't a surprise. She had said she would give the man up. She made me promise not to tell you. I said I would help. I stayed as long as I could. But then I had to go. Frank was ill. I love him.' Her hands were out of her pockets now, reaching for him. 'I didn't tell you because I didn't want to hurt you. I thought it would be all right. She promised when I left.'

He hit her then, turning, slapping her across the face, then pushed her backwards, and again, gripping her coat as she almost fell.

'But you promised me, Rosie. You promised me that you would stay. Then you get a letter from this bugger and you go. What have you done? What has Mum done?'

He was holding her now, hugging her, crying because he had wanted to cry like this when Ollie had rung, when he had caught the train home, gone into the empty house. But Maisie had already gone and Rosie wasn't there and she was his friend and his love and he needed her.

She held him close, though her mouth was bleeding and her face throbbed. She held him because for this moment he was hers again and there was so much sorrow, so much love. 'I did nothing with Joe. I've let you down though. Lee's gone. I can't bear that either but I had to go.'

She felt his breath in her hair, the wetness of his tears. 'I love you. I thought I'd helped. I thought it was safe to go. I had to go.'

But now she felt him stiffen again and tried to hold him as he pulled away.

'I know. You went. Maisie went. Lee went. Over there where Ed is. I trusted you all. I loved you all and now it's just Dad and me.'

He walked back to the road. He could hear the wind in the trees. He could hear his voice, Ed's voice. He had lent him his bike. Ed had given him sweets. They had laughed and talked and Jack had told him that his dad was changing, becoming mean and strange, and Ed had put his hand on his arm. Don't worry, he had said. It's the war.

'And all the time he was laying my mum,' he shouted, laughing, turning to Rosie who was dabbing at her mouth. 'Is that what you were doing with Joe?'

He didn't know where the words were coming from. He didn't know what to do with the anger which filled him, spilled over, made him crazy, made him hurt her. Made his head go round until he felt ill.

Her mouth was bleeding. His Rosie's mouth was bleeding and he went to her again, holding her, telling her he was crazy. He didn't know what he was doing. He loved her, he hated her. He hated them all. He loved them all. She wasn't here when he needed her. She was with Joe, and Maisie was with Ed. He loved her. He loved his mother, and Ed. But he hated them. Christ, how he hated them. They had taken Lee. They've . . . taken . . . Lee.

He was howling now and he could taste the blood on her mouth as she kissed him. She drew him to her, stumbling, falling, taking him with her on to the soft grass, and he kissed her, his tongue in her mouth. He pulled at her coat but she stopped him and, he undid her buttons. Then he ripped at her blouse, he wanted her to tear, to feel his lips hard on the softness of her skin. Had Joe done this too, while Ed took Maisie and Lee from him?

'I love you, Jack,' Rosie said. 'I'm sorry. I'm so sorry.'

He looked up at her then. 'Has Joe done this to you?'

The wind was clawing at the branches, the clouds were whirling across the sky. Rosie looked at him, deep into his eyes, into the pain that all the lies had brought.

'Yes,' she said. 'But long ago and it was not what I wanted. I was confused.' She held his face between her hands, making him listen, making him look into her eyes. 'It was long ago. I love you. I've always loved you. All my life I've loved you.' She was kissing his lips, his eyes, his skin. There was blood on his face and the warmth of it in her mouth and she didn't know that it was hers. Slowly he began to kiss her back.

But the anger hadn't gone. It took hold deeper, stronger. Other hands, American hands, had touched her. Touched his Rosie, the girl who had played flicksies, the girl he had pushed on the swing. The girl he had taken to fetch the cheeses. American hands had touched his mother, taken his brother. Christ, it was all too much. It was all too strong. The rage was too strong.

He pushed up and away, but she pulled him back.

'Don't leave me,' Rosie said against his mouth.

He pushed away again, because he wanted her, but he hated her, loved her, wanted to hurt her, wanted to hold her and the rage was still there; his head felt as though it would burst.

She pulled back at him again.

'Don't leave me,' she said again and now her kisses were on his lips and her hands were on his back, and the wind was all around and he couldn't think, he couldn't see her, and he held her, moved on her, dragged at her skirt, her pants, hauling them down, pushing her legs apart, heaving at his own clothes. He sank down on to her, and she cried out as he tore and entered her. And he cried out as he came because all the love and the hate were still there, and the rage too. And then it was over.

Suddenly it was cold, and they moved, pulled at their own clothes, neither helping the other. Then they sat with their backs to the wind, separate, alone, and he wanted to wipe the last minutes from their lives, but it was too late and he was glad that he was leaving England, taking this rage away from her.

They moved without speaking into the trees where the wind was not as strong. The damp had soaked into their coats. Jack lit another cigarette.

'I'm going to Korea. I've volunteered.'

The branches were cracking, shaking, twisting, and the sheep across on the other slope were moving, baa-ing, Rosie saw them, heard them. He couldn't go. No, he couldn't go.

'You can't. I love you. You can't leave me.' She felt the ache between her legs, the feel of him inside her. He couldn't go. Those were the only words left in the world – he couldn't go.

'You love me,' she insisted, catching at his arm as he lifted the cigarette to his mouth, watching as he drew its nicotine deep into his lungs and then out again, his lips pursed, his eyes on the trees in front.

'I do love you and I hate you and if I stay I'll do what Ollie did. I feel as though I'm going mad inside. Everything's gone bad. I'll destroy us both.' He took her hand. 'I've got to go. I've got to get the anger out of me. It's been building since she went. Ollie cried and I held him and then I held him while he tried to tear the house apart. I wanted to do it too.' He pinched out the cigarette. 'I can't think. There's so much hate. I miss Lee so much. I missed Ed so much.' He dropped her hand.

'I've got to get away. That's all.' His voice was angry again. He stood up. 'Let's get you back.'

He walked in front of her, down the road. There was no train that late so she had to stay in a hotel, alone. He left her there, outside. Not touching her, not smiling.

'I'm sorry,' he said. 'About . . . well, you know. If you're in trouble, let me know.'

She gripped his arms. He couldn't go. Not out there. He couldn't leave her. They loved one another. She knew they did. This anger would pass . . . wouldn't it? But then she thought of Ed and Lee, of Maisie, of Joe, of America and she didn't know.

There was light from the hallway, falling out on to the street, there were soldiers walking past, one being dragged. He was singing 'Roll Out the Barrel' and she wanted her grandpa.

She said nothing. She let her hands fall, made herself watch as he walked down the street, made herself nod as he called back, 'I'll write. When I've sorted myself out, I'll write. If I sort it out. If there is anything worth sorting out between us any more.'

Then he was gone and there was no one left in her life. 'Oh, Jack,' she called, but it came out as a whisper. 'You and your goddamn anger. Your pain. What about mine. What about mine?' She was shouting now but he didn't hear.

CHAPTER 14

Jack sailed from Liverpool at the beginning of October on a troop ship with Regulars, Reservists and National Servicemen, and he was glad to be amongst them, to be leaving England, to be leaving Rosie and the memories. He was glad to be leaving for The Land of the Bleeding Morning Calm as the Sergeant had called it when he marched them up the pier.

He was glad to be on board, to be drilled, to be exercised. He enjoyed the orders, the bull, because it was familiar, like the scar on his hand was familiar. Like the other men were familiar, though he knew none of them. He just knew their language, their style, their habits, because they were like him. He was Army now.

There were no women. There was no tenderness. No betrayal, because if anyone broke the trust, out there on the hills of Korea, they all died.

He enjoyed pushing the ammunition into his rifle, hearing the click. It was cold, final. He enjoyed the storm which lashed the ship for four days, pitching and tossing, throwing him from his bunk, making him sick, making him wheel and fall, because it stopped him thinking and feeling.

He enjoyed the lectures, because then he could not hear her voice in his head. He learned how the North Koreans with Russian-built tanks and weapons had poured across the 38th parallel into South Korea in June.

'Will the West really resist the spread of Communism? is what the Russians will be asking themselves,' the instructor said. 'And I can tell you that we will. They've challenged the UN. They must be stopped.'

Jack listened when Captain Norris said that the Korean War had come when the international outlook was already bad, how the cold war was at its height, how Eastern Europe was under Russian domination. How West Berlin had just escaped this fate. How the Chinese Communists had triumphed in China. He knew all this from Frank's letters to Rosie. But, no, he wouldn't think of her.

He took out a cigarette, smelling the match, thinking of the oast-houses, the fag-ends they had collected as children. But he wouldn't think of that. He must listen to the officer with the moustache now, standing as Captain Norris sat. He must look at the Padre sitting upright, one leg crossed over the other. He must not think of her.

The second Captain was pointing at the board where a map hung.

'In June the South Koreans had a small army, no tanks or heavy artillery and only a small airforce. The North would have conquered South Korea if the United States hadn't had access to their occupation forces in Japan. These, though under strength and ill equipped, were mobilised but were still pushed back to the South East Corner along with our men when they also reached Korea.'

The officer slapped his cane down into his hand. Jack pinched out his cigarette. The Corporal next to him sighed.

'Get a bloody move on,' he murmured. 'I want me bleeding lunch.'

Jack grinned. The Captain was looking at his notes, the men were stirring. The man in front of Jack rubbed his neck. His hair was very short. L O V E was tattooed on his fingers. But there wasn't such a thing, was there?

'As you know, men, General MacArthur launched an invasion in September at Inchon while those in the Pusan perimeter, in the South East, went into the offensive. Now the North Koreans are on the run. We have pushed them back almost as far as their capital Pyongyang. Well over the 38th parallel. The border.' Captain Mackin coughed and looked up as another officer left, papers in his hand.

'It was a hard slog, don't think it wasn't. The harbour was mined, the roads were mined. There are still mines. That took a toll of tanks and men. The casualties have been heavy, but General MacArthur has turned down an order from Washington cancelling their issue of one can of beer a day.'

He stopped for laughter. There was some but the reservist

Tom, on Jack's left, was quiet. He had served in the Far East. He had been a POW at Changi. His war should have been over, he told Jack as they went for food. His wife thought so too.

'It's worse for the girl you've left behind,' he said.

Jack didn't reply. He hadn't left anyone behind, had he? But he didn't want to think about it. He couldn't get past the anger, the hate, to the love. He didn't want to any more. Not now, not yet. It was easier this way.

They sat through another lecture that afternoon and the sea was calm, there was only the vibration of the engines, the smell of diesel, and the Captain's voice again as he told them that the biggest fear was that Communist China would become involved.

But then he swept on quickly, telling them of the country and its people, but all Jack could think about was whether the Chinks would come in, because if they did, it would be tough. Very tough. Tom's hands were shaking and Jack wondered how the Government could send people back into the ring who had already been through so much.

Would the Americans send Ed over here? He had done a lot, hadn't he? They should send him. He should be killed. But he was too old.

'Old enough to be my father,' he said that night as he leaned on the rail and spat into the waves and wondered when the ache inside his head and chest would fade.

The days wore on. They listened, they trained, they wrote to their families, their lovers, their friends, but Jack only wrote to Ollie. He had no lover. But in the darkness of the night, when the only sounds were the grunts of men and the throb of the engines, he felt her warmth, her passion, and turned away from the memory of his own savagery. He wanted to feel love again, as it had once been. But he could not. And so he didn't write.

They arrived in Korea at the beginning of November. It was cold. They could see their breath on the air as they stood at ship's muster. They could see the buildings, the jeeps. They could see the hospital ship too, moored alongside. At Pusan they heard that the Chinese had come in, fiercely, briefly, but everyone knew they would come again. It was only the UN Command who refused to believe it, a Sergeant said as he passed them, grey and tired.

They entrained for Seoul but not before the Red Cross hospital train drew in from the forward battle areas. Tom watched and so did Jack. The red was sharp against the white of the bandages. The orderlies carried the drips beside the stretchers, the nurses checked labels, soothed, gave drinks, listened to a man shout that he could still hear the bugles.

A GI hobbled past. 'Yes, it's the bugles. You know it's them then. It's the bloody Chinese, they attacked us near the Manchurian border. Your turn next, buddies.' He was smiling but it didn't reach his eyes.

'Bloody Yanks,' said Jack. The GI had been big like Ed.

He pushed Tom on. 'Come on, let's go.' But he didn't want to. The Chinese were involved now, up on the border, but they wouldn't stay there. He wanted to go home. This wasn't drilling, exercising, smoking, drinking. This wasn't a scarred hand. This was vivid, stark, shocking. The fear made his voice rough.

'Come on, Tom, get on.'

The wooden seats were slatted, dusty. But he didn't want to go forward. He wanted to go home. This was real. God, Rosie, this is real. He slung his kit on to the floor. The dust caught in his throat. More were heaped on top. Tom was close. He could smell his sweat. But what was there at home any more? Who was there?

Seoul was damaged, bombed like London had been. But Jack wouldn't think of London, only of Korea and the tents they lived in, the mobile Naafi, the mist which changed to sharp cold almost overnight. It was all right, they were told, they weren't moving forward.

They stayed, smoked, bulled, smoked, trained. Felt nothing but boredom. Filled days which went too slowly, watched American troops lurch by in jeeps and Jack felt nothing but hate. In Seoul the hotels were functioning. There were drinks at night, Korean bar-girls who sat on stools with slits up their skirts, but he didn't want them. He didn't want anyone's lips against his. He didn't want anyone near him ever again.

Tom didn't want them either. These girls were Koreans. Koreans had guarded his camp. Their cruelty had been worse than the Japanese and so they bought drinks only for themselves. They sat sipping the beer, watching the flares in the sky. Watching the refugees pulling carts piled high, their faces numb.

The men wore white robes, baggy trousers and straw hats similar to the women who dragged their long hair back into buns. They drank another beer. There had been no more talk of the Chinese and it was 20 November. MacArthur had said they would be home for Christmas. He had to sort himself out before then. He had to write. But he didn't know what to say. He didn't know what he felt.

On the 22nd ten of them were sent north to the forward position as Infantry replacements, along roads girded by frozen paddy fields, and on either side were snow-dusted mountains and hills; shrub-covered, desolate.

Troops were dug in. Smoke rose from the fires. There was a wind. Always a wind and as they travelled the squad talked, but of nothing because they all remembered the boys on the hospital train.

'But the Chinese haven't come and MacArthur said we'd be home by Christmas, didn't he?' Jack repeated.

He shifted on the seat, peering out of the canvas-covered truck, listening but hearing only the wind. He laughed, they all laughed because they had all been listening too. For bugles.

They smoked, looked out at the cottages made of wood and mud and thatched with straw. Three were scorched and ruined. Even in this cold they could smell the human excrement used to feed the soil.

They passed peasants who carried loads on A-shaped frames, women who carried loads on their heads and babies on their backs. The roads were dirt tracks with pot holes which were frozen over. The truck cracked the ice, splintering it, frosting it. Jack threw out his cigarette stub. It arced away, bright in the cold air.

Tom sat, his hands loosely between his knees, his rifle leaning into the crook of his arm.

'I wish I wasn't here,' he said.

'No good saying that when you're sitting on top of a bleeding hill.' The Sergeant opposite nudged his leg. 'You just remember to keep your head down, your eyes open, and pray you get home. You've been in it before. You should know. Help this lot of nigs. Anyway, we're here. Home sweet home.'

187

The truck stopped at the base of Hill 12. They hauled their kit up on foot, catching on to shrubs, pulling themselves along, slipping, their rifles clattering. A stream ran from the top to the river below and ice crusted the overhang.

The unit they were to join catcalled them at the top. A Lieutenant met them. They saluted. He was grey and lined too, although, they learned, he was only twenty-two. The Sergeant led them to the field kitchen. Others were there before them, warming their hands around their mess tins, moving from foot to foot, nodding as they dug out their tins. At least the beans and stew were warm.

'More shit-diggers. Just what the Chinks want for tea,' a Lance-Jack grinned.

Jack nodded, laughed, and when they had eaten they were shown the hoochies they would sleep in, fight in, shit in. They were shown the machine guns, the mines, the booby traps. That night he and Tom slept in sleeping bags. Dave, John and Simon didn't.

'We've been here too long,' they said. 'You might need to run. Those buggers are like a bloody avalanche.'

The hoochie was heated by an ammunition box into which petrol dripped from a copper tube fed from a can fixed high on the outside. The chimney was made from shell cases, and prodded up through the roof made of branches. It was still too cold for Jack and Tom but there was no firing. There had been none for many days.

But there was the cold and it ate into him. He zipped up his sleeping bag, pulling it over his head, but the cold eased through the ground, the air. It kept the sleep from him and he thought of the ice on the inside of Rosie's boxroom, the damp of the ground when he had held her, driven harshly into her, felt her warmth, her love, and he felt ashamed.

But she had left Maisie, she had gone when Joe had written. Joe had kissed her breasts. Ed had taken Maisie and Rosie had let him and he turned again and again but he couldn't find warmth, he couldn't find sleep and neither could Tom because the Chinese might come. But they didn't. Not then, and not the next day or the next.

'And they probably won't,' Jack said, digging another

perimeter fox-hole, cursing the frost-hard earth, the ice-cold pickaxe.

'Get your bleeding weight behind it,' the Sergeant growled. 'A Chink would shoot your backside off in that pathetic little hole.'

So he dug further and so did Tom, hearing the clatter of stones, looking out across the valley, the river, the hills. Seeing nothing. No Chinese, no birds, just the cold which stabbed into your lungs but didn't stop you thinking. He dug again. He wouldn't think of her. He wouldn't write. He wouldn't write to Maisie either.

On 24 November it was Thanksgiving Day and they watched as trucks brought out turkeys, and planes dropped the trimmings to US troops, and he wondered if Maisie was eating turkey too. He pushed the thought of her from him, but for a moment he stopped and leaned on the barricade he was building from the rocks, not seeing the planes, not seeing the trucks or the snow-frosted world. Just remembering Lee's laugh, the feel of the little boy's arms around his legs in the back alley on his first leave.

Still the Chinese didn't come but there was no sense of ease. Only of waiting. He had spent his life waiting. Should he write? No, he couldn't.

They went on patrol that night as the snow started to fall, heavily, silently. Five of them, the Sergeant leading, Tom second. He knew so much about survival. He had fought the Japs, he had survived the camps. He was quiet, calm, except when his hands shook.

They slid down the slope, digging in their heels, not speaking, not clinking, looking, listening, and Jack's hands were wet inside his gloves and his breathing was rapid.

He was frightened out here, beneath the sky, away from the holes, the others. And no, he wasn't thinking, he was breathing with his mouth open, tasting the snow, straining to hear the enemy, if they came. He was looking, always looking, but what could you see through all this snow which drove in and around him? Christ, he was frightened. These weren't manoeuvres. This was real. And what the hell was he doing here?

He put his feet where Tom's had been, he slipped, recovered. His feet hurt with the cold but that was all right. It was when they didn't hurt that you had frostbite, it was then that you lost your feet.

He looked and listened. His throat hurt from the cold air. There was nothing, just the sound of breathing, and soon the hill had flattened and the going was easier as they crept to the shore of the river.

They set up a listening post behind scrub and rocks where they could sometimes see the river as the snow hurled itself in a different direction and the curtain lifted. Tom linked up a field telephone. They spent three hours watching, listening, feeling the cold bite through their clothes, their balaclavas, their gloves, feeling it stab into their lungs with each breath. It had been minus thirty-five when they left. They could hear the snow cracking the branches of the shrubs and the Sergeant's breath froze on his moustache.

The next patrol came down to relieve them at 2300 hours. They edged up the hill again. Watching, scrambling. Christ, be quiet. Using their hands, shaking the snow which caked their gloves and faces, and always they listened, even as they thawed in the 'warm tent'. But the enemy didn't come and no one relaxed, though MacArthur had said they would all be home for Christmas.

The sound of firing woke them the next night, it was down by the river.

'Thank God, thank God,' he whispered when he woke. 'That could have been me.' Now there were bugles, rattles, whistles and drums, grenades and small arms fire.

But his hands were too cold to unzip his sleeping bag and he wept as John and Dave and Simon ran out, rifles in their hands, ducking and weaving as the Sergeant shouted, 'Take that side and keep your heads down.'

'Christ, I can't get out.' He was going to die. They were coming for him and he was going to die. But Tom was there, calm, leaning over him, unzipping the bag for him, helping him as Ollie had done when Jones's man had beaten him at the warehouse, as Rosie had done with the cheeses. Tom gripped his shoulders.

'It's OK, Jack. You're OK. They're not here yet. Remember what you've been taught and stay with me.' He turned and moved out into the snow. There was firing all round, from the hills ahead and around them.

The fear held Jack still. Dad, where are you? Rosie? He wanted to run. Just run and hide because he could hear screams and shouts and the bugles at the base of the hill and they were getting nearer, the firing was louder. The snow was heavy, and he couldn't see. He hadn't been able to see in the fog either. Dad, where are you?

But the barricades were there. They would keep them away. Jack was out in the open. Following Tom, running, the snow in his eyes, his nose, his mouth. The breath was sharp in his chest. He slipped, scrambled up again, ran to where the Sergeant pointed, heaving the Sten gun up on to the wall he had built, firing down at men who fell as the ducks in the fairground had fallen, but more took their place. For God's sake. More took their place.

His gun was hot. Tom was firing. There were tracers in the air. Flashes from grenades were bright against the snow. Still they came. On up the hill. And he wasn't killing men, he was killing ducks. Ducks which flipped back up, no matter what he did.

They were closer now, scrambling where he had scrambled, firing, blowing their bugles. The Sergeant was behind them. They were much closer.

'Stand your ground,' the Sergeant shouted, but they were so close. He would see their faces soon. They were at the first barricade, leaping over, shooting, stabbing, killing. This was real, for Christ's sake. People were dying. There were screams and groans all round and there was sweat on his face, dripping on to his coat. But he was cold. How could he sweat?

The Sergeant screamed, 'The buggers are through. Over here, you two.'

They crouched and ran back to the next fox-hole. Jack lay down, fired again, heard Tom do the same. It was cold, for Christ's sake. The ground was cold but the Chinese were coming on, falling, dying. Jack fired, Tom lobbed grenades, but more came.

'Where the hell are they coming from?' It was Tom. He was standing, his body exposed. Jack pulled him down.

'Keep firing.' His mind was cool now. It was Tom's hands that were shaking, not his. There was no hate, no love. Just the gun, just the Chinese, and they were closer. For God's sake, they were so damn close.

191

'You've got to hold.' The Lieutenant was behind them, his breath short. He was shouting. 'Got to hold, let Hill 16 complete their manoeuvre. Then we can go, if we have to. But hold.'

John was with them now. They dug their knees in deeper. It didn't matter that it was cold. They wanted to live. They held for five hours.

At 0300 hours the Sergeant slapped Jack on the back, took over the Sten.

'Get out now, over there.' He was pointing to where other men were leaving, stumbling and running, while others still fired, still fought. Jack took his rifle, crouched, ran. Tom was with him, passing him a Luger he had taken from a fallen soldier.

The Chinese were breaking through. They were fighting. He saw arms lifted, guns and knives which twisted and plunged. Tom turned, his head down, his gun up.

'Get out, Jack!' His voice was faint against the noise but Jack heard him, stopped.

'Come on, Tom. Your wife. Get home.' He grabbed him, pulled him, turned him and they ran on together.

They skidded down the hill, ducking and weaving, looking forward, behind, to the side. There were others, friends and enemies. A Chinese lunged for Jack, he dodged, drove home the rifle butt, felt the jolt through his body, but they went on, down the slope, slowing, easing, creeping at the base, sidling off to the side of the road, but there were more and they were firing and Jack felt a punch high up in his arm.

He turned. Tom was down too. There was blood on his chest, on his stomach. He had been shot four times. His mouth was open, his eyes too. He was dead. Snow was already settling. He was warm and Jack took him in his arms, tried to lift him, carry him home to his wife, away from all this, because he had been in too many wars.

But the punch had been a shot and he could only move one arm and the pain was beginning now. He tried to drag Tom, but he had no strength and so he had to leave him, there, in the snow, alone but not alone for there were other dead around him.

Jack felt the anger and the pain rage and he screamed, 'Rosie.'

The Sergeant was there then, pulling, dragging him towards the road where tanks were retreating. He shoved Jack up on to the body of one.

'Hang on or you'll die. Hang on, son.'

There were others clinging, hurting, panting, and he did cling on but not for long because the road was blocked by blazing vehicles and a tank which had lost its track.

He dropped to the road. His coat was too heavy. It dragged at him. He pushed at the tank with the other men but there was too much fire from the hills each side and behind them and so he walked, and another man took his rifle, struggling on ahead.

They passed a soldier on fire from burning phosphorus. How could he burn with so much snow? The flames were so bright. How could he burn when it was so cold? Jack felt as though his head were bursting.

'Shoot me,' the American was screaming. Jack shook his head, stumbled on. Christ, that could have been him. Oh Christ. Dad, where are you? Rosie. He stopped, turned back.

'Shoot me,' the man whimpered now, holding out a blackened claw. 'Shoot me.'

The snow was still falling. The man carrying his rifle had gone, walking on, not waiting. There was just this man here, crying, burning. There was no war, no firing, just the two of them, and one was dying, slowly, and his whimpers seemed so very loud.

Jack did shoot him, with the Luger. The whimpering stopped but pain blossomed in Jack and he cried as he walked because he had shot a man with a blackened, burning body and he would never be free of the smell or the sight of it.

Many others straggled back as the days went by. The UN were in retreat again. He didn't mind the pain in his arm. He didn't mind the throbbing, it was better than being dead. Tom was dead and he had a wife. Jack had no one and he was glad. There was too much pain in loving. Tom's wife would know that now. There was always too much pain. He was glad it took all his strength to put one foot in front of the other. He was glad it took all his mind to breathe in and out. In and out because he didn't think of Rosie, or the burning man, or Tom.

They passed blazing villages, and always the enemy was close behind and to the sides of them in spite of the US airstrikes. There were mortar bombs arcing through the freezing sky. They walked with refugees, then passed a burned out field hospital. A jeep came, doling out hot chow. 'Hurry up. For Christ's sake, hurry up,' the Corporal said, ladling hot cereal and powdered eggs into their helmets because they had no mess-kits any more.

The firing was as close as it had been before, but no closer. Why was the Corporal panicking? He wasn't dead. It was all the others that were dead. Jack dropped his helmet. He was hot, so hot. The food spilled on his boots, into the churned snow.

He sank to the ground. It wasn't cold as it had been when he was shooting the ducks on the hill.

Jack felt the jerking of the jeep, the rattle of the train, and it was like the one that had taken them hop-picking and he knew he must think, he must write to Rosie. But what would he say? He didn't know. He was too tired. Too hurt.

The field ambulance carried him from the train to the ship. A stretcher took him from the ambulance to the gangway. The Medical Officer and Wardmaster lifted the blanket, looked at his shoulder. He screamed as they touched him.

'No gangrene. Those maggots have done a good job,' the Medical Officer said, not looking at Jack, just at his arm. The Wardmaster wrote medical instructions on a label which he tied to Jack's wrist. He was sick of labels. They had tied one to him when he went to Somerset. He wasn't a parcel, he was a person. Rosie hadn't liked hers either. But he wouldn't think of that.

He was carried on a stretcher by South Koreans to the ward on the water line, one deck below the air-conditioned quarters for those seriously injured. They didn't see a doctor on the trip to Japan. There were too many operations needed. Too many amputations because of gangrene.

Jack wouldn't think of the maggots which had been cleaned from his wound. He couldn't bear to think of them in his body. He lay and listened to the throb of the engines, felt the vibration in his wound, his arm which was hot and swollen. He talked to the others as they limped, or sat, arms bandaged, heads bandaged, but they all had their limbs, they all had their lives. Tom hadn't any more and soon his wife would know.

Love hurt.

It was hot. So damn hot. He sat up, but he had no strength, so he lay again. It had been so cold up there on the hill and as they ran away. Pyongyang was burning now. The UN troops were scorching the earth, burning the supplies, stopping the enemy from gaining anything. They were retreating to the 38th parallel. How much further would they go back? Would it all have to be done again?

The trip took three days because the channels could not be guaranteed free of mines and the heat grew worse. The wards were over the main generators. The portholes were secured when at sea.

There were no washing facilities. They were dirty, they were in danger of dehydrating. There were large jugs of water and lime-juice and the boy next to Jack poured him some because he couldn't stand. The ship's engines were so loud. They throbbed in his head, in his wound. All over his body.

He was given more penicillin. He knew there were more maggots but he must wait until Japan to have them scraped away.

An American died and the boy next to Jack told him that they were going to store the body in ice which had to be replenished every two hours, because the Americans returned the corpses to their homeland. Jack turned away from him. They took too many things back to their homeland. They had taken his mother, his brother.

They drew into Osaka and Jack thought that perhaps it was better that Tom was dead, not here with him, because these were the people who had beaten and struck him. These were the people he had hated. As Jack hated Ed. Did he hate Rosie?

The dead went off first, covered with the flag of their country, while the band played. Then the wounded, but not the walking wounded yet. They waited but when it came to their turn Jack still couldn't walk. He was carried on a stretcher and shared an ambulance with a man who had been burned but Jack wouldn't look because he had shot a man with burns. He had been an American. He had pleaded to die.

Jack felt the gun in his hand again. He had shot him. He had looked into a man's face and killed him. Seen the agony go from his eyes, but the light too. An American had asked that of him.

An American had taken his mother. An American had kissed Rosie's breasts, and as the ambulance drew away from the docks towards the hospital he knew he still couldn't write to her.

CHAPTER 15

Rosie walked into the hotel when Jack left, lifting her head and ignoring the gaze of the woman behind Reception, taking her key, climbing into the bed which had not been aired. There was frost on the inside of the panes. He had left her, goddamn him. God damn him. And now she was crying.

Jeeps passed, their headlights flashing into the room, across the ceiling, lighting up the pictures which hung from thin chains. She couldn't sleep. She wouldn't cry. She could scarcely breathe. She lay with her hands on her breasts where she could still feel his mouth.

She wanted to go from the bed, out into the town, to the camp, find him, make him love her, make him push his hate away, her anger, her pain, but she stayed, watching the sky through the window, feeling the throbbing between her legs which had become an ache by the morning. There were drops of blood on the sheet. She sponged them. Each breath hurt. She didn't speak as she paid for her room. She didn't nod. She couldn't.

At the station were the same kiosks selling rolls and newspapers, but she bought nothing, not even tea, and she didn't turn as the train took her away from him. But everything was dark.

She took a Tube and bus and then walked to Middle Street. She walked slowly. She put one foot in front of the other carefully because she ached inside, and she was going home and there was no point to it. And he might come running up behind her, catch her arm, pull her round. Tell her he was wrong. He was sorry. He loved her. But he didn't. And still it hurt to breathe.

She entered the house before Norah and Harold returned from work. The fire was banked. There was a faint heat. She dropped her coat on the floor, her bag too. She dragged the tin bath from its nail on the yard wall.

She smelt the gas before it lit, she heard it hiss as it heated the water in the boiler, she saw the steam beating up to the ceiling, layering the room, clouding the window.

She tipped the water into the bath, poured in cold. There were only two inches. She poured in more cold. Then she peeled off her clothes, leaving them where they fell. It didn't matter that the water was cold. She barely noticed, but she knelt in it, feeling the ridges of the bath on her knees, heaping the water into her cupped hands, splashing it over her body, between her legs, because she had to remove the smell of him or she would die, from anger and from loss.

She splashed again and again, wetting her hair, her body, her arms, her legs, everything. Soaping, rinsing, crying because they had loved but it had not been as she had dreamed. They had loved, but there had been hate, and love without tenderness, only pain. And he might have gone for ever and she didn't know how this had happened. She didn't know how her world could change like this. She didn't know how she could love someone as much without them loving her back.

She dropped her head to her arms, and sniffed. Then to her legs. There was none of him left. Would that help the minutes, the hours, without him? She would not think of longer, of for ever. Now there were more tears, racking sobs which dug deep into her chest and still it was difficult to breathe.

She dressed in fresh clothes, dragged the bath to the yard, tipped the water down the drain. She washed her clothes, hung them on the line where they dripped. She set out the candy she had brought back for Norah on the kitchen table. She hung the scarf she had brought for Harold on the chair and looked at the shirt which had been for Jack, the blouse which had been for Maisie, the car which had been for Lee.

She carried round the bourbon which she had bought for Ollie and left it on the doorstep. What did it matter if he drank it all too quickly? What did anything matter? There was only anger, only pain.

Norah came back at six-thirty and Harold too.

'You're back then. So, how's lover boy? Ollie said you'd gone up there. He said you know all about Maisie's man. Bet

Jack didn't like that.' Norah shrugged out of her coat, nodded towards the candy. 'It'll make me fat.'

Rosie made tea, slicing up the tin of ham she had brought back, boiling potatoes, cutting tomatoes into quarters. She put a fruit cake that Nancy had made on a plate in the centre of the table.

She couldn't eat but she made herself put food in her mouth. She made herself chew until the plateful was finished because Norah was watching.

'So, Jack's volunteered?' Norah was smiling, looking at Harold who pushed his glasses up on the bridge of his nose.

'Yes,' Rosie said, and felt Jack's weight on her body, inside her, but she wouldn't cry, not now. Not here.

'Left you, has he?'

'He's going to Korea. For a while. Only for a while.' Rosie took her plate to the sink. Washed it, dried it. She could smell the soda but not him. At least she could not smell him.

'Have you still got your job?' Norah was wiping her plate with bread she had torn off the loaf.

'Leave the girl alone,' Harold said as he stood up, leaving his plate for Norah to clear, moving to Grandpa's chair, opening his paper, stretching his legs out.

Get out of my grandpa's chair, Rosie wanted to shout, but he had been kind. For a moment he had been kind. She stood with her back to the sink. She had given Lee's present to his friend, who had been playing footie in the alley. He was lonely, he had said.

'Don't know why you don't get yourself a live-in job.' Norah pushed a crust that was too large into her mouth.

'This is my home, for as long as I need it. Don't you ever goddamn forget that. I have a right to be here.' Rosie moved to the back door, lifting her coat off the hook, putting it round her shoulders. 'I'm going out.'

'Where to, now Jack has gone?'

Rosie turned the handle, opened the door, walked out into the cool of the evening and the fragrance that still hung on the air from the last of the roses. She didn't answer. She didn't know. Jack wasn't there, nor Maisie, nor Lee. What *was* there, without them all?

As she passed the yellow rose she stooped, smelt its scent,

199

touched its petals, picked it, held it to her cheek. It was soft, fragrant. Some things never changed.

She walked to the rec. She sat on the swings and heard the laughter of their childhood. She leaned against the chains. His hands had held these. She pushed lightly, her feet rocking against the ground. He had to come back. In spite of everything. He was her life. He must see that. He must see that she couldn't have stopped Maisie. One day his mother would have had to live her own life. Or could she have stopped her? Perhaps she could.

She pressed her forehead against the chain, hard, rocking sideways now, crushing the rose, the stem with its thorns, but nothing helped the pain then, or that night or any night, or the anger.

Nothing helped the panic which caught and held her, pushing her up from the bed, making her walk, rubbing her hands up and down her arms at the thought that he might never want to hold her again. He might never want to look at her smile. How could all that love go, so quickly? How could all that love be pushed aside by hate? How could such anger and pain live inside her too?

The next morning she walked to see Mrs Eaves and thought she saw his head amongst the crowd. But it wasn't him and the pain was too sharp and she turned, looked in the tobacconist's window and cried but the tears didn't make anything better.

The store was bright and warm in a world that was cold, empty and dark. Glenn Miller was being played by a girl with neat peroxided hair and Mrs Eaves saw her, waved, took her by the arm to her office. Her keys jangled as she walked. They talked and Rosie cried again and said that Frank was better but Jack had gone. Hating her, loving her, unable to decide.

'But he'll write. I know he will,' Rosie said, watching as Mrs Eaves nodded, pressing out her cigarette in the ashtray which had Margate written on the edge.

'Of course he will, but it'll take time. And if he doesn't it's not the end of the world.'

But it would be. Rosie knew that, though she said nothing.

She did still have her job, though, and they liked the piece she had written about small-town America. Its fears, its guilts. Its hysteria. They edited it down to half and ran it. For a few days that took her mind from the ship that was taking Jack to Korea but for no longer than that. But now at least she would not hope to see him come towards her as she walked to the bus. Now he had gone but he would be back. She had to believe that, she told Mrs Eaves.

She wrote to Frank and Nancy, telling them that Jack had volunteered, that he was on his way.

She didn't tell them that he might never come back to her because she didn't dare to write the words. She loved him in spite of the pain, the anger. She would never love anyone else and all his love couldn't just disappear, could it?

The day she wrote her letter to Frank she received one from them and read it in her lunch break sitting on a bench in the park.

Lower Falls
26 September

Dearest Rosie,

We miss you so much. How are things? Is it sorted out with Maisie? How did Jack take it? You must not think it is your fault. You couldn't babysit the situation for ever, you know. I trust that Jack understands that.

Here's good news anyway. Frank has had details through of the Inchon landings. It seems MacArthur got it right. He came in strong, surprising the North Koreans but had to ride out a typhoon on the way. They had to time it exactly to land during high tide or they would be wading ashore in mud. As it was, some Marines had to do just that as they attacked Wolmi-do which guards the approaches to Inchon.

There were fierce battles as other forces landed on the mainland but they advanced rapidly, as you will know. Those in the South East are on the offensive too.

This success seems to have quietened down the zealots in our area which is a good respite for us both. Frank continues to do well. McCarthy is still stirring things up nationally.

Come back, my dear, whenever you can, whenever you want to. We love you so very much. We miss you. Give our love to Jack. Bring him too. Joe sends his regards to you.

Nancy

Rosie tore it up, dropping it into the bin over by the seats. She didn't want to read about the war, not now, not ever, because Jack would be there soon. She wanted to go back to Frank and Nancy, to their arms and their gentle voices, but not yet. Not until she heard from Jack. He might write. He would write. He might be injured. She must know. She must stay, and fear began, at last, to dull the anger.

In the second week of October, Sam and Ted were buying a record of Frank Sinatra's in Woolworths when they saw her. They came over, laughing, joking. They were older, much older. They were men but Jack was a man too.

'Ollie says he's gone, the daft bugger,' Sam said, his smile wide but his eyes serious.

Rosie took the ribbon the salesgirl handed her. It was blue and wide.

'Yes, he's gone. He is a daft bugger.'

'Ollie says his missus has gone?' Ted was looking at her now. 'Wasn't your fault. Everyone knew. You couldn't stay with her for ever, you know.'

Rosie touched the ribbon. It was soft and cool. Write to Jack, tell him, she wanted to shout but couldn't. She knew now that he must realise that on his own.

'Come up the Palais. It'll be like old times,' Sam said, looking at the ribbon. 'Not your colour,' he added.

They went that night but it wasn't like old times. Sam and Ted drank beer. She drank sherry. It was too sweet. They danced but Sam and Ted met girls they knew and she was one too many but they had been kind and they knew Jack and for a moment it had been good.

At the end of October she received a letter from Nancy telling her of the UN advance in Korea, and how the North Korean forces had crumbled in the face of the UN forces. In the space of a few short weeks the UN had occupied virtually the whole of Korea.

'Frank is worried that MacArthur cannot now be reined in. He might try to end the threat that Communist China poses to American interests in the Far East by not stopping at the frontier. Truman has to insist that this is a "limited action" against a specific Communist act.

'Maybe it will be over by Christmas. If so, Jack won't fight. He won't be there long enough. Keep hoping, my dear.'

The Features Editor had been working her hard. She typed, took shorthand, read the slush pile, wrote short pieces and slowly the career that she had always striven for was within her reach, and that, at least, gave her pleasure, gave her purpose.

She took the letter into the park and read it again. Even though it was cold she brought her lunch here every day. It gave her some peace. An elderly woman sat next to her, eating ham sandwiches. She wondered where the pig had come from. There was almost no bacon or pork left in the country, or so it seemed. She looked at the snoek between her bread. The Government was pushing these tins of fish at a protein-hungry public but the smell made her feel sick. The taste was rank and salty. It had upset her for days. So had the whalemeat which Norah kept for sandwiches. The taste of cod liver oil was too strong.

The old woman saw her looking, smiled, patted her leg and passed her one.

'Thanks,' Rosie said. 'But no. I'm not very hungry.'

But the old woman insisted and she took it and tasted the fresh ham, but she felt the nausea begin again. She waited until the old woman had left the park, then fed it to the birds, watching as they flapped their wings, listening as they squawked.

The next morning she woke early, eased herself from the bed, put on her coat, crept down, heated the kettle, and ate a biscuit, but it didn't work. She rushed to the privy, leaned over the pan, and vomited. She leaned back against the wall, sweat-drenched, cold; the sickness was in her stomach, her throat. She vomited again and again, but quietly. For God's sake be quiet. She pulled the chain to drown the noise.

She dressed, and made bread and marge for her sandwiches, ignoring the snoek tin with its blue fish, ignoring the whale-meat and the cheese. She worked, and came home through the fog which was sulphur thick. Slept. It was the same all that week and the next but there was no letter from him. Still no letter.

There was one from Frank though.

Lower Falls,
1st November

My dear Rosie,
I got it wrong. I thought things were cooling down a bit.
I've been pulled up before the Un-American Activities
Committee. Interviewed, hectored, treated with contempt,
shouted at until I couldn't think straight. It's this Anti-Nazi
League thing and because I know a Hollywood screenwriter
who's been blacklisted. You know. You met him.
They wanted me to name friends of his and mine that we
knew at College. How can they do this? How can people
believe all this garbage about good people? He claimed the
5th Amendment. He hasn't worked for four years as far as
they know. But he writes for me under another name. They
don't know that of course. Thank God. But am I a coward
for saying that?
I thought things were improving. I guess they're not.
McCarthy is still fuelling the fire with that goddamn bulging
briefcase of his which never actually pulls in any 'spies'. Just
ruins good folk. Thank God I don't have an employer. I
would have been sacked. People think you're guilty if you
stay silent. Have they all gone mad to believe this bunch of
lunatics? Haven't we just spent years fighting this in Europe?
Have you heard from Jack? Things still seem to be going
OK out there. You are our bright spot. My health is OK so
don't worry. I'm just mad.
Maybe you can come out for Thanksgiving, or Christmas?
The fighting will be over by then, the troops will be home.
Our love always,
Frank

But Rosie couldn't go. Two days later, on 17 November,
she fainted as she shopped at Woolworths, and Mrs Eaves took
her into the office and pushed her head between her legs.
'When did you last have a period, Rosie?'
She was stroking Rosie's hair, her other hand was on Rosie's
wrist. It was a plump hand, like Nancy's, and now Rosie
leaned her head against this woman and wept but said it was
only the snoek because that had to be the truth.
That afternoon they took two hours off and travelled by

204

taxi to a doctor that Mrs Eaves knew. There was a brass plate
on the wall, polished so that the letters were smoothed almost
to flatness. The bell didn't sound outside but a nurse opened
the door, showed them upstairs, and gave them magazines to
read while they waited on amber-covered chairs.

Mrs Eaves didn't come into the consulting rooms with her.
She went alone. There was a large desk, a letter rack, a blotting
pad. There was no ink on it. It was white, pure white. The man
who rose and shook her hand was Ollie's age. He had a bald
head, a moustache, and kind eyes beneath full, bushy brows.
How could someone with no hair on their head have so much
above their eyes? Rosie wondered, sitting down, feeling too
tired to be here. To be anywhere.

'So, we have a problem, eh, Miss Norton?' The man steepled
his hands, rested his mouth on his forefingers, pressed his lip
up into his moustache.

'I don't know,' said Rosie, bunching her hands inside her
coat pockets. She felt nausea rising. She swallowed, watching
the signet ring on his little finger.

'Let's have a look shall we?' he smiled, pointing to the back
of the room. 'Just leave your petticoat on. The nurse is there
waiting.'

She lay still on the couch behind the curtain at the back of
the room, looking up at the coved ceiling, feeling strange hands
pressing her. She lifted her legs as he asked. She answered his
questions, not looking at him. Tracing the crack which wound
up the wall, beneath the coving, then on to the ceiling until it
was finished. This could not be happening to her. This man
wasn't real. The nurse, who would not meet her eyes, wasn't
real.

She dressed, and walked to the chair again.

'Well, my dear. You are almost certainly pregnant. We'll
run a test, just to confirm, but there's really no need.'

His hands were steepled again. He tapped his teeth this
time. She watched that, listened to that. She didn't think of the
words which had been in her own mind for six weeks. It wasn't
possible. It couldn't be possible. What would she do? For
God's sake, what would she do?

She stooped to pick up her bag from the floor. She said
nothing. She couldn't speak. There was too much fear.

'There are things that can be done.' The man was playing now with a paperknife, turning it over and over, the light flashing on its blade. He stopped, looked up at her. 'You aren't married?'

Rosie covered her left hand but then said, 'No.' He knew that already. He had called her Miss Norton. Oh God. What would she do?

'How will you support the child?'

She shook her head. Until those words she had not thought of a child, only of the shame.

'I don't know.'

The doctor hesitated, looked at her, then down at the desk. 'I can help but you realise it must be discreet. It would be quick and painless. Not in a seedy room in some dirty street. But it will cost a hundred guineas.'

Rosie thought of the hop-yards, the sticky smell on her hands, the gypsies who brewed potions. The Welsh girl who had drunk some on a hot and heavy night and then screamed in pain all night but smiled for the rest of the picking because there would be no disgrace, not this time.

But Jack had been at the hop-yard, Jack had smiled and held her. Jack had thrust himself inside her on the cold damp moors and she had wanted him. Not like that, not in that way perhaps. But she had wanted him and she loved him, even if he no longer loved her. This child was part of him. She counted the breaths she was taking, they were in time with the clock on the mantelpiece.

'No, thank you.' Rosie stood up, handing him his consultation fee. The movement made her feel faint. She sat again. He came round the desk, put his hand on her shoulder.

'Will the father marry you?'

'I will be quite all right, thank you,' Rosie said, rising, but slowly this time.

She went to the GP. The next week she collected iron tablets from the chemist in her lunch hour and nodded to Mrs Eaves.

'The baby is due at the end of June,' she said quietly.

Mrs Eaves told her she must sit with her feet up and rest as much as she could at work. She must carry nothing heavy, but a shorthand pad wasn't heavy, neither were the articles she had to sift. Mrs Eaves also said she should go back to America but Rosie said she couldn't. Frank and Nancy had enough to worry about and she couldn't face their disappointment, the ending of all their hopes for her.

'How would Jack find me, when he comes home?' she said and wouldn't allow herself to see the doubt in Mrs Eaves's eyes or acknowledge the same doubt herself.

It was at night that the fear grew and cut the breath in her throat, when she was away from the lights of the office and the smiles of the other girls. It was when she was alone that she allowed herself to think of the child that was growing and she didn't know if Norah would let her stay until Jack came back at Christmas. Because she had to believe that he would, just as she had to believe that he would write. Goddamn it, Jack, write. You must write. Because there was still an anger that swept her as well as fear and love and it helped to keep her strong.

In the first week of December Frank wrote with the details of the Chinese assault which had pushed the UN forces back, slaughtering them in the narrow valleys, even though they marched on only a handful of rice. How Mao's men had marched on through the snow, capturing, fighting. How the British Forces had carried out rearguard duties. How brave they had been. Had she heard from Jack? Was he all right? They would not now be home for Christmas.

Rosie went round to Ollie who opened the door, his face setting when he saw her.

'Is he all right?' she asked because there was no place for anger or her own fear. There was only the thought of Jack and Korea.

Ollie looked at her. 'I'll let you know if he isn't.' He shut the door.

That night she fainted as she stood to take her plate to the sink. Her cheese was still on the plate. She hadn't been able to eat. Harold carried her to the armchair by the fire, Grandpa's chair, and Rosie cried, her head down in her hands, because Grandpa wasn't here and neither was Jack. But Norah was, standing in front of her, her stockings rolled down round her ankles, her slippers trodden down at the back.

'You're pregnant, aren't you?' Norah's hands were on her hips.

Rosie wiped her face with the back of her hands and nodded. 'Does that Jack know?'

Rosie shook her head.

'Then you'd better write and tell him.'

'I can't.'

Norah slapped her face then hard, catching Rosie's hair, jerking her head to one side.

'You're a bloody little slut. Why not? Isn't it his? Is it that Joe's?'

Rosie gripped the arms of the chair. She pushed herself back into it, away from Norah who was leaning forward, her face ugly. She would stay in Grandpa's chair, then she would be safe. It would all go away. All of it. It would roll away to the time before all this.

'Go on then, whose is it?' Norah insisted.

'It's Jack's, but I can't tell him. He's left me. He wants to make up his mind whether he loves me. He'd come back if I told him, but I'd never know whether he wanted to.' Rosie reached out her hands. 'Can't you goddamn understand? I love him. I can't do that to him.'

Rosie looked at Harold now. He was kind sometimes but now his face was filled with contempt.

'So you're alone. Lovely little Rosie hasn't anyone to love her. Now you'll know what it's like.' Norah was reaching down, pushing at Rosie, pulling at her, forcing her from the chair. 'I was left with you and Grandpa. I was alone.'

Rosie clutched at her, she felt sick again. 'But Grandpa loved you, and Grandma. You know they did. Grandma most of all. What the hell are you talking about?' Norah was still pushing her out of the kitchen, towards the hall, and Rosie didn't have the strength to stop her.

Norah shouted in her face now, pulling her back, jerking her to a stop. 'But you had the best. You still have. You go to America, you bring back candy. Push it in my face. You little slut. Well, you've got more than you bargained for out of all this love, haven't you? You're an alley cat.' She pushed her towards the foot of the stairs.

Rosie felt her legs growing weak, her head heavy. The blackness was gripping her again. Sweat drenched her body. She clung to the banister, sank on to the stairs.

'Get out by the morning,' Norah hissed, standing above her, watching.

'I can stay as long as I need to,' Rosie said, anger driving the sickness back, but only for a moment. She leaned her head down on her knees. 'Grandpa said.'

'And what do you think Grandpa would say to this bastard you're bringing into the world? You don't think he'd want it in his house, in his neighbourhood. Where it'd bring disgrace. Where his rose growers would know.'

Norah left her, went back into the kitchen, shut the door. There was no light left. Just darkness. And Rosie knew Norah was right. There were too many memories here. There was too much of the past which needed to be guarded for Grandpa. She must go. It was Christmas in three weeks and it was time for her to go. To find some privacy.

CHAPTER 16

The hospital was clean and white and light. And so cool. Jack was eased on to the bed. The pain was all over him now, sweeping, cutting, and he groaned, turned his head, watched the naval nurse as she smiled. Looked at the bag on top of his locker which contained toilet necessities, playing cards, cigarettes and sweets. There was writing paper too.

He looked away. He wouldn't need that. Not to write to Rosie. Not now, not ever. He wouldn't write to Ollie either. Why tell him?

'You'll be going up to theatre soon. There'll just be a small prick now.' The nurse smiled at him again but his lips wouldn't work to smile back.

It was two weeks before the pain left him and then only in snatches in which he watched the ward, heard the clatter of trolleys, the murmur of voices. But then it claimed him again so that he didn't know which was morning, which was afternoon. He didn't know which was night, which was day.

All he knew was that Korea seemed further away than a three-day boat trip. There were no flares, no bugles. There were no screams. There was no Tom. There was no American dying of burns. No American he had to shoot.

But there was the smell of disinfectant, the gentle hands of the nurses who soothed the boy across the way when he groaned, who soothed Jack when he woke screaming from dreams in which he shot the American, again and again, but the flames kept burning, the hand kept reaching out and the face which called to him was Ed's. Yes, Korea was far away and England even further.

But now the times without pain were longer. He watched the clock move round and the nurses with charts, and smiles, and soft voices, and it was all so clean, so ordered. There were no decisions to be made, no questions to be asked except, 'What day is it?'

'It is December eleventh. Now rest.'

Each morning he was a little stronger and each day and night the dreams faded until at last he did not sleep in the day, or cry out at night.

That morning he ate breakfast, biting into crisp toast, and smiled at the boy opposite who smiled back. There had been no groans from him either.

He watched as the doctor did the rounds, first one bed, then the other. The sheets were starched and correctly turned, the pillowcases too. The Sister coughed, the doctor nodded and then they came to him and he felt the tension rise in him. He was better. He knew that. The doctor would know too. He would send him back, into the battle.

The doctor checked his bandage, talked to the Sister, laughed when Jack said he would be ready to do the town by the evening.

'Maybe next month. Maybe,' the doctor said.

Jack touched the bandage, feeling the tension relax, feeling his face smile. Thank God, he would be here for that long at least. He wouldn't be returning to the snow, the cold, the fear. He could stay here where there was no life outside the ward, outside the cool drinks, and the kind nurses, and the ache of his arm.

The Staff Nurse smoothed his sheets as the doctor moved on. 'A little bit longer then,' she said.

'You knew I was frightened?'

'You all feel the same. Why not? I would.'

'Each day,' the boy across the ward shouted, 'there are letters delivered. I bet my girl sends me one.' Jack had written none. He would receive none and so he turned from the Sister who stopped at each bed but his. Everywhere there were letters, three for the boy across the ward. All his had SWALK written round the flap.

Now there was silence as they read them and further silence as the letters were replaced in the envelopes and visions of home came too close.

He had none of that. He had none of their pain. The ache that he felt deep inside wasn't love. He had told himself that. It was anger. There was no love any more. He knew that. He remembered Tom. His wife must know by now.

He watched instead the Japanese flower girl who came to the ward with a trolley heaped with flowers and foliage. She wore bobby sox, and a skirt and blouse, and she almost looked American, but not quite. There was the golden skin, the lowered eyes, the small steps.

He wished that she wore a kimono like the girls he had seen on the way to the hospital. He didn't want anything American in here.

She took flowers and leaves to the central table. Her hands were small and quick. She undid the copper pulley, and lowered the existing arrangement which hung above the ward's central light. He hadn't noticed it before.

She tipped the faded blooms into a basket, emptied the water into a bucket on the trolley, refilled the vase, arranged the flowers, slowly now, and the foliage, then raised the arrangement back up above the light. That night, a small blue spotlight illuminated the flowers and he dreamed of the hopyards and heard the bees, smelt the hops. Then the scent of roses, the scent of the past, filled the air and he woke crying, but he told the Sister it was the pain.

With each day he grew stronger and the nurses began to decorate the wards as Christmas approached. He and Bill from the bed across the way held the ladders while the nurses climbed and pinned streamers and foliage and the other men whistled and cheered.

That night he dreamed of Rosie making streamers because it was 20 December and in the morning he was running a fever and his wound had become infected. He was too ill to notice Christmas, too ill to open the presents forwarded from Ollie; the tie from Maisie, the letter from Lee, the shirt with no card, which he knew was from Rosie.

'I'm too ill,' he shouted to the nurse and pushed them all from the bed, making her take them from the ward, but keeping Ollie's card and the money he sent and looking up at the flowers which glowed throughout the night.

It wasn't until the middle of February that he was able to move to the convalescent ward and now he knew, they all knew, that though the Communists were pushing them back in the centre, the Chinese supply lines were in doubt.

In the west of Korea US and British troops had recaptured the port of Inchon which had been taken when the Communists carried forward their attack. UN troops were also shelling Seoul which was yet again in the hands of the Communists. On the east coast the South Koreans, supported by naval bombardment, had driven up the coastal highway to the 38th parallel.

They all knew this, but they didn't talk about it. They didn't want to remember, nor did they want to go back.

The next week they had a private in who had been injured when the Allied forces took up positions in a twenty-five-mile arc to the south of Seoul. He told them that Communist resistance had stiffened. That the fourth battle for Seoul was about to begin. That he hoped it would be over before he was returned as fit for active service. He was a conscript. He was nineteen. Jack felt old at nearly twenty-one. He didn't want to go back either, but neither did he want to go to England.

The flower girl came to this ward too while letters were delivered and so Jack heaved at the pulley for her with his right hand. His left was still bandaged, still in a sling which dragged at his neck. Each day he pulled it and smiled and they spoke of the coldness of the weather, the beauty of the flowers, and her voice was sometimes harsh as voices were in the Japanese tongue she told him. But her lips were shaped and gentle, her eyes demure and black. And he didn't have to look at the men opening their mail.

They talked of the summer and the sun that would come and she told him of the giant fish fashioned from bamboo and covered with painted cloth which is launched each July by Toyahama fishermen in honour of the ocean gods. She told him how the Japanese people bore gifts of rice to the dead in the graveyards and he thought of Rosie taking roses to her grandpa, but he didn't want to think of her. She was the past. She was where the pain was.

So he listened again to the flower girl, whose name was Suko, and she told him that their language could mean different things, that their symbols had many meanings. How the white dots of flowering plum and the red dots of camellia keep the

213

Japanese winter from ever being quite dead. He should travel to one of the unbombed cities, she said, when he was more able, and search for the outward signs of the Japanese spirit which had survived defeat and Hiroshima and Nagasaki. The spirit which had sought and found peace.

'For, Jack-san, you have need of that spirit,' she said as she lifted each leaf, each petal, and put them into the bag before pushing the trolley from the ward.

Jack did not help her again. He walked down the corridors, into other wards, talking to the men, looking out at the deep snow, sensing the cold which crackled in the air. He had no need of peace. It was the others who struggled and lashed and betrayed.

In March he took a small Japanese cab into the town and the cold was still sharp in the air. He had three weeks' Rest and Recuperation and would return to a hostel each night, the Sister had said, smiling, unless, of course, he found something more pleasurable to do.

'Sort yourself out, soldier,' she said as he stopped and looked back at her. She was Australian, big and kind, but Jack walked away from her and did not look back. There was no room for that sort of pleasure in his life now.

He looked out from the cab windows at the snow which had been pushed from the road and the pavements. He saw the street walkers, the Cadillacs, the Buicks, the American enlisted men who stood in groups on the street corners, chatting to the Japanese girls, kissing them, linking arms. He turned from them.

He paid the cab driver as they pulled up outside the hotel where he was to meet Bill, and was glad that Tom wasn't here to see this wealth amongst the people who had imprisoned him. Glad that Ollie wasn't here because there were no new cars available in England.

He climbed the marble steps, nodded to the Japanese bellhop, walked through to the bar. Bill was there, he was drunk, and there was beer on the counter where he had slopped it. There was a glass chandelier above them, soft music playing, nuts and crisps in bowls on the bar. Whisky lined the wall behind the barmen. There was no hint of a war being played out on their doorstep. Was there any hint in England?

'Let's eat,' Jack said, taking Bill's arm, steering him through the tables where beautiful people sat, staring.

'Don't you know there's a bloody war on?' Jack said to one girl with blonde hair and a wide mouth sitting with an American Captain. Their hands were linked. They both wore wedding rings.

'Sure, honey, but not in here,' she drawled and laughed. 'And not back in Iowa either.'

Bill lurched and Jack steadied him, walking him through, past the Japanese head waiter towards a spare table. There were flowers on the thick white tablecloth. There was an arrangement carved out of ice up near the stage. A band played a selection of Frank Sinatra's songs.

They ate a steak which was tender and rare and rice cooked in saffron and Jack didn't order wine, only water, and watched as Bill ate and then drank, slowly, carefully, and only when his plate was empty did they leave.

Jack drove him back to his room. Put him to bed, sat with him because the boy was laughing, then crying, and it was only when he slept that he returned to his own bed.

The next day he drank beer in the town with Bill, but not much, and then they walked past underwear shops full of GIs buying lingerie for the Japanese girls on their arms. They stopped at a restaurant which smelt of beer and fried fish.

They climbed narrow stairs and sat on large cushions, cross-legged. There were other soldiers there, laughing, drinking. There were geishas with white corn-starched faces and sticky hair who danced with them when they had eaten the fish which the chef had cooked in a deep pan of oil, swishing it round with long chopsticks.

The Sergeant who sat at the end told them that these girls were 'after the war' geishas who were not trained but who bought a kimono and pretended for the Americans.

Jack left then. He wanted nothing that the Americans sought or had possessed.

He borrowed a jeep the next afternoon and drove to the address that the Australian sister had given him when he called on her first thing that morning. She had kissed him on the cheek too, saying again, 'Just sort yourself out.'

As he drove he looked at the paddy fields pressed up against the tarmac, seeing through the thawed and muddy snow that every space had been cultivated, even the tiny gap between the ditch and a filling station where GIs were buying petrol for their jeep which was full of Japanese girls. He remembered Suko saying that there were too many people and not enough land.

There were no straggling copses, no hedges. In Japan, Suko had said, there were only disciplined, trained trees. There was no space for wanton growth. He passed small paper-windowed houses which soon became jammed together as he approached a village which was more like a town. They were jammed too tightly for fields, too tightly even to breathe it seemed. There were people walking, so many people. As the road narrowed and the houses took the light from the street he looked at the piece of paper in his hand. He stopped the jeep. He asked directions of an old man dressed in black, slowly, in English.

The man pointed. 'Leave jeep. Walk. Ask. Police.'

Jack did, passing tiny shops with paper doors, all with lights which shone through the paper, out into the street. There was a police box on the corner. Jack asked again.

'Keep on. Don't turn. It on right.'

Children ran past in quilted coats, shrieking, laughing. Was Lee doing that in the cold of America?

There were restaurants on either side of the narrow alleys he walked along. One opened on to the street, revealing people eating fish at small tables. So many people and they were all so small, like Suko.

He was there now. He stopped but the door was paper. How did he knock? He couldn't so he called out instead, 'Suko, it's Jack.' He waited, then called again. 'Suko. It's Jack. I've been rude. I ran away from you. In the ward. I'm sorry. I've come to say I'm sorry.'

The door slid back, and Suko was standing there in a kimono, not bobby sox. Her blue-black hair was pulled back. She bowed, three times.

'Jack-san, this is an honour.' She stood to one side. 'Please put your shoes here.' She pointed to the left of the door.

Jack stopped, looked at her. She wore no shoes. There was a Shinto shrine in the room. He stooped, unlaced his boots, placed them next to hers and entered.

He felt too big, too white. He nodded at the old lady who came forward and bowed. He bowed too. Christ, he was so *big*.

They sat on tatami cushions and his ankles hurt as he crossed his legs. Suko laughed, then covered her mouth with her hand.

'You will eat with us?'

Jack nodded and watched the old woman cut each item carefully. The brazier exuded heat, the charcoal had a sweet smell. She tossed and turned the fish and the vegetables, and Jack could find little to say, but Suko didn't speak either. They both watched her grandmother.

They ate with chopsticks and Jack was awkward and clumsy but no one laughed and so he tried again and it was good.

'Perhaps you would come with me tomorrow to find that unbombed town?' Jack said, but Suko shook her head.

'No, Jack-san, that is for you alone. But I take you to see Japan. I take you to puppets, to Osaka with its canals. I take you to the theatre.'

Her voice was soft but the harshness was still there. It always would be. Was there still that faint drawl in Rosie's voice? But what did it matter? She meant nothing to him now.

The next day they drove to Osaka and then along the roads where the piled up snow was melting. Men trudged up and down alleys with wicker baskets on their back. Women passed with babies strapped to their backs. An old battered car passed with Japanese bobbysoxers singing.

What would Tom think?

The next day they watched a puppet show where the Punch and Judy he had remembered from Southend paled into insignificance. These puppets were life-size with their puppeteers alongside, visible. There was no laughter, only tears. No farce, only tragedy, and Jack sat back and waited to be bored. But Suko sat still beside him, her golden skin smooth and pure, and soon the puppets took over the puppeteers and became savage, harsh, too strong, and Jack clenched his hands and believed.

They ate at a restaurant and Suko smiled and nodded and her hands were as delicate with the chopsticks as they had been with the flowers.

As they drove back alongside the fields she told him that in

217

the spring the farmers would pull harrows and the women would dig, then sow. She told him how the farmers had always sold their daughters, in order to have fewer mouths to feed, in order to survive.

'Where are *your* parents?' he asked.

'They were in Nagasaki,' she said. 'They did not survive.'

Jack didn't visit Suko for a week. He didn't know what to say, what to do, but when he called outside her house again she slid back the door and smiled, took him in, gave him green tea. As they sat cross-legged on the floor he said, 'I'm sorry. I couldn't come. I didn't know what to say about your parents.'

Suko nodded. 'I know. One day you will be able to face pain, even that of others. For now you cannot. You must wait.' That was all.

They drove to the theatre, where actors took over the role of the puppets, and Jack listened to Suko explaining as they roared and laughed and cried that the message of this play was blind loyalty, whatever cruel and bloody acts this might require.

Jack watched the disembowelling and could not understand the pleasure it gave the audience, the pleasure it gave Suko. He watched the dancing and was glad when they returned to her small house, away from the colour of the pageant, away from the turbulence, and as he drew up to her house he turned and kissed her mouth. It was soft, small, and so was the body he held and stroked, and so was the hand which smoothed his hair and touched his lips and brought feeling back into his life.

'I've only one week left,' he breathed into her hair.

'You will come tomorrow and we will love,' she said.

Suko's grandmother was not there in the house when he arrived and Suko led him into the room, holding his hand in hers, not kissing him, not allowing him to kiss her.

'Not yet, Jack-san. You are in Nippon now. You must be slow. You must take time.'

He sat down on the cushions and she smiled and bowed, then left the room, and he watched her move with her short steps, one in front of the other. He watched the neatness of her body and wouldn't think of Rosie. She was dead to him now. The ache in his heart was anger, not love.

He drank the saki that Suko had left, first one glass and then another, and then another until there was softness in the room and an easing of his body.

It was then she called.

'Jack-san.'

He rose, his mouth dry, and walked into a small room which was filled with steam from a bath in the centre and the damp heat smothered him, but she was there too, in a white bathrobe, beads of sweat on her face, on her neck, beads which ran down on to her breasts.

She undid his buttons, slipped his clothes from his body, washed him down with soap, her hands gentle, probing, and he wanted her but she kissed his mouth, then pointed towards the bath. He climbed into the water which was almost scalding.

She rubbed his back with soft bark and it was as though there had been no past, there would be no future. There was only the present.

He rose from the water and slid her bathrobe from her shoulders, letting it fall from her body, and the heat he felt was not from the steam, but from within. She was golden, soft and smooth. So small. So very small.

He held her to him, wetting her, kissing her, tasting her sweat, tasting his on her. Then he carried her out into the room where the futon was already laid on the floor, and there, in the heat and smell and the light of the charcoal fire, he made love to her, gently, softly and then with a passion which swept him from the paper house to the cold hillside in Yorkshire, and when he cried he knew why, but he pushed his knowledge away.

He was to spend his last days at Suko's house, she told him. Her grandmother was not there. She had left because Suko asked her to, she told Jack at dawn as they sipped tea from the cups without handles.

'For us to be together, Jack-san,' she said, then set her cup down, took his from him, and they made love again, and again.

Suko worked each morning and wouldn't stay in the village with him.

'I make the flowers bring joy. It is my peace, Jack-san,' she said, her eyes lowered as she stood before him. 'You go to your friends. You return at night.'

219

Jack drove again to the theatre, walking over the bridge, looking down into a stream with ice clusters at the edge. He looked back down the path. There were cherry trees.

An old man stopped. 'In the spring the blossom blooms. Life begins again.'

Jack nodded and made himself walk into the theatre. He sat and listened and shrank from this culture which was Suko's.

They made love that night and the next and there was nothing that was savage, only everything that was gentle. They had four nights left and he whispered that he would come back when the war was over. He would never leave her.

'You're so beautiful.'

Jack held her, feeling her slightness against him, seeing the blackness of her hair against the pillow. She shook her head, then told him of her childhood, of her life with her grandmother as the bombs rained down. She told him of the American who had come with the occupying forces and he stiffened. He could smell the charcoal, feel its heat.

She kissed his mouth. 'I loved him. He loved me. He went back. He died on a plane which crashed as he landed. I loved him. I will always love him. You love someone. You will always love them. We find comfort with each other, that is all, Jack-san. You will not come back to me.'

He was standing now, standing over her, seeing her golden skin against the futon. Had her American seen her like this?

'Has he?' he screamed at her.

She stood now. 'Come and lie with me. We are happy together because we both have a heart which belongs to another. We give comfort.'

She was stroking him now. 'We give comfort, Jack-san. We cast the shadows from our lives for a while, the pain deep inside is soothed.'

He felt her hands, her lips on his chest, his belly, his thighs and knew why he had been back to the theatre. It was there, watching the Kabuki, watching the warrior, his face contorted, his limbs stiff and cruel, that he had recognised the savagery that was in his own heart.

The next day he travelled to Kanazawa, where there was no sign of bombing, where it was as it had stood for centuries. He

220

walked. He stood and looked at the mossy stillness behind an ancient wall. Children were laughing and playing in the distance but he barely heard them.

He walked on to a cottage, and stood in the doorway as a peasant bowed. He smelt the sweetness of the rush matting, and saw the white of an early-flowering plum set as a symbol of stillness in a world which was mad.

He walked in the garden which nestled against the base of the eastern hill. It was walled, self-contained, still. There was an ordered stream, a bridge and no wind stirred.

He could smell again the hops, see the bines, trace the initials on the gate with his fingers. He could see Rosie.

He drove back to the village, back to Suko, back to her arms and her bed and she held him as he slept and that night it was as though he was a child again and the next night, and the next.

He flew back on Monday. His shoulder was stiff but what did that matter? He strapped himself into the bucket seat. All around was the smell of the disinfectant that had been sprayed on the plane's arrival. He clutched the seat belt as the engine roared, swallowed as the plane clawed through the sky. He looked down at the Straits of Korea, and thought of Suko, her body, her sweetness. He thought of the hills he was returning to and then the hills where the bines grew. He had a letter to write.

He looked at the sea again, and heard a distant echo of Chinese bugles.

CHAPTER 17

Norah did not say goodbye the morning Rosie left but Harold came to the end of the yard while Norah dressed in the bedroom. He took Rosie's arm and told her that he would forward any mail if she let him know her address. He gave her two pounds towards her fares.

She took it, kissed his cheek, remembered Butlins and told him that he must keep on with his brass rubbing.

'You mustn't let her take that away from you.'

Now, as she walked to Woolworths, she remembered how Grandma had tried to stop Grandpa's visits to the Rose Club, how Norah had tried to cut down his rose bushes. She dropped her cases and ran back, down the street, down the back alley, into the yard, into the kitchen. Harold was packing his rubbing wax into a grip. He wore cycle clips.

'Harold, what about the roses? Can you stop her?' Rosie was holding the door. She felt the nausea rise but she wouldn't be sick. Not here, not now.

He did up the buckles on the bag, walked to the doorway, then into the yard, strapping his bag to the back of his bike, looking round at the roses then back at her.

'I think so. I like them too. Don't worry. I'll think of something.'

He nodded, pushed his bike out into the alley, stopped, looked back.

'I don't agree with what you've done. With the baby and all that. It's a disgrace. But good luck.' He mounted the bike, then nodded towards Ollie. 'Don't worry. We won't tell him. Norah doesn't want anybody to know.'

He was off then, and Rosie left, looking back, remembering Grandpa shelling peas, his big fingers pushing their way up the pod, her small ones too. And Jack's hands taking five, throwing

222

them up into his mouth. For a moment she could smell Maisie's bread and dripping and hear the echoes of the past.

At the store Mrs Eaves wanted to come with her to look for a bedsit but Rosie shook her head.

'No, I must do it alone but would you ring my office, please? Just tell them I'm ill and I'll be in tomorrow.'

She left her bags though, then caught a bus to Soho because that was where she had been with Jack. That was where the music still played, where there was still hope, warmth. It was a place where she would not be judged as she would be elsewhere, down each street, in each shop.

On the bus she felt sick, she felt alone, because Jack had always been with her before. She took slow breaths, pushing her hands against her mouth, feeling the clammy sweat on her forehead, the cold which swept through her before the vomit. She pushed herself from her seat, out on to the platform, ringing the bell, stepping off, ignoring the shouts from the clippie. She walked into a side street, and leaned against the wall, breathing, counting till at last it passed.

She caught another bus and this time the nausea did not reappear. She walked down Berwick Street where they were putting out the rubbish from the restaurants. She stopped, asked if they knew of any accommodation. They shook their heads.

It was so different in the day. There was no music sweeping out of the cellars, no tarts touting for custom. Instead they were collecting the milk from their doorsteps along with old ladies doing the same. She passed the baker's where people were queuing for their morning bread and barbers who were already open, already snipping.

A violinist played in the alley which connected the two street markets. A man stood opposite shouting that Jesus Saves. He grabbed at her arm, pushed a leaflet into her hand. She dropped it like others had done amongst the rotting vegetables and the woodshavings. She walked along the stalls, listening to the woman in a headscarf shouting.

'Christmas is coming, the goose is getting fat, but what about bleeding me if you don't buy me spuds?' The woman was digging into the money pocket of her apron, she wore fingerless gloves, her skin was shiny from the coins, her nails dirty, and

Rosie turned away. Jack had been able to charm the birds out of the bleeding trees, one woman had said.

She walked along the dirty streets, climbing steps to the peeling front doors of four-storeyed houses, knocking on doors but always there were no rooms. She stopped and had Camp coffee in a café. The teaspoon was chained to the counter. The sugar was clumped on the spoon. It was warm, it was sweet. What more did she need?

She walked in the other direction. It was lunchtime, the pubs were open. Music came from them and laughter. A newspaper seller was packing up for the day.

Rosie was hungry, tired, but she had nowhere to sleep for the night. She walked on past a newspaper shop. There were advertisements in the window. One was for a room to let. She wrote down the address, asked in the shop for directions.

'Just down the road. Second on the left,' the man said, serving a Cypriot with a packet of pipe cleaners.

She found it. Climbed the steps which were crumbling at the edges. There was a basement beneath her, a blanket strung up on a string. The courtyard smelt of tomcat. There were three dustbins. She looked away towards the door which was opening.

A small woman stood there, with neat hair, neat clothes and a smile which she flicked at Rosie when she asked to see the room.

They climbed the brown-painted stairs to a room on the top floor at the rear that looked out over the backs of other houses, pubs, and clubs. But she could see the sky. She took it.

Mrs Eaves came back with her to carry her bags. It was cold and dark as they left the bus but now music was soaring from the basements, castanets from one, swing from another, and Rosie smiled. They used the key that the woman had given her. The light went out before they reached the first landing and they switched it on again but again it went out before they reached her room. Rosie laughed. Mrs Eaves didn't.

'Come to us, Rosie. Please. You can't stay here. You might fall. Does she know about the baby?' She dropped her voice to a whisper.

Rosie felt the laugh die. 'No.'

Mrs Eaves put down the cases while Rosie unlocked the

door. 'Well, she said no children on the card. She might throw you out when it begins to show. Come to me then.'

Rosie nodded, but she wouldn't. She was alone now. She would be alone until Jack came back.

There was only a forty-watt bulb in the light and no shade. There was one blanket on the bed but Rosie had brought her jumper-blankets, and her own sheets.

There was a sink and a wooden draining board that was sticky with other people's soap and mess. There was a gas ring and a gas fire which Mrs Eaves tried to light, but the meter had run out. They put money in and it plopped as Rosie held the match to it, flaring blue, then yellow. Its hissing filled the room. There was a table covered in oilcloth, only one chair.

Mrs Eaves took her to an Italian café for tea. She knew the owner and his wife. They had met in the war when she had come here with her GI.

They ate baked beans and chips but could smell nothing but coffee. There were onions hanging against the pine-covered walls but Rosie wouldn't let herself think of Jack and the onion seller in the pub. The other tables were full. Young men with scarves trailing on the floor, wearing old coats, laughing, talking, flicking out rhythms on the tables, talking jazz.

There was a phone on the wall. It rang. The small Italian who had served them threw his teacloth over his shoulder, grabbed the receiver, and, waving his hands in the air, shouted across the room.

'Luke, for you again. You give them my number. Always my number. You all give them my number. I try to feed you. How can I when you make me your office too?' He dropped the receiver, it swung on its wire.

Mrs Eaves laughed and called across, 'Just the same, Mario, eh?'

'Worse, Anne. Much worse.' Mario was shaking his head.

'You need more help.'

'I know, I know. You'll come then, Anne?' He laughed, and walked through to the back.

Rosie moved the Worcester sauce and the salt and pepper into a neat line.

'Everyone is so young,' she said, looking round, moving the sauce bottle behind the pepper then back again.

'You're young, Rosie.' Mrs Eaves's hand was plump and warm and Rosie clung to her for a moment and then sat back, watching Luke at the telephone, laughing, putting his thumbs up to his friends at the table.

'We got the gig. Five pounds!'

They cheered.

'Not any more,' Rosie said, touching her stomach.

That night as she lay in the room, moonlight came in through the gap in the curtains which didn't meet. She listened to the noise of the house, the banging doors, the shouting from the room next-door. There was a smell of cabbage everywhere.

She pulled the blankets around her head. The bed was damp. She was alone. But at least she had her job and that would enable her to go forward, to carve out a future for herself and the baby.

There were shadows as clouds passed in front of the moon. There was the faint sound of a trumpet and she thought of his arms around her, holding her. She ran her own hands across her shoulders, held her arms, pretended they were his hands.

The next morning she took the bus back to Middle Street and left her address with Ollie and with Harold, then rushed in to work, travelling back to Soho in the evening. She wrote to Nancy and Frank, telling them she had found a place of her own, giving them her address, telling them she wanted her freedom, telling them she was happy. They mustn't know of the baby. They would be worried and they had enough.

At eleven the next morning, the Editor called her into the office to offer her the job of Assistant Features Editor. Rosie felt the sudden thrill of success, the pleasure which those words brought, but she knew, clasping the arms of the chair, that she would have to tell the elegant woman in front of her that she was pregnant.

'Will it matter, Miss Stephens?' she asked.

It did matter. She was sacked on the spot and told to take her things from her desk and leave at once.

She did. She packed her shorthand pad and her pencils and walked out of the office and it was not until she was walking in and out of the Soho shops, asking for work, that she really believed that her future had been snatched from her and she had to lean against a pub wall and turn her face to the bricks, because it was all too much.

It seemed hours that she stood there, but it was only minutes. Then a man came up and asked her for sixpence for a cup of tea and she dragged one out of her purse, and gave it to him. He was dirty and old. At least, she thought, she was young, and so she pushed herself away from the wall, repeating that to herself.

She asked in more shops, more pubs for a job.

'We need a washer-upper,' said a man with a moustache, flicking his ash on to the floor. 'You'd need to clean the lavs too.'

She said she'd call back. She walked and asked again, crossing Archer Street where musicians were gathered outside the doorways of the agents' and managements' offices.

She stopped outside the Italian café where it was warm and clean and light. It was lunchtime. There was jazz oozing out of a cellar two houses away. She listened, holding the icy railing, putting her hand to her mouth, pushing back the nausea.

The café was full. She pushed through to the counter. Luke was there again, buying coffee for three tables, laughing, throwing shillings on to the counter.

'And one for this girl too,' he shouted to Mario, nodding at Rosie, who flushed. He smiled and she wanted to say, you might not want to, I'm pregnant. But she didn't because there was warmth in his look and in Mario's as he wiped the counter and winked at her.

'I don't know. A bit of success. It goes to their heads.'

Rosie nodded, taking the coffee. 'Thanks.'

She sat by herself on the bench near the counter, watching the ebb and flow of the young men, and young girls. She couldn't join in. She wasn't young any more. How could you be young if you were pregnant? She remembered the contempt in Harold's eyes and in Miss Stephens's too.

Luke sat with the others, then stood up, raising his coffee.

'First gig tomorrow. First bloody gig.' He was laughing, waving to the others at his table to stand. They did. There was a girl with them, long-haired. She hugged a boy with a beard and he kissed her on the mouth and Rosie turned away, burning her tongue on the hot coffee, but it didn't matter.

She ordered toast but with no butter. It made her retch. Mario looked up at her.

'Can you wait? We're so busy. It gets worse and worse. You no want a job?'

She did want a job but she leaned across and said, 'Yes, I need a job. But I'm – '

Mario interrupted. 'I know. Mrs Eaves tell me. I no mind. My wife no mind. You come. She say you good worker. I trust her.'

Rosie looked down at the sugar clumped on the spoon. Jack had trusted a lot of people.

She started work on the spot. She walked through the streamers into the back room piled high with old tables and boxes. On into the kitchen where Mrs Orsini smiled at her, her eyes sweeping down her body.

No, it doesn't show yet, Rosie wanted to scream at her, her face rigid as she looked at the small fat woman, not lowering her glance, though she wanted to.

'Oh, these things happen,' Mrs Orsini said. 'Mrs Eaves, she tell us you are a good girl. You love this man. He leave you.' Her arms were folded, she leaned against the table piled high with rolls. Toast was grilling, spaghetti simmering in a large pan.

'No,' Rosie said as she hung her coat up on the hook along the wall and washed her hands, scrubbing them hard, and then scrubbing them again. 'No, he hasn't left me. He's gone to Korea. He'll come back. He'll write. I know he will.' There were tears running down her face but they didn't reach her voice. That was calm, but not calm enough, for Mrs Orsini held her, patting her back while Mario called from beyond the swing door.

'Where my spaghetti bolognese? You women. Where my spaghetti?'

Rosie wrote to Nancy and Frank that evening when the café had closed and she had made tea in her room, that she had taken a job as manageress of a restaurant and that she would freelance for the magazine.

She walked to the window, pushing up the bottom sash, listening to the jazz, to the shouting, to the drunken singing. Her legs ached, her back ached but she had a room of her own and a job. At least for now, she was all right. She wouldn't look into the future, there was no point.

On 20 December she heard from Frank and Nancy.

Lower Falls
December 1950

Dearest Rosie,

Have you heard anything from Jack? We worry about him. It's been so cold out there. The frost was 45 at its worst. Rearguard duties fell to the new British brigade just arrived in Korea. That would be Jack.

Over here it is cold too. Joe has suggested that Frank writes under a pseudonym. We are losing readers. The reversal in Korea will not help. McCarthy is shouting louder each day. Our Local Administrator has an alarmingly large chest filled with importance. I just hate him.

Let us know your news about Jack. Let us know how the new job is going. It must be good for you to give up the magazine. We understand that you can't leave right now but come when you can. Frank is fit. He's fighting back. He's angry but not strained, if you know what I mean.

All our love darling girl.
Nancy

PS. The enclosed $40 is your Christmas present. It comes with love.

Rosie went into the café early that day and Mario nodded as she asked him about the decorations. She cut strips, coloured them, stuck them and wouldn't think of the fighting. Mrs Orsini helped and it was almost like being with Maisie again. They pinned them up. Customers came in and helped. Luke held her waist, steadying her beneath the holly which Mario had rushed out and bought in the market.

They drank coffee, and ate toast and omelette in the kitchen when the lunchtime rush was over, and Rosie walked to the post office for Mario at three in the afternoon, looking at the people walking past. Looking at the market traders shouting, dipping their hands into their aprons. The religious man pushed another leaflet into her hands and she turned.

'Don't you know there's a goddamn war on in Korea? Tell them all about that instead of pushing paper in people's faces.'

He turned from her, thrusting his leaflet at an old man. She grabbed him. 'There's a war on and nobody cares. Go on, get your mouth round that.'

But he pulled from her and she dropped the letters. An old man helped her pick them up. They were dirty and she was crying, standing in the street crying. The old man patted her hand and walked away. Everyone walked away in the end.

But then Luke came with Sandy, the girl with the long hair, and they walked back with her to the café, and then on home because the tears would not stop, because the world wouldn't stop either. Because life was too difficult.

She lay on the bed, and felt pain sweep across her back, and then her belly. She breathed slowly, and watched Luke boil the kettle on the ring and Sandy put tea into the pot, smelling it brewing, watching the milk being poured from the bottle, and the pain was still there and she was wet between the legs.

They called a doctor. He came and asked what she had taken. Luke held her hand as she thought of the consultant and his brass plate, his hundred-guinea offer. She thought of the gypsies and their brew and knew she might be losing the baby. All this could be over. She looked round the bedsit. She could go to America. She could stay here. Anything. She could be as young as Luke again and free.

Luke was squeezing her hand. It should have been Jack but he had gone, though her love for him had not. It never would. She turned to the doctor, who was standing over her. No one was taking the baby from her. No one had taken her career. She had done that. She had become pregnant. No one had taken Jack. She had helped to bring that about. It was time she got angry. It was time she began fighting again. It was goddamn time.

'I fell. This baby's part of Jack. It's all I've got of him. Just do your goddamn job. Please.'

Luke squeezed her hand again and Sandy smiled but the pain was too bad. She watched as Luke went to phone for an ambulance from the box on the corner, digging into his pockets for pennies, then looking in her purse. The doctor had to give them the money in the end.

She was in hospital, there were more doctors. There was Mrs Orsini and Mrs Eaves and there were days of rest when Christmas came and went and there was no card from Jack, though she had sent a present to Ollie for him back in November. But she wouldn't grieve because she was back in there, fighting.

In January she was back in Soho and Mrs Eaves and Mrs Orsini had put flowers in the room, and the baby was still inside her. She was fit, the doctor said, but mustn't leap over windmills. She had laughed because for now the world was good. Her baby was alive. She was alive and so was Jack because no telegram had come to Ollie.

There was a letter from Frank and Nancy when she got back to her room, and she returned to work knowing that the Chinese offensive had been halted. The United Nations were on the attack, but no one else that she passed seemed to care.

She served coffee, cooked, smiled, and laughed when Mario pushed a chair beneath her as she cut up the vegetables and asked if she had taken her iron today.

'And what about that soldier?'

He banged the pans when she shook her head.

Luke and Sandy made her sit too when she went out with them on a January evening to hear Luke's band's first gig and the warmth of these people made it seem as though the sun was shining through the fog which drifted and froze on the paintwork.

They sat at candle-lit tables in the basement of Chloe's and Sandy pushed her long hair back from her face, as Luke and the band worked their way down through the tables to the small stage.

'They've worked hard for this, all of them.' Her nail varnish was black. It was chipped. She was smoking in quick sharp bursts.

'Are they good?' Rosie asked.

Sandy smiled. 'You wouldn't know about jazz; I suppose. But yes, they're good.'

It was becoming crowded now. Rosie moved her chair closer to Sandy as a young man squeezed another round the table. Sandy was stubbing her cigarette out in the ashtray.

'It's hard, though, for them. They have to work too *and* fit this in. They need more time to practise. They need a place to practise. The flat's too small. The landlord doesn't like it.'

Rosie bought a beer for Sandy, a lemonade for herself from the girl behind the bar. But then the band was playing and Luke blew a trumpet as Uncle Bob had always dreamed. He explored the middle range, digging out melancholic tones, drawing pictures in the air, dredging feelings out of each person who sat and listened.

His eyes were closed, his foot tapped. He blew bends which broke her heart, he played a break while the others rested, improvising, soaring, growling, the sound beginning in his throat and forcing itself up through the instrument and out into the tone of the note. She smelt the steak on Frank's barbecue, saw Uncle Bob moving towards his band and had to turn from Sandy because of the tears in her eyes.

Luke played, Stan and Jim too, the clarinet and the trombone picking up the rhythm, Jake on the saxophone sliding in but he needed to be more mellow, throaty. She made herself listen again, watching the group through the spiralling cigarette smoke from the young man next to her.

Dave played block chords on the piano which was effective in small doses, but Dave knew that, she could tell, because he used it sparingly. Luke played a solo.

'Maybe he improvises too much,' Rosie said to Sandy, who looked at her through the hair which had swung back across her face.

Yes, Jack would think so, Rosie thought, because he liked Duke Ellington. Did he still?

When they broke for a beer and the clapping had died she spoke to Luke, telling him that she thought he used too much verbal agreement on the arrangements. 'It needs to be written out at this stage. It would be smoother, clearer.' And Jake, on the saxophone, needed improving. But the band was good, very good.

She felt the excitement rise in her as Luke looked at her and nodded.

'You know about jazz, don't you?'

'Yes, Frank taught me. Uncle Bob too. And Jack.'

She looked round as the band left to play another set. The excitement was there in everyone. One day they would be good enough for Bob, she'd make sure of that, but there was a great deal to be done before then.

The next day she poured Luke a coffee, Sandy too, as they came in for their lunch, and then she talked to Mario in the kitchen about the back room. She pointed to the packing cases, to the tables, to the extra space that could be used to bring in customers. She spoke to him about a Jazz Night where the bands could practise in front of an audience who would buy coffee and food.

Mario shook his head but Mrs Orsini nodded, slapping him on the back.

'Why not? Rosie knows what she's doing. That young Luke. He is good, is he not? You will hear all bands and decide. OK.' Mrs Orsini looked at Rosie and then at Mario who spread his hands wide.

'I will go upstairs when it starts. I will lie with my head beneath pillow. You are satisfied?'

'Not quite,' said Rosie, putting the dishes in the sink, talking as she washed. 'The boys are getting calls. They are being taken for a ride. They play for too little money. I want to take the calls for them, act as their manager, their agent. If they agree.' She turned.

'So you want to set up another business. Why not? They use my phone already, why not my staff? You would like a small dance floor. You would like me to swing from the ceiling in a tutu?'

Rosie laughed and so did Mrs Orsini.

'Yes, why not?' Mario said. 'For once there is a light in your eyes. Your Jack should see that. And don't forget you have clinic appointment this afternoon.'

Rosie went along. The nausea had almost stopped. There were mothers with young children in the waiting room. They clung to their mothers' legs as Lee had clung to hers and Jack's. As she had clung to Grandpa. She had forgotten that. She smiled at a blonde child and then at the mother, who looked away and tutted.

She was given iron by the doctor and told by the nurse it would be sensible to wear a curtain ring. Her voice was cold, correct. She gave Rosie details of a Home for Unmarried Mothers.

Rosie bought a ring from Woolworths. She went back to her room, climbed the stairs, breathed in the cabbage. Her legs ached, her back ached, but there was still the jazz.

She stood at the window. The sky was grey, full of snow. There would be snow on the mountains of Korea and he hadn't written. She lay on the bed. It was cold. He still hadn't written. She pushed the ring on to her finger. God damn you, my darling love.

She didn't go into work again that day. She lay on her bed but didn't sleep. All she could see and feel were his arms, his lips, his smiling eyes. All she knew was that she loved him. That night she allowed herself to cry, but only that night because she had his child to work for, to protect. A child who would put his arms around her legs. A child she had not pictured until today.

The next day Mario, Luke and the boys turned out the back room, and set up the tables while she and Mrs Orsini wiped the tables, chairs, the walls that she could reach without stretching. Luke would do anything high.

She stood behind the counter and served coffee and tea and food, listening all the time to the banging, the heaving, telling the customers that Thursday was to be a regular Jazz Night. The playing was free, she said, smiling, but the refreshments were not.

Over thirty came the first night and as people left at midnight a man approached Luke to play a gig at Chertsey on 1 March and offered him five pounds. Luke beckoned to Rosie.

'You'd better talk to my manager, Rosie Norton.'

The man smiled. 'Well, Mrs Norton, I'm Tom O'Toole. So, you manage these boys. Strange job for a woman, isn't it?'

Rosie brought out her drawl. 'It runs in the family. You might have heard of Bob Wallen from Pennsylvania.' She didn't wait for him to acknowledge the name which he might or might not have known. 'These boys can't work for that sort of money. Not now. They were offered twice that last week. I turned it down.'

She waved at Mr Orsini.

'Mr Orsini has had to pay ten pounds tonight and he got them for that because I know him well.'

She nodded to Mr O'Toole.

234

'Give me a ring sometime. On this number.' She handed him a card. 'But I can't stop now. I have to arrange their itinerary with them. Nice meeting with you.'

She shook his hand, and walked past him to Luke and Mario, gathering the boys around her until Jake said, 'He's gone. You've lost us five pounds.' He was smoking grass and she took it from him, and ground it into the floor, taking him to one side. Her back hurt, her legs ached, she had served coffee until the steam had dampened her hair, until she could stand the ringing of the cash register no longer. She was angry.

'If you ever smoke that goddamn stuff in here again you're out.'

'You don't own us.' Jake's head was down, his shoulders hunched, and it was like Sam again in the rec when she had first come home, but this time there was no Jack to stand by her. This time she was alone but it didn't matter, she was still angry.

Rosie looked round, called Luke over. 'He's smoking grass in here. Mario's been good to us. He could be in trouble. I've told him he's not to do it again or he's out. This is your band. Your decision. But if you want to play here again, smoking is out. Right?'

They had no choice. She knew that. They couldn't practise anywhere else. Luke took Jake to one side. She waited. She saw Luke pat Jake on the shoulder then look round and nod. She smiled, and she knew that there would be good days and bad days, but for now, she was strong enough to carry herself through.

'He'll be back. Don't worry. He'll phone. I know he will.'

He phoned back in March when her skirt was too tight to be done up any more. He offered the band twelve pounds to play in Surbiton, expenses on top of that, and so one night Rosie asked Luke to stay late at the café and told him that they must practise much harder. They were in the real world now. They could go on, even to the US, but there was a great deal of work to be done.

She told him that he should write out more arrangements, then maybe he should try the cornet. Luke agreed, kissed her cheek, said he was sending another band along to see her.

The next day the baby moved, for the first time, and a call

came through from Stone's Club near Birmingham. She talked the fee up to fourteen pounds and now she took a ten per cent cut which the band agreed was really not enough, but she wouldn't take more.

That night she wrote to Frank and Nancy and told them of Luke, glad that at least there was one lie less. But as she sat in front of the gas fire which plopped and hissed, the room seemed empty and bare. There had been no letter from the father of the child that had fluttered inside her and no one to share her pleasure.

CHAPTER 18

A truck took Jack straight towards the North. The enemy were in flight, the Sergeant told him and the twenty others who sat either side of the vehicle, lurching and bouncing past refugees and burnt-out tanks from the earlier United Nations retreat.

Jack leaned on his rifle, looking out at the snow which still covered the rice fields. He would write when he arrived. He would tell Rosie that he loved her, that he always had and always would. That he was coming home, when this was over.

'Shouldn't be long before we're home then, Sarge?' he called out to Sergeant Rivers.

'Who knows? Let's hope you're right,' the Sergeant answered.

They travelled for hours jolting along in the wake of the enemy, passing supply trucks returning empty from the forward positions. There were ambulances, too, but they didn't look at those. Jack flexed his shoulder. It was stiff but that was all. He looked out again at the hills splashed with snow. He wouldn't think of Tom either. He had to get home to Rosie.

He lit a cigarette, the match flame was fierce in the cold. He lit Bert's too, then tossed the box along to the Sergeant. There was a heavy smell of sulphur. He and Rosie would go to the hop-yards when he returned. He drew on his cigarette, jigging his feet to keep warm. Christ, it was cold. But it would be cold for the Chinese too.

They reached camp, leaping down and moving in single file off up the track to Hill 81, hearing the revving of the truck, the grinding of gears as it reversed then turned, leaving them, heading back to Pusan to pick up more troops, more supplies.

'Get on up that hill,' the Sergeant barked. 'Might be a bit of nice digging to welcome you back, work you little invalids in before you go running off towards the border doing your good deed for the West.' He was pointing, jerking his hand, his eyes red with tiredness, his voice hoarse. He looked old.

They headed on up the hill, straining their heads forward, carrying their rifles in both hands across their body, then, as the going got steeper, in one hand as they dug in their boots and their rifle butts, cursing, sweat pouring down their backs.

'Great to be bloody back,' Bert groaned in front of Jack, his boots thick with mud where so many feet had thawed the snow. The sun had gone by the time they reached the top. They went straight to the field kitchen, eating where they stood, looking round at the supplies piled up; the ammo, the Stens, the mortars.

There were look-outs on all sides and there was staccato firing in the distance, to the right and left and dead ahead.

'We move out in the morning. Chase the little buggers. Get your 'eads down where you can,' the Sergeant said, pushing past, cleaning his mess tin with a crust of bread.

Jack did the same, then swilled it with water, put it back in his pack, heaved that up on to his back again and headed towards the fox-hole where Bert was standing, beckoning to him.

At least there was no digging. That had all been done on the last advance and their hole was crowded but there was room against the sides. He didn't sleep in his sleeping bag. He had thrown that away. It was cold, bloody cold, but he slept. But not before he had thought of Rosie and the words he would write when the sun came up.

The Sergeant called them at first light and Jack ate breakfast, heaved at his pack, hearing the thuds and clinks all around. He could hear firing and now there were Mustangs high overhead.

'Keeping the pressure on,' an older regular said, nodding at Jack as he wrote his letter, standing up, pressing on Bert's pack, telling him to stand still for Christ's sake, while he told Rosie that he loved her, that he was coming home when his National Service was over. Begging her to forgive him, sure that she would because he knew she loved him too.

'Come on, get over here,' the Sergeant called and Jack stuffed the letter into an envelope, then pushed through the men to the Padre who had held a service as the field kitchen was packed up. He took letters from the men, waving to them as he set off in one direction and they in another, down the hill, taking up the pursuit, heading towards the firing.

It was then, as he dug his heels into the slope, looking out towards the peaks and snow-shrouded shrubs, that he felt a hand grip his shoulder and heard Nigel's voice say, 'Well, you old reprobate, here we are again. Bet you wish you were back cutting the grass with those scissors.'

Jack swung round, stepped out of line, gripped Nigel's arms, wanting to hug him but their eyes said it all and it was enough. Jack saluted then, heard the Sergeant shouting, 'Come along, if you don't mind, Sir.'

Nigel grimaced, and moved on down the hill as Jack fell back into line.

'Catch up with you later, Private,' he called back.

Jack laughed. 'Yes, Sir.'

And it was not until that evening, when they set up camp, bivouacked between boulders, crouching into the existing hoochies, taking two-hour watches, straining their eyes, cursing the men behind who stumbled on old tins left by the previous occupants, that they had time to talk, pressed up against the perimeter look-out.

'Too much pressure, dear boy. Simply had to take a commission.' Nigel was grinning but he didn't turn, he didn't take his eyes from the land around.

'Yes, Lieutenant Sanders. The pips look exquisite. How long have you been out here?'

'Just two weeks.'

Jack knew it could not have been longer. There was no fear in Nigel's eyes and there was still youth in his face.

'We'll soon clear those gooks,' Nigel said.

'Maybe, but they can march on rice, oatmeal, dried peas. They've been fighting with Mao for years. They plan and execute. They're professionals, mobile, take advantage of the terrain. They may be poorly armed but they take weapons from the dead. And they keep on coming.' Jack remembered the bugles, the screams. He remembered Tom and the burning man. 'Just keep your head down, especially now you're leading my platoon.'

They were whispering, listening. There were tracers in the distance. There were flares but he felt better now that Nigel was here, especially with Tom gone.

Nigel looked at him now. 'You're different, Jack.'

'I've been here longer than you and I've grown up a bit. That's all.'

He punched Nigel's arm when their relief came and crawled into his hole, thinking of Rosie, thinking of Suko, thanking her for all that she had shown him.

They set off the next morning as dawn broke. There had been no bugles, but then there wouldn't be. They were the ones chasing this time, weren't they? They marched all day, between hills, alongside paddy fields, the snow and mud clinging to their boots, their thighs sore from the slapping of their wet trousers. Patrols were sent out. The way had been cleared by the troops up ahead. They marched, they slept, they listened.

On the fourth day they were up with the forward troops and the firing was closer and all around. As evening came they straggled through dark hills. There were trees, there were shrubs and large boulders, and Jack looked to each side, straining his eyes.

The Sergeant came along, speaking to them all, but quietly. 'Seems like a good place for a bloody ambush. Keep your wits about you.'

Jack looked ahead to Nigel, who turned. 'Did you tell them, Sergeant?'

'Of course I bloody told them,' the Sergeant said under his breath and then, more loudly, but not too loudly, 'Yes, Sir.'

No one spoke, they were all listening, walking, praying. So far so good. Jack was breathing through his mouth. The air was cold. There was enough light to see his breath. It was crazy. No one would hear his breath over the noise his bloody feet were making. And over the noise the Centurion tanks that had joined them this afternoon were making as they came up the pass behind them.

He turned. He could see their antennae waving. He looked ahead at Nigel, his head turning from side to side. His shoulders were rigid. Jack's were too. Everyone's were.

Then the firing started, small arms thwacking into the ground around them, mortar thudding, screaming.

'Return fire, get some cover. Keep your heads down,' the Sergeant was shouting, waving his arm towards the paddy fields. They were wet, cold. Jack ran, then sprawled down, full length. The tanks were firing, but one was hit by mortar and exploded. The track was slippery and another tank keeled over into the paddy field.

The Chinese were swarming down the hill now, firing burp guns, throwing grenades, and the bugles were blowing. The endless bloody bugles. Jack looked across at Nigel.

'Get your head down, Sir,' he called and Nigel spun round, then ran crouching towards him, throwing himself down beside Jack. Firing as he did so. The rifle butt rammed hard against Jack's shoulder as he fired, again and again, but he couldn't even feel the pain.

The barrel was hot. He reached for more ammunition. Nigel moved along the line of men, talking, helping to reload the Sten. The Chinese were falling but more were coming in their place.

'Don't they know they're supposed to be retreating?' Jack ground out.

Bert lay on his side reloading. 'Bloody little buggers,' he said again and again, but now they were fading. Fewer came to replace them, and Nigel called, 'We're to make our way across the base of the hill on our left. Orders from HQ. Meet up there with a US Infantry Brigade, or what's left of them. Take casualties with us.' He was speaking in short bursts, as though he'd been running, but Jack was panting too. It was fear.

The first squad moved east while Nigel stayed with the rearguard. Jack ran with the first squad, then set up a rearguard under the Sergeant while Nigel and his men broke out, and ran past them. Now Jack, Bert and six others held the Chinese again who faded and left.

'That's what the book says should happen,' grunted Bert.

'Make the most of that piece of perfection then, sonny,' shouted the Sergeant as he passed.

They marched through the night towards the US Infantry Brigade and ate breakfast with men who drawled and looked like Ed, and Jack, though he loved Rosie, could not speak or eat with them.

The UN forces pushed north relentlessly day after cold day and Jack's platoon slept, ate, and marched, forcing the Communists back, seeing the airstrikes on the hills in front, the burning napalm, and he turned from that, feeling sick.

At night he watched the mortar scoring across the cold sky and wouldn't smoke the American cigarettes which Bert had been given.

It became commonplace to storm an enemy-held hill, firing, gripping the shrubs, pulling themselves up, hurling grenades, fighting hand to hand, plunging their rifle butts into heads, hearing screams all round, Chinese and British. Each time they took the hill, they herded prisoners into lorries then sat, their legs weak, vomiting, their stomachs churning from the smell of death. But at least Rosie would soon have his letter and, at least, soon, this war would be over.

At the end of March the Chinese were pushed across the 38th parallel and Jack's unit dug in on a hill which was scattered with the debris of previous battles. They stepped over abandoned Chinese and American equipment, they picked up pay books and identity tags and the Captain sent these back to Seoul which was once more in the hands of the United Nations.

Digging in was difficult in the sandy, frost-hard ground but none the less they tried.

Nigel and Jack talked on watch and Nigel said that the UN and Truman would be looking for a political settlement after throwing back the enemy, but MacArthur wanted to carry the war to Manchuria.

'He'll have to go,' Jack said. 'Or there'll be another war, with atom bombs this time.' He stared across the quiet sky, thinking of Nagasaki, and Suko's parents.

In April they watched the hills bloom with a profusion of colour which he had never dreamed could exist in this land where there seemed only harshness and poverty.

They watched from the hill as the transport became bogged down in the spring mud, they cleared out the fox-holes and cursed it. Their uniforms were wet from the rains, their skin sore from the chapping, but the war was as good as over, they would be going home soon. So they laughed and smoked, leaning on the stone-built barricades, hearing the rain on their tin hats, on their capes, and thought of England. Of its greenness, its rain, its fog, its rationing, and longed to be there.

They heard that the Gloucesters held the most exposed position on the direct approach to Seoul across the Imjin River but surely the Chinese wouldn't come again. They were beaten. There would be peace, MacArthur had been sacked on 11 April.

But they did come again, at the end of April as green was sprinkling the rice fields and new life was beginning all around. They came with their bugles blowing and the Gloucesters saved the left flank of the UN Corps and held up the advance of the Chinese so that the line could be reformed and held. Out of a force of 622, forty-six officers and men returned.

But Jack didn't have time to grieve, because the Chinese were storming his hill, too, and the air was rent with bugles and cymbals and screams, but Jack wasn't screaming, he was lining up the Sten, hearing it clink against the stones of the barrier, and now he was firing it, as the first wave of Chinese rushed up the hill.

How did they move so fast, for God's sake? He heard the gun, felt it judder, concentrated on that, not the bugles, nor the cymbals. He just fired, while Bert fed in the ammunition and threw water on the barrel to cool it as the night wore on, and there was no sense of surprise any more. He was getting used to all this.

He saw four Shooting Stars scream into the valley and bombard the enemy with rockets and cannon fire and napalm and this time he didn't feel sick. He was angry because he should be going home to Rosie. Not firing through showers of mud thrown up by mortar, not lifting a water bottle to his parched lips, not looking at the men he killed, feeling nothing because more would come in their place to kill him and he would never see Rosie again.

They fought all that day, keeping them at bay, waiting for reinforcements but none came. There were too many Chinese storming the whole line. There were supplies though.

'Thank God,' Nigel said as he slapped Jack's shoulder, telling him he would send a relief to take over the Sten soon.

Jack could see the parachutes with ammunition cases dropping amongst the Chinese instead.

243

'Oh Christ,' Nigel groaned.

They fought into the evening. They fought as the sun dropped, brilliant red, behind the hills and now, in the dark, they fired by the light of flares, picking out the Chinese, who were still crawling across the valley and up the base of the hill, getting closer to them now.

Nigel came running out to him, crouching, looking at the rain-sodden maps. 'Can you both hold out for a while longer? They're coming up three sides. No relief teams to spare.'

Jack nodded. 'Keep your bloody head down, Nigel.' He turned. He hadn't called him Sir. They looked at one another and smiled. There was no time for anything but friendship now.

Bullets were thwacking into the mud in front of them as Nigel ran back, dodging, shouting to the Sergeant, 'Get that man down.' But he was too late. Jack saw the radio operator fall, blood spurting from his chest, his radio set blown apart on his back.

There was so much mud flying into the air from mortar explosions, and there was the noise. So much noise and so many Chinese.

At midnight the order came through to pull out, down the hill, deploy six hundred yards to the rear.

They moved, each acting as rearguard, each doing as they were ordered without question, each saving the lives of their friends, and the parade ground flashed into Jack's mind as he skidded down the hill, taking up position as others slid past, then moving again.

They took up positions along the further side of a stream, wading through the water, holding their weapons above their heads, spreading out, flanking the valley, waiting because they knew the Chinese would keep on coming and that their own reinforcements would not.

The enemy came with the dawn. The machine gunners found their targets, and now the British counter-attacked, roaring towards the Chinese as they forded the stream, bogged down in the mud. The rain was in Jack's face, he could taste it, but his mouth was still dry as he ran towards the enemy, firing.

There were no bugles now and the British pushed back towards the valley again, yard by yard, until the day passed and the evening came again but the Chinese rallied and stormed, wave upon wave, as the last of the sun lit the spring flowers, and Bert was killed and Nigel dropped, wounded, his arm useless, and the Sergeant didn't shout any longer, for he was dead.

Jack dragged Nigel towards the base of the hill, ignoring his screams. There were too many all around to listen to just one.

'Break out, all of you that can,' the Captain shouted.

Jack heaped Nigel on to his back, but he was too heavy. He slapped Nigel's face. There was a bullet graze on his forehead and a flesh wound on his arm. He stirred.

'Stand up or die, Nigel,' he shouted, holding his face, looking around, then back at Nigel. 'Stand up, damn you.'

Nigel stirred, groaned. 'Stand up,' Jack repeated. Nigel stumbled to his feet, and Jack slung his arm over his shoulder, taking his weight, moving through the mud, slipping on the stones, but they were moving. At last they were moving.

He dragged Nigel, hearing his breathing, feeling it on his neck. His mouth was still dry from fear and exhaustion. His eyes were sore as he peered into the moonlight. God, Nigel was heavy.

He stopped, and lay down with Nigel beside him at the edge of a paddy field. He could smell the mud, the generations of excrement, and so he thought of the hop-fields, the gentle hills, and when he had rested he moved again. But this time small brown young-looking men loomed up in front of him in the moonlight and the green lush fields of Herefordshire were gone as they shouted and pushed and made Jack walk with his hands on his head in front of Nigel.

When he turned to look at his friend he was prodded with a rifle butt and he was afraid because he had heard of the cruelty of the North Koreans and this is what these men were.

Nigel moaned with every step and Jack breathed in time with his moaning. They could barely see the ground but there was enough light from the cloudless night to avoid the boulders, to stay with the track, and now there were others with them and Chinese soldiers too and Jack breathed more easily.

They were allowed to drop their hands but their fear remained. He stopped and looked back at Nigel, whose feet were dragging, who dripped blood with every step, and the Chinese guard nodded. Jack took his friend's weight and the man behind stepped forward and eased his arm round Nigel's body.

'Let me give you a hand, soldier.' It was a drawl, but Nigel needed help and so Jack nodded but didn't look.

They walked all night and came to a village as dawn broke. They were lined up in the courtyard and there were other Chinese soldiers there. They were given sweetened rice to eat and Jack pushed it into Nigel's mouth, waiting while he gagged, then giving him more.

'Prop him up between us,' the American said, nodding to a cart which was taking other wounded. 'We've heard that they're never seen again. They shouldn't know that he's wounded.'

So they pulled Nigel up, tying the sleeve of his shirt round his arm, needing water to wash the wound, but not daring to ask.

They were searched. Mirrors, scissors, knives were taken by the Chinese who didn't speak and who didn't notice Nigel's arm with the American's jacket slung over it. All the time the North Koreans loitered at the edge of the courtyard, watching.

A Chinese officer came into the courtyard in the cool of the morning sun. He stood before them.

'You are prisoners of the Chinese People's Volunteer Forces in Korea. You have been duped by the American imperialists. You are tools of the reactionary warmongers, fighting against the righteous cause of the Korean people.' He paused, looked around.

Jack tightened his hold on Nigel's good arm. He saw the American clasp his arm more tightly round his body. There were ten men in front of them. Nigel's head was lolling.

'Hold your head up,' Jack hissed and Nigel did.

'You are hirelings of the Rhee puppet government but you will be given the chance to learn the truth through study and you will correct your mistakes. We shall not harm you. At home your loved ones await you. Obey our rules and regulations and you will not be shot.'

They were allowed to sit down and Jack found some shade near the edge of the compound. The mud was deep. It soaked

246

through their clothes but all Jack thought of was Rosie reading his letter, waiting for him, and it gave him strength. But only until a peasant came and struck two prisoners in front of Jack and then turned, hitting him and Nigel with a stick, again and again until blood burst from their lips and heads, because his family had been killed in a raid.

The American, whose name was Steve, stood up and took the stick from the Korean, then the North Koreans moved, pushing through the seated ranks. The mud was in Jack's mouth and nose and he pushed up with his hands and saw the North Koreans take the Yank, pushing him before them towards the edge of the village. He looked for the Chinese but they had gone.

Jack rose, staggered and almost fell but then he was on his feet. He followed Steve and clutched a guard. 'Leave him,' he croaked. 'Leave the Yank.' He was grabbed too. He pulled away but was hit again by the peasant and the blood was running down his face. He turned, called, 'Look after Nigel,' and thought of Rosie as they hauled him, shouting, their breath sour, in his face.

'Hang on, bud,' the American shouted over his shoulder.

They were hauled to a pit, pushed in and there was white blossom on the branch of a tree which hung between them and the sky. Rifles were fired at the walls so that the bullets ricocheted around them, but they were not hit. The North Koreans laughed and the earth smelled of urine, of faeces, but Jack didn't look at the base of the pit, or into the dark flat faces. He thought of Rosie and the bines which swung as though in the sea. And white blossom.

Steve was silent. He stood with Jack, unmoving, until the bullets ceased, and still he said nothing and Jack had no voice with which to speak. Fear had taken it from him.

They were hauled from the pit and a revolver was placed at the American's head.

'Confess your crime, imperialist dog,' the largest North Korean said.

The American said nothing and the hammer clicked but the chamber was empty.

The North Korean opened the chamber and showed Jack. There were two bullets. He spun it, closed it. He held it to Jack's head.

'Confess your crime,' he said again.

Jack looked across the space to the other men, some of whom were visible between the village huts. He thought of Rosie, her mouth, her eyes, and said nothing because there was nothing to say.

But there was no bullet, only the noise of the hammer striking the empty chamber reverberating along the barrel, through the skin into his mind, but Rosie was there, and there was no room for the scream which wanted to leave his mouth.

The Chinese came then, pushing the North Koreans to one side, shoving Steve and Jack before them, back to the village square, and they sat on either side of Nigel and neither spoke because now their legs and their hands were trembling.

They drank the water that the Chinese soldiers passed round and when they had gone Jack cleaned Nigel's wound with the sleeve he had soaked, and dripped water into his friend's mouth, careful not to let the guards see because one man had been beaten for washing his face with the water. He had insulted the guard by using it in that way.

They stayed in the village during the day, pressed up against the hut walls in case the US planes strafed the village. Jack lay listening to the bullfrogs, listening to Nigel's groans, but Steve said little, especially when the North Koreans were near because, he explained, he was American, and the gooks hated them above all else. Jack was glad of his silence. He didn't want to speak to this man.

Each soldier in turn was taken to a hut and interviewed by a high-ranking Chinese officer who asked his rank, name and number, and asked why he supported the Wall Street warmongers who had helped South Korea invade North Korea in July 1950. Jack didn't answer.

'We Chinese believe in a lenient policy to preserve lives so that you imperialist tools can learn the truth. The North Koreans are different. Do not try and escape. They wait for you to do so.'

When Jack came out the North Koreans were there, waiting.

They took Steve too and now they knew that he was American, but there were others who were aircrew and they became the targets of the interrogation instead.

The day passed and at six p.m. the guards came round with

248

sorghum which Jack and Steve ate from cigarette tins because they had lost their hats in the mêlée. A British Sergeant came round too and said that more marching was expected tomorrow and there'd better be a better exhibition than there was today or he'd want to know the reason why.

It raised a smile, it raised morale, and Jack watched the flares and the tracers in the sky, and wondered how this could have happened when they thought they were going home, when he thought he was going home to Rosie.

CHAPTER 19

The landlady stopped Rosie in the hall in March as she searched the wire letter-box for the letter that just might be there. The woman's hair was newly permed and smelt as Norah's had. She wore lipstick and an overall and crossed her arms over her sagging breasts. There was a cigarette in her left hand and the ash drooped, then fell on to the linoleum.

'You've put on a lot of weight. You must think I'm daft. You'll have to leave when that baby you're carrying's due. I wouldn't have that sort of thing here, even if you were married.'

The woman sucked on her cigarette again. There were lipstick marks against the white of the paper. 'This is a decent establishment. No place for the likes of you. You've got to go before it's born.' She exhaled smoke as she spoke, nodded and turned, dropping more ash.

It was the ash that Rosie watched, not the woman who walked back into her room which opened on to the hall. As she opened the front door she watched it blow, then crumble to nothing. She shut the door behind her. She wanted to slam it against the words which she could still hear. Mrs Eaves had said this might happen.

She walked down the steps to the pavement, then turned and looked back at the house, at the peeling balustrade, at the door with its bubbling paint. Where could she go? Fear swept through her. She tugged at her skirt, easing it around her swelling waist where two safety pins were now clasped together. Who would take her and a baby?

The pavement was damp and footsteps were muted all around. She couldn't go to Mrs Eaves; it wasn't fair and there wasn't room. She called in to the butcher's where the smell of meat made her want to retch. There was a queue, there was always a queue, and the woman in front of her wearing a headscarf knotted at the front over her curlers laughed when the butcher brought his cleaver down on to the scarred and stained wooden block and shouted, 'It's 1951 and it'll take three books this morning, ladies, to buy a pound of meat.'

We know that, Rosie wanted to shout. But where can I find somewhere to live and what about the boys fighting out in Korea? Who knows about them, or even cares? And now the Chinese have been routed, will they come home? Oh God, I wish he'd come home. I wish he was safe.

She picked up Mario's order, and carried it to the shop, heaping it on to the table, laughing as Mrs Orsini shouted upstairs to her husband, 'So now the meat is here, Rosie is here, a customer is here, but you are not.'

Yes, she laughed but the laughter was empty because the fear inside her was building, making her weaken and she mustn't do that. She eased herself through the streamers between the kitchen and the café, smiling as she poured coffee for the three young men who stood waiting, knowing that there would be no tips from them. They were in worn coats and shapeless sweaters.

One of them stirred his coffee at the counter. His hands were red and chapped. He looked up at her. His glasses were steamed up and she smiled again as he took them off, rubbed them, replaced them.

'Luke said you might be able to help,' the boy began. 'We play New Orleans style.'

The others at the table behind weren't drinking, they were listening, and Rosie nodded. She mustn't think of Jack coming home, she must think only of fending for herself and the child. 'Tell me about yourselves. What have you done so far? Where have you played?'

As she listened the panic subsided. Yes. It was all right again. She must always believe that Jack was safe. She must concentrate on the new life. That was her job. She must work now, that was all, harder than she had ever done in her life before. She must save enough to tide her over for the birth and a few weeks afterwards and then she would manage. Mrs Orsini hadn't said yet that she could bring the baby to work with her, but she might.

But where to live while she had the baby? She pulled herself away from that thought. It was March, she had until June and she must listen to this boy because bands like these were her future. She would be like Bob, manage, guide, but always care. That's where she must put her energy; not into thoughts of Korea, not into fear for herself.

'We're playing at a club two blocks away tomorrow,' the boy told her.

'I'll come and listen.' Rosie smiled. 'We'll talk some more after that.'

She served all morning and in between made bookings over the phone, dropping in her coins, holding a hand to one ear, haggling, always raising the offers to something better while Mrs Orsini clucked and made her eat sandwiches because now she was eating for two.

'But it's too much. I haven't got an army in there.' Rosie smiled at the plump Italian woman. She wasn't hungry but she ate because this was Jack's baby and hers.

After the lunchtime rush she took a bus to Middle Street, slipping down the alley, letting her scarf hang down over her body because no one must know, least of all Ollie whom she was going to see. Perhaps Jack had written and Harold hadn't forwarded the letter.

She pushed open the gate into Jack's yard. Paper had blown into the corners. Lee's old bike was rusted and broken, lying on the ground with the wheel at an angle. The curtains were drawn. The door was locked but she knocked anyway. She wanted to hear some sound, and to touch something that Jack had touched. She wanted to stay where he had been, just for a moment, and hear the echoes of their laughter.

Harold came then, out through Grandpa's yard. He stood at the entrance to Ollie's. 'I thought I heard something.'

He was looking at her body and Rosie held her scarf in a bunch. 'Hello, Harold. I just wondered if any mail had come?'

He looked up at the house where the windows were like blank eyes. 'No. I'd bring it to you, honestly I would.' He was looking at her face now, not at her body, and she believed him, and everything hurt within her. But how could there be so much pain when she knew deep inside there would be no letter? Was she very stupid?

'It looks so empty.' She looked back at the house.

'Ollie's gone. He's got a job building the new town outside London. Norah wants to go when it's finished.' Harold nodded his head towards Grandpa's house. 'I don't though. It grows on you.'

Rosie nodded. 'What about the mail, though? What if it comes to Ollie, not to Number 15?'

Harold nodded. His moustache needed a trim. 'She's picking it up. Don't worry. I'll see you get any news.' He turned, then looked back over his shoulder. 'I'd ask you in but . . .'

'She still feels the same then?'

'Yes. Says your grandpa would too.' Harold shrugged. 'You're OK, though, aren't you?'

'Oh yes, no worries. I'm fine.' She walked out of the gate, watching as he turned back into the yard where she could no longer go. She could see that the roses were still there.

'Prune them for me, Harold,' she called softly and he nodded.

'I will. I like them. It's the scent, you know.'

Yes, she did know.

She walked to the rec, sat on the swings and wanted to go to Herefordshire again, paddle in the stream or go back to Pennsylvania and swim in the lake, let it soothe, listen to the ripples, but now was not the time. Now she must work. The wind was cold, too cold, and so she walked back to the bus, past the warehouse where she and Jack had walked with the cheeses and she could hear their laughter again, feel his closed-mouth kiss.

Back in Soho there was music coming from the basement clubs and she pushed her way through to the bars of the pubs which lined the road to the café. She took a job as barmaid three nights a week, starting when the café closed, leaving the other evenings free to listen to groups, practise with them, build up the business.

It would be good for her, she told herself. There would be less time in the bedsit, less time listening to the hissing fire, to her own breathing, to her loneliness. Less time to worry about where she would live, because so far none of the landladies she had asked would take a child.

The next night she listened to the new band and the pale young man who played the banjo. She heard its sharp tones cutting through the collective improvisation, through the murmur which continued from the dimly lit tables all around, and later they talked over glasses of beer and he told her that he played the guitar too and Rosie was glad.

'It's more flexible, but keep the banjo too. You can play well. Come to Mario's Club on Thursday. I'll have fixed you a few gigs by then. I take ten per cent.' She looked away as she said this. His coat was so shabby, all the musicians were poor, but so was she, and so would her baby be, unless she charged the rate that Luke said was fair, unless she worked until she dropped.

The boy smiled, and shook her hand, and they sat up talking about the clean and emphatic rhythmic backing that the banjo had always given, about the Big 25 Club in New Orleans where he had always wanted to play. Rosie nodded, her eyes sore with tiredness, but she needed to know her groups, to care about them, to find out their strengths and their weaknesses.

She worked at the bar the next night, pulling pints, smiling, wearing loose clothes to hide her shape, but her legs ached and her arms and her face from the smile that had to be there.

There was a letter in the wire rack on her return but it was not from Jack, it was from Nancy. She read it by the light from the small table lamp Mario had given her, hearing the plop of the gas, smelling it. Sipping cocoa, which was all she could face after an evening of beer-laden breath and nicotine-heavy air.

Lower Falls
March

My dearest Rosie,
  Do hope that all is well with you. Your groups seem to be coming along well. Uncle Bob tells us you've written about this guy Luke and his band. Sounds interesting. Maybe if he comes over, you could come too. Perhaps with Jack when the war's over.
  I hope to God it comes soon. It might take some of the panic out of things over here. Then 'pinkoes' like us might just be able to get some sleep at night without some nut

ringing up and shouting – Reds go home – over the line! Then we might get back to being fifty instead of ninety.

It's not being helped by the Rosenberg trial in New York City. My God, how tempers are rising all around.

It would cheer us both so much if you could come out to see us. But maybe you need to put in time at work, especially when you're just trying to get the restaurant on the road and the groups too. We understand.

All our love,
Nancy

The paper was cold. The heat didn't reach across to the bed and Rosie wanted to read of the maples and oaks at the lake, the target on the garage, the barbecue, Mary. She didn't want to hear of tension, of heartache, because she couldn't go back. All she could do was lie to the people she loved. The people who needed her right now.

Her legs were throbbing, her head ached. She lay down and pulled the knitted blanket up round her head. She wanted to be in her bedroom at Lower Falls, she wanted to be back where Nancy's arms could take away the pain, where her laughter broke into her loneliness. But she wanted to be here more, waiting for Jack, in case he came, in case he wrote.

That night she dreamed that he wrote, but March became April and there was no letter. There was just work, but the money was mounting and she sent in an application for an Unmarried Mothers Home. She was accepted but the letter was cold and the list of garments and equipment required was long.

So she worked on Sunday at the pub also and they said they would take one of her groups on a Friday night, unheard, because her reputation was growing. She slept well that night but couldn't face more than cocoa.

Towards the end of April, the UN forces retreated as the Chinese poured in reinforcements, and the newspaper ink came off on her hands as she read the piece again and again at the Orsinis' kitchen table and cried because now he wouldn't be coming home soon, the UN forces would have to go on fighting and there had been no letter.

She cried and couldn't stop and Mrs Orsini held her.

'He won't be coming home yet,' she whispered as she felt the heat from the older woman's body.

'One day he will. I know he will, if he loves you as we do,' Mrs Orsini said. 'You are a good girl. He cannot fail to love you. You must wait. You must be patient. You must not give up.'

That night as she lay in bed she wondered how long hope lasted. How long she could bear such loneliness. And how could she bear it if he died and she was never told? But Mrs Orsini said that Ollie or Harold would tell her and Rosie knew that she was right.

She worked throughout April, barely noticing the leaves sprouting on the clubbed trees, barely noticing the blocks of ice melting outside the French restaurants along the back streets. She listened to groups, listened to booking managers, and always increased the fees so that the ten per cent she took left the boys with the original offer.

She and Luke spent one evening a week with Jake, coaxing, nagging, drawing him on, because now they were both convinced that his playing could be brought up to the standard of the others, but still it was not quite right. She wrote again to Uncle Bob, telling him that Luke's group was almost ready. That he would want them when he heard the middle range, the melancholia, the dexterity, the heart.

She went to the clinic and they said she was underweight but the baby was strong. They gave her more iron. Mrs Orsini gave her soup, sandwiches, salads, but she was too tired to eat and Mario couldn't understand the circles under her eyes and neither could Mrs Eaves. She didn't tell them about the bar work, they wouldn't understand how necessary it was. She said nothing to Luke either, or to Sandy, who made her sit down now when she phoned because her legs were trembling for much of the day and so were her hands.

She still pulled pints though, in the evening, and it was here one night that Luke found her, pale, tired, bending, stretching, and he waited outside until the doors were locked and the customers had left. He waited beneath the street light, his leg crooked up behind him, until she came out of the side door and

256

for a moment she thought he was Jack and ran towards him, but then stopped.

'Why are you doing this?' Luke said, his arms crossed, his voice hard. 'You're more than seven months pregnant. Are you mad?'

The light cast shadows on his face and Rosie walked past him. She didn't need this. She needed money for her baby. She needed a future. Not this. Not now. She didn't turn but he followed her, grabbing her arm.

'Are you mad or just greedy? Why this on top of everything else? What do you want to do? Go back to America a rich woman? Show off to your friends about how well you've done? You're killing yourself. You're killing the baby.'

She pulled from him. The stars were clear in the sky. There was no cloud, no breeze. She would think of that, not his words.

'I'm going home because for now and for now only it is home. When the baby's born I have to leave. I have nowhere to go, no one to go to.' She wasn't looking at him, she was looking at the sky above the rooftops. 'That's why I'm working. I've got to pay for the goddamn Home, I've got to survive afterwards until I can work. I'll see you tomorrow, Luke.'

She walked on, back to the house by herself, climbed the stairs by herself, but then the baby stirred and she smiled. No, not by herself.

Luke didn't come into the café the next day, or the pub in the evening. Neither did the rest of the group, or Sandy. They didn't play on Thursday night but it didn't matter, because the new group did and the applause was loud, though Rosie had been too tired to tap her foot. Too tired to feel the hurt of Luke's rejection, because that is what his absence meant.

Mrs Orsini was quiet too, and busy. There didn't seem time for her to smile and Mario was in and out. Rosie served coffee, made phone calls, took phone calls, added gigs in the book, totalled up the figures. Served spaghetti bolognese to Mrs Eaves who came and smiled but left quickly with Mrs Orsini, and Rosie told herself it didn't matter.

She served in the pub that night and she had never been so tired. The Chinese and the North Koreans had been held on a line to the north of Seoul and the Han River. Where was Jack? Was he safe? Would he write?

As she left the pub she looked towards the lamppost but Luke wasn't there and the walk home was cool and quiet and empty. But the wire box for letters wasn't.

There was one from Frank saying that Joe was coming over to cover the Festival of Britain which had started at the beginning of May. He was also coming to hear Luke's group and to see her, to put their minds at rest that she was well and happy. Frank wanted her to write a feature on the Festival as well since she was doing freelance features in Britain.

Rosie read it again, lying fully clothed on the bed, then she tore it up, into smaller and smaller pieces. How could she hide this baby now and why was there no letter from Jack? And she hadn't written anything since she had left the magazine – her skill had gone, absorbed by the life she now led.

She slept, dragged herself from the bed when the alarm rang at seven a.m. She made tea and toast but couldn't eat, she was still too tired. She pushed her swollen feet into her shoes, and took her coat because the wind was still cool. The landlady was by the front door, holding it open for her.

'Made other arrangements yet?' she asked.

'You've had my rent until the end of May,' Rosie said, pushing past her, buttoning up her coat, knowing that the hem rose at the front and dipped at the back because she was so large.

When she arrived at the café the Closed sign was still up though the door was unlocked. The chairs were still upside-down on the tables and she moved slowly, setting them down, thinking of Joe, working out the letter she would write to stop him coming, the extra lies she would tell, but then Mario came into the room, his white apron smudged, and Mrs Orsini was behind her with Mrs Eaves.

Mario took the chair from her, set it down, took her by the hand, led her behind the counter, through the kitchen, up the stairs. Past the Orsini flat, right up to the top where the attic was. He said nothing and Rosie was too tired to ask.

He opened the door to the rooms which had housed packing cases, old chairs, rubbish. Luke and his band were there, with Sandy too. There were no packing cases any more. There was a carpet on the floor. There were chairs, a table, a cooker. Mario showed her this and the bathroom with the white suite. Light flooded in through the eaved windows.

There was another room with a white-sprigged muslin bedspread draped over a bed. There was a dressing-table. No one spoke. Rosie turned. Mrs Eaves had followed them up and stood with Mrs Orsini.

Luke said, 'This is yours, Rosie.'

Rosie stood but her legs were trembling, and now Luke moved over to the side of the bed where a sheet hung over something. He pulled it back and there was a cot with blankets cut down and freshly ironed sheets.

'And this is the baby's,' he said.

She walked over to the cot, stroked the bedclothes then the headboard. Frank's grandfather had carved the headboard on her bed at Lower Falls out of maple. She heard again the jazz from the open window flowing across the shadowed lawn.

She turned. 'I don't deserve it.' She laid her hand on her stomach. 'I can't take it.'

The sky was blue behind the rooftops and the chimneys. There were white clouds. How strange. There had only been darkness for so long.

She said again as they all stood, silent but smiling still, 'I can't take it.' But how she wanted to be able to.

Mr Orsini spread open his hands. 'Then you look for another job, my Rosie, because the person that works with us now has to live above. It is better for business. We are putting a phone up here.' He turned, the others were grinning now. 'But, you want to leave. You leave. We want you to stay. We want the baby too. We want you live here. Work here, with baby.'

Mrs Eaves came then, took her arm, moved her through into the other room, pushed her towards the chair beside the fire which had been hidden beneath an old sheet up to now. It was Grandpa's.

'We brought it over from Norah's. Harold helped us.'

Rosie sat. She looked at her own hands clutching the arms of the chair which his had held and now she looked up. His books were here too, on shelves along the wall.

'Thank you.' It was all she could say, but it was enough because there were so many tears in her eyes and everyone else's and she wanted to hug them, tell them how much it all meant to her. Mrs Eaves stooped and kissed her head.

'We know, my dear,' she murmured.

Mr Orsini clapped his hands and laughed. 'Good, good. Now downstairs, everyone. The café should be open. There is much to do. You too, Rosie, and there will be no more job at pub. There will be no more nasty woman at house. There will be no talk of Home for you and baby.'

He was taking her arm, helping her up while Mrs Orsini nodded and Mrs Eaves smiled. They followed Luke and the group down the stairs and everyone was talking at once but Rosie listened to Mr Orsini. 'You will go now to clinic. You will have baby in nearby hospital. You will come home to us.' He put up his hands. 'No arguments. That is as it should be. We help until Jack comes back.'

Rosie walked to the clinic and there was blossom on the trees, there were children running in the streets, laughing, shouting, as she and Jack had done. As their child would do, and one day they would take her to the hills of Herefordshire and the lake in Pennsylvania.

On 20 May Rosie went to the market for vegetables. She chose spring greens, with the dew still on the leaves, carrots, onions but left the potatoes for Luke to bring later. She listened to the man who sold crockery, dipping his hands into the money pocket of his apron. He wasn't as good as Jack.

She stopped, bought a paper and read of the British and Australian troops who had defended their positions and thrown back the Chinese. People pushed past her. They didn't care that there was a war on. Rosie put the paper into the litter bin and looked up and down the street. Was there fresh spring growth where Jack was? Was there blossom against blue skies as there was here? Was he thinking of her?

She walked on. She knew he wasn't dead. Ollie would have had a telegram and so she thought of him as she had known him, selling his plates, laughing, throwing the cheeses over the wall, and the sun was warm on her face and she didn't see the dog until it was too late.

It ran at her, caught her behind the knee. She fell, the carrots bursting out of their newspaper as her bag fell with her, and for a moment there was no pain, just surprise, just dirt on her hands and in her mouth. Then there were hands lifting her, voices, faces that cared, that were worried, shocked, and now the pain came, passing over her in waves.

'Sit down, missus.' Someone brought a chair out of a shop and an ambulance was called but the carrots were still all over the pavement. Someone must pick them up. The newspaper was lifting and flapping. It was dirty. Her hands were dirty and her mouth. She could taste the grit.

At the hospital she held out her hands through the fog of pain. They were dirty, so dirty, and the Sister smiled and washed them and asked how they could get hold of her husband.

'Jack's in Korea,' Rosie whispered because there was too much pain to use her voice properly.

The doctor tried to stop the baby coming because it was four weeks too soon, but the contractions were stronger, coming too quickly, and Rosie lay on the bed and called for Jack, again and again, because his baby was coming too soon. Mrs Eaves and Mrs Orsini came and patted her hand, soothed her forehead but they weren't allowed to stay.

'We'll be in the corridor. We'll wait,' Mrs Eaves said and there was a smile on her face, but not in her eyes.

The pain came again. 'Don't go,' Rosie called. 'Everyone goes.'

Lucia Anne was born at one a.m. She was small, but strong and beautiful, so very beautiful, and Rosie held her before they took her to an incubator. She stroked the small hands, the perfect nails, the soft hair, the skin. She kissed her cheek. Mrs Eaves and Mrs Orsini saw the baby too and cried when they heard the names because they were theirs.

The Sister came into the ward the next day, her face stern, her lips thin. She pulled the screens round the bed. 'There is no husband, is there?'

Rosie shook her head.

'Then you should have the baby adopted. It would be better. There would be two parents, a settled home.' The Sister straightened her apron. 'You're young enough to start again. Forget all about this.'

'I have a home. The father will come back from Korea. I know he will.' Rosie turned away to face the screen and would say nothing else.

At visiting time the husbands came and she looked away, out of the window at the blue sky. She was glad she had been to see Grandpa when he lay in hospital. She was glad she had carried the roses until her hands were raw because there was a loneliness here like no other.

Mario came, and Luke, and then Mrs Eaves and Mrs Orsini and they said they had told Norah. She did not come. The doctor spoke to her the next day about adoption but Lucia Anne was hers, she told him. She loved her.

'But my dear, love is not enough,' the doctor said.

'Love is everything,' she replied.

She took Lucia home and there were flowers in the flat and light, so much light. And there was love. So much love, from them all. But Jack wasn't there.

And Joe was coming soon and what would happen then?

CHAPTER 20

Jack's long march to the 'safe rear' began at seven p.m. as spring edged into the summer of 1951.

'To prevent strafing from UN planes,' the Chinese guard said.

They carried sacks of sorghum and Jack and Steve helped Nigel, who was stronger now but his arm was swollen and stiff. Jack still couldn't smile at the American, because he was a Yank like Ed, but he took the help he gave because the Yanks had taken so much from him.

They marched through mud and the Sergeant at the head of the column set up the rhythm and it helped, it made them feel human after the Korean children had giggled and stared and the North Korean guards had spat.

The mud dragged at their boots, Nigel lost the rhythm. Jack chanted left right, left right, and the Korean guard lunged at him with his rifle butt, screaming.

'OK, buddy, keep your shirt on,' Steve drawled and the guard turned on him and thudded the butt into his ribs.

Jack kept silent because the American had taken the blows which should have come to him. The bruises would have been easier. Steve kept silent too and now Nigel was back in rhythm, they were all in the rhythm, cursing with each step, cursing, counting, cursing, counting, but only in their minds, and Jack thought of this, not Steve and his long loping strides in which he saw echoes of Ed.

Trucks passed them, their lights picking out the road, spewing up mud, leaving the sickening smell of gasoline hanging on the air. Planes sometimes soared above, dropping flares which illuminated the road and adjacent hills, and each time the men had to break and scatter into the roadside ditches, sinking into the stinking mud as rockets hit the hills and the road. Then, as the planes disappeared, they clambered out again, marching on in sodden clothes, which rubbed against their skin. Christ, how they rubbed.

All along the hilltops bordering the roads the Chinese air-raid wardens fired rifle shots into the air when other planes were sighted and again and again they were back in the ditches, cursing the American air crews but cheering them too, if only in their minds.

They crossed bridges and were made to run for the length of them, their breath jerking in their chests, the sorghum sacks breaking their backs, deadening their legs. Jack could hear Nigel groaning but the guards couldn't hear above the thud of boots.

'Better than the assault courses,' he said as they ran. 'Do you remember? Just keep going.' And Nigel did.

Their mouths were dry. There were no drinks, but the guards had nothing either and they carried packs too.

They halted in a village before it was light, crouching in the centre, their bodies cooling quickly in the morning chill. Nigel was groaning but Jack gripped his good arm.

'In your mind, Nigel. In your mind.' Because the prisoners who had been in the Japanese camps in the last war could understand the North Koreans. They understood that the ox-cart which followed them meant death for the injured placed upon it.

Steve checked Nigel's wound. 'It's OK. The maggots are in it now.'

Jack nodded, swallowing. He couldn't have lifted the bandage, seen the writhing mass, but he wouldn't think of that. He would think of his mouth which was dry, of water which had not yet been given. He would think of the stream below the hop-yards, of Rosie standing, letting the water ripple about her legs.

The Chinese officer was shouting at his men and there were bullfrogs in the paddy fields which lay all around them. They were given water to drink and hot watery sorghum to eat, then herded up into the hills before dawn broke and there they lay during the long daylight hours.

They slept on the sandy ground, sheltered from planes by rocks and shrubs, and in the village he could see trees with white blossom bursting from their branches, symbols of stillness. He thought of Suko and the avenues of trees he had not stayed to see in Japan. But most of the time he thought and dreamed of Rosie and hated himself for hurting her.

But then the Chinese would come and sit and talk of their sins, of their crimes against the Korean people, of the right of the Chinese people to Formosa, and all the time the North Korean guards sat and lay on the perimeter, watching the men, fingering their guns, their knives, and no one tried to escape on that first night or day, or indeed the whole journey.

They marched again at seven p.m. when the rain was pouring. It was in their eyes, their fatigues, their mouths and so they weren't thirsty, but tired.

'So goddamn tired,' Steve drawled and Nigel nodded, but Jack looked straight ahead.

They stopped in the morning and this time there was room to stay in village shacks but it enabled the Chinese to talk to them more easily. A smooth-faced lecturer in well-pressed olive greens came by truck and harangued the prisoners as they slumped with knees crossed on the floor, looking out of the door at the blossom.

For two hours they sat and listened and their backs ached, their heads too, and then they were allowed to rest but the children of the village threw stones into the shacks, then beat sticks on the walls so there was no sleep for any of them. They marched again at seven p.m. and the lice were itching.

By ten p.m. they were lying in ditches, scattered before a strafing plane, its roar filling the air which was full of flying cartridge cases. One guard was killed and two prisoners. They were so tired, they barely noticed, but when they arrived at the next village they turned their clothes inside-out and squashed what lice they could between their fingernails.

There had been lice in Middle Street before they'd bought the houses. He and Rosie used to crush the lice there too. Steve checked Nigel's arm again, because Jack could not, and it was then that Jack said, 'Thanks. I couldn't do it.' It was the first time he had said thank you to an American since Maisie had left, but he couldn't look at him when he said it. And it was for Nigel that he spoke, not himself.

That day, they heard a cuckoo call as they lay on the hills

which were drenched in colour. Jack eased himself on to his back and thought of the Somerset village, the hill, the May blossom, the camp he and the other evacuees had made. He thought, too, of the cuckoo which he and Ed had heard. But then he thought instead of Rosie.

Each night they marched, each day they hid, drinking boiled water, eating sorghum, rice. Each day all the prisoners cracked lice and Steve checked Nigel's wound. They listened to the Chinese and wondered how long this would go on for.

For weeks they marched with the ox-cart trundling behind and more prisoners joined them until there were eighty of them. They brought news, but it wasn't good. The Chinese were advancing.

Dysentery had killed fifteen of them after four weeks and still they marched. The heat sapped their energy and now the flies were thick around them as they hid on the hills, resting, lying on the dry ground. They crawled in their ears, their eyes, their noses, their mouths.

When they covered their faces with squares of shirts they felt them crawling on the surface, heard them buzzing, but Nigel's arm was better, the maggots were gone, and he carried his own sack of sorghum. They had no need of Steve now, but he continued to march with them, though Jack barely spoke.

In the second week of June they entered a camp which was set on a peninsula, in a valley between two hills beyond which was the sea. There were barely any soles left on their boots. Their skin was burnt, their hair and clothes were thick with encrusted dirt. Their lips were cracked.

'This is exquisite,' Nigel said, bracing his shoulders, marching in step.

Jack laughed, looking up at the blue sky.

'Hardly exquisite, dear boy,' he answered, looking down now at the single strand of wire which marked the perimeter of the camp, knowing that the geography was the real restriction. He, too, braced his shoulders and marched in step to the huts, then gave news to the prisoners who had been there over the winter; who were thin, bruised, hungry, but who said the regime was kinder now. Indoctrination was the order of the day. It wasn't very successful. Jack looked at Nigel and they smiled. Steve smiled too.

They ate corn and millet that evening. They wanted to sleep but were taken out into a large hut and lectured and Jack looked at his thumbs which were black with the ingrained blood of the lice, but still he itched, still he scratched. They all did, but tomorrow they wouldn't march. At least there was that.

In the morning they were put on a wood rota and Steve and Jack went up into the hills with eight others but Jack talked to the others, not to Steve. They collected wood, brought it back, boiled water for drinking, but it was too late for some. Five of their men died of dysentery in the camp that first day.

They were broken down into companies by the Chinese for daily political study sessions. Nigel, Steve and Jack were kept together and there was nothing Jack could do about it. They sat in rows, cross-legged, trying not to listen.

'You soldiers have come here as dupes of the imperialists, the warmongers, the Wall Street big-shots who have tricked you to leave your countries and fight this war to increase their profits,' the lecturer told them. His voice droned on and on.

There were flies everywhere. Jack dropped his head on to his chest and thought of the cool breeze of England, Rosie's soft hands.

They were given paper to write an essay on the lecture they had received. Nigel wrote, and Steve and Jack copied his words. They were all sent for that evening. They stood before the Commandant and confessed their copying crimes as the Commandant insisted they must. But Steve and Jack couldn't write the essays that the Commandant now insisted upon because they had not been listening. They were taken to cells in the village.

The North Korean guards pushed them inside the clay and wattle building which smelled of excrement, urine, and the gasoline which was stored in drums at the end of the passage. There were doors either side. It was dark. Steve murmured, 'This looks kinda fun.'

Jack looked at him now, really looked, because there had been no fear in his voice and he wondered how that was possible. But now he saw the fear in the American's eyes. There was youth too, and kindness, and Jack smiled but then he was pushed alone into a cell.

The uneven dirt floor was soaked with oil. It was dark. So dark. The door opened and he turned. A North Korean guard stood there, a pistol in his hand.

'You come.'

Jack left and Steve called, 'Good luck, buddy.'

He was taken to a wall which flanked the square outside the cells. His arms were tied with wire. He was turned to face the guard. The sun was too bright, the shadows so sharp. For Christ's sake! He was going to be shot. Shot, now. Jack put up his hand. *No*, but the word was silent. There was no time. The guard had levelled the pistol, pulled back the hammer. The gun fired into the wall behind him and Jack's legs shook and he nearly fell.

The guard returned him to the cell and Steve tapped on the wall.

'You OK?'

'I'm fine. Just fine. What else can you do on a quiet afternoon?' But he wasn't OK. He sat on the floor, his arms round his knees, trying to stop the shaking and the tears, listening as Steve in his turn was taken, but he also returned and so the shaking stopped and the tears too. Because he hadn't died today and he wasn't alone.

The guard handed in a blanket, rice bowl and spoon and took their boots, and he couldn't sleep that night because he didn't know when they would come again to take him. The cells were full, and he knew the others couldn't sleep either because they tapped and talked in whispers. So, although there was no light, there was comradeship, and that kept the fear from all their voices.

The next day the guards came and took them one by one, barefoot, to the earth latrine at the end of the passage, then back to the cells. They were made to sit bolt upright from five-thirty a.m. onwards. Jack's back stiffened, burned. He slouched. The guard looked through the grille and shouted. He sat up again, back rigid now, until eleven a.m.

There were no more trips to the latrines. A young American air navigator had dysentery and Steve told the guard, who hit him in the face with his fist, and Jack wondered how he could ever not have liked this man.

The navigator used the corner of his cell.

'That is good. You need to learn humility,' the Chinese officer called through their doors.

At eleven breakfast arrived. They stepped three paces outside the cell to collect the food, but one at a time so they saw no familiar face. Jack forced it down. Boiled water was brought. Jack filled up his bowl, sipped it. Tipped a little on to his fingers, wiped his face, his hands.

At midday the flies and the heat rose. The Chinese bugles blew and the guards shouted that they must lie down for one hour. Jack pulled the blanket over his face, lying on the dirt floor. He heard and felt the flies, felt the sweat soak into the blanket, but it was better than having them in his mouth, crawling heavy and bloated across his skin.

They were then made to sit again, bolt upright, and there was comfort in the knowledge that others were having to do the same. There was such comfort in not being alone.

Each minute seemed an eternity. He thought of Rosie, of the coolness of the bines, the softness of her lips. He didn't think of the cold ground in Yorkshire because it made him feel so disgusted with himself, and so grateful that she could still love him. The shirt had shown that and it was more than he deserved. But at least there had been no child for her to struggle with alone. She would have told him.

At twilight they were ordered to lie down and sleep. They were inspected at nine p.m. A torch was shone in his face. He pretended to be asleep. He pretended to be asleep when Steve tapped, and when he spoke, because the disgust was still with him.

As he walked to the earth latrine in the morning he watched a guard carry a bucket towards a sheet of wrought iron on the ground. He saw him kick the sheeting to one side. An American officer emerged wearing flying boots. He was white and haggard and stumbled to the latrines ahead of Jack.

Jack's guard laughed. 'He not confess to crimes.'

'Good luck, buddy,' Jack called and the man turned, dazed, his eyes deep sunken. He smiled before Jack felt the blow of the rifle, felt it thud into his ribs, felt the dust in his mouth as he fell.

He was dragged back to the cell before he could use the latrine. He was made to sit all day without food, without water, and there was only the corner of his cell as a latrine. But it was worth it to have reached out, for that one moment, to a boy, an American, who was suffering more than he.

That evening, after twilight and after inspection, he talked to Steve about Ed and Maisie and Lee because all the anger and the bitterness were gone. They had disappeared when Steve had spoken without fear and when the American had crawled from the pit.

They were out of the cells within a week and at the end of June the Chinese danced as evening came, swaying in weaving columns to the discordant sound of a drum and clashing cymbals in celebration of a festival only they understood.

'How exquisite,' Nigel murmured and Jack nodded.

'Kinda strange, out here,' Steve said. 'Can't quite catch the tune, but I've heard those cymbals before.'

They had all heard them, but then they had been almost drowned by bugles and guns.

There were fewer North Koreans now and less brutality. They were allowed to wash but there was no soap or towels. They were given anti-malarial tablets and louse powder. They were fed twice a day from the Chinese troops' kitchen. They knew it was all to re-educate them through leniency but by now Nigel had dysentery and none of this helped that.

So each day they listened to lectures, wrote essays, but thought their own thoughts and clung to their own dreams, their own memories, and longed to be home.

In July the Commandant spoke to them. He smoked Dragon cigarettes from China and shouted when Nigel had hiccoughs and couldn't stop.

He told them that some of them were righteous progressive men who were self-consciously learning the truth.

'You are our friends and we will help you to struggle free from the toils of the warmongers.' He looked at Nigel who was still hiccoughing. 'Others of you are semi-righteous, uncertain. You are swayed by every wind that blows. You listen to both sides but cannot make self-conscious decisions.'

Nigel was still hiccoughing, clenching his hands into fists, holding his breath. Men were laughing now, but not the Commandant.

'Others of you are bad men. You believe slanderous things.

270

You close your minds against the truth. You distract others from learning.' He motioned with his swagger stick to Nigel and the guards came and took him and now there was no laughter.

Steve looked at Jack. 'He's too weak. That dysentery. He ain't fit enough to take that cell, or the pit.'

Jack nodded. He began to stand but Steve pressed him down.

'That won't help. We'll have to wait.'

They didn't take Nigel to the pit though. They took him to the Commandant's hut where he spent the evening writing a self-criticism which he had to read the next day to the camp.

It was clever, very clever, Jack thought, grinning. It was a criticism of the Commandant, not capitalism, but written in a way which made this impossible to grasp. Afterwards Nigel told him that he wanted to go to university when this mess was over.

At the end of the week they were given paper to write a letter home, c/o The Chinese People's Volunteers' POW Corps. Jack wrote to Rosie, telling her that he loved her, that his friend Nigel was here, and Steve, an American. That all the anger was gone, that he would survive. That he was ashamed. That he hated himself for hurting her. That this couldn't go on for too long and he would be back.

They handed them in but an American who knew Korean heard the guards say that they would never be sent and home seemed very far away.

The wood-gathering parties had to scavenge further afield now but suddenly the trips became more popular because Mexican POWs had discovered marijuana growing on the hillsides and now they rolled the leaves between book pages and smoked them to ease the boredom of the days. But Jack and Steve refused to smoke because they needed to care for Nigel who was weaker each day from dysentery and beri-beri.

There were no medical supplies, though there was a doctor who tried to help. The Chinese had no drugs for themselves either.

They still sat through lectures, listening just enough to be able to answer questions, but they also talked to the Puerto

271

Ricans who knew and understood the herbs which could save lives. Steve and Jack used the remains of the paper which they had been given for their essays to write down descriptions of the plants.

The following week they strayed from the wood-gathering party, searching, picking, stuffing the herbs into the pockets of their trousers, remembering to carry wood under their arms as well. They brewed the mixture up behind the hut and no guards stopped them because boiling up water was common. Nigel drank it from his cigarette-tin and he seemed a little better and they talked of home, and of Oxford where he would go when the war was over.

They did the same the next week, and the next, and then it was the beginning of August and new prisoners said that talks were being held in a tea-house in Kaesong on a ceasefire in Korea. That this must almost be the end, and that day the wood party looked up at the hills, felt the heat and the dust, and because the war would be over soon it didn't seem so important to stretch themselves beyond endurance. They were late mustering, slow in leaving and Jack watched them straggle in on their return. He watched the Commandant too, standing frowning, and waited for what he knew would happen.

The Chinese herded all the prisoners into the square. They were lectured on their negative attitude to labour and made to sit in the sun for the afternoon and Nigel became worse as the heat increased. The herb gatherer had forgotten to gather.

Jack and Steve went out on the wood detail the next morning, even though they were tired and weak and it wasn't their turn, but Nigel was worse. They needed herbs, they needed to make sure the squad were brisk and that Nigel didn't need to sit in the sun again.

They took the sloping paths, lifting the wood which was already hot though it was only eleven a.m. They found the herbs, bitter, sweet. The smell clung to their hands. They moved further from the others, picking, leaning over for wood, glancing behind, checking the guards, picking, always picking. And others did too now for their own friends.

They came out the next day too, and the next, picking for Nigel, and for others, but on the Sunday afternoon Jack and Steve were not cautious enough as they searched and picked.

They didn't check how close they were to the squad. Jack heard the shouting of the guards first, then the warning from Steve, then bullets thwacked into the ground at their feet. There was the sound of running feet and they were pushed face down and kicked, then dragged back to the camp.

They were brought before the Commandant, who accused them of trying to escape. They said nothing. The scent of herbs was still on their hands. Steve looked at Jack who shook his head. They couldn't admit to the herbs in case others were stopped too. In case the marijuana smoking was discovered and men punished.

'You must admit your error,' the Commandant said.

'I'm kinda sick of admitting to errors,' Steve said. 'Why don't you go take a powder.'

The Commandant didn't speak, he just nodded and the guards took Steve across the square. He dropped the herbs on the ground. They were picked up by another prisoner and taken to Nigel.

Jack saw this. He also saw the flies around his head. Then he watched the smoke rising from the Commandant's cigarette and there were no flies near the smoke. Power brought advantages, that was for sure.

'And you. You will admit your error? Your attempt to escape.'

Jack stood to attention. He rubbed the scar the scissors had made. He was tired too, of obedience, of humility. Yes, he was tired and the war was nearly over anyway.

'I have made no errors,' he said.

He also dropped his herbs on the ground and they were picked up too and the soldier who did so said, 'I'll get them for Nigel until you're back out.'

He was thrown into the pit near the latrines and Steve called out from the other, 'You'll like the privacy, Jack.'

He didn't, though, and neither would Grandpa, he thought, smiling wryly. It was dark, it was hot, so hot. The sun beat down on the iron, the guards banged with sticks and he sat crouched, hugging his knees, feeling the sweat rolling off his body. He stripped off his clothes, held his head in his hands while it ached enough to burst.

As the heat of the day beat on the steel covers he took shallow

273

breaths, panting, seeking air, lifting his head, but there was none. He rolled on to his side. The earth was cooler. He buried his face in it but the dust entered his mouth, his nose. He crouched, he wept and the tears were salty and then he sat, still and straight, as Suko had done before the Shinto shrine. He thought of white blossom, of the cool of the stream about Rosie's legs.

They lifted the covers at twilight. He staggered to the latrines, heard Steve's voice as he returned. It was cracked and dry.

'Kinda like a long holiday, eh, Jack?'

Jack slipped down again into the pit. The guard handed him sorghum in a tin and half a can of boiled water. It was warm. They pushed him down. Some of the water spilt. They slid the sheeting over again.

He heard Steve being taken now and when he returned he called out to him.

'Better than a deckchair at Southend, eh, Steve?' His voice was cracked and dry too.

The next night was cold and the morning took so long to come, but then the heat came too and the flies and the noise of the sticks and because they had spoken to one another their arms were tied behind their backs after they had been taken to the latrines. Food was still passed in, though, but they had to bend over and lick it from the tin like animals.

They didn't call to one another again, but they shuffled their feet or they coughed and that was enough. And it was enough, too, for Jack to sit still now and hold his body upright, to ignore the bindings and think of blossom, Rosie and the cool of England.

After two days the guards untied their arms, but pushed them back down again into the pit. There were deep raw grooves in their skin from the rope but these didn't touch the thoughts inside Jack's head, the memories, the echoes of the life he had lived, the people he had loved.

In the second week he pictured the pebbles in the stream below the hop-yards. He picked them from the water. The water was cool, the pebbles wet. He built a pyramid. The pebbles dried. He walked amongst the cool green fountains of hops, and saw the yellow dust beneath his fingernails. He picked the hops, flicking them into the bin. He smelt them, felt them. Kissed Rosie, laughed with Ed, smelt the lavender on Maisie's neck, threw Lee up into the air, heard his laughter. Heard Ollie's too.

In the third week he breathed slowly, emptied his mind, and on each trip to the latrine he coughed with a dry throat, and each time he heard Steve do the same he knew he could go on. They were released at the end of August.

Jack could barely stand. The light hurt his eyes as it had hurt them each time he had walked to the latrine. He was marched back to the compound, through North Koreans who threw stones at him and called him a murderer.

They did the same to Steve, whose beard was dark against his white skin. Jack rubbed his own beard. He watched the stones hit his friend. But Steve didn't notice. He was thin, his legs trembled as Jack's did. They met at the gate, nodded, smiled, held one another's arms.

'The war must be nearly over,' they called to a prisoner who brought them water. They lifted the cans to their lips.

The young boy shook his head. 'New POWs in say the talks will go on and on, maybe for years. There's no truce, only more fighting.'

They felt sick with something deeper than anguish and couldn't move as they watched the boy walk on, his head down, dust scuffing up with each step. The hop-yards were fading. Jack couldn't hold on to them.

They walked towards Nigel's hut but he wasn't there. He had been moved to the officers' camp, another prisoner told them.

'He didn't want to go. He wanted to wait for you, but he had no choice. They're trying to destroy the old leadership system, demoralise everyone, so the officers have been separated from the ranks. He died there last week. We've only just heard.'

CHAPTER 21

Joe came at the beginning of June, when Rosie had only been home a week. He walked into the café as Lucia slept in her pram outside the kitchen door in the small sunswept courtyard. Rosie was talking on the phone to a promoter who wanted Luke at whatever cost.

'Though within reason, my dear.'

Rosie laughed. 'Twenty pounds. Excluding expenses. I don't think I can be more reasonable than that, Harry.' She knew he would take far more in profit for she had been to the function room behind his pub, seen his gold rings, his expensive watch.

Rosie grinned as he sounded her out about a national tour for the band. She turned to write the date in the book. Joe moved and she looked up, saw his blond hair, his tanned skin, his white teeth. She saw the watch which gleamed against his skin. It was new. Everything went quite still and then jogged into motion again as she put her pen down, carefully. There was ink on the nib. It had smeared her finger.

She didn't kiss him but shook his hand, feeling cold, wishing he hadn't come. Her world had been intruded upon. The lies were about to be exposed and she was ashamed. For the first time for weeks she was ashamed.

He grinned, looked around. 'So this is it?'

'Yes, this is it.' She poured him coffee, nodded towards Luke. 'We're on for Saturday. Expenses excluded. Twenty pounds!'

Luke whistled and Joe looked at her. 'From what Frank said I imagined the restaurant would be bigger.'

'Remember you're in little old England now,' she said, wiping the counter.

276

'You're looking good.' He sipped the black coffee as he leaned against the counter.

Rosie didn't know what to say to this man who didn't belong here. Who shouldn't have come. 'You must meet Luke,' she said, her voice cold and crisp, because she could remember that the hand that lifted the cup had stroked her breasts. It had been a mistake.

Joe arched his eyebrows. 'Have I said something wrong? Burst in on you? I should have rung. I didn't think.' He looked unsure suddenly. She hadn't seen this in him before and she smiled, reaching out her hand, touching his.

'No, I'm just busy. Too much to do, too little time.' She had pushed the thought of his trip away, unable to think of any lies strong enough to make Frank change his plans, too engrossed in Lucia. And now she relaxed. What did it matter? Lucia was with her, safe, beautiful. That was what was important.

'Luke,' she called. 'Meet Joe. Uncle Bob's scout.' She laughed and Joe relaxed, shook hands and passed Camels round while Rosie collected cups, took orders, and passed them through to Mrs Orsini.

She then took Joe out to the yard. There was no point in wasting time but she had to make sure he didn't tell Frank and Nancy.

She walked to the pram, and pulled back the blanket. 'This is my child. Jack's child,' she said.

She watched Joe flush. He looked from the baby to Rosie but said nothing. He just stood, his hands in his pockets, and then he murmured, 'Quite a surprise. No wonder you didn't want to visit Frank and Nancy. They've got quite a bit on their plates already. This might shake them up a bit.'

Rosie touched her child's hair. It was always so fine, so soft, so warm. 'I'll tell them when things are easier for them, but you must say nothing. You must promise me that.'

She waited, wondering whether he would agree, wondering how she could make him, if he refused. But he agreed and she was surprised, but why should she be? He was kind, wasn't he? He had sent her money to go over to Frank. But she was still surprised and didn't know why.

Joe touched the baby, who woke.

'I thought you hadn't heard anything from Jack?'

'I haven't. He doesn't know, but I'll tell him, when he writes, because one day he will.'

He laughed as Lucia gripped his finger. His shirt was so white against the tan of his skin and he had promised he would say nothing. Rosie was grateful. He had touched her child and smiled and she was pleased.

He didn't stay long but came again in the evening to hear the band. Luke played while Joe drank Coke and listened, his finger tapping on the glass. Luke's band played for an hour and the music was good, mellow, haunting, penetrating. They listened to the chord held at the end of the chorus, heard the crescendo as Luke led the band into an all-in section. They heard the growl, heard his improvisation but it was a carefully planned one. He was so good, and Jake was better. So much better, but he still needed to go a little further.

'He'll get there though,' she told Joe. He nodded.

Luke sat with them in the interval. There was smoke in the air and candle wax on the table. Rosie checked her watch. Mrs Orsini was looking after Lucia but she would need a feed at ten.

'Great, really great. This club is good too, better than I expected,' Joe said, and Rosie winked at Luke, who sat back in his chair and smiled. 'You're right, Rosie. Bob'll really go for this. It's what he's been looking for. The guy on sax will have to go though.'

Rosie felt cold. It was as though there was no laughter in the room, no murmur of voices. Hadn't he heard her? Hadn't she just said that Jake would make it? Joe was still smiling, lifting the glass to his mouth, and she could picture him at the Lake Clubhouse, smart, adored, arrogant, ruthless. But he had agreed to keep her secret. There must be some softness there, maybe?

'But Jake is almost there. He's getting better every day,' Luke protested, and Rosie nodded, looking at their clothes, looking at Joe's. But no matter how slick he was, he was wrong.

'He'll make it. I'll stake my reputation on it. I'll pull in favours from Uncle Bob,' she added quietly.

Joe put the glass back on the table, and looked towards the group who were edging their way back through the tables.

'Look, Luke, you're a commodity. Bob can package you but you've got to get rid of the weak link. There's no room for

278

feelings in this game.' He turned to Rosie. 'This is business. You need to toughen up, Rosie.'

Rosie stared at Joe, then at Luke. She waited.

'No,' Luke said getting to his feet. 'Thank you, Joe, but no. We all go, or no one goes. No package without Jake.' His smile was ironic.

Joe shrugged. 'I think you're wrong.'

Rosie put up her hand to stop Luke. She could fight for Luke now that he had made his decision. And she would fight because there was more than one way of doing business. You didn't have to be hard, just fair, and Joe could be fair. He had shown her that this afternoon.

'He's not wrong. Bob thinks of his bands as people. You're wrong, Joe. Think of the group who played at the barbecue, Bob nurtured them. Jake needs confidence, that's all, and a little time.' She wanted to shout at him, but she kept her voice calm. 'Bob wouldn't thank you if you passed this group over and they made it elsewhere, because they will.'

She watched him as he crossed his legs, picked at a thread on the sleeve of his jacket, rolled it between his thumb and forefinger. His nails were short, clean and square.

'Have you a lot invested in these guys?' Joe asked her quietly, leaning forward, talking behind his glass.

'A lot of time, a lot of effort, a lot of pleasure. Why not give them until you leave England? See what happens.' Why did he equate everything with money? She thought of his family. How could he be otherwise? But he could learn. She remembered his hand on her child. She still held on to Luke's jacket.

Joe looked at her and grinned. 'Why not? Bob's in no rush. OK. You got a deal. Just one condition.'

Rosie felt Luke relax, she let her hand drop from his jacket, feeling the relief surge in her too. She nodded. 'What?'

'I've got to write a feature for Frank on the Festival. You're expected to send one back too. Show me round. Let's have some fun.' He was smiling, his voice was lazy again as it had been on the beach by the lake.

She didn't want to celebrate while Jack was fighting, but she nodded. He knew about Lucia. He was going to report to Bob and he had been fair. There was no choice, but they wouldn't be alone. She would take Lucia, Jack's child.

But before she went anywhere, with Joe or anyone else, she took Lucia to Middle Street one morning when Norah would be at work. She pushed the back yard gate open, and picked up Lucia, taking her to Grandpa's roses, their fragrance heavy on the mid June air.

She walked along by The Reverend Ashe, took a matchbox from her pocket and tipped out the ladybird she had found, easing it with her finger on to the underside of the bud where too many greenfly were flourishing. Poor Grandpa.

'This will never do, will it, Lucia?' she said softly, bending to kiss the head of the sleeping baby. She heard the back door open and turned. Norah wasn't at work, she was standing in the doorway with a mouth like a sparrow's bum. Nothing changed.

'Hello, Norah.'

Her sister looked her up and down and then the baby in the fine white crocheted shawl which Mrs Eaves had made.

'I heard you'd had it.' She stood with her arms crossed over her breasts.

Rosie moved closer. 'I thought I would bring her to see Grandpa's roses, and now to meet you.'

Norah shook her head. 'I don't want to see your by-blows and now you've fiddled with the roses you can go. That fool Harold spends enough time on them as it is.' Her face was tight.

Rosie gently brushed away a bee that was hovering over Lucia. No, nothing changed. 'I'm sorry I bothered you.'

She reached out and picked the dark red rose from the raised bed. It was loosely budded. She smelt it, put Lucia back in the pram, and laid the rose on her blanket. Before she left she turned. 'There have been no letters for me then? No news for Ollie about Jack?'

Norah shook her head. 'He won't come back for you. You're on your own now.'

Rosie nodded. 'I'm not on my own any more, Norah.' She looked at Lucia, then pushed her from the yard, towards the rec where she sat on the swing with Lucia in her arms and watched the children playing, the mothers sitting knitting, talking. Thinking of Lee and of herself. Of Jack, of Norah. Listening to the echoes.

Norah sat in the kitchen, stirring her tea. The door was shut against the sun and those bloody roses. Shut against the sight of her sister with the baby that she and Harold seemed unable to produce.

Yes, there had been a letter from Jack. She had destroyed it. Yes, there had been a letter to Ollie informing him that Jack was a prisoner of war. She had told Ollie that Rosie had been informed.

She sipped her tea, looking at the space where Grandpa's chair had been, at the shelves devoid of books. How dare she take things from this house? How dare she have a child and a new white shawl? How dare she be loved, because Norah had read Jack's letter before she had burnt it. How dare she be loved when Harold no longer sat opposite her in front of the fireplace, and instead went out rubbing brasses or pruning roses. How dare she?

It was a hot day when Joe and Rosie went to the Festival, and as they approached the South Bank and the Skylon that seemed to hang in the air above them, Rosie said, 'I wonder if this isn't some sort of paternalistic exercise in educating the masses. There are so many exhibitions here which seem designed to present British Society as a family divided, not by class, but by a rift between the imaginative and the practical.'

Why was she talking like this? she wondered. Lecturing and pointing towards the twenty-seven acres which lay between County Hall and Waterloo Bridge.

'Casson and the other architects have laid it out like a miniature wonderland. It's crazy when there's still so much hardship, so much ruin. There's still so much fighting in Palestine and Africa and Korea.'

That was why she was lecturing. Because she was with another man and that man was pushing her child. He had been kind, and it was good to have someone with her, but it should have been Jack.

There were thousands of others strolling with them, stopping, investigating here, by the red, white and blue awning, the role of the British in exploration and discovery. Over there, by the yellow stand, was the geology of the country. Over there by the brown was the history of the monarchy.

'This is some kind of a pat on the back, is it?' Joe said, cupping his hand round the cigarette in his mouth, protecting the match from the wind which lifted his hair. He stood with his back to the crowds, one of whom nudged him. He dropped the match. Began again.

'Yes, I suppose so. We deserve it. You just have to look around.' Rosie pushed Lucia on. 'You haven't got this kind of damage back in the States, have you? You don't have to queue for basic foodstuffs. You just call in your loans.'

Joe laughed, drew on his cigarette, flicked the match into a litter bin. 'Point taken. But this really is quite something.'

He was taking photographs now, of the piazzas, the terraces, the murals and modern sculptures. Rosie looked in one pavilion, saw the new design in furniture, the chairs with spindly legs and the spidery staircases rising into the air. They looked as though they would take no weight.

An exhibitor smiled and called her over. 'Come on, madam, try the chair.'

She looked at Joe, who nodded. 'Go on then.' He took a photo and she pulled a face and then another and he was clicking all the time and then they were laughing.

They looked at the plan of the exhibits, following the red dotted line with their fingers, and Joe said they must retrace their steps and start at the beginning or they wouldn't get any sort of an article out of all this.

They began then at The Land of Britain and Rosie took notes on how the natural wealth of the British Isles came into being. She told Joe that she was going to slant her feature by comparing the new architecture – the piazzas, the modern sculpture – with damaged Britain, utilitarian Britain, the Nissen huts, the pill-boxes. He called her a 'goddamn pinko'. They laughed and she waited but he didn't tell her how he was going to write his feature.

They moved along, listening, looking, writing, talking, and he told her that Frank was well, much better than anyone had hoped.

'More important, though, are the circulation figures. They're right up again now that he's started using a pseudonym. The money's rolling in again.'

Rosie looked at him, at his smiling face, his assured manner, the hands which carried his notepad. A woman was in the way of the pram and Rosie stopped, waited.

'Excuse me, ma'am,' Joe called. 'We're trying to get through here.'

The woman turned. Rosie smiled. 'Don't hurry, we're looking too.'

She was embarrassed that Joe had wanted to force his way through. They had all day, there was no panic. She looked at the small models of the Skylon, the symbol of the Festival, which a trader was selling. Rosie bought one, and put it on the end of the pram, and the woman came over, looked at Lucia and smiled.

'You're a lucky couple, she's lovely.'

Rosie nodded and Joe flushed. 'I know,' Rosie said and it was only later as they were looking at the photographs representing the wide range of British manufacturers that she said gently, 'You said that the circulation figures were more important than Frank and that the money is rolling in. I hardly feel that either of these things is more important than Frank. Now I must find somewhere to feed Lucia.'

She looked around. There was a tent for lost children with a red pennant on the top. Her breasts were full and heavy, they were aching. She was angry with Joe.

She pushed the pram into the tent, sat on a folding chair, put Lucia to her breast and thought of the woman who had looked at the baby and said how lucky *they* were. And though she had been angry with Joe it had been so good to pretend for that short moment that she was one of a pair. She looked at the ring on her finger. Was she always going to be alone, or would he come?

They ate sandwiches and tea at a stall and Joe said, 'I didn't mean to say that the paper was more important than Frank. I guess you must know that.'

Rosie ate the moist bread, the Wensleydale cheese.

'Do I?' she replied. 'I'm not sure that I know anything any more.'

Joe put down his cup and asked for coffee because he couldn't drink the tea. It was ninepence. 'Gee, that's a lot.'

He took it and turned back to her. 'It's just that it's everything he's worked for. He loves that paper. I love it. I work real hard now. It's coming up good. It's going to be a good investment.'

'And what about McCarthy? Do you write against that poison, Joe? Do you shout that it's wrong to victimise innocent people?'

Joe bought another coffee and they moved away to let others near. 'Frank writes against it. That's enough.'

They finished eating, then walked further but Rosie was tired and there was something wrong. She was still angry and she didn't understand why.

'I must get back now, Joe. I've some calls to make, some details for Luke's tour to tie up and the other bands too.'

He nodded, pushing a path through the crowds. 'You shouldn't have to work like this, not with a baby. It needs two.'

Rosie shrugged. 'I'm doing just fine.'

'You sure are but it's a lot to handle. You're just swell.' He leaned over and propped the Skylon upright, but it fell over again as she mounted the kerb on their way out.

'Is it still OK for this evening?' he asked.

Rosie nodded. They had planned to go with Luke and Sandy downriver to Battersea Park to see the open air sculptures and then on to the fun-fair. She hadn't wanted to go alone with Joe.

Mrs Orsini looked after Lucia that evening and they took a cab to Battersea Park which exuded so much light that it bounced off the clouds and for a moment Rosie was with Frank and Nancy in New York again.

As they arrived fireworks soared high into the air. They heard the bangs and the whizz and Joe said, 'Guess they knew we were coming and this is the welcome mat.'

Tonight he was different somehow, he talked of Frank's expertise, his kindness. He said how much he respected him, how empty life would have been if anything had happened to him, and Rosie looked at him and smiled, her anger dying.

'I'm glad you feel the same as I do.'

They linked arms with Luke and Sandy and marched in step to the fun-fair singing 'Roll Out the Barrel', and by the time they arrived Joe knew the words.

They sat on painted horses, clutched the spiralling poles, and couldn't talk because the music was so loud, but they laughed. They all laughed and then they swung in boats, the ropes slipping between their hands. They shot ducks and she wouldn't think of Jack. They threw darts and she won a teddy bear and Joe carried it for her. They laughed, sang, drank and she felt young again. So young and the lights were on the river and it was as though she was by the lake. She felt Joe's arm around her, felt his kiss on her cheek.

'It's sure good to see you again, Rosie,' he murmured, and she smiled.

'Yes, it's good to see a friend from America. It's been so long. You were kind to tell me about Frank, and send my ticket over. I shall always be grateful to you for that.' She touched his face. 'Thank you.'

Luke grabbed her, pointed towards a striped tent. 'This we have got to see.' He dragged her off and she laughed and touched his cheek too. It was good to have friends.

They tried to guess the weight of the fat woman in the striped tent and ate candy floss which stuck to their faces in melted strands. They stood and watched the horses again, then had another go, and another. In the hall of mirrors they pulled faces, stuck out their legs, lifted their arms, and laughed until they ached.

They went on to the Fairway of the South Bank and danced, she with Luke, Sandy with Joe. They jitterbugged, and there was no Palais MC to tap her on the shoulder, no forbidding notices pinned to walls.

Joe tapped Luke's shoulder and she danced with him. They jived and his arms were strong as he pulled her towards him, steered her back, moved with her and with the music. His wrists were dark against his shirt. He pulled his handkerchief from his pocket, wiped his face, threw back his head and laughed.

'This is just great.'

And it was. Then the music slowed and they danced cheek to cheek and he told her of the drive-in movies they had in the States now. How kids would drive in, take a bay, honk their horns to bring the girl car-hops to their windows, order their food, which was brought to them on a hook-on tray. How the kids kissed and loved and hooted their horns when they had gone all the way.

She didn't want to hear this. Not from Joe. He was too close. So she talked instead about the growing popularity of jazz in Britain. So many loved it and all the time she could feel his breath on her hair, the heat of his skin as he held her hand. All the time she could remember the feel of his lips and hands on her breasts and she was angry at Jack because he wasn't here. Because he hadn't written and she was lonely.

But then she was angry at herself because she was dancing to music, swaying with the rhythm, laughing, when there was a war on. And nobody seemed to care. And she didn't understand herself.

'The Gloucesters' casualty figures came in as the King inaugurated this Festival,' Rosie said against Joe's shirt.

'Speak up, Rosie, I can't hear you,' he said, quickening his pace because the music was faster now, but they were jitterbugging again and she didn't repeat her words.

They danced until midnight and she wasn't tired but her breasts were full again. They caught a cab, then walked home, all of them, and Soho was still awake and they all wanted to go on to a club, but her dress was wet from the milk and how could she tell them that? She asked them in for a coffee while she checked on Lucia, and asked Mrs Orsini if she would mind staying for longer. Mrs Orsini sat in Grandpa's chair and smiled.

'You look happy. You look twenty-one at last. That is good.'

Rosie said again, 'We'd like to go to a club. I know it's very late, but I'll do the kitchen in the morning.'

Mrs Orsini smiled. 'You feed her now then you go back down and you go to a jazz club with them and we will share the kitchen. I like to see you like this.'

She put down her knitting and held up a hand as Rosie thanked her. 'No. No thanks. You just do as an old witch tells you and be happy. Tonight you are young and you are free. Go and explore yourself. My Mario says the same.'

Rosie picked Lucia up, felt her suck the nipple and she stroked the head of Jack's child.

They went on to the 51 Club. Luke knew the man on the door. Joe bought champagne and the ice clinked in the silver bucket. Rosie ran her finger down it. It was so cold. Joe eased off the stopper with a light thud. He poured the brimming bottle, letting the froth subside in each glass, then topping them up.

'To us all,' he said and they lifted their glasses.

'To us all,' Rosie repeated and included Jack.

They listened to the jazz. The air was thick with smoke and with laughter, theirs included, and Luke said that perhaps there should be dancing at Mario's. It was happening in other clubs. He nodded towards the floor.

'Not enough room, unless we open up the annexe,' Rosie said. 'Still, no reason why not. I'll talk to Mario. But I want to talk to this group first. They're good.'

Luke laughed, but Joe didn't. 'Can't you leave your work behind for one night?'

Rosie looked at him. 'It's work I love. It's work I need. There's Lucia, you know.'

He paused, then smiled, lifting the glass to her. 'I understand,' he said, but she wondered if he did.

She worked her way through the tables, catching up with the saxophonist, a young man with glasses, as he led his group to the bar, and booked them for Luke's tour that she and Harry, the promoter, were organising. She had a full programme now and she and Luke bought the next bottle of champagne because life had been good to them this summer. Rosie nodded, she had eight bands to organise now. It felt good.

They joined the other dancers on the floor and the beat was insistent, the lights revolved, she was young, she was free and tonight she had friends and more than that, she had a partner to hold her, swirl her round, pour her drink, toast her, and the tiredness dropped from her as they danced until nearly dawn.

Joe walked her home, waving to Luke and Sandy, shrugging away their thanks. Rosie was quiet because it was different now that they were alone. It was not so safe, so easy.

The streets were emptying as they walked from one pool of light to the next and there were no ropes hanging on the lampposts. Rosie told Joe that when she and Jack had been children there had been some in Middle Street. They had tied them. She looked at her hands. She could still feel the rope.

He stopped then, caught her arms, held her to him, stared into her face.

'He's gone. He hasn't written. He won't come back. Surely you know that now. You must make a life for yourself.'

Rosie pulled away, looking up at the sky where the clouds still hung. 'I don't know that. I don't know anything. If only I knew where he was, what he's doing, what he's feeling, I would know where I was going. No, I don't know anything, Joe, only that I love him.' She wished Luke and Sandy were still here, that they were all dancing and laughing again.

She looked down again at her hands, then at Joe. 'You're going to Japan. Frank told me. See where he is. Find him for me?'

He took her hands in his. He was warm, gentle. 'We were friends, Rosie. It would have been more if you hadn't left. Do you remember the beach?'

She shook her head, but she did. Goddamn it, she did. She said, 'I know he'll write. I know he loves me. Find him for me, Joe.'

She walked back towards the flat, back towards Jack's child. Joe walked with her, his strides long, easy. He said nothing but kissed her cheek at the door.

'I'll be back in December. I'll find out what I can.'

CHAPTER 22

It had been hard to accept Nigel's death, to think that he would never go to Oxford or punt on the river as he had talked so often of doing. That he would no longer wake up in the morning and look towards the hills and say, 'It's quite exquisite.'

Jack and Steve sat against the hut wall together in the baking heat of early September and marvelled that it was still only 1951. It seemed a very long time since they had first arrived in Korea. They felt so old and they were only twenty-one.

As more days passed Steve talked of college, of the history course he would take. His parents farmed in the Mid-West and couldn't understand that he wanted to move to New York, to feel cluttered by the buildings, to hole himself up and write novels.

'They say, get a proper job. OK, so I will, but one day I'll get there.'

Jack threw pebbles at the marker Steve had dropped. He had struck twice. If he did it again it was Steve's turn.

'I've never really thought what I'd do. It was all going to wait until I finished the draft.' He threw again. The pebble missed.

'You got a lot of time to think now, bud.'

The next pebble hit. They heard the click, heard a man rush past them with his arms outstretched, his mouth pursed, roaring like an engine. Two more men came close behind him. They looked at one another and grinned. It was silly time. They stood up, kicked down the pile of stones and joined in the swooping and whirling, dodging in and out of the others. One Corporal became a helicopter.

The guards stood and watched, bemused. But then the planes started making staccato gun noises and the guards moved forward, pushing, shouting, and at a signal from the

Corporal the men stopped dead. Their arms still outstretched until there was another signal, the jerking of a head. They stood to attention, their protest made for today; confusion generated. It made them feel less powerless.

They were made to dig holes as punishment for the gun noises. The soil was dry and stony but they had all done this at basic training. There was nothing new in the world. They were ordered to fill the holes in. They had done this in basic training too.

The next week they watched a tennis match, all the men lining either side of an imaginary court in the compound. They moved their heads in unison, watching a non-existent ball, clapping as the scores were called. This time there was no punishment but it would have been worth it, even if there had been. Jack wrote it down on the extra paper that he stole during essay writing.

'Rosie might be able to make something of it,' he told Steve.

'You make something of it. I'll help.'

Jack shook his head. 'We won't be here *that* long. I'm better suited to the market stall.'

They were still there in November, though, when the cold crackled in the air. By then the ground was too hard for them to dig as punishment and so they were made to stand upright until what little sun there was had gone from the day and frost coated their clothes. A man laughed at the Chinese guards who walked by, holding hands.

Jack allowed Steve to help him draft out an article on the escapade because he wanted to discuss the confusion between cultures, the cruelty of laughter. They knew now that the fighting would go on for a long time and, therefore, they would be here for a long time too. They understood that now and were trying to stay sane, trying not to think of the news the new prisoners had told them when they had been marched into the compound.

The peace talks were being held up by the Communists who wanted all their captured men to be returned, irrespective of whether or not they wished to be. The West remembered Yalta, and would not agree to this. It was insane that they were all kept here, day after day. But they mustn't go insane, they knew that.

'It's like the First World War back there, mate,' a Lance-Jack had told them. 'We're ranged in two lines along a static front lobbing everything we can get at one another, while the politicians talk. It's a laugh a minute. Nice and quiet here, though.'

But that was before he had sat through two hours of indoctrination in Chinese, two hours of translation, then attended interviews, then written essays. They spoke to him two weeks later when he was thinner, bored, restless, longing for a home which was very far away, longing for a letter, though no mail had yet been distributed. No, none of them must go insane. They must have something to work towards, to hang on to.

A new Commandant arrived. He called each of them in for an interview. He smoked but Jack didn't. There was no tobacco any more, only that which was offered by the lecturers, the interrogators, to those who volunteered to give propaganda interviews.

The man had smooth olive skin. His voice was soft. He smiled. Jack smiled. Would it be the same as it had always been?

'What does your father do?'

'He sells vegetables.'

'What does your mother do?'

No, it was not the same.

'My mother does nothing,' Jack said, not knowing now what Maisie did. Was she still laughing with her head thrown back? Did she still make bread and dripping? Do Americans eat that? He must ask Steve. He smiled because it didn't hurt to think of her any more.

'Why you smile? You are proud that mother not work? That mother lazy?'

'My mother is not lazy. I'm smiling at something private.'

'There is nothing private. You are being cleansed here. All is open. Why you smile?'

'I smile because I love my mother.'

The Chinese looked at the interpreter, then back at Jack. Then down at his sheet.

'Why your mother not work?'

'She has a child.'

291

'She could work with your father.'

'Maybe.' Jack shrugged. He couldn't tell this man his mother had gone away with a GI. That she lived in the land where the capitalist warmongers thrived. That she had chosen to do this. He had learned here that truth was sometimes best avoided. Rosie had known that. She had been right.

'How much land your family got?'

'As big as this room.' Jack looked round. 'Yes, as big as this room.'

He could see the shed, the fence, Lee's toys. He could smell Grandpa's roses. Were they still there?

'How many cows your family got?'

'We get milk in bottles.' Yes, he could still smell the roses, and yes they would still be there. Rosie would make sure of that. And no, he wouldn't go insane, not when he had her to return to.

'How many pigs?'

'No pigs.'

'What jewels you own?'

'No jewels.'

'What coins you own?'

'No coins.' But there was the nailer's penny. Did Rosie still have that? He knew she would.

The Commandant wrote, his head down, dandruff on his shoulders, then he sat back in his chair. 'You poor peasant. You should like our ways. You should fight the capitalists.'

Jack shrugged. The questions had begun differently but the end had been the same.

He told Steve not to mention his horses, his acres, his cows. He told him not to be too generous with the truth, not to get angry, not to shout, because he knew his friend dreamed of the pit and woke groaning. Jack did too.

'Don't let him sting you into saying anything,' Jack said.

But the Commandant did sting Steve and he did shout and rage and was dragged to the pit, stripped to the waist when the cold was deep in their bones. He was there while the Americans celebrated Thanksgiving with a service and songs, not feasts.

Jack wrote about the service, about the handfuls of millet which they had cooked to eat that day, and most days. He wrote about the Pilgrims. He drew parallels between the two.

But it was muddled and that was how he wanted it to be because he would need it like that when Steve was released.

He showed it to Steve when he came out. He made him sit and read it, while others threw their jackets over him, and blankets too, all donated by the men who had heated water for him to drink.

'Get away, Jack,' Steve said, pushing the paper aside, trying to curl over. 'Just get away. I've had enough. It's never going to end.'

But Jack had known he would say this. It was what he would have felt and he also knew that if he took the paper away it would be the beginning of the end. So he dragged Steve upright.

'Come on, Steve, I can't get it right. It's confused. You can help.'

Steve was pushing him away again, but Jack came back, shoving the paper in his face. Steve took it, scrunched it up, threw it across the room, and lay down. Rob, another prisoner, brought the paper back to Jack and helped to support Steve.

'Read this, you goddamn give-upper. You bloody Yanks, you're all the same.' Jack wasn't shouting, but his face was close to Steve's. He wasn't angry either, but Steve wasn't going to be allowed to give up. Those who did so died and Jack wasn't going to lose this friend who was so like Ed.

He straightened out the paper but again Steve knocked it from him, and it took an hour to force him to look at it. He stabbed at the second paragraph with a dirt-choked finger.

'Take it out. Who wants to know that garbage? Ain't you got no sense, Jack?' His voice was tired, angry, but he was reading it. Jack rewrote it in the morning and again Steve turned it down and it wasn't until the evening of the second day that he nodded, but Jack didn't care whether it was good or not, Steve was back on side. That was what mattered.

They attended lectures as before, threw stones at markers, as before, and Steve said, 'No more pit for either of us, eh?'

Jack nodded. 'Yep, let's get to the end of all this, then go out and get blind drunk, once in England, once in New York.'

They rose. It was time for afternoon lectures and the young men who filled the camp wondered how the minutes could drag so slowly, how their bones could ache with boredom, but they did. Day after day after day.

293

The next week they were all called into the big hut and saw a prisoner sitting alongside the Commandant. There were Chinese cigarettes on the table in front of him. The Commandant rose.

'You not have group study this morning. You have morning to self because one has behaved with great satisfaction.' He pointed to the prisoner who stared ahead.

'This man has seen the truth. He will go now from the camp and he will tell the world on the radio of the crimes of the Imperialists. He will tell of the wrongness of his attitude which has given way to correctness.'

There was silence in the room.

'You too can leave this camp. You too can see the truth. Your countries are not interested in you. You are still here. The war goes on. You are behind wire, play foolish tricks while warmongers eat in restaurants. Your wives live well without you. The years pass. Even if you do go home, we can reach you. You are never free of us. It is better to be a friend than enemy.'

He took a cigarette from the pack and gave it to the man, who put it between his lips. He was thin, drawn and his eyes still looked straight ahead. The Commandant lit the cigarette, smoke spiralled up to the wooden roof. Jack watched it disappear.

There was still silence, even when they were dismissed. The words were the same as they had been on previous occasions and there had been silence then. No one booed, no one blamed the man. It was his way of surviving.

'Gets to you, though, doesn't it?' Steve said as they crouched on the ground and threw stones at the marker. Jack had won thirteen games, Steve eighteen. 'Guess the months could become years.'

Jack nodded, looking round at the hills dusted with snow. It was so cold. He looked up at the sky, it was cloud-heavy. There might be snow tomorrow. Where could they throw their stones? It was better to think of that.

But the next week they were told it was over. The guards herded them into columns, the Commandant stood before them, the snow falling on his cap, his pressed olive green uniform, his soft golden skin, as he told them 'All prisoners go home'.

It was too sudden. He could not believe it, but then he felt Steve's hand on his arm. 'We're going to make it, Jack.' And then the joy came, coursing through him from deep inside.

They were dismissed. For a moment they could not move, then they leaped in the air, whooping, cheering, some crying. They were going home, goddamn it, they were going home. Jack thought of Rosie, of running down the alley towards her, of her arms as she came out of Grandpa's yard. Then he thought of the prisoner who had taken cigarettes in return for survival. Would he go home?

Joy pushed the hunger and the cold away. It brought smiles to faces which had stiffened into grim endurance. It brought hope into faces which had been without for too long. They were going home.

They were marched to a train, the snow soaking into their worn uniforms and through the split seams of their boots, but they marched in time, their few possessions slung on their backs.

The Sergeant called out the drill orders. Their shoulders were straight. They took the walking wounded, helping them, bearing their weight, and Jack felt the stones he had thrown at the marker in his pocket. They could be kept with Grandpa's penny.

He turned and looked back at the mountains. 'How exquisite,' he said.

Steve nodded his goodbye to Nigel too.

They were marched to a train. There were no seats but it didn't matter. They would be home for Christmas. They headed south in the last of the daylight, looking out across the country, seeing the ruins, the devastation, the napalm-damaged hills. The people were living in dugouts, hovels. There was nothing but poverty, but they were working, stolidly clearing the snow, cooking over open fires, ignoring the train. Jack wrote about this for as long as the daylight lasted, asking what the fighting had been about, but soon it was too dark to see the page.

There was no light then, no food, no drink. They sat on the floor, moving with the train, huddled together for warmth.

'My mom'll be pleased,' Steve said, his voice a murmur like all the others.

'I'll write to mine but first I'll see Rosie,' Jack said.

Before daylight broke they eased into a tunnel and stayed there throughout the day to avoid the air strikes. So the fighting wasn't over, the Sergeant asked the guard, looking uncertain.

'No, you being exchanged,' the guard said.

They had water, they had food, but they were colder now and blew on to their hands, draping old blankets over their shoulders. But did any of it matter? They were going home. They were bloody well going home.

Bob sat with them, talking of the food he would cook on his wife's stove in their prefab.

'I don't know, you retreads. You've all gone soft,' Steve laughed. 'Let her do the cooking.'

Jack laughed too, wondering how reservists could bear to be called up, having already done their bit, and then he thought of Tom. He would not be going back. He thought of Suko too and hoped that she would find happiness.

Bob told them how he would cut the rind off the bacon, fry that until it was crisp, then the bacon, then the mushrooms picked the evening before from fields behind the house. He would take the sharp knife from the drawer, slice the tomatoes, grown against the wall behind the house, and fry them too. He would walk up the ash path to pick the warm eggs from the coop, the straw still on the shells. Soon the whole wagon was listening, hearing the fat spitting, tasting the bacon, the British not caring that it was the wrong season for tomatoes, not caring that bacon was still on ration. It was home, and that was where they were going, and now they cheered and laughed even when the guards swung back the door and said, 'Quiet. You should sleep. Quiet.'

How could they sleep? They were leaving here. The big man himself had said so.

They travelled on south as darkness came. On the fifth night they were shunted into a siding near Pyongyang where they stayed for a week, asking the guards each day when they would be released.

'When Captain come,' they said.

The men used a bucket as a latrine, pushing it far into the corner. They squashed lice which still bit them in spite of the cold, but none of this was for long and so it didn't matter.

296

On the eleventh day a Chinese Captain slid open the wagon door and they clambered to their feet, pushing towards the entrance. Other guards put up their rifles as the Captain said, 'You go north instead. Prisoner-of-war camp. A mistake has been made.' He smiled and slammed the door shut and there was only darkness, only silence. It had been a trick, but a darker trick than the ones they had played. It was a pitch black trick.

It broke three of the men. It nearly broke all of them. Hope had gone. Hate had come for many of them, but not for Jack. He had had enough of hate. He just wrote it down and Steve helped. They made Bob help too because he cursed and swore, beating the side of the wagon with his fists. He wasn't the only one who came close to despair as the train swept north again. There were tears too, in the darkness of the night.

'Funny trick, eh?' Steve whispered to Jack, his voice full.

'Capped our games in the camp, didn't it? Quick learners, eh?' The tears were dry on Jack's cheeks now, there would be streaks in the dirt. He rubbed his skin.

'The goddamn bastards.'

'Maybe we could try and escape,' Jack whispered. He couldn't bear to think of the train taking him further and further from Rosie. He wanted to break from it, hurl the guards to one side, rush for the South. 'Can't be too far from the lines now, but with each day, it's further. We'll talk as we march.'

A guard had told them they were leaving the train the next morning. They waited, sitting with their arms around their knees, resting their heads, but not sleeping. No one was sleeping. How could they when the disappointment was so sharp, the anger so raw?

They were marched from the train, out into a road cleared of snow.

'To another camp,' the guards said, pointing north.

The Sergeant lined the men up before they left, ignoring the guards who gestured for them to begin. He stood before them, looking as thin as they did, but ramrod straight, his eyes sweeping the men. 'You'll march in step. You'll remember who you are. You'll not let these buggers beat you, or I shall have your heads for my breakfast and your danglies for my lunch. Is that quite clear?'

The men smiled and nodded.

The Sergeant barked, 'About turn.' He ignored the guard who was pulling at his clothes and shouting at his men to hurry. 'Forward march.'

It was only then that the men moved, and they did so in perfect unison. It was only after the first mile that the pace slowed but they were still in time. They would be until they dropped now.

Before Steve and Jack could make their move, two Americans ducked out of the line as it passed between wooded slopes. They sneaked off into the undergrowth. Jack watched them snake across the snow-covered rice field to the base of the hill. They were stark against the white and their footsteps were clear.

Ten minutes later, the alarm was raised. North Korean guards found them two hours later and beat them to death.

Later Jack looked up at the condensation trails behind the shooting stars as the north-west jet streams pushed the planes home and nodded when Steve said, 'Seems kinda pointless. Might as well get through school, buddy.'

They both nodded, still marching, still watching the men in front, blocking out the two beaten bodies which had been thrown into the ox-cart. Those men would never go home now.

They marched until January, through deep forests where all sound was deadened, dragging their legs through thick snow, pulling their balaclavas low. Snow fell from branches, whooshing through the frost-laden air.

'It's quite exquisite,' Steve said and Jack nodded.

Finally, in driving snow, they reached the camp and were pushed into a large barn.

Their Sergeant was saluted by men who were already gathered in the building. One stepped forward.

'Fellow students, we welcome you to this college of correction. I am Sergeant Howe,' he said and bowed.

'How exquisite,' said Jack, bowing back, and they began to laugh, all of them, too loudly and too long, but it was a laugh.

They were given padded overcoats by the Communists which they thought was a trick, but which Sergeant Howe said was part of the 'lenient policy'. They waited in the barn for the interrogation which they knew must come, and then there would be the lecture and the translation.

It came and Jack looked at the Chinese who asked him how much land he had. What his mother did. What his father did. Jack answered him, wanting to ask in return, 'And what have your people just done to our hopes? Did you think it was funny?' but he just answered the questions as they all did, then sat and listened to the lecture, and to the translation, because this was their life now until they left it on an ox-cart or the war was over.

It was eight in the evening before they were released from the barn to their clay and wattle huts which were heated by tiny wood-burning stoves. The floorboards were covered by straw mats with a narrow aisle down the middle.

They slept shoulder to shoulder. The wind swept through gaps in the clay and their breath froze on their blankets, on their lips, as the night hours passed. No one talked, but no one slept either. They had been so close to escape and now they were back at the beginning again.

Early in the morning loudspeakers blared Soviet and Chinese revolutionary music over the compound and Jack leaned up on his elbow.

'I think I prefer Butlins, on the whole,' he said and pushed the despair away, because it was a new morning and he must live each day, if he was to return to Rosie. And he would return.

Before roll-call at seven a.m. the new men, including Jack and Steve, were put on the wood-collecting rota.

'I guess everything's back to normal now,' Steve muttered and he, like Jack, began again. They all did.

They ran across to the lean-to communal latrine in temperatures which were forty degrees below zero and ran back because it was too cold to walk. They had to stand, though, for roll-call and thought that they would die.

Then they did physical jerks as the Commandant ordered. The snow glistened at the edge of the compound and the twilight of the winter morning turned into daylight and the cold air cut into their throats and chests.

One hour before breakfast the squad leader, Corporal Jackson, read a Communist publication aloud in their hut with a guard at the door. He read without pausing for full stops, for correct pronunciation, but used his own. It lightened the morning.

299

Four men collected the food from the camp kitchen where it was cooked in pots, carrying it back to the hut in a large bucket. The men placed their rice bowls and cups round the bucket and millet was spooned out into each. They ate it standing or sitting on their straw mats, talking quietly.

Another four men drew water into another bucket and wash-pan from the kitchens, where there was a gasoline drum full of water which was kept full over a fire which burned from dawn to dusk.

A bell rang at 10.00 hours and they went with the other men of their squad to the lecture room, where they sat with legs crossed on the bare boards and listened while they were instructed on the Marxist philosophy in Chinese, and then again in translation whilst their ears and noses felt that they would drop off with the cold.

They broke at midday, ate rice which contained a few tiny pieces of pork.

'It's a better camp,' Steve said.

'The Commies have officially decided that they'll not convert us all by cruelty. They're trying kindness to turn us into eager little beavers who will spread the message back home, when we get back. Make the most of it. Who knows how long it will last,' the Sergeant said.

They sluiced their bowls, then walked in the compound, taking note of the sentry at the gate and the sentry posts at intervals around the perimeter. They watched the village life which went on outside the wire and Jack remembered the Italian prisoners and how they had given the evacuees apples and showed them pictures of their children. He thought of the hot meal he had eaten. The prisoners probably ate better than the villagers. The whole thing was crazy.

At 14.30 hours they were back in the unheated hall and now the prisoners were made to read aloud from Marxist books and they did so, with no regard for punctuation or meaning.

The lecturer then picked Jack out to give his opinion on the chapter that had just been read.

Jack had listened to the beginning and the end so he stood up and repeated, 'The philosphical basis of Marxism is dialectical materialism which is hostile to all religion. Marxists feel that religion defends exploitation and drugs the working classes.'

He sat down.

'Proper little swot, aren't we?' grinned Bob.

'But what is your opinion of it?' the lecturer insisted.

'Oh-oh,' whispered Steve as Jack rose to his feet.

'Love is an opiate, so is alcohol. They exist. Religion exists. It gives ease as the others do and comfort. Therefore my opinion is that as religion exists so does its use as an instrument of peace and comfort.'

There was silence as he sat.

'Didn't understand much of that,' Steve murmured.

'Neither did I,' Jack replied.

'Neither did he, from the look of him.' Bob was looking at the lecturer who looked at the guards, then shrugged and asked another man for his opinion of Jack's opinion.

The hours crept on and in the evening they were issued with Russian and Chinese papers, translated into English. They used the paper to roll marijuana cigarettes in the summer, the Corporal told them, tearing the outside edge of three of the sheets, but only three, because the guards took the papers back at the end of the evening.

The next afternoon they were issued with paper and pencils and ordered to write an essay on 'Why the unjust aggressor is in Korea'. Jack managed to take two pieces of paper and, writing on both sides of one, he kept the other so his lessons could begin again that night with Steve.

And so the hours and the days slowly passed. Sometimes there were letters though none from Rosie, but then many people had none. They wrote letters too, but doubted that any were sent.

January became February and then it was March which limped into April and the days were still filled with boredom, with hunger, with cold and nothing changed with the coming of spring but the weather.

CHAPTER 23

By mid December '51 Rosie and Mario had extended the club, using the annexe for tables, leaving space in the back room for dancing. Luke and Sandy had left to tour Britain, along with the Larkhill Boys Rosie had met in the club with Joe.

'Bookings are good,' Luke rang to say. 'Full houses everywhere. Harry's bought himself another gold watch. You'll be able to do the same.'

'Or maybe Father Christmas will do that for me,' Rosie laughed. 'See you in January. Take care, all of you.' She put the phone down and looked round her small flat.

The table lamps lit the room softly, illuminating Grandpa's books. He would like it here, not as much as in his own home, but he would like it. There was a small half-knitted cardigan lying on the workbasket. She reached for it, began knitting, listening to the fire which hissed in the grate. She missed Luke and the boys. She measured the length of the cardigan then decreased for the armhole. It was ten o'clock. She was tired. She should sleep but each day and each night she waited for Joe to phone with news of Jack. He hadn't yet.

She finished the armholes, caught the remaining stitches on a holder, cast on for the left front, knitted up to the armhole, but her eyes were dry and sore. Rosie looked at the clock again. Eleven. She put her knitting away and went to bed, hearing Lucia breathing quietly in the cot beside her. The baby hadn't stirred since her feed at ten. She would sleep through until seven. She was perfect.

On 19 December she received a Christmas card from Frank and Nancy together with a present of a $50 bill which she put into the bank with the rest of her money. There would be no gold watch for her. There was a long future to build. She read their letter as she waited for the spaghetti to cook in the café kitchen.

Lower Falls
15th December

Dearest Rosie,

Well, your skis are still in your room, the snow is here but you aren't. We understand though, really we do. Joe told us how busy you are and we can remember how hard we worked when we took over the paper. One day, we'll come to you.

Frank is well. He writes his columns, and edits the paper unofficially, makes his 'pinko' stand for common sense. Two of his friends still can't find regular work but pick up whatever they can. They will never write again, as long as McCarthy can stand up and give the performances that he does.

It is thought that maybe Eisenhower will throw his hat into the ring for the elections. Maybe he will be able to bring him to heel. Enough of that. We survive. I hope it isn't that which keeps you from us? But even as I say that, I know it can't be. Forgive me. It's just that you start leaping at shadows some days, so many friends have turned their backs.

It was so strange, wasn't it, the way the shooting stopped in Korea at the end of November following the establishment of the truce line along the 38th parallel. Joe filed his copy on it, saying no one ordered it, it just happened. For a moment there was peace.

I can't hold out much hope on a full armistice for a long while. The repatriation of the prisoners of war is the stumbling block. Have you heard from Jack? What is that boy playing at? How did you get on with Joe? He's a good reporter. He's sending back some good copy.

Have a wonderful Christmas, Rosie. The house will be empty without you, darling. Dare we say we will see you in 1952?

Your ever loving
Nancy

Nancy did not mention the feature Rosie had written about the Festival. Perhaps there was too much happening with them over there. Rosie wished she could go, but she couldn't.

Mrs Orsini, Mario and Rosie decorated the café and the club the next day, tying together holly with red ribbon bought from Mrs Eaves, pinning it up in corners, sitting Lucia up in her pram so that she could see, stringing streamers across the room. The customers helped. Mrs Eaves helped too and somehow there was enough laughter to wash away another Christmas without Jack, without news even.

On the evening of the twenty-second Rosie cut, coloured and pasted chains for her flat, showing Lucia who banged her rattle on the blanket in front of the fire, turning from her front on to her back, kicking her feet, pushing the rattle into her mouth, dribbling. Rosie kissed her cheeks, they were wet, pure.

She picked up her child and held her, seeing Jack in her movements, in her smile. She carried her to the window, looking out over the rooftops, hearing the jazz, the shouting and the laughter.

'Where are you, Jack?' she called, breath clouding the window.

A telegram came from Joe the next day, while she was serving customers and Mrs Eaves with mince-pies.

'Have news stop Be with you 24th stop Joe'

Rosie put it down. Mrs Eaves read it, folded it, put it away, then asked Mrs Orsini to babysit for Lucia while Rosie came with her to the West End.

Rosie looked at her, then started to put sugar into bowls. They were too full. There would be news tomorrow. It would be Christmas Eve and there would be news. How could she wait that long? Why was it so hard to breathe?

'Come on then, get your coat,' Mrs Eaves said, picking up her handbag and her gloves, pulling them on, pushing up between her fingers. 'Come on, get your coat, I said. Let's get you through this evening anyway. And don't worry. It can't be bad news or he would have cabled you earlier.'

They walked out into the crisp air. There was jazz all around, coming up from cellars, mingling with calypso, with swing. Tomorrow there would be news and she couldn't bear the minutes that had to pass until then.

Chestnuts cooked on braziers, sailors on leave entered the pubs, finding accommodation for their leave, amongst the homosexuals or the girls. Tarts lingering in doorways called, 'Merry Christmas, Rosie. I'll be in later for a coffee.'

Mrs Eaves took her arm and pointed to the Christmas tree outside the pub. There were streamers on it and candles which weren't lit. 'They'll light them at midnight on Christmas Eve, as they always do, now the war's over,' the publican said, as he waved to them from the doorway.

But the war wasn't over. Not the one Jack was fighting and the thousands of other young men.

They caught a bus, singing carols with the Salvation Army band as they waited. They went up to the West End, walked along Oxford Street, then, catching another bus, walked along Shaftesbury Avenue, looking at the billboards; and then they went back to Soho which they both preferred, which they both knew now. At least the evening was passing. There was only the long night to get through and some of the next day.

Joe didn't come until six p.m. on Christmas Eve when the café had closed. Rosie stood at the door of her flat, watching as he climbed the stairs. There was a small decorated Christmas tree fixed into a log in his hand. He held it out. Rosie's breath was shallow again.

'For Lucia,' he said. His mac was open, his belt dragged on the floor. It was dirty, muddy.

Rosie nodded, stood aside to let him enter. The tree smelt of pine. She placed it beneath the window. By the morning the room would smell too. It would be fresh and clean and pure but she couldn't wait any longer. She turned.

'Tell me,' she said.

Joe smiled, shrugged. He looked tired, there were bags under his eyes, lines across his forehead. 'Well, the good news is that he's safe. He's a POW. His father should have been notified. I don't know why he didn't let you know. Something went wrong somewhere. Anyway, Jack is one of the lucky ones. At least he's been named as a prisoner by the Communists. Thousands of them have just been sucked in and lost.'

Rosie turned to the bright sky, to the stars, to the jazz which she could hear drifting up, along with the steam from the clubs and pubs. It was going to be a good Christmas, she thought, as the joy surged within her. He was safe, he was out of the

305

fighting. He had not come back because he couldn't, that was all.

'So that's why he hasn't written,' she murmured, putting her hand to her mouth.

Joe wrestled with his tie, pulling it loose, unbuttoning his collar. He looked around, saw the bottles on the table and asked, 'Can I pour myself a drink?'

Rosie came across the room, poured the bourbon Mario had found for her and then one for herself. Joe could have the crown jewels for bringing that news.

'I've no ice,' she said, feeling the smile broaden on her face.

'Drink up, Rosie. I said that was the *good* news.' Joe swirled his drink round in the glass. It was amber in the soft light. The fire was hissing. She looked at the tree. She shouldn't have smiled, that was it. Or made the streamers. If she hadn't made the streamers it would have been good news only. No, she didn't want to hear any more. She knew the important news, didn't she?

'Take your mac off, Joe,' she said, sipping the bourbon. It was harsh in her throat. The glass was cold. She put it down on the small table by Grandpa's chair, carried the mac across to the hook on the back of the door. It smelt of Joe, of America. It should smell of Korea. Why was it so hard to breathe? Why did her throat ache like this?

She walked back, sat in Grandpa's chair.

'Tell me now, then.'

She didn't look at him, but at the Christmas tree, at the chains she had made, but which would have been better left unmade. Then she looked at the fire as he told her that he had discovered in Japan that Jack had fallen in love with a Japanese girl called Suko. That they had had an affair, that he was to marry her on his return. That he would never be coming back to her and that was why he had never written.

She looked at the glass of bourbon on the table, she pulled it to the edge, tipped it, breaking the vacuum as they had done at the Lake Club when they were so very, very young. There was no vacuum, but what did it matter?

She drank, then looked at the tree, at the fire, at the chains, at Joe who stood there, looking down at her.

He moved towards her, knelt, touched her knee, her arm. 'I'm so sorry. So very sorry.'

'At least he's safe,' she said but she didn't want Joe there. She didn't want anyone there. She wanted to push him away, he was making the room dark. He was taking what air there was. She couldn't hear the hissing of the fire while he was there. She couldn't see the chains. She couldn't see the tree, but it was his tree. He had bought it for Jack's daughter. He had been kind. And there was no pain yet. For God's sake, the pain hadn't come yet.

'Come for Christmas,' she said. 'For lunch. You mustn't be alone. No one should be alone.'

She stood now, keeping the glass in her hand. She walked to the door, took the coat off the hook and gave it to Joe, because the pain was beginning and it was hard to breathe. So hard to breathe.

He left, walking softly down the stairs.

She called, 'There can be no mistake?'

He stopped and turned. 'No, Rosie, no mistake. I can vouch for that.' And what did it matter, he thought, as he moved down the stairs, what did it matter if he had lied. That man didn't deserve her. She was far more suited to him.

The Christmas meal was held in Mario's flat. Mrs Orsini drank sweet sherry and gave some to Rosie because the older woman had heard the news. They pulled homemade crackers and Joe gave her a gold watch and she smiled, felt its coolness against her skin, felt his fingers as he did up the catch. She held it up to the light.

'Luke will be pleased,' she murmured. 'Thanks, Joe.' She wished that Luke and Sandy were here.

She heard her voice from a distance, saw his smile. She gave Lucia Grandpa's nailer's penny, hung now on a silver chain. She pulled her cracker, ate turkey, ate Christmas pudding, found silver sixpences, fed Lucia, sat by the fire, listened to the King's speech but was dying inside.

Joe came the next day and the next and the next, helping, talking, comforting. He played with Lucia who laughed and held her hands out to him. He took the baby to the park, then hoovered the flat for Rosie, typing out his copy, talking to her about her writing, about the Cougars, about the tennis courts

307

at the lake, about Frank and Nancy, about a world which did not include Jack.

She worked in the café, she played with Lucia, she wrote a letter of thanks to Frank and Nancy and on New Year's Eve she stayed up until midnight in the Orsinis' flat and Joe clicked his glass against hers when the clock struck twelve.

'Happy 1952,' he said, and smiled and both their gold watches glinted in the light from the Orsinis' lamps but Rosie wanted her own lamps, her own fire, and could bear all this no longer. She ran from them, taking Lucia, running up the stairs, laying her child down in her cot, stroking the hair that was Jack's, kissing the smile that was his too.

Now the pain broke and she stood at the window, hearing the music. And she cried, great racking sobs, because he wouldn't be in her life again, but how could he not be? He was part of her. His memories were hers. They had swung on the rope tied to the lamppost together. They had smelt the hops, they had stolen the cheeses. How could he do this?

Then she felt terrible rage, searing violent rage. He had shared her life, hated her, loved her, thrust himself into her, torn her, taken her in his confusion and now he had forgotten her and all their years together. Goddamn you, Jack. I hate you, I hate you.

She leaned against the window and hated him, loved him, wanted him, wanted Nancy, wanted the comfort of arms about her. And then Joe came. He held her, his arms were strong, and they had memories too. The lake was there as he soothed and stroked. The lake and the sun and the long sloping lawns where she had known peace and love. Where everything had been so much easier.

He carried her to the bed, he undressed her and undressed himself and she clung to him because he was part of Frank and Nancy's world. He was kind, he was here, he wanted her. Jack didn't. His hands had found someone else's body; his mouth, someone else's mouth.

But Joe was too fast for her, and it was as if they were at the barbecue by the lake again with his lips on her breasts, his hands on her body. She knew she only wanted comfort, nothing more than that, but what did it matter? What did any of it matter? She shut her mind to the face which loomed over her, to the body too close, too heavy. The body which wasn't Jack's and which was entering her, filling her, and now she held him, because passion of a sort was sweeping her too. Passion born of anger, of pain.

In the morning they walked Lucia in her pram across the frost-hardened grass, carving out patterns on the ground. Her hand was warm in his, her lips too, from the kiss he gave her, and it was good not to be alone. But Jack was still everywhere and her love for him was too, and her anger and her pain.

But as the weeks wore on and Joe was seconded to a Fleet Street paper it became easy to be with him. He laughed, he joked, he tossed Lucia in the air and took her back to the time she had shared with Frank and Nancy.

At night she forced herself not to think of Jack as Joe kissed her and held her, because Jack had held another, he loved another. The waiting was over. Their love was over.

But she dreamed of him. Each night she dreamed of him and woke up crying, wanting to clutch at the image, wanting to shake it, hurt it, as she was hurting.

In February the King died and Frank wrote asking for a feature from each of them. Separate ones please, he said, which Rosie thought was strange, because how else would they do it? She left Mario to take any messages and wrote about the black armbands the children were wearing, the adults were wearing, she was wearing. She wrote of the simple oak casket which was moved from Westminster Hall to St George's Chapel. She wrote of the thousands of subjects who paid their last respects to this man who had brought them through war and peace.

The coffin left Westminster on a gun carriage. Big Ben rang out one beat a minute to mark the fifty-six years of the King's life and many of the men and women who stood with Rosie wept. And Rosie wept too.

The Household Cavalry, in ceremonial dress, walked in slow time to Paddington station where the royal train was waiting. As the cortège passed Marlborough House, Queen Mary, the King's mother, stood at the window and bowed her head and the crowd wept again.

Rosie wrote about the woman who turned to her while she was writing and asked who all the words were for. Rosie told her. 'Tell them we loved him,' the woman said.

Joe was covering the story at the Windsor end and when he arrived back that evening he hugged her, kissed her, his lips eager, his tongue searching her mouth. His nose was cold from the frost-full air, and so were his hands as he slipped them beneath her shirt. She laughed and kissed his neck and felt his hands become warm as they stroked her back, her breasts.

'You had a good day then,' she murmured, glad that someone was coming home to her each day, glad that she was becoming used to it, welcoming it, wanting Jack to know that she was not alone either.

Joe kissed her forehead, tucking her shirt back in, moving away, laughing.

'I sure did, so let's have your notes, I'll put this together and then we have the evening left for better things.' He laughed again and reached forward, rubbing his finger around her mouth.

Rosie smiled. It was good to be wanted at last. 'No. I'll write mine. You write yours. That's what Frank asked for.'

She moved to Grandpa's chair and began to write. Joe came towards her. 'Oh, come on, Rosie. Let's put it into one. It'll make a better feature. Won't take me a minute.'

But she refused because George VI had been *her* king, not his.

'Perhaps you should write about the return of the Duke of Windsor for his brother's funeral. That might appeal to the Americans,' she said, wanting to soften her refusal.

'Trying to teach me my job?' His voice was cold.

Lucia called out from the bedroom Rosie had made for her out of the boxroom. She moved towards the door. She didn't want this row. She didn't want any rows. There had been enough struggle already, hadn't there?

'No, you know your job. I know mine.' She didn't want to talk about this any more. She was too tired.

'I still think it would make a better feature. We'll split the fee.'

Rosie stopped. 'Look, Joe. It's not the goddamn money. I don't need the money so much any more. It's just that I have something I want to say from the British point of view. You wouldn't understand.'

Joe moved towards her, pulling her back towards the chairs. 'Oh, come on. I don't give up easy. Let's talk this over.'

'I've told you. No.' Rosie pulled away. He had hurt her wrist. Her watch had dug into her skin. She rubbed it and returned to the door. Now she was angry. 'Goddamn no.' She was shouting. Lucia cried.

Joe left her then, picking up his mac, thudding down the stairs, pushing aside Lucia's pram, scoring the hall wall, and by the time he returned she had finished her feature and posted it. He was drunk. He was sorry. So was she, because he was a good man, a kind man.

Joe knelt by Grandpa's chair and kissed her and she kissed him back because he had soothed her, comforted her, and there was some sort of caring growing inside her for him, though she didn't know how much.

February grew colder and Rosie pulled the blankets up around Lucia's shoulders when they went out. Lucia was sitting up now, pulling herself forward, pointing, her nose red in the cold. Joe never again drank as much as he had on the night of the King's funeral. Instead he talked of the future, of Frank's paper, of the need to keep it in the family, of his love for her.

At night his body sought hers and she liked the feel of his hands and his lips and now she stroked him too, held him, kissed him, and the dreams of Jack were not so fierce. But still they came.

Lucia was pulling herself up, using the table, and it was good to share these moments with someone else. But Rosie still read the news about Korea.

Nancy wrote to say that she was sorry, so sorry about Jack, but it didn't seem like the boy Rosie had loved. Was she sure of her facts?

But Rosie wouldn't allow herself to think about Jack any more, at least while she was awake. She had been working harder in these last few months than she had ever done before. She took phone calls late into the night and made them too, adding to the stable of bands, moving more and more into the

311

promotion side, enjoying the battles, enjoying the triumphs, pushing away the failures.

Joe didn't like it. He didn't like the phone ringing when he was stroking her hair, when he was kissing her mouth. He put on the radio too loud so that she had to strain to hear. But he was so kind and he comforted her, she told herself. He had found out about Jack for her. And it was better than being alone, wasn't it? And after all he had said he would listen to the band again now that Luke was coming home and send his final report to Bob. Rosie planned a party and Joe helped to lay out the drinks in Mario and Mrs Orsini's flat, because her own wasn't big enough. And then Luke was home and the gramophone played Bix Beiderbecke. Luke and Jake kissed her, held her, gave her a package. It was a gold watch.

She took it from the box, held it and couldn't speak but then Joe came up.

'Beat you to it, fellers.' He lifted Rosie's arm, pulled back her sleeve.

Luke and Jake flushed, then laughed, but Rosie didn't laugh. She took off Joe's watch and put it in her bag. She offered her wrist to Luke and he slipped the new one on.

'I'll wear one today, one tomorrow,' Rosie said, knowing that Joe had stiffened. Jack would have waited until he saw whether or not she could cope. But she mustn't think of him.

She took Joe's arm, kissed his cheek, led him away, poured him a drink and told him he was handsome, kind, loving. Soon he was laughing again and asking her to book Luke for Mario's club so that he could hear the group again.

The music was softer now and Luke came and danced with Rosie, holding her. He was familiar and he was safe. She told him that she was sleeping with Joe. She told him that the memory of Jack still hurt so much. He nodded.

'Don't rush into anything. Remember what your grandpa said.'

She didn't rush anywhere. She woke, worked, loved, slept and the days passed, but it always seemed dark. It had seemed dark since Christmas. She was tired. She ached inside. Joe was with her but the loneliness remained.

*

At the end of March Rosie received a letter from Frank enclosing $50 for the article on the King's funeral.

Lower Falls
20th March

Dearest Rosie,
    Yes, this is what I wanted. All your own work. I didn't tell you that the paper spiked your feature on the Festival. You copied Joe's ideas about drawing comparisons between the new ideas and the Nissen huts, the austerity etc. I faced him with it. He'd been having some trouble handling domestic features, you know. He told me he had talked his ideas over with you. That you must have 'borrowed' them.
    I was sorry you did that but he said things were tough, you might have become confused. I can understand that happening. I've done it myself. I was worried about you. You must have been real upset, real tired, but I guess things are better.

I wanted you to know I love you.
Frank

Rosie waited for the day to pass. Waited until Joe came home. She worked, she phoned, she cancelled one booking because the manager of the theatre was known to pass drugs. Her boys were too good for that. She took a taxi to Middle Street. She walked past 15 and 17 down to the rec. The wooden fencing was still up around the bombed houses.

'Will it ever be finished?' she murmured into Lucia's hair, sitting on the swing, hearing her laugh.

She cooked a meal for herself, not for Joe. Not ever again for Joe.

He came in at seven. Lucia was in bed.

Rosie stood by the window. He slung his mac over the arm of the chair, poured a bourbon with his strong tanned hands. His cuff was white against his skin, his teeth white too. His watch golden. He was such a golden boy. He belonged at the Lake Club, not here. He moved towards her, kissed her, put his arm about her.

She handed him the letter, not watching as he read it but knowing when he had finished because he moved away.

For a moment there was silence, and then Joe said, 'I know what this must look like.'

'You must go,' Rosie said, looking at him now. 'You really must go.'

There was no anger in her voice. Just as there was no anger in it when she was dealing with difficult promoters and managers. That was business. This was business. Nothing else now.

'I'm not going. I belong with you. I love you. Together we can do things. We can build up the paper. Take over from Frank. It's all I've ever wanted, you know that. Married to you, that's possible.' He moved to her now, gripping her arm. 'We need each other. Jack's gone. You need me.'

She looked at his hand on her arm and then at him. He dropped his hand.

Rosie said, 'I've packed your bags. They're in the café, by the counter. I'm surprised you didn't see them.'

His lips were thin now and there was no love in his face. There never had been, she could see that now. 'If you do this I'll tell them about Lucia. I'll tell Bob to turn down Luke.' Joe was shouting, gripping her arm again.

Such short clean nails, suitable for the Lake Club. So very suitable. She moved away and again his hand dropped as she picked up his mac. It was still cold, damp and smelt of Joe. It meant nothing to her.

'Get out, Joe. I can't trust you, so there's nothing left.'

'I only wanted you so I'd get the paper.' He was spitting out the words, his shoulders rigid, his hands clenched into fists.

'And I've used you too, and I'm sorry,' Rosie said, holding the door, nodding to him as he stood there, large in this small room where he was now an intruder. 'Please go now, Joe.'

He started to say, 'You're a bitch . . .' but then stopped, shaking his head. 'Rosie, can't we . . . ?'

She shook her head, handing him his mac. He snatched it from her, turned, flung it at the window, driving a glass ashtray to the floor. It broke and only then did he leave, his mac lying crumpled on the sill.

Rosie quietly closed the door, knelt and picked up the splinters. She wouldn't need an ashtray now. She didn't smoke. Grandpa was right. Second best was no good.

She carried the broken glass through to the kitchen in Joe's mac, dropped them in the bin, then stood at the window listening to the sounds of the streets, to a soft cough from Lucia. Yes, he was right, it was better to be alone.

Rosie wrote to Frank and Nancy, telling them that she and Joe had quarrelled, that the report about Luke would be bad, but that *she* vouched for the band. Please would they tell Bob that? She also said that the Festival feature had been her idea. Joe had copied it.

She didn't tell them about Lucia because Joe might not and they had enough heartache now. And she had enough too.

In April she went again to Middle Street and slipped in through the back gate at a time when Mrs Eaves said Norah would be out. She pruned the roses, cutting them back to the healthy buds. She returned to Soho, and bought three rose plants from the market, planting them out in pots in Mario's yard. These were in recognition that the past had gone. There was to be no more waiting for anyone.

In May Frank and Nancy wrote to her, full of love, full of guilt at what they saw as their betrayal of her. They could not write fully until Joe returned from the POW camps where the North Koreans and Chinese were housed. Things were supposed to be bad there, he said. When Joe arrived in Lower Falls in the summer they would tell her what had been decided for that young man.

In the summer Frank wrote to her:

Lower Falls
June 1952

My dearest Rosie,
    We have spoken to Joe. He no longer works for the paper. I now write again under my own name. There has been enough subterfuge. It's time I got out there fighting again. McCarthy can't go on for ever. When the Korean war ends my guess is that he will lose his appeal. All this talk about betrayal by the leadership because of the reverses and then the stalemate is just too easy to spout.

God giving that man a mouth was like giving a lunatic a gun.

The report on Luke was bad. Yours has over-ridden it. Bob trusts you.

But now I write about really important things. The first being that I know now that I am a grandfather. Joe told us. How can you think that this would bring anything other than joy? How can you think that it would have made our problems worse? We love you. We shall love Lucia. But your pain is our pain.

Think carefully, Rosie. Joe vouched for the news he brought about Jack's love affair. I have checked the POW list. He is on that but that doesn't mean the rest is true. Give him the benefit of the doubt where love is concerned. Just wait until the end of the war when you will know one way or the other. Please. I know it is what your Grandpa would want.

Incidentally, we are coming over to see you in July.

Frank

CHAPTER 24

The year had passed slowly; tortuously slowly. The lectures didn't change as 1952 slipped into 1953, neither did the nature of the seasons. The cold was extreme, the spring came with its usual glorious explosions of colour.

'Exquisite,' Steve said and they remembered Nigel, but Steve couldn't really see the colour. The lack of vitamins had given him twilight blindness. He groped his way if Jack wasn't with him, and he didn't sleep because he thought he would never write now.

The Doc said he would. That vitamins would reverse the situation.

'But when will he be able to have those, Doc?' Jack had asked.

'When this lot is over.'

But no one knew when that would be. Sometimes they doubted that it would ever happen.

The peace talks continued. New prisoners, conscripts who had not volunteered, told them so. The newcomers told them about the guns which blasted from the trenches and showered shrapnel and earth on to the men of both sides. It was trench warfare again. In this age of great might, they had returned to static trench warfare.

Conditions improved again as the blossom bloomed on the trees. The men were given two larger meals a day, with rice and soya beans. Once a week they had a piece of pork. There was steamed bread, Korean turnip, cabbage leaves which Jack made Steve eat raw because Maisie had always said that cooking boiled the vitamins away. They also had potatoes now.

Jack told Steve how he had picked potatoes in Somerset, how Rosie's grandpa had grown some one year in a bucket in the yard. They had been small and translucent and good enough to eat on their own.

There were no letters from Rosie. Steve had none either though he was sure his mother would have written. Some men had letters, though, and between the news of births and deaths the words which cut deepest were those of everyday life. The sink that was cracked. The bulbs that had been planted before they left. The bike that was rusted.

Jack wrote about all this with a journalist's eye. 'Keep at it. You'll do well,' another American whose father was a Sub-Editor on the *Washington Post* said when Steve showed him.

Each day they threw stones at the marker, because why should they change the ritual of their life, just because one of them no longer saw clearly, Jack asked? He forced his friend to concentrate while he gave him instructions. 'Same direction, not so hard this time.' Jack told Steve that as long as he could still hit the marker he would also be able to write.

'Just you wait and see. You'll use all these months, these years. The times in the pit, the times when the blossom has bloomed and filled us with wonder, and one day you'll win the Pulitzer Prize.'

Steve threw another stone, hitting the target. He aimed in exactly the same direction for his next throw.

'There you are, and just you wait, it'll be over soon. You'll get those vitamins.'

But would it soon be over?

It was for Steve. In April 1953 the North Koreans agreed to repatriate a number of wounded and ill prisoners and they included Steve on the list that they called out at roll-call. They included Bob too because dysentery had taken its toll of the older man and a stomach ulcer was suspected.

Jack scribbled a note to Rosie and gave it to Bob to post. It was hurried because the trucks were already pulling in. The men had thirty minutes to grab their belongings and say their farewells. As the others were being helped to the truck Steve hugged Jack, slapped his back. They held one another and couldn't bring themselves to say goodbye until the guard started shouting at them, pulling at Steve to move.

318

'See you, bud,' Steve said. 'I almost don't want to go. Don't want to leave you. It's been so long. But I'll see you.'

'You will. You get those vitamins inside you and you goddamn will,' Jack said, helping him up into the truck.

They clasped hands as the truck jerked away. Jack ran along behind waving to Bob, waving to Steve, watching as the mud spun from the wheels, swallowing his envy and his loss, wondering how he could go on without his American who was more than a friend, who had known the horrors of the pit alongside him. Who had defecated in the corner of the same rail-truck, who had washed Jack's rags when he had dysentery. Whose rags Jack had washed in turn.

He turned away as the truck eased into the haze and now the Sergeant shouted at him and the others. He lined them up. Told them that they were a motley shower, a bloody disgrace to their countries and he didn't want to see any long faces. Their friends had left. Soon they would all leave this godforsaken country, and they would leave with their spirits intact, their health intact, even if he had to break their bloody necks.

'And don't you forget it,' he bellowed. 'Dismiss.'

Throughout April the routine remained the same as it always had been and the men stopped looking up each time the Commandant left his house outside the compound. Nothing had changed. They weren't going home, yet.

The days were lonely now for Jack. He threw pebbles at the marker. He sat through lectures, using them to sharpen up his précis. Using them to dream of Rosie. Using them to rest. They were all so thin and tired and more fell ill with beri-beri but no more were shipped out.

Jack remembered the train ride to Pyongyang and feared that the same trick had been played again and maybe Steve would be trucked back. He didn't return though as April turned into May. In the camp they were given sleeping bunks, chairs and tables. Razors, mirrors, combs, nail-clippers, toilet bags, cigarettes, wine and beer. They shaved away the unkempt beards and looked almost young again.

The food had improved so much that the British were more able to play soccer, the Americans to play baseball. Jack wondered if Frank still had the target on the garage that Rosie had told him about.

Each day he threw pebbles at the marker because it was part of his routine and then he squatted in the compound and listened as the Americans threw, batted, ran.

'Now whad'ya gonna do, batter, batter?' was the chant from the supporters.

'Stay loose, baby, stay loose.'

'Whad'ya say? Whad'ya say?'

But solitary confinement still continued too and manual labour outside the compound: hauling logs, unloading trucks, digging channels – and the wood detail, the never-ending chopping of wood.

Peking Radio's English broadcasts continued too, including interviews with those UN troops who had turned, and although most of the men in the camp scarcely listened, the tone of the reports was different and some of them became convinced that the end was near. But Jack, and those who had been with him, could not forget the train journey to Pyongyang and refused to think of home.

On 27 July their Sergeant lined them all up at 1400 hours and, as the sun beat down on the compound square, the Commandant addressed the camp in Chinese.

'The bugger,' breathed Jack, because he knew the Commandant spoke English well. There was a pause.

Then the interpreter said, 'Both sides in the Korean war have agreed to a cease-fire to take effect from now. You will be returned to your own side.'

There were cameramen with the camp staff and Jack knew that they were there to record the scenes of joy, but none of the prisoners moved. They looked at the Sergeant and waited.

He gave his orders. They obeyed. Attention. About turn, quick march. Back to their huts, denying their captors any emotion. Denying themselves any as they sat on their beds and wondered if this was another trick.

One week later, in pouring rain, trucks came and took them to the railhead. They travelled in cattle wagons until they reached another camp. They lived beneath canvas for another two days eating beans and rice. Jack would not believe that he was going home and neither would many of the others.

Small groups departed each evening. Red Cross observers

320

were there now. Jack watched the yellow moon push up over the mountain crest. Where were they going? Back to the camp? Even with the Red Cross he could not bring himself to believe.

But then it was his turn. He pulled himself up into the truck and wished that Steve was here and Nigel, Tom, Bob. And still he couldn't believe. He couldn't feel. A Chinese Captain stood in the rain, urging them to turn from the warmongering capitalists and stay where there was truth.

Jack said, for Steve, for Tom, for Nigel, 'Why don't you take a powder.'

They drove into Freedom Village three days later and passed lorry after lorry taking Communist POWs back north.

There's nothing left for you up there now, Jack thought, the ruined countryside still raw in his mind. It was the people that suffered, always.

They drove into the encampment beneath a 'Welcome Home' arch and slipped down from the lorry. Someone directed them towards doctors who examined them, then on to the interrogators, who examined them. Then on to the psychiatrists who gave them ice-cream, and examined them.

'I just want to get home,' Jack said, because now he believed it and the joy was racing through him. He had been asked to fill in too many forms, been asked too many questions for it not to be the truth. It was over. He was going home. He was bloody well going home.

A woman in WVS uniform came to him as he sat on his bunk. She gave him a shirt and sat and talked to him. It was too long since he had heard a woman's voice, too long since someone had done up the buttons on his shirt, and his eyes filled with tears.

'It's so long since I've seen Rosie,' he said to the woman and then he cried.

The next day he boarded the troop ship, felt the wind in his hair and stood by the rail, with so many others who were too thin, too old, to be twenty-three.

'It was exquisite,' he called out as the ship left, not caring about the looks from those at his side. He was saying goodbye to Nigel and to Tom. 'It was goddamn exquisite.' And he was crying again, the tears smeared across his cheeks.

*

The year had passed slowly for Rosie too. Frank and Nancy had come in the summer of '52. They had held Lucia, they had held Rosie. They walked in the park, they looked at the ruins, at the rosebay willowherb which covered some still-unfilled craters. They gazed at the re-building which was slow, very slow. They took her to shows, to restaurants where there was still a maximum price. They went back with her to Somerset but not to Herefordshire because she must go there alone one day.

They travelled through the Somerset lanes, visited Montacute, Martock, Crewkerne, Stoke-sub-Hamdon. They climbed the hill and looked across the Levels. They looked down on the orchard where Ed had camped. They stood outside the school where Jack had been taught. They heard the laughter through the peaked windows and Frank put his arm round Rosie, chewing his empty pipe.

'He'll come back,' he said, but none of them really knew whether he would or not.

Frank and Nancy had left for the States again in August and when they took Luke and the group back with them it was as though they had taken the sun. Winter had come and gone and Bob had sent for the Larkhill Band too. They were all playing in New Orleans which Luke said 'was heaven come early'.

There had been no letters from Jack though she had written. Nancy said that much of the mail did not get through.

In April 1953 Frank telegraphed her: 'Repatriated POWs arriving RAF Lyneham, Wiltshire. May 1st. Meet them. Ask them. Frank.'

He arranged for her to have admittance but when she arrived and saw the plane land, saw the men being helped to the ground, sick, tired, injured, she turned away. This was a time for the families that surrounded her, families that now held back tears that had been falling all morning.

She wouldn't intrude. She would wait. She would work.

Promoters started coming to her with propositions in spite of her youth and because of her honesty, her reliability. On 2 June she covered the Coronation for Frank's paper because it kept her in contact, it kept the paper in the family. She took two-year-old Lucia with her and she sat in the pushchair, waving a flag, turning and laughing at Rosie, with Jack's mouth, his laugh.

322

She wrote of the golden coach, the eight grey horses and wished that Lucia was old enough to remember it all. It was wet and it was cold but wasn't England so often wet and cold? Rosie laughed and so did Mrs Eaves who was with her.

'Will you go back to America?' Mrs Eaves asked.

'It depends if he comes back. And if he does, will he want the stall? It all just depends. Both countries are my home.'

They waved at Queen Salote of Tonga, that huge brown smiling figure whose open carriage, Mrs Eaves said, must have been filled with rainwater.

Each Commonwealth Prime Minister had his own carriage and that led to such a shortage of professional coachmen that, Rosie wrote, businessmen and country squires had dressed up and were now driving some of the coaches. Rosie and Mrs Eaves laughed again and moved to Buckingham Palace where the Queen and the Duke of Edinburgh waved from the balcony at midnight by which time Lucia and most of the other children around them were asleep in their pushchairs.

Rosie said to Mrs Eaves as the crowd roared, 'I missed VE Day. I'm glad I caught this.'

Mr and Mrs Orsini had been watching it on their new television and when Rosie and Mrs Eaves returned they toasted the new Queen in iced champagne which Mario had saved since the beginning of the war. They talked until two, with Lucia asleep in Rosie's arms. Life was good, she thought.

On 15 June the Chinese launched a new Korean offensive and she cried all night because there seemed to be no end to this waiting, this killing.

Then Frank rang her from America. 'It's me. Take no notice. It's these goddamn Commies trying to gain some sort of propaganda success before the armistice is signed. We're close, Rosie, very close. Hang in there, goddamn it. See you. Bye.'

The line was crackling, she had hardly been able to hear. But it was enough.

The roses in the yard behind the kitchen were blooming well by July and Lucia pointed to Rosie's pocket each time they went out, wanting to be shown the matchbox which they always took for the ladybirds.

On 27 July the armistice was declared and a few days later

Rosie rang her jazz groups and her contacts and told them she would not be available for at least two months. Mr Orsini would handle everything. She took a cab to Middle Street and dropped a letter in through Ollie's door. It said:

Dear Jack,
    If you come back and want to see me I shall be in Herefordshire until the end of September. I love you.
                                                    Rosie

She didn't go into Grandpa's yard because Norah was there, the windows were open. She walked to Woolworths and heard Frank Sinatra singing, felt the warmth, basked in the light, fingered the glasses, the jewellery, the same sort of ribbon which she had bought when she met Sam.

'I'm going to Herefordshire. I can't wait here. I shall give myself two months and then that's the end. I've left a letter. I haven't told him about Lucia. He must come because he wants to,' she said to Mrs Eaves, speaking in short sentences because it seemed to hurt too much to speak, to breathe.

Jack's troop ship arrived at dawn on 18 September. He felt better, he had eaten well and there was a little more weight on him now. All he could think of was Rosie and he rushed for the train, sat in the carriage looking out of the window at the greenness of this land. He had forgotten. Somehow he had forgotten how green it was. He leaned out of the window as the train rattled through fields which had been ploughed, through fields in which cows grazed. There was sweetness to the air. He was home.

A woman was knitting opposite. She looked at him as he sat down again. 'Been posted abroad have you? Must have been nice to get a tan like that. I don't know, you young people. Away from the shortages. You don't know you're born,' she tutted.

'I've been in Korea.'

'Oh, that's the one my Harry said was a waste of time.' She was looking at her pattern, tracing the line of instructions. It slipped and fell to the floor. Jack picked it up.

'Yes, you could say it was a waste of time,' he replied and

324

looked out of the window again. So many years had passed, so many men had died. There had been so much waiting, for them all. But there was Steve, there was Bob, and he had learned to write, learned about himself. He shrugged. 'Some of my friends will have thought it a waste of time,' he said. 'They didn't come back. They'll never come back.'

But the woman wasn't listening, she was counting her stitches. There was no point in talking any more. He just sat and watched the country unfold, the towns cluster, the suburbs of London approach. He ran down the platform, out to the taxi-rank. There was a queue. There was always a bloody queue. He was laughing and the man behind him smiled.

'Been away then?'

'Yes.' Jack didn't say where to. 'Going back to see my girl.'

'That's what makes it all worth while, ain't it, mate?' the man said.

Jack nodded, climbing into the taxi which drew up. 'Yes, that's what makes it all worthwhile,' he called back. 'Middle Street,' he said to the cabbie.

He looked out. The ruins were still there, but progress had been made. He smelt the air. It was the same old smoke, the same familiar skyline, the same streets which were becoming narrower. It wouldn't be long now. The taxi was turning into Albany Street, past Woolworths, down into Middle Street. Jack tapped on the glass partition. 'This'll do, mate.' He pushed open the door outside Rosie's house. He paid, tipped, ducked down through the alley, into Grandpa's yard, then stopped. Dropped his kitbag. He was home. At last it was all over. They could begin again, if she would have him.

He knocked on the door, pushed it open, calling, 'Rosie. I'm back.'

There was only Norah there, washing clothes at the sink, her hair permed, her mouth pursed. Grandpa's books were gone from the walls, his chair too. Norah turned from the sink and said, 'Thought you'd be here one day. She's gone. Back to America with that Joe. Gave you up a long time ago. Ollie's gone too, up north of London. Building the new towns.'

Norah didn't watch him go, she just heard his feet run out through the yard. She knew he'd try Ollie's house. She'd left the key there in the usual place but she'd burned the letter he'd got his friend from the camp to post. She'd taken the letter Rosie had pushed through the door. Thought I wouldn't see, I suppose, she thought, scrubbing harder at the dirt ingrained in Harold's trousers from kneeling on those church floors. Well, that'll teach her to tell my husband to go back to his hobby. That'll teach her to take him away from me. She turned back to the sink.

In Herefordshire, the sun was still warm, though it was nearly five p.m. Rosie paddled with Lucia in the stream, taking the pebbles as her daughter handed them to her. They were wet. She carried them to the bank, adding them to the pile of those which were drying.

Two weeks to go until the end of September and Jack had not come.

She looked up at the slopes above her. The bines were half picked. The pickers were using the last of the light, flip-flipping, not looking. Chatting, laughing.

When she had arrived the barley had still been in the fields all around the cottage she had rented. The combine had worked up until the end of August, shaving off the last tuft before the farmer sent in the plough. Seagulls had clustered over the furrows and Lucia had stood with her mouth open, waving at the birds, calling back when she thought they called to her.

Rosie had gone for a walk with her daughter the evening before the pickers came, and climbed the stile into the kale, hearing the partridges as they whickered in the hedge.

They had passed the blackberry bushes, still ripe with fruit, and looked across the sloping fields, down to the stream they were paddling in now. Seeing the thistles, the cows grazing, she had felt the peace of the place, the echoes.

She had waited, then walked her daughter through the bines which swung in the gentle breeze, telling her that one day they would all come and pick hops and then dance like she and Grandpa had once done. She had taken Lucia to the gate, shown her the carved initials. Her daughter had rubbed her hand over the letters her father had cut and laughed.

And each day they had waited.

Rosie turned back to the stream now, easing her feet through the water, over the stones, as Lucia, her dress tucked into her knickers, laughed and held up more pebbles, drips running down her plump arm.

Rosie turned and threw them towards the pile. Yes, they had waited but not for much longer. If he didn't come she knew now what she would do. She would spend half her year in England, half her year in Lower Falls and she would survive and prosper. But . . . But . . .

They waded towards the bank, ate sandwiches which were warm from the sun. Rosie remembered the lake, then Lee at Wembley, and touched the letter in her pocket which he had written, now that he was 'a big boy'. She lay back on the grass, pulling Lucia on top of her, hugging her, rocking gently, hearing the buzz of nearby bees.

There were moths at night, beating against the window, trying to reach the light. Didn't they know it was hopeless? She kissed Lucia fiercely.

'Water, Mummy, water,' Lucia said and laughed, pointing to the stream.

The water was cool against their legs as they waded in again and they scooped pebbles and threw, again and again, and the pile grew bigger as Rosie told Lucia how Daddy had lain on the bank and told her of Somerset and how Grandpa had picked hops that year as though he was a young man again.

Her hand was cold now but the pyramid wasn't high enough and so she threw again.

Another, larger pebble came through the air, hitting the pile before hers did. 'I hit the marker every time now,' Jack said.

Rosie saw his smile, his thin face, his thin hands that he held out to her and to his daughter. Then she was running with Lucia clutched to her, through the water, over the pebbles which bruised her feet, but which she didn't feel. Running as he came down the bank and into the water too, and at last his arms were round them both, his lips were on hers, the same soft gentle lips, the same skin, the same words.

'Mrs Eaves told me you were here. I love you, little Rosie.' And then, into her neck, 'Forgive me.'

'God damn you, my darling love,' was all she said, because the waiting was over.

Also available in Arrow

Somewhere Over England

Margaret Graham

War will not break her spirit...

In England in the 1930s, eighteen-year-old Helen Carstairs braves the prejudice of friends and family to marry Heine, a young German photographer who has fled the growing horror of the Nazis.

But the storm clouds are gathering in Europe. When fighting breaks out, Heine is interned, their small son is evacuated and Helen is left to face the Blitz alone.

And the agony of war threatens to divide a family already tormented by conflicting passions of loyalty, shame, betrayal – and love.

Previously published as *A Fragment of Time*

arrow books